Happy Bir~~ ~~ ~~
I Lon~~ ~~
mare
aug. 25th 1992

THE
LADY'S
CONFESSION

THE
LADY'S
CONFESSION

GEORGE MACDONALD

Michael R. Phillips, Editor

BETHANY HOUSE PUBLISHERS

MINNEAPOLIS, MINNESOTA 55438

A Division of Bethany Fellowship, Inc.

Originally published as *Paul Faber, Surgeon* in 1879 by Hurst & Blackett
Publishers, London, as a sequel to *Thomas Wingfold, Curate* (now *The
Curate's Awakening*).

Copyright © 1986
Michael R. Phillips
All Rights Reserved

Published by Bethany House Publishers
A Division of Bethany Fellowship, Inc.
6820 Auto Club Road, Minneapolis, Minnesota 55438

Printed in the United States of America

Library of Congress Cataloging-in-Publication Data

MacDonald, George, 1824–1905.
 The lady's confession.

 "Originally published as Paul Faber, surgeon in 1879 by Hurst & Blackett
Publishers, London, as a sequel to Thomas Wingfold, curate (now The
curate's awakening)"—T.p. verso.
 I. Phillips, Michael R., 1946–   .   II. Title.
PR4967.P38   1986   823'.8   86–8243
ISBN 0–87123–881–0 (pbk.)

BETHANY HOUSE PUBLISHERS
Minneapolis, Minnesota 55438

The Novels of George MacDonald Edited for Today's Reader

Edited Title	Original Title
The two-volume story of Malcolm:	
The Fisherman's Lady	*Malcolm*
The Marquis' Secret	*The Marquis of Lossie*
Companion stories of Gibbie and his friend Donal:	
The Baronet's Song	*Sir Gibbie*
The Shepherd's Castle	*Donal Grant*
Companion stories of Hugh Sutherland and Robert Falconer:	
The Tutor's First Love	*David Elginbrod*
The Musician's Quest	*Robert Falconer*
The Maiden's Bequest	*Alec Forbes of Howglen*
Companion stories of Thomas Wingfold:	
The Curate's Awakening	*Thomas Wingfold*
The Lady's Confession	*Paul Faber*
Stories that stand alone:	
The Baron's Apprenticeship	*There and Back*
A Daughter's Devotion	*Mary Marston*
The Gentlewoman's Choice	*Weighed and Wanting*
The Highlander's Last Song	*What's Mine's Mine*
The Laird's Inheritance	*Warlock O'Glenwarlock*
The Landlady's Master	*The Elect Lady*
The Minister's Restoration	*Salted with Fire*
The Peasant Girl's Dream	*Heather and Snow*
The Poet's Homecoming	*Home Again*

MacDonald Classics Edited for Young Readers

Wee Sir Gibbie of the Highlands	*Sir Gibbie*
Alec Forbes and His Friend Annie	*Alec Forbes of Howglen*

George MacDonald: Scotland's Beloved Storyteller by Michael Phillips
Discovering the Character of God by George MacDonald
Knowing the Heart of God by George MacDonald

Contents

Introduction

By this time, those of you who have grown to love the novels of George MacDonald through the edited editions in the Bethany House series probably know how seriously I take my work. As I have shared in Introductions to other books in the series, each story is a whole new experience in my spiritual walk, giving me new awareness and expanded vistas of growth and insight.

In the spirit of this candor concerning my own reactions, therefore, I must confess that the first time I read MacDonald's *Paul Faber, Surgeon* (now *The Lady's Confession*), I was disappointed. It cannot be helped, I suppose, that we all have favorite books—and this one was not one of mine!

However, in the process of editing *The Curate's Awakening*, to which this book is a sequel, I became so caught up in the character of Thomas Wingfold that I resolved to complete the entire Wingfold trilogy. How glad I was, therefore, as I began work on this book, to discover that in my first reading some years ago I had missed entirely the meaning of the story. All at once, as I have experienced many times with other MacDonald books, I found myself swept up with the theme, characters and spiritual truths which struck right to the root of my thinking. "How could I not have appreciated this book?" I asked myself with something akin to shock. "How could I have been so blind? These truths are incredibly *profound*."

And yet perhaps my original lack of understanding should not surprise me. For the themes of this book are indeed like those concerning which Paul wrote, "Their minds have been blinded with a veil over them" and "the wisdom of God is a hidden mystery which the world cannot know." "The deep things of God" found here follow appropriately after *The Curate's Awakening* and expand upon its theme of salvation. For now that Wingfold has passed through his crisis of doubt and emerged as a gloriously maturing man of God, MacDonald focuses his attention on the next likely candidate for conversion, the village doctor and atheist, Paul Faber. Faber and Wingfold become close friends and the stage is set for many illuminating discussions.

However, now MacDonald probes still deeper into the essence of sin itself, man's need, and the nature of man's heart in relation to God. Faber is the classic example of a "good" man, more kindly and compassionate and loving than many so-called Christians. He sees no need for God. But his very goodness is also his downfall. For with his goodness comes a fierce pride which, as the story unfolds, reveals the spiritual and even moral bankruptcy of mere "goodness." No human being is *good enough*. We are *all* sinners.

But not only does *The Lady's Confession* offer a parable of pride on the individual level, but on the church level as well. Pride exists within the human heart to keep individuals from God's salvation. And pride also exists within church bodies, keeping them from unity with each other and with God. Faber's perceptive criticisms of Christians are especially disgraceful in that love and unity among them are the trademarks Jesus has given us to demonstrate to the unbelieving world that the gospel is true. In exploring the unbelieving heart of Faber, therefore, MacDonald also brings to light the impact of spiritual pride and division between Christians.

If this is a parable of salvation, it is equally a parable of unity in the Body of Christ. Scripturally the two are intrinsically linked. The only way, according to Jesus, that the world will come to know His Father is through the love Christians demonstrate, toward one another and to the world. When people see division, unbelief is the result. The breaking down of church and doctrinal walls—one of the strongest themes running through many of MacDonald's books—is the fabric of this story which centers around an Anglican curate, an atheist, a Congregationalist minister, the minister's doubting daughter, a believing dwarf who acknowledges no particular church alliegance, the rector of the Church of England, and "the lady" caught between them all, not knowing what she believes.

Though the walls between the Anglican and dissenting church groups in the town remain firmly in place, when the walls crumble and love and unity begin to flow, the whole town—the believers and unbelievers alike—is swept into the redemptive current. So strong is the force of love that no unbelief can stand where true unity between brothers and sisters exists.

First published in 1879, *Paul Faber, Surgeon* may have provided the germ for Thomas Hardy's classic published twelve years later, *Tess of the D'urbervilles,* for the plots are remarkably parallel except for the endings. Though he gave no indication as to his reasons, George MacDonald once commented that he thought *Paul Faber, Surgeon* the best of his novels.

The Lady's Confession is the ninth in the ongoing *George Mac-Donald Classic Reprint Series* from Bethany House Publishers. As you may know from other introductory material I have written, when the series began several years ago George MacDonald was a name few in this century had ever heard. Only a handful of his books were then in print—none of them his full-length novels. Bethany House believed in the concept, took the project in hand, and, because of their fine artwork, their commitment to promotion, and the excellence of their editorial staff, have succeeded in accomplishing in our generation what George MacDonald himself did in his. Never since his own lifetime have George MacDonald's books enjoyed such a widespread audience. I would like to publicly thank Bethany House Publishers for the Spirit-led dedication and diligence in this effort. Now that MacDonald is once again "popular," many additional editions of his books are being released, for which all MacDonald loyalists are grateful. But it remains the original Bethany House series which has paved the way, so to speak, and opened the door to this new wave of interest. And I personally, and all who love MacDonald's books, will always remain in their debt.

My own personal vision has always been to slowly work toward the release of all of MacDonald's novels, working on them at a rate which enables me to diligently represent the original author, to whom and to whose Lord I desire above all to be faithful in my editing. Sales and promotion have never been my primary concern, but a true representation of the originals, in language understandable for today's reader. I take both encouragement and guidance from a statement made by MacDonald himself concerning an edited edition of *Letters From Hell* by Valdemar Thisted (1886). In the book's preface MacDonald wrote:

> ". . . The present English version is made from this German version, the translator faithfully following the author's powerful conception, but pruning certain portions, recasting certain others, and omitting some less interesting to English readers, in the hope of rendering such a reception and appreciation as the book in itself deserves, yet more probable in this country."

And such remains my present goal as well.

Finally, I encourage you to remember the driving motivation in George MacDonald's life: to turn his readers toward his Lord. In obedience to his Master do we most faithfully carry out the vision of George MacDonald's life and the message of his books.

God bless you all!

Michael Phillips
One Way Book Shop
1707 E St.
Eureka, CA 95501

Characters

John Bevis—Rector of the parish on behalf of the Church of England

Mrs. Bevis

Paul Faber—Glaston's surgeon

Thomas Wingfold—Curate of the abbey church (Anglican—Church of England)

Helen Wingfold

Mr. Drew—A businessman of Glaston; a draper

Mr. Drake—Former Congregationalist minister in Cowlane Chapel (a dissenting congregation, to be distinguished from the Anglican state church)

Amanda Drake—Adopted daughter of Mr. Drake

Miss Dorothy Drake—Mr. Drake's daughter

Mrs. Ramshorn—Aunt of Helen Wingfold and widow of Dean Ramshorn who had held rank within the Anglican church

Juliet Meredith

Mrs. Puckridge—Juliet's landlady, resident of Owlkirk

Mr. Jones—Butcher; a member of the abbey church

Mr. Barwood—Deacon of Cowlane Chapel

Joseph Polwarth—Dwarf gatekeeper of Osterfield Park

Rachel Polwarth—Joseph's niece

Dr. May—Faber's friend in Broughill

1 / The Rector

The rector sat on the driver's box of his carriage, guiding his horses toward the grand old abbey church of Glaston. His wife was inside, and an old woman he had stopped to pick up along the road sat on the footboard, a bundle beside her. The rector's coachman sat beside him; he never took the reins when his master was there.

Mr. Bevis drove like a gentleman, in an informal yet thoroughly businesslike way. His horses were black—large, well-bred and well-fed, but not showy—and the harness was just the least bit shabby. Indeed, the entire effect—including his own hat and the coachman's—gave to the observer that aspect of indifference to show, which, by the suggestion of a nodding acquaintance with poverty, gave it the right clerical air of being "not of this world."

Mrs. Bevis had her basket on the seat in front of her. Beneath an upper layer of flowers, it contained some rhubarb, the first of the season, and a pound or two of fresh butter for a poor relative in the town.

The rector was a man about sixty, with keen gray eyes, a good-humored mouth, and a ruddy face suggesting plain living as well as open air. Altogether he had the look of a man who knew what he was about, and who was on tolerable terms both with himself and his neighbor. The heart under his ribs was even larger than indicated by the benevolence of his countenance and the humor in his eyes. As for his wife, her placidity sank almost to dullness.

They were passing at good speed through a varying country—here a thicket of hazel, there open fields, occasionally well-kept farm hedges, and now and then clumps of pine, the remnants of an ancient forest. A recent rain had cleared the air and left the morning as nearly perfect as it could be. Halfway through a very narrow lane, the rector's horses suddenly started, throwing their heads wildly. Sailing high over the hedge bordering the road just in front of them, hardly touching the topmost twigs with his hoofs, appeared a great red horse. Down he came into the road, bearing a rather tall and certainly handsome rider. A dark brown moustache on a somewhat sunburnt face and a stern settling of the strong yet delicate features gave him a military look.

His blue eyes sparkled as he drew up close to the hedge to make room for the carriage. When Mr. Bevis had neared the rider, he slackened his speed.

"Hey, Faber," called the clergyman, "you'll break your neck someday! You should think of your patients, man. No one in his right senses would make a jump like that."

"It's only fair that I turn the tables and give Fate his chance with me now and then," returned the surgeon jovially. As he spoke he moved gently along in the same direction as the carriage, with just room to keep clear of the front wheel.

"Upon my word," declared Mr. Bevis, "when you came over the hedge there, I took you for 'Death' in Revelation!" He glanced back with momentary uneasiness, for he had found himself guilty of a little irreverence, and his conscience sat behind him in the person of his wife. But that conscience was a very easy one, being almost as incapable of seeing a joke as of refusing a request.

"Any special cases in your charge this week?" concluded the rector.

"Nothing too unusual," answered the surgeon. "But *you've* got one in your care, I see," he added, gesturing over his shoulder.

"Poor old thing!" responded the rector, as if excusing himself. "She's got a heavy basket, and we all need a lift sometimes—eh, doctor?— both into the world and out of it at the other end."

There was more reflection in this statement than the parson was in the habit of displaying. But he liked Faber, although he knew as well as everyone else that the doctor was no friend to the church or to Christianity, or to religious belief of any sort. Therefore, this liking, coupled with a vague sense of duty, had urged him toward this most unassuming attempt to cast the friendly arm of faith around the unbeliever.

"I plead guilty only to the former," answered Faber. "A lift out of this world from me would be mercy killing, and I have always leaned away from that practice. The instincts of my profession, I suppose, are against it. Besides, helping people out of the world ought to be your business."

"Not mine altogether," said the rector with a kindly look from his perch atop the carriage, a look which, however, fell only on the top of the doctor's hat.

Faber seemed to feel the influence of it nevertheless, for he returned: "If all clergymen were as liberal and good-natured as you, Mr. Bevis, there would be more danger of some of us giving in to your way of belief."

The word *liberal* seemed to rouse the rector to the fact that his coachman was sitting on the box beside him—yet another conscience, listening to every word; and above all, one must not be *too* liberal. With a word he quickened the pace of his cleric steeds, and the doctor was left parallel with the carriage window. There, catching sight of Mrs. Bevis, he paid his compliments and made his apologies, then trotted his gaunt Ruber again beside the wheel and resumed talk with the rector, but not the same talk. For a few minutes it turned upon the state of this and that ailing parishioner. For while the rector left all the duties of public service to his curate, he ministered himself to the ailing and the poor immediately around his own little property, that corner of his parish farthest from town.

"You don't seem to feed that horse of yours very well, Faber," the rector pointed out at length.

"I imagine it does seem that way, from the look of him," returned the doctor. "But you should see him feed! He eats enough for two, but it all goes to muscle and pluck. That's why you see so little fat on him."

"I must say, the less fat he has to carry the better if you're in the habit of jumping him over such hedges onto the hard road. In my best days I would never have faced a jump like that in cold blood," said the rector with a shudder.

"Well, at the worst it's but a knock on the head and a longish snooze," replied the surgeon.

The careless words, defying death itself, wrought in the rector a momentary terror.

"Take care, my dear sir," he warned solemnly. "There may be something to believe in after all, though you don't believe it yourself!"

"I must take the chance," replied Faber. "I will do my best toward long life by keeping the rheumatic and epileptic and other ailing persons alive as long as I know how. But as to the afterlife where nothing can be known, I prefer not to intrude."

A pause followed. At length the rector remarked: "You are so good a fellow, Faber, I wish you were better in the area of belief. Won't you come and dine with us sometime?"

"Yes, soon I hope," answered the surgeon. "But I am too busy at the present. For all her sweet ways and looks, the spring is not friendly to man's health and my work is to wage war with nature."

A second pause followed. The rector would gladly have said something, but nothing would come.

"By the way," he finally managed, "I thought I saw you pass the gate—let me see—on Monday. Why didn't you stop in?"

"I hadn't a moment's time. I was sent for in the village."

"Yes, I know. I heard about it. What is your impression of the lady? She is a stranger here.—John, that gate is swinging across the road. Get down and shut it.—Who is she, Faber?"

"All I know is that she is a lady."

"They tell me she is a beauty," said the parson.

The doctor nodded his head emphatically. "Haven't you seen her?" he asked.

"Only her back. Don't you know anything about her? Does she have anybody with her?"

"Nobody."

"Then Mrs. Bevis shall call on her."

"I think at present she had better not. Mrs. Puckridge is a good old soul and pays her every attention."

"What is the matter with her? Nothing infectious?"

"Oh no! She caught a chill. Yesterday I was afraid of pneumonia."

"Then she is better today?"

"I confess I am still a little anxious about her.—But I should not be dawdling like this with half my patients to see. I must bid you good day.—Good morning, Mrs. Bevis."

As he spoke Faber drew rein and let the carriage pass, then turned his horse's head to the other side of the road, scrambled up the steep bank to the field above, and galloped toward Glaston whose great church rose high in the sky. Over hedge and ditch he rode straight for its tower.

"The young fool!" said the rector, looking after him admiringly.

"Jolly old fellow!" exclaimed the surgeon at his second jump. "I wonder how much he believes of all that religious humbug. But, then, there's that curate of his who believes everything and would humbug the whole world if he could. How any man can fool himself so thoroughly is a mystery to me!—I wonder what the rector's driving into Glaston for on a Saturday?"

Paul Faber embraced all the natural laws of science with great energy. He was so afraid of any kind of intellectual error or mistake that he would rather run the risk of rejecting any number of truths than of accepting one single error. In this spirit he had concluded that, since no immediate communication had ever reached him from any creator of men, he had no ground for believing in the existence of any such creator. Besides that, he reasoned, a thousand inconsistencies clearly evident in the world made the existence of one Being, perfectly wise and good and powerful, impossible. He had never asked himself which was the worst deception—to believe there was a God when there was none, or to believe there was no God when there was one.

He did possess, however, a large measure of the lower but equally indispensable share of religion—namely, that which has respect to one's fellowman. Not a person in Glaston was more ready day or night to run to help another. And the help he gave was not merely by way of professional capacity, but as a true neighbor, whatever sort of aid was needed.

Thomas Wingfold, the curate of the abbey church, had a great respect for the doctor. Having himself passed through many phases of serious and painful doubt on the way to his own spiritual awakening, he was not shocked by the surgeon's unbelief. He seldom tried to answer Faber's objections directly. He sought instead to cause the roots of those very objections to strike into the deeper strata of his being, hopefully there to disclose truth to the man himself, to wake in him that spiritual nature, which alone is capable of coping with such questions.

The first notable result, however, of the surgeon's relationship with the curate was that, whereas before Faber had kept his opinions to himself, he had now grown to the point where he spoke his disbelief with plainness. This did not come of aggravated antagonism but of admiration of the curate's openness in expressing his own doubts to his congregation.

There had arisen therefore between the doctor and the curate a certain degree of camaraderie which had at length come to the rector's ears. He had before this heard many complaints against the curate, but he had shrugged them aside. He was no theologian himself, and he had found the questions raised about Wingfold's teaching altogether beyond the boundaries of his interest or grasp. He could not comprehend why people should not content themselves with minding their own business, going to church, and so feeling safe for the next world. What did opinion and theology matter? The rector did not exactly know what he believed himself, but he hoped he was none the less of a Christian for that.

But somehow it didn't seem right to him that his curate should be on such friendly terms with one who denied the very existence of God. That was going a bit too far. The rector himself enjoyed a bit of sparring with the surgeon. But a casual *tête-à-tête* as had just occurred was certainly different than the friendship his curate and the agnostic surgeon shared. Besides, the rector had taken the opportunity to remind Faber of the hereafter; was Wingfold likely to do that and remain on amicable terms? Not for a moment did Bevis doubt the faith of Wingfold. But a man must have some respect for appearances; appearances were facts as well as realities were facts. An honest man must not keep company with a thief. Neither must a clergyman keep company with an atheist.

Something must be done. Probably a word would be enough, and the rector* was now on his way to say it.

---

*The curate was the clergyman who conducted services in the church, while the rector, occupying a higher rung on the organizational ladder within the ecclesiastical structure, was responsible for overseeing the affairs of the parish on behalf of the Church of England.

2 / The Minister

Everybody knew Mr. Faber, whether he was riding his red or his black—known by the names Ruber and Niger—and many were the greetings given him as he passed along Pine Street. Despite his atheism, he was popular. The few ladies out shopping bowed graciously, for both his manners and his person were pleasing and his professional standards unquestioned. The last person to address him was Mr. Drew, the principal draper of the town, who had been standing for some time in his shop door when the doctor rode up.

"I wish you would look in on Mr. Drake, sir," the draper urged. "I am quite uneasy about him. Indeed, I am sure he must be in a bad way, though he won't admit it. He's not been himself since he quit his church.* But he's not an easy man to do anything for, you know."

"I don't see what I could do," returned Faber. "To call on him without his ever having called for me!—No, Mr. Drew, I don't think I could."

It was a lovely spring day. The rain that had fallen heavily during the night lay in flashing pools about the street. Here and there were little gardens in front of the houses, and the bushes in them were hung with bright drops, so bright that the rain seemed to have fallen from the sun itself, not from the clouds.

"Why, goodness gracious!" cried the draper, looking past the rider. "Here's your excuse for a visit to the Drakes right here!"

Up to the very nose of the doctor's great horse walked a little girl, who now stood staring straight up at the huge red-maned head above her.

Now Ruber was not altogether gentle, and it was with some dismay that his master pulled him back a step or two.

"Where did *she* come from?" he asked.

"From somewhere they say you don't believe in, doctor," answered the draper shrewdly. "It's little Amanda, 'Ducky' as she is fondly called, the minister's own darling.—Whatever do you mean by splashing through

---

*Mr. Drake had formerly been the minister of a "dissenting" (non-Church of England) chapel in the town. *Dissenting* churches took many forms—Presbyterian, Methodist, Baptist, Reformed, etc., all descendants of the great reformers such as Calvin, Knox, the Wesleys, Edwards, etc.—while the Church of England's roots extended back to Henry VIII's break with Catholicism in the early 16th century. In the United States and the rest of Western Europe the distinction between *Catholic* and *Protestant* is more familiar, while in Great Britain the parallel differentiation is between *Anglican* and *Dissenting*.

every gutter between home and here," he continued, his round, good-humored face wrinkled all over with smiles as he picked up the tiny truant. "Why, your apron is as wet as a dishrag! And your shoes!"

The little one answered only by patting his cheeks, which in shape resembled her own, while Faber looked down in amusement and interest.

"Here, doctor," the draper went on, "if you take the little mischief-maker up on the saddle in front of you and carry her home, that will be your excuse to call on Mr. Drake."

As he spoke he held the child up to him. Faber took her, and sitting as far back in the saddle as he could, set her in front of him. She laughed joyously, her mouth stretched wide to reveal dainty little teeth. When Ruber began to move she shrieked with delight.

Holding his horse to a gentle walk, the doctor crossed the main avenue and went down a side street toward the river, where he entered a narrow lane. There with the handle of his whip he managed to lean over and ring the doorbell of a small old-fashioned house. The door was opened by a ladylike young woman with smooth, soft brown hair, a white forehead, and serious, rather troubled eyes.

"Aunty! Aunty!" cried the child. "See! I'm riding!"

Miss Drake looked a little surprised. The doctor lifted his hat. She gravely returned his greeting, then stretched up her arms to take the child. But Amanda drew back, nestling against Faber.

"Amanda, come dear," appealed Miss Drake. "How kind of Dr. Faber to bring you home. I'm afraid you've been a naughty child again, running about in the street."

"Such a big ride!" cried Amanda, heedless of the reproof. "A real horsy—Big! Big!"

She spread her arms wide, indicating the vastness of the body upon which she still sat. But still she leaned back against the doctor, and he awaited the result in amused silence. Again her aunt raised her hands to take her.

"I want another ride!" cried the child, looking up and back at Faber.

But her aunt caught her by the feet and, amid struggling and laughter, drew her down and held her in her arms.

"I hope your father is well, Miss Drake," said the doctor.

"Ducky," said the young woman, putting the child down, "go and tell Grandpapa how kind Dr. Faber has been to you. Tell him he is at the door." Then turning to Faber she replied, a quaver in her voice, "I am sorry to say he does not seem at all well. He has had a good deal of trouble lately, at the chapel, and at his age that sort of thing tells."

As she spoke she looked up at the doctor with a curious trepidation in her eyes. Nor was it any wonder she should look at him strangely. For to her he was like an apostle of evil, yet at the same time perhaps truth. Terrible doubts lately had been assailing her—doubts which she could in part trace to him. And as he sat there on Ruber he looked like a beautiful angel who *knew* there was no God—an evil angel whom the curate, by his bold speech and troubling questions, had raised and now could not banish.

The surgeon had scarcely begun a reply when the old minister made his appearance. He was a tall, handsome, well-built man with strong features. But the hat hanging on his head and baggy, ill-made clothes and big shoes gave an appearance of weakness and oddity. He greeted the doctor with a thin smile.

"I am obliged to you, Mr. Faber," he began, "for bringing home my little runaway. Where did you find her?"

"Under my horse's head."

"She is a fearless little damsel," said the minister in a husky voice that had once rung bell-clear over crowded congregations, "—too fearless at times. But the ignorance of danger seems to be the protection of childhood. And indeed, who knows what evils we all walk in the midst of—evils that never touch us!"

What platitudes! thought the doctor.

"She fell in the river once, and almost a second time," Mr. Drake went on. Then turning to Amanda he said, "I am going to have to tie you with a string, my pussie! Now come away from the horse."

"How do you stand this trying spring weather, Mr. Drake? I don't hear the best accounts of you," probed the surgeon, drawing Ruber a pace back from the door.

"I am as well as perhaps I should expect to be—at my age," answered the minister. "I am getting old—and—and—we all have our troubles. But I trust our God to see us through them," he added casting a significant look at the doctor.

By Jove! speculated Faber to himself, *the spring weather has roused the worshiping instinct! The clergy are on the prowl today! I had better look out or it will soon be too hot for me.*

"I can't look you in the face, doctor," resumed the old man, "and believe what people say of you. It can't be that you don't even believe there *is* a God?"

"If there is one," Faber replied, "he has never given me grounds sufficient to think so. You Christians say yourselves that he has favorites to whom he reveals himself. The *chosen,* I believe you call them. Well, I am not one of them, and must therefore of necessity be an unbeliever."

"But think of it, Mr. Faber—if there should be a God, what an insult it is to deny his existence."

"I don't see it quite as you do," returned the surgeon, suppressing an inclination to laugh. "If there be such a one, would he not have me speak the truth? I only state a fact when I say that I have never seen him or seen evidence of him. Anyhow, what great matter can it be to him that one man should say he has never seen him, and can't therefore believe he is to be seen? A god should be above that sort of pride."

The minister was too shocked to find any answer beyond a sad, reproving shake of the head. But he felt almost as if the hearing of such irreverence without making a bold retort made him party to this blasphemy against the Holy Spirit. Was he not now conferring with one of the generals in the army of the Antichrist? Ought he not to turn his back upon him and walk into the house?

But a surge of concern for the frank young fellow who sat so strong and alive upon the great horse broke over his heart, and he sorrowfully looked up at him.

Faber mistook the cause and object of his evident emotion.

"Come now, Mr. Drake, be frank with me," encouraged the doctor. "You are not in good health; let me know what is the matter. Though I'm not religious, again I speak the truth when I say that I would be glad to help you. A man must be neighborly, or what is there left of him? Even you will allow that duty to our neighbor is half the law. Your Book says that. And there is some help in medicine, though I confess it is no perfect science yet, and we are but dabblers more often than I would like to admit."

"But I don't choose to accept the help of one who looks upon everyone who thinks as I do as ludicrous and regards those who deny everything as the only honest men in the world."

"By Jove, you are forthright man!" exclaimed the doctor. "What I say of such as you is that, having inherited a lot of humbug and bad ideas, you don't know it for what it is, and you do the best you can with it."

"If such is your opinion of me, I should like to ask you one question about another," said Mr. Drake. "Do you in your heart believe that Jesus Christ was an impostor?"

"If the story about him be true, I believe that he was a well-meaning but enormously self-deceived man."

"Your judgment of him seems altogether illogical. How could any good man so totally deceive himself? That appears to my mind altogether incredible."

"Ah! but he was an extraordinarily good man."

"And you say that makes him all the more likely to think too much of himself?"

"Why not? I see the same thing in his followers all about me."

"Undoubtedly the servant shall be as his master," responded the minister and closed his mouth, resolving to say no more. But his conscience prodded him with the truth that had come from the mouth of its enemy—the reproach his disciples brought upon their Master. For in the world's judgment, the master is as his disciples.

"You Christians," the doctor went on, "seem to me to make your-selves the slaves of an imagined ideal. I have no such ideal to worry about. Yet I am not aware that you do any better by each other than I am ready to do for any man or woman. I can't pretend to love everybody, but I do my best for those I can help. I try to be a good and decent man in all I do. And, Mr. Drake, I would gladly serve you."

The old man said nothing, his emotions in turmoil. Would he accept life itself from the hand of one who denied his Master?—go to the powers of darkness for a cure?

He had turned and was on the point of walking silently into the house when he thought of the impression he would make on the unbeliever if he were thus to reject the offer of his kindness. Half turning, he stood hesitating on the threshold.

"Doctor, you have the great gift of a kind heart," he began, still half turned away.

"My heart is like other people's," interrupted Faber, but not rudely. "If a man wants help, and I've got it to give, what more natural thing than that we should come together?"

There was in the doctor an opposition to everything that had about it even the faintest odor of religion. But it must not be supposed that he was a proselytizer to his cause. He was content to let everyone have his own opinions of things. Say nothing, and the doctor said nothing. But equally he believed that others should allow him his views. So when the verbal pistol was fired against him, off went his own gun in answer.— But with no bravado, for the doctor was a gentleman.

"Mr. Faber," said the minister, now turning toward him and looking him full in the face, "if you had a friend whom you loved with all your heart, would you place yourself under obligation to a man who counted your friend as only folly?"

"The cases are not parallel. What if the man merely did not believe your friendship was alive? There could be no insult to either."

"If the denial of this friend's living opened the door to the greatest wrong that could be done him, and if that denial seemed to me to have its source in some element of moral antagonism to him, *could* I accept— I put it to you, Mr. Faber—*could* I accept assistance from that man? Do not take it wrongly. You prize honesty—so do I. I would ten times rather stop living than to accept life at the hand of an enemy of my Lord and Master."

"I am very sorry, Mr. Drake," relented the doctor, "but from your point of view I suppose you are right. Good morning."

He turned Ruber from the minister's door, went off quickly, and entered his own stable yard just as the rector's carriage appeared at the farther end of the street.

3 / The Manor House

Mr. Bevis drove up to the inn, threw the reins to his coachman, stepped down and helped his wife out of the carriage. Their passenger had already stepped off the footboard with her belongings and departed. Then the Bevises parted, she to take her gift of flowers and butter to her poor relation, he to call upon Mrs. Ramshorn.

Everyone knew Mrs. Ramshorn. The widow of a dean, she considered herself the chief ecclesiastical authority in Glaston. Yet her acknowledged friends would have found themselves compelled to admit that her theology was both scanty and confused and that her influence was not of the most elevating nature. But she spoke in the might of the matrimonial aura around her head, and her claims of churchly authority were undisputed, at least in her hearing, in Glaston.

There was quite another reason, however, which prompted the rector's visit on this particular day. His curate, whom his business in Glaston this Saturday concerned, had some nine or ten months before married Mrs. Ramshorn's niece, Helen Lingard. Helen had lived with her aunt for many years. Mrs. Ramshorn had been plentifully enough provided for, but Helen certainly had added a great deal to the comfort and style of the housekeeping. Therefore, when all of a sudden the girl calmly insisted on marrying the curate, and transferred to him the entire property inherited from her father and brother, the disappointment of Mrs. Ramshorn in her niece was equalled only by her disgust at the object of her choice. He was a man obnoxious to every fiber of her aunt's ecclesiastical nature.

With a firm, dignified step the rector paced the pavement between the inn and the manor house. He knew of no cause why he should not stand as tall as the next man before any human being. It was true, he confessed to himself in a moment of soul honesty, he *had* closed his eyes to certain faults in the man of good estate who had done him the honor of requesting the hand of his only child. Indeed, he had withheld from his daughter the information which might have led her to another choice. He had satisfied himself that the man's wild oats were sown; he made no inquiry as to the crop. It was also true that he had not mentioned a certain weakness in the last horse he had sold; but then he hoped the severe measures he had taken had cured the animal. He was aware that at times he took a few glasses of port more than he would have judged proper to carry to the pulpit or the communion table.

Yet as I say, he was conscious of nothing to cause him real shame, and in the sound of his step there was certainly no lack of confidence. It was true he performed next to none of the duties of the rectorship; but then neither did he turn any of its income to his own uses. Part of the money he paid his curate, and the rest he laid out on the church building, which might easily have consumed six times the amount in desirable and needful repairs. What further question could be made of the matter? The Church continued her routine, and one of her most precious buildings had been preserved from ruin in the bargain, thanks to him.

How indignant he would have been at the mere suggestion that he was, after all, only an idolater, worshiping *The Church* instead of the Lord Christ. But he was a very good sort of idolater, and some of the Christian graces had filtered through the roofs of the temple upon him— especially those of hospitality and general kindness toward humanity. Indeed, he did less to obstruct the religion which he thought he furthered than some men who preached it as on the housetops.

It was from policy, not from confidence in Mrs. Ramshorn, that he went to her first. He liked his curate, and everyone knew she hated the poor fellow. If two interpretations were possible concerning anything he did, there was no doubt which one she would adopt and spread about. Not even to herself, however, did she admit the one chief cause of her hatred: having all her life been used to a pair of horses and a fine carriage, she now had to put up with only one pulling a small buggy.

The rector pulled himself erect, approached her house and sent a confident announcement of his presence through the house with the brass knocker on the door. Almost instantly the long-faced butler, half un- dertaker, half parish clerk, opened the door wide and invited the rector to step into the library, as the butler had no doubt Mrs. Ramshorn would be at home to see *him*. And it was not long before she appeared and gave him a hearty welcome. By no very wide spirals of descent, the talk soon swooped down upon the curate.

"The fact is," voiced the memorial shadow of the deceased dean at length, "Mr. Wingfold is not a gentleman. It grieves me to say so of the husband of my niece, who has been to me as my only child, but the truth must be spoken. It may be difficult to keep such men out of holy orders, but if ever the higher positions of the church come to be freely bestowed upon them, that moment the death-bell of religion is rung in England. My late husband said so. While such men keep to preaching in barns we can despise them; but when they creep into the fold, then there is just cause for alarm. The longer I live the more I see my poor husband was right."

"I should scarcely have thought such a man as you describe could have captivated Helen," remarked the rector with a slight smile.

"Depend upon it, she perceives her mistake well enough by this time," returned Mrs. Ramshorn. "A lady born and bred must make the discovery within a week. But poor Helen always was headstrong. And in this out-of-the-world place she saw so little of true gentlemen!"

The rector could not help thinking that birth and breeding must count for little indeed if nothing less than marriage could reveal to a lady that a man was not a gentleman.

"Nobody knows," continued Mrs. Ramshorn, "who or what his father—not to mention his grandfather—was! But—would you believe it?—when I asked her *who* the man was, she told me she had never even thought of inquiring. I pressed the question, and she told me she was content with the man himself and was not going to ask about his family. She would wait until they were married! She actually said so, Mr. Bevis. What could I do? She was of age and independent means. And as for gratitude, I know the ways of the world too well to look for that."

"We old ones"—and as he said the words Mrs. Ramshorn bridled a little, for she was only fifty-seven!—"have had our turn, and now it is theirs," maintained the rector rather inconsequently.

"And a pretty mess they are likely to make of it!—what with infidelity and blasphemy—I must say it—blasphemy!—Really you must do something, Mr. Bevis. Things have come to such a pass that, I give you my word as a lady, there are some wonderings about the rector himself for committing his flock to the care of such a wolf."

"Tomorrow I will listen to him preach," assured the rector.

"Then I sincerely trust no one will give him warning of your intention: he is so clever."

The rector laughed.

"But," the lady went on, "in a place like this, where everybody talks, I fear the chance is small that he won't hear of your arrival. Anyhow, I would not have you form your opinion on the basis of just one sermon. He will say just the opposite the next week, for he contradicts himself incredibly. Even in the same sermon I have heard him say things diametrically opposite. The man has not an atom of consistency. He will say and unsay as fast as one sentence can follow another, and if you confront him with it he will support both sides."

"Then what would you have me do?" asked the rector. "The straightforward way would undoubtedly be to go to him."

"I fear you would gain nothing by that. He is so devious. The only safe way is to dismiss him without giving him a reason. Otherwise he will certainly prove you in the wrong.—But don't take my word for it. Get the opinion of your churchwardens. Everybody knows he has made an atheist of poor Dr. Faber. It is sadder than I have words to say. He *was* such a gentlemanly fellow!"

The rector took his departure and made a series of calls on those he judged the most influential of the congregation. He did not think to ask why they were influential, or why he went to them rather than the poor. What he heard embarrassed him considerably.

Wingfold's friends spoke highly of him, his enemies did not. The rector made no attempt to weigh the integrity and character of the curate's friends with that of his enemies. Neither did he make the observation that while Wingfold's enemies differed in the things they said against him, his friends closely agreed in what they said for him. The fact of the matter was that those who found their consciences roused by him more or less understood the man and his aims. Conversely, those who would not submit to the authority he brought to bear upon them, trying all the while to measure and explain him by their own standards, failed totally to understand what he was about.

The churchwardens told the rector that ever since Wingfold came, he had done nothing but burn the ears of the congregation. They told him also that some of the principal dissenters declared him to be a fountain of life in the place. To a Church of England rector like Mr. Bevis, that seemed to be the worst accusation of all, for Mr. Bevis was strongly opposed to dissent in any form. He regarded it as one of the highest of merits that a man should be what he termed "a good churchman."*

---

*For our 20th century "Americanized" ears to fully grasp the import of these complaints, we must recall that the difference between the Anglican *Church of England* and "*dissent*" is similarly parallel to the distinction between *Catholic* and *Protestant*. The complaints Mr. Bevis heard against the curate suggested that he was obliterating the former walls between two absolutely opposite church systems. For dissenters to be attending Wingfold's church had caused a commotion equal to what might be the case today were half the leaders in a protestant evangelical church in a small town to suddenly rally around the Catholic priest, while at the same time the staid traditionalists of the priest's own church sought to have him removed. Though the Church of England had no ties whatever to Catholicism, the impact would be similar and would cause an unrest equally in both camps. It was this sort of general hubbub Wingfold had stirred up in Glaston.

4 / Paul Faber, Surgeon

The curate remained in his study all morning. When his wife came in shortly before noon, one look on his almost luminous face told her the thought-battle was over and his sermon for the morrow was at hand. She gazed at his expression a moment, then took his hand and led him down the stairs to their midday meal.

He had not spoken to his wife about the text on which he had been reflecting for several days. After they were married, he found in this respect he could not separate her from one of his congregation. Therefore he could not involve her in his sermon before he saw her in the church, with rows and rows of pews and faces between him and her. She still remained, during those few moments, one more of the flock, the same one over whose heart he had so often agonized, pouring words of strength and consolation during her trouble with her brother Leopold.*

On Saturdays Helen would let no one trouble him unless she saw some good reason—solely if some person was troubled. His friends knew this and seldom came near him on a Saturday. But that evening Mr. Drew (who though a dissenter was one of the curate's warmest friends) called rather late, when he considered that the curate's sermon must certainly be finished. He told Helen the rector was in town, had called upon several of the parishioners, and undoubtedly would be in church in the morning.

"Thank you, Mr. Drew. I perfectly understand your kindness," acknowledged Mrs. Wingfold, "but I don't think my husband needs to know tonight."

"Excuse the liberty, ma'am, but—but do you think it well for a wife to hide things from her husband?"

Helen laughed merrily.

"Certainly not as a rule," she replied. "But my husband and I think married people should be so sure of each other that each should prefer not to know what the other thinks it's better not to tell. If my husband overheard anyone calling me names, I don't think he would tell me. He knows, as well I do myself, that I am not yet good enough to behave better to anyone for knowing she dislikes me. It would be but to further the evil; and for my part too, I would rather not be told. I think on Monday my husband will say, 'Thank you, wife. I am glad you kept this from me till I had done my work.' "

The Curate's Awakening, George MacDonald, Bethany House Publishers, 1985.

"I quite understand you," answered the draper.

"I know you do," returned Helen.

The curate slept soundly that night and woke in the morning eager to speak what he had to say.

Paul Faber fared otherwise. Hardly was he in bed before he was called out again. A messenger came from Mrs. Puckridge to say that Miss Meredith was worse, and if the doctor did not start out at once, she would be dead before he reached Owlkirk. While he quickly put on his clothes, he sent orders to his groom to saddle Niger and bring him round to the house instantly. He was vexed that he had taken Ruber out both in the morning and the afternoon and could not have him now. But Niger was a good horse also. He was only two-thirds Ruber's size, but he was only about one-third his age and saw better at night. On the other hand, he was less easily seen. However, that would be of little worry since Glaston nights were so still and deserted. In a few minutes Faber and Niger were out together on a lane dark as pitch. They would have to keep to the roads, for there was not light enough to see the pocket compass by which the surgeon sometimes steered cross country.

Could we but see the boyhood dreams of a man, we would have a great help toward understanding the character he has developed. Those dreams of young Faber were almost exclusively of playing a prince of help and deliverance among women and men. Like most boys that dream, he dreamed himself rich and powerful, but the wealth and power were for the good of his fellow creatures. He had always wanted to help people.

That spirit of help had urged him into the medical profession. But it would have taken one stronger than Faber to listen to the scoffing materialism from the lips of authority and experience at the medical school and not come to look upon humanity with a less than reverent regard. But Faber escaped the worst. Despite the influence around him, he learned to look on humanity with respect and to meet the stare of appealing eyes with genuine sympathy.

Yet before he had even begun his practice, Faber had come to regard man as a mere body and not as an earthly home for an immortal soul. The highest and best things in the human animal were to him dependent on nothing but chance physical organization. But his innate poetic nature was always ready to play havoc with this view, keeping the delicacy of his feelings intact. This sensitivity preserved him from much that most vulgar natures plunge into; it kept alive the memory of a lovely mother, and fed the flame of that wondering, tender reverence for women which he shared with most men.

A few years of worthy labor in his profession had done much to develop him. His upright character, benevolence, and skill were already highly regarded by the people of Glaston and its neighborhood, where he had been practicing only about a year. Even now, when in a fever of honesty he had declared there *could* be no God in such an ill-ordered world, his heart was so full of the human half of religion that he could not stand by the bedside of a dying man or woman without lamenting that there was no consolation available at such a moment.

Faber's main weak point was, that though he was indeed tender-hearted and did kindnesses not to be seen of men, he did them to be seen of himself. The boy was in the man, doing his deeds and seeking the praise of his own conscience. Though perhaps this was not a *grievous* wrong, it was poor and childish and obstructed his higher development. He liked to think himself a benefactor. Such a man may well be of noble nature, but he is a mere dabbler in nobility, for a certain degree of pride is always inherent in such a view of oneself. Faber delighted in the thought that, having repudiated all motives of personal reward in the future which came of religious belief (which he in his ignorance took for the main essence of Christianity), he ministered to his neighbor and did to him as he would have others do to himself. Without any hope of divine recognition beyond the grave, he prided himself on the fact that he performed such ministry in a fashion at least as noble as that of the most devoted of Christians. It did not occur to him to ask if he loved his neighbor as well, or if his care about him was equal to his satisfaction in himself. Had he analyzed the matter in any depth he would have discovered that the belief he so disdained had carried some men immeasurably further in helping their fellows than he had yet gone.

But in spite of all that, Faber was both loved and honored by all whom he had attended. He was in the world's eyes a *good* man. With his fine tastes, his genial nature, his quiet conscience, his good health, his enjoyment of life, his knowledge and love of his profession, his activity, his tender heart—especially to women and children—and his keen intellect, if any man could get on without a God, Faber was that man. He was now trying it, and as yet the trial had cost him no great effort. He seemed to himself to be doing very well indeed.

And why should he not do as well as the thousands who counted themselves "religious" people and who got through the business of the hour, the day, the week, the year without once referring to the will of God or the words of Christ in anything they did or did not do? If he was more helpful to his fellows than they, he fared better as well. For actions which are in themselves good, however imperfect the motives, react wonderfully upon character and nature. It is better be an atheist who does the will of God than a so-called Christian who does not. The atheist will not be dismissed because he said *Lord, Lord* and did not obey. What God loves is only the lovely thing, and he who does such a thing does well and is on the way to discovering that he does it very badly. When one begins to do the will of the perfect God, then that person is on the road to doing it perfectly. Doing things from duty is but a stage on the road to the kingdom of truth and love. But because it is but a stage, not the less must that stage be journeyed; every path diverging from that road is "the flowery way that leads to the broad gate and the great fire."

With more than his usual helpful zeal, Faber was now riding toward Owlkirk to revisit his new patient. Could he have mistaken the symptoms of her attack?

Mrs. Puckridge, anxiously awaiting the doctor's arrival, stood by the bedside of the young woman who had been lodging with her for only a short time. The lady tossed and moaned, breathing very quickly. Her color was white more than pale, and now and then she shivered from head to foot, though her eyes burned feverishly.

She lay in a little cottage room, cut low on one side by the slope of the roof. The night was so dark that when Mrs. Puckridge carried the candle out of the room, not even a trace of light came in through the unshaded dormer window. But light and dark were all alike to the one who lay in the little bed. In the midst of its white covers and white pillows, her large black eyes were like wells of darkness throwing out flashes of strange light. Her hair, too, was dark, brown-black, of great quantity, and so fine that it seemed to go off in a mist on the whiteness as if the wind had been blowing it about. Some of it had strayed more than halfway to the foot of the bed. She was clearly beautiful, with a regularity of features rarely to be seen. Though her face was distorted with distress, suffering had not yet flattened the delicate roundness of her cheek or sharpened the angles of her chin.

When Mrs. Puckridge came into the room, she always set her candle on the sill of the storm window. As the doctor drew near the village, the lone light guided him to the cottage gate. He fastened Niger to it, crossed the little garden, gently lifted the door-latch, and ascended the stair. He found the door of the room open, and Mrs. Puckridge wringing her hands in helpless ignorance. He signalled to her to be still and softly approached the bed. He stood for a moment gazing in silence on the sufferer, who lay at the moment apparently unconscious. But suddenly, as if she had become aware of a presence, she flashed wide her great eyes, and their pitiful entreaty went straight to his heart. Faber always felt the anguish of his patients, particularly children and women. He would serve them like a slave. The silent appeal of her eyes nearly brought tears to his.

"I am sorry to see you so ill," he murmured as he took her wrist. "You are in pain. Where?"

Her other hand moved toward her side in reply. Everything indicated pleurisy—such that there was no longer room for gentle measures. She must be relieved at once; he would have to open a vein. It had seldom fallen to Faber to perform the very simple operation of venesection to open a vein, allowing the blood to flow and relieving pressure. But his relative inexperience had little to do with the trembling of his hands as he proceeded to undo a sleeve of his patient's nightdress. Finding no button, he snatched a pair of scissors from his pocket, cut ruthlessly through the linen and lace, and rolled back the sleeve. It disclosed an arm so beautifully formed it would have made a Greek sculptor ecstatic at the sight of it. Faber felt his heart rise in his throat at the necessity of breaking that delicate skin with the shining steel which was already poised between thumb and forefinger.

But he hesitated only a moment. A slight tremble of the hand he held was the only acknowledgment of the intruding sharpness as the knife slit the whiteness and the red flow instantly rose in the bowl he held underneath. He stroked the lovely arm to help its flow, and soon the girl once more opened her eyes and looked at him. Already her breathing was easier. But presently her eyes began to glaze over with approaching faintness. He put his thumb on the wound to stop the blood. She smiled and closed her eyes. He bound up her arm and laid it gently by her side, gave her something to drink, and sat down. He sat until she sank into a deep, quiet, gentle sleep.

"Thank God!" he breathed involuntarily, and stood up. What he meant, God only knows.

After various instructions to Mrs. Puckridge, to which she seemed to pay the strictest attention but which I fear she probably forgot the moment they were uttered, the doctor mounted and rode away. The darkness was gone, the moon was rising, slowly mounting through a sky freckled with wavelets of cloud. All was so soft, so sleepy, so vague, it seemed to Paul as he rode slowly along, himself almost asleep. It was as if the night had lost the blood he had caused to flow, and the sweet exhaustion that followed had from the lady's brain wandered out over Nature herself.

Was he in love with her? I do not know. I could tell, if I knew what being in love was. I think no two loves were ever the same since the creation of the world. I know only that something had passed from her eyes to his. But what? The Maker of man and woman alone understands the awesome mystery between two of them.

It must be a terrible thing for a man to find himself in wild pain, with no God to whom his soul can go. But to a man who can think as well as feel, it is even more terrible to find himself afloat on the tide of a lovely passion, with no God to whom he can cry. Will any man who has ever cast more than a glance into the mysteries of his being dare think himself sufficient to rule his nature?

5 / Thomas Wingfold, Curate_____

Before morning it rained hard again, but it cleared at sunrise, and the first day of the week found the world well washed and bright. Glaston slept longer than usual, however, despite the shine, and in the rising sun looked deserted. No cheerful shop windows reflected the sun's beams or filled them with rainbow colors. There were no carriages or carts— only one rider—Paul Faber again, on Ruber now, the horse aglow in the morning.

No children played yet in the streets or lanes; but the cries of some came at intervals from unseen rooms, as the Sunday soap stung their eyes, or the Sunday comb tore the matted locks of their hair. As Faber rode out of his stable yard, Wingfold took his hat from its peg and began his walk through his churchyard. He lived nearly in the churchyard, for, happily, since his marriage the rectory had lost its tenants, and Mr. Bevis had allowed him to occupy it in lieu of part of his salary. It was not yet churchtime, but he had a custom of going quite early every Sunday morning to sit for an hour or two alone in the pulpit, amidst the absolute solitude and silence of the great church. It was a door, he said, through which a man who could not go to Horeb might enter and find the power that dwells on mountaintops and in desert places.

He went slowly through the churchyard, breathing deeply of the delicious spring morning air. Raindrops were sparkling all over the grass and moss-covered graves, and in the hollows of the stones they had gathered in pools. Every now and then a soft wind awoke, like a throb of the spirit of life, and shook together the scattered drops upon the trees, and down would come diamond showers on the grass and daisies of the mounds and feed the green moss in the letters of the epitaphs. Over all the sun was shining, as if everywhere and forever spring was the order of things. And is it not so? Is not the idea of the creation an eternal spring ever trembling on the verge of summer? It seemed so to the curate, who was not given to sad or sentimental moralizing over the graves. No grave was to him the place where a friend was lying; it was but the place where the Lord had once lain.

"Let those possessed with demons haunt the tombs," he declared as he sat down in the pulpit; "for me, I will turn my back upon them with the risen Christ."

While he sat thus in the pulpit, his wife was praying for him while she yet lay in bed. She had not come to love him in the vestibule of society but in the chamber of her own spiritual temple. For there a dark vapor had hidden the deity enthroned until the words of his servant, her husband, had melted the gloom. Then she saw that what she had taken for her own innermost chamber was the dwelling place of God. Therefore the wife walked beside the husband in the strength of a common faith in absolute Good.

She loved every hair on her husband's head, but loved his well-being infinitely more than his mortal life. A wrinkle on his forehead would cause her a pang, yet she would a thousand times rather have seen him dead than known him guilty of one of many things done openly by not a few of his profession.

And now, as one sometimes wonders what he shall dream tonight, she lay wondering what new thing, or what old thing fresher and more alive than the new, would this day flow from his heart into hers.

The following is the substance of what she did hear from him a few hours later. His rector, sitting between Mrs. Bevis and Mrs. Ramshorn, heard it also. The radiance of truth shone from Wingfold's face as he spoke, and those of the congregation who turned away from his words were those whose lives ran counter to the spirit of them.

Whatever he uttered grew out of a whole world of thought, but it grew before his listeners. That is, he always thought afresh in the presence of the people, and spoke spontaneously concerning the things about which he had been thinking and praying during the previous week.

" *'You cannot serve God and mammon.'* " A few stirred uneasily at the authority in his voice.

"Who said this?

"Is he not the Lord by whose name you are called, in whose name this church was built, and who will at last judge every one of us? And yet how many of you are trying your hardest to do the very thing your Master tells you is impossible? I appeal to your own conscience. Are you not striving to serve God and mammon?

"Do you say to yourselves that it cannot be? Surely if a man strove hard to serve both God and mammon, he would soon see that it was impossible. It is not easy to serve God, but it is easy to serve wealth. Surely the incompatibility of the two endeavors must quickly become apparent. But the fact is there is no strife in you. With *ease* you serve mammon every day and hour of your lives. But for God you do not even ask yourselves the question whether or not you are serving him at all.

"Some of you are at this very moment indignant that I call you materialistic. Those of you who are assured that God knows you are his servants know also that I do not mean you. Therefore, those who are indignant at being called the servants of mammon are so because they are indeed such.

"Let us consider for a moment the God you do not serve, and then the mammon you do serve. The God you do not serve is the Father of Lights, the source of love, the maker of man and woman, the head of the great family, the Father of fatherhood and motherhood, the life-giver who would die to preserve his children but would rather slay them than they should live as slaves of evil, the God who can neither think, nor do, nor endure anything mean or unfair, the God of poetry and music and every marvel, the God of the mountaintops and the rivers that run from the snows of death to make the earth joyous with life, the God of the valley and the wheat field, the God who has set love between youth and maiden, the God and Father of our Lord Jesus Christ, the perfect, the God whom Christ knew, of whom he declared that to know him was eternal life.

"The mammon you serve is not a mere negation but a positive Death. His temple is a darkness, a black hollow, ever hungry, in the heart of man. His wages are death, but he calls them life, and many believe him. I will tell you some of the marks of his service—a few of the badges of his household—for he has no visible temple. No man bends the knee to him; it is only his soul, his manhood, that the worshiper casts in the dust before him.

"When a man talks of the joys of making money, or boasting of number one, meaning himself, then he is a servant of mammon. If when you make a bargain you think only of yourself and your own gain, you are a servant of mammon. If in the church you would say to the rich man, 'Sit here in a good place,' and to the poor man, 'Stand there,' you are a mammon server. If you favor the company of the popular and those whom men call well-to-do, then you are serving mammon and not God. If your hope of well-being in times to come rests upon your houses or lands or business or savings, and not upon the living God, whether you are friendly and kind or a churl whom no one loves, you are equally a server of mammon. If the loss of your goods would take from you the joy of your life, then you serve mammon. If with your words you confess that God is the only good, and yet you live as if he had sent you into the world to make yourself rich before you die; if it will add a pang to the pains of your death to think that you have to leave your fair house, your trees, your horses, your shop, your books all behind you, then you are a server of mammon and far truer to your real master than he will prove to you.

"The moment the breath is out of your body, your master has already deserted you. And of all that for which you did rejoice, that which gave you such power over your fellows, there is not left so much as a spike of thistledown for the wind to blow from your sight. For all you had, there is nothing to show.

"Some of you are saying in your hearts, 'Preach to yourself and practice your own preaching!'

"And you say well. And so I mean to do, lest having preached to others I should myself be a castaway. God has put money in my power, through the gift of one whom you know. I shall endeavor to be a faithful steward of that which God through her has committed to me. Hear me, friends: to none of you am I the less a friend because I tell you truths you would hide from your own souls."

Those most uncomfortable dared only turn their eyes in sideways glances. The atmosphere was sharp with tension, but Wingfold went on, his voice warm, "Money is not mammon; it is God's invention. It is good and the gift of God. If it were not for money and the need of it, there would not be half the friendships in the world. It is powerful for good when divinely used. Give it plenty of air and it is sweet as the hawthorn. But shut it up, and it rots and breeds worms. Like the earth itself, like the heart and mind of man, it must be broken and turned, not heaped together and neglected.

"Money is an angel of mercy, whose wings are full of balm and dews and refreshings," Wingfold explained. "But when you lay hold of him, pluck his wings, pen him in a yard, and fall down and worship him—then, with the blessed vengeance of God his Master, he deals plague and confusion and terror to stop the idolatry. If I misuse or waste or hoard it, I pray my Master to see to it and punish me. I would undergo the pain of any fire rather than be given over to the disgusting idol! And now I will make an offer to my fellow townspeople in the face of this congregation—that whoever will, at the end of three years, bring me his accounts, to him also will I lay open mine, that he may see whether I have made a friend of mammon.

"Friend, don't be the slave of materialism, of greed, of selfishness. Be wary. Don't hoard the gold when it is in your purse. Instead, in God's name, spend—and spend more. Take heed *how* you spend. But take heed that you *do* spend. Be as the sun in heaven; let your money be your rays, your angels of love and life and deliverance. Be a candle of the Lord to spread his light through the world. If up till now you have radiated darkness in any fashion, humble yourself, then arise and shine.

"But if you are poor, then don't mourn over your purse when it is empty. He who desires more than God wills him to have, he also is a servant of mammon, for he trusts in what God has made and not in God himself. He who laments what God has taken from him, he is a servant of mammon. He who cannot pray because of the worldly cares pressing in on him is a servant of mammon.

"Certain men in this town love and trust their horses more than the God who made both them *and* their horses. None the less confidently will they expound on the doctrine of God. But a man who does not surrender his soul to the living God and live in him, his religion is worth the splinter of a straw. A man's views on the things of God can only be trusted to the extent that man is himself walking with God.

"Friends, cast your idol into the furnace. Melt your mammon down, coin him up, make God's money of him, and send him out to do God's work. Make of him cups to carry the gift of God, the water of life, through the world—in lovingkindness to the oppressed, in rest to the weary who have borne the burden and heat of the day, in joy to the heavy-hearted, in laughter to the dull-spirited. Let them all be glad with reason and merry without gloating.

"Ah! what gifts in music, in drama, in the story, in the picture, in books, in flowers and friendly feasting, what true gifts might not the mammon of unrighteousness, changed back into the money of God, give to men and women, bone of our bone, flesh of our flesh. How would you not spend your money for the Lord if he needed it from your hand! He *does* need it, for he that spends it upon the least of his fellows spends it upon the Lord.

"To hold fast to God with one hand while you open wide the other to your neighbor—that is true religion and undefiled, that is the law and the prophets, that is to live the life Jesus came to teach us about and to demonstrate to us.—Lord, defend us from mammon. Hold your temple against his foul invasion. Purify our money with your air and your sun that it may be our slave, and you our master. Amen."

6 / Mixed Reactions

The whole time Wingfold spoke the rector never took his eyes off the preacher, but the preacher never saw him, for he dared not let his eyes wander in the direction of Mrs. Ramshorn. He was not yet so near perfection but that the sight of her haughty, unbelieving face tended to stir up bitter thoughts within him.

Church over, the rector walked in silence between the two ladies to the manor house. Mr. Bevis courted few greetings from the sheep of his neglected flock as he went, and returned those offered with a constrained solemnity. The moment they stood in the hall together, Mrs. Ramshorn turned sharply on the rector and exclaimed, "There! What do you say about your curate now?"

"He *is* enough to set the whole parish on its ears," he answered in a rueful tone.

"I told you so, Mr. Bevis."

"Only it does not therefore follow that he is in the wrong. Our Lord himself came not to send peace on earth, but a sword."

"Irreverence hardly becomes a clergyman such as yourself, Mr. Bevis," scolded Mrs. Ramshorn. She regarded any practical reference to our Lord as irrelevant, therefore naturally irreverent.

"And, by Jove!" added the rector, heedless of her remark, and falling back into an old college habit of speech, "I fear he is in the right. And if he is, it will go hard for you and me on the last day, Mrs. Ramshorn."

"Do you mean to say you are going to let that man turn everything topsy-turvy, and drive the congregation out of the church, John Bevis?"

"I never saw such a congregation in it before, Mrs. Ramshorn," he returned mildly.

"It's little better than a lower class dissenting assembly now. And what it will come to if things go on like this, God only knows. The congregation you speak of is nothing but low-breds *he* has brought into what was once a grand and mighty place." Her righteous tone combined with the unrighteous sentiment would have been comical except for the gravity of her unchristian attitude.

"Well, I must confess the fellow has quite knocked the wind out of me indeed by his sermon, and I haven't quite caught my breath yet. Have you a bottle of sherry open?"

Mrs. Ramshorn led the way to the dining room where the Sunday dinner was already laid and the decanters stood on the sideboard. The rector poured a glass and drank it down in three mouthfuls.

"Such buffoonery! Such coarseness! Such indelicacy!" cried Mrs. Ramshorn while the parson was still occupied with his sherry. "Not content with talking about himself in the pulpit, he must talk even about his wife! My poor Helen! She has thrown herself away upon a charlatan! And what will become of her money in the hands of a man with such levelling notions, I dread to think. And then, worst of all—to offer to show his account books to every inquisitive fool itching to know my niece's fortune! Well, he shan't see a penny of mine, that I'm determined about."

"You need not be uneasy, Mrs. Ramshorn. You remember his condition."

"Stuff and hypocrisy!"

Mr. Bevis checked his answer. He was beginning to get disgusted with "the old cat," as he called her to himself.

He too had made a good speculation in the money market. Otherwise he could hardly have afforded to give up the practice of his profession. Mrs. Bevis had bought him the nice little property at Owlkirk, where, if he worshiped mammon—and after his curate's sermon he was not at all sure he did not—he at least worshiped him in a very moderate and gentlemanly fashion. Everybody liked the rector, and several loved him a little. Though he had never yet in his life consciously done a thing because it was commanded by Christ, he was not therefore a godless man. And through spiritual infiltration, he had received much that was Christian.

The ladies went to take off their hats and their departure was a relief to the rector. He helped himself to another glass of sherry and seated himself in the great easy chair which had formerly been the dean's. But what are easy chairs to uneasy men? Dinner was at hand, however, and that would make a diversion in favor of less disquieting thought.

Mrs. Ramshorn also was uncomfortable. With no little aggravation she sensed that the rector was not with her in her deprecation of Wingfold. She did her best to play the hostess, but the rector, while enjoying his dinner despite discomfort in the inward parts, was in a mood of silence altogether new both to himself and to his companions. Mrs. Bevis, however, talked away in a soft continuous murmur. She was a good-natured, gentle soul, without whose sort the world would be harder for many. But she did not seem to have much mollifying influence on her hostess, who continued to snarl and judge and condemn and did not seem to enjoy her dinner any the less for it. When it was over, the ladies went to the drawing room, and the rector, finding the company unpleasant, went to check his horses at the inn.

They neighed a welcome the moment his boot struck the stones of the yard, for they loved their master with all the love capable of their strong, timid, patient hearts. Satisfied that they were comfortable, for he found them busy with a large feed of oats and chaff and Indian corn, he threw his arm over the back of his favorite and stood leaning against her for several long minutes, half dreaming, half thinking. In that dream, however, he had been more awake than any hour for long years, and had heard and seen many things. At length he patted the mare lovingly, went into the inn where he enjoyed a cup of tea, and then set out to make his call upon the curate.

It was years since he had even entered the rectory. He had scarcely known the people who had last occupied it, and even during its preparation for Wingfold he had not gone near the place. Yet his dreaming thoughts as he stood in his mare's stall had been of that house, and it was with a strange feeling of the past that he now approached it.

All his years with his first wife had been spent in that house. She was delicate when he married her and soon grew sickly and suffering. One after another their children died as infants. At last came one who lived, and then the mother began to die. She was rather melancholy, but hoped as much as she could. And when she could no longer hope, she did not stand still but walked on in the dark. I think when the sun rises upon them, some people will be astonished to find how far they have got on in the dark.

Her husband, without verifying for himself the things of God it was his business to teach others, yet held some sort of spiritual communion by his love for his suffering wife and by his admiration of her goodness and gentleness. He had looked up to her with the same reverence with which he had regarded his mother, a woman with an element of greatness in her. Though she lived more according to the severity of her creed than the joy of Christ, she was yet a godly woman. It was not possible that he should ever have adopted her views or the doctrines she accepted as the truth of the gospel, for he was more *liberal* in his outlook. But there was yet in him a vague something not far from the kingdom of heaven. Some of his wife's more fundamental friends looked upon him as a wolf in the sheepfold. But he was no wolf, only a hireling. Many neighborhoods might have been the better for having such a man as he for the parson of the parish. And yet for one commissioned to be in the world as *He* was in the world, Mr. Bevis nevertheless fell far short. Why, he knew more about the will of God with respect to horse's legs than to the heart of man.

As he drew near the house, the spirit of his departed, suffering, ministering wife seemed to overshadow him. Tears began to well up in his eyes. He was not sorry he had married again, for he and his present wife were at peace with each other. But he had found he could not think of the two women with the same part of his mind. They belonged to different eras of his life. For one thing, his present wife looked up to him with perfect admiration, and he, knowing the poverty of his soul, could not help looking down on her as a result, though in a loving, gentlemanlike way.

He was shown into the same room, looking out on the churchyard, where in the first months of his married life he had sat listening to his wife sing her few songs with the little piano he had saved hard to buy for her. Such happy times had lasted only through those few months. After her first baby died she had rarely sung. Now all the colors and forms of the room were different, and that made it easier to check the lump rising in his throat. It was the faith of his curate that had brought back thoughts of his first wife, although the two men would hardly have agreed in any confession narrower than the Apostles' Creed.

When Wingfold entered the room, the rector rose, went halfway to meet him, and heartily shook hands with him. They seated themselves, and a short silence followed. But the rector knew it was his part to speak.

"I was in church this morning," he stated, with a half-humorous glance into the clear gray eyes of the curate.

"So my wife tells me," returned Wingfold with a smile.

"You didn't know it, then?" rejoined the rector, with an almost doubtful, quizzical glance. "I thought you were preaching at me all the time."

"God forbid!" exclaimed the curate. "I was not aware of your presence. I did not even know you were in town yesterday."

"You must have had *someone* in mind as you spoke. No one could say the things you did this morning if he were simply addressing abstract humanity."

"I cannot say individuals did not come into my mind as I spoke. How can a man help it when he more or less knows everyone in his congregation? But I give you my word, I never thought of you."

"Your message would have been just as fitting if you had," returned the rector. "My conscience sided with you all the time. You found me out. I've got a bit of the muscle they call a heart left in me yet, though it has gotten rather leathery.—But what do they mean when they say you are setting the parish on its ears?"

"I don't know, sir. I have heard of no quarreling. I have made some enemies, but they are not very dangerous, and I hope not bitter ones. And I have made many more friends, I am sure."

"They tell me your congregation is divided—that they take sides for and against you. Surely that is a most undesirable thing."

"It is indeed, and yet it may be a thing that cannot be helped for a time. Has any man ever attempted to help cure souls without stirring up a certain amount of such division? But if you will have patience with me, I am bold to say, believing in the force and final victory of the truth, there will be more unity in the end."

"I don't doubt it. But come now—you are a thoroughly good fellow, and I'm accountable for the parish, you know. Couldn't you state your case a little more mildly? Couldn't you make it just a little less peculiar? Only the way of putting it, I mean—so that it looked a little more like what they have been used to? I'm only suggesting this, you know. I'm sure that whatever you do, you will act according to your conscience."

"If you will allow me," said the curate, "I will tell you my whole story. And then if you should wish it, I will resign my curacy without saying a word more than that my rector thinks it best."

"Let me hear it," agreed the rector.

"Please take a chair," suggested the curate, "that I may at least know you are comfortable while you listen."

The rector did as he was requested, laid his head back, crossed his legs, and folded his hands over his worn waistcoat. He was not the neatest of parsons. He had a wholesome disregard for the outermost man and did not even know when he looked shabby. Without a hint of pomposity he settled himself to listen.

Condensing as much as he could, Wingfold told him how through great doubt and trouble of mind he had come to hope in God and to see that there was nothing really left to man but to give himself, heart and soul and body, to the love and will and care of the Being who had made him. He explained how he now regarded his profession as a call to use every means and energy at his command for the rousing of men and women from that spiritual sleep and moral carelessness in which he himself had been sunk for so long.

"I don't want to give up my curacy," he concluded. "Still less do I want to leave Glaston, for there are some here whom I teach and some who teach me. That which has given ground for complaint seems to me to be but common sense. If you think me wrong, I have no justification to offer. We both love God—"

"How do you know that?" interrupted the rector. "I wish you could make me sure of that."

"I know that I do," replied the curate earnestly. "I can say no more than that."

"My dear fellow, I haven't the merest shadow of a doubt of it," returned the rector, smiling. "What I meant was that you could make me sure *I* do."

"Pardon me, my dear sir, but judging from sore experience, if I could influence you one way or the other I would rather make you doubt it. The doubt, even if an utter mistake, would in the end be much more profitable."

"You have your wish then, Wingfold. For I do doubt it very much," confessed the rector. "I must go home and think about it all. You shall hear from me in a day or two."

As he spoke, Mr. Bevis rose and stood for a moment like a man greatly urged to stretch his arms and legs. An air of uneasiness pervaded his whole appearance.

"Will you not remain in town and have tea with us?" invited the curate. "My wife will be disappointed if you do not. She tells me you have been good to her for twenty years."

"She makes an old man of me," returned the rector musingly. "I remember when she was such a tiny thing in a white frock and curls. Tell her what we have been talking about and beg her to excuse me. I *must* go home."

He took his hat from the table, shook hands with Wingfold, and walked back to the inn. There he found his coachman away, nobody knew where.

To remain overnight at the inn would have given pointed offense to Mrs. Ramshorn. Because of her supposed authority in the church, she would expect them to stay at the manor house. But he could not tolerate hearing his curate further abused. Therefore, with the help of the barmaid, he hitched the horses to the carriage himself, and to the astonishment of Mrs. Ramshorn and his wife, soon drew up to the door of the manor house with his carriage.

Mrs. Ramshorn strongly urged him to stay, but it was in vain. And Mrs. Bevis was content wherever she was, so long as she was with her husband. Mrs. Ramshorn received their good-byes very stiffly, somehow sensing rebuke.

Mrs. Bevis enjoyed the drive; Mr. Bevis did not. Doubt was growing stronger and stronger all the way that he had not behaved quite like a gentleman to the Head of his church. As I have already shown, he had an honorable nature, and the eyes of his mind were not so dim with good living as one might have expected. And now in the mirror of loyalty, he was coming to see himself falling short. He weighed himself in the scales of honor and found himself wanting.

Simply put, he had not behaved like a gentleman to Jesus Christ. It was only in a spasm of terror that Peter had denied his Lord. But for nearly forty years John Bevis had been taking his pay, and for the last thirty he had done nothing in return. If Jesus Christ did not care, then what was the church?—What was the whole system called Christianity? But if Jesus *did* care, then what was John Bevis in the eyes of his Master?

When they reached home he went neither to the stable nor to the study, but immediately walked out onto the neighboring heath where he found the universe rather gray about him. When he returned he tried to behave as usual, but his wife saw that he scarcely ate his supper. She assumed it was because of the annoyance the curate had caused him, and wisely did not trouble him with questions.

7 / Mr. Drake

While the curate was preaching that same Sunday morning, Walter Drake—"the old minister," as he was now called by his disloyal congregation—sat in a little arbor looking out on the river that flowed through the town to the sea. Green grass went down from where he sat to the very water's edge. It was a spot the old man loved, for there his best thoughts came to him. A good deal of the stuff of which poets are made lived within him, and since the troubles in his church had overtaken him, the river had more and more drawn him. And often, as he sat thus almost on its edge, he fancied himself waiting the welcome summons to cross life's river and go Home. A weary and rather disappointed pilgrim, he thus comforted himself as he sat.

The softened sounds of a singing congregation came across gardens and hedges to his ear. They sang with more energy than grace. Were they indeed singing to the Lord, he asked himself, or only to that usually unseen idol, Custom?

Then a silence came. The young man in the dissenters pulpit was reading his text, and the faces that had once turned themselves up to Walter Drake as flowers to the sun were now all turning to the face of the one they had chosen to replace him, "to minister to them in holy things." He sat motionless, his eyes fixed on the ground.

But why was he not at chapel himself? And if he could not show his face in his former congregation, what was to stop him from going to the church to hear Mr. Wingfold? Could it be that he yielded to temptation, actually preferring the long glide of the river and his own solitude to the worship and the hymns and the sermon? Had there not been a time when he condemned any man who did not go to the chapel every Sunday? Yet there he sat, the church on one side of him and the chapel on the other. His daughter Dorothy was at the chapel; she had taken Ducky with her; the dog lay on the porch waiting for them; and the cat thought too much of herself to make friends with her master.

He was not well, it was true, but he was well enough to have gone. Was he too proud to be taught where he had once been a teacher? Was it that the youth in his place taught doctrines which neither they nor their fathers had known? It surely could not be that he was resentful they had retired him in the prime of his old age with but a third of his former salary.

In truth it was impossible for the old minister to have any great esteem for the flashy youth, proud of his small Greek and less Hebrew—

one of the hundreds whom the devil of ambition drives to preaching. Whether the doctrines he taught were in the New Testament or not, certainly he never found them there, being but the merest disciple of a disciple of a disciple. His fiery words displayed only a glimmer of divine understanding. And yet at the same time Drake might have seen many points of resemblance between his own early history and that of the shallow man now speaking from his pulpit.

His people had behaved badly to him, and he could not say he was free from resentment or pride. But he did make for them what excuse lay in the fact that the congregation had been dwindling ever since the curate in the abbey church began to preach in such a strange, outspoken fashion. Now there was a different sort of preacher! No attempted oratory with him! No studied graces in waving of hands and uplifted eyes, no tricks, no gimmicks. And yet at moments when he became possessed with his object rather than subject, every inch of him seemed alive. He was odd—very odd; perhaps he was crazy—but at least he was honest. He was certainly incomparably superior to the young man who had replaced him at Cowlane Chapel. Expecting the young man to draw great crowds, the deacons of his own church had retired Drake, who had for more than fifteen years ministered to them the bread of life.

Bread! Yes, I think it might honestly be called bread. True, it had had bits of chalk in it, with an occasional morsel of potato peel or dirt, and badly baked. But the mass of it was honest flour, and those who did not recoil from the look of it, or recognize the foreign matter, could live upon it. But a great deal of it was not of his baking at all; he had merely been the distributor—crumbling down other bakers' loaves and making them up again in his own shapes. In his declining years, however, he had really begun learning the business. But many in his congregation not only preferred bad bread of certain kinds, but were incapable of digesting any of high quality.

He would have liked to attend the abbey church that morning; only that would have looked spiteful. His late congregation would easily excuse his nonattendance with them. They would even pitifully explain to each other why he could not make an appearance in their midst just yet. But to go across town to the church would be in their eyes *unpardonable*—a declaration of a war of revenge.

But there was another reason why Mr. Drake could not go to church that morning; and if it was not more serious, it was a much more painful one. Some short time before he had any ground to suspect that his congregation was faltering in its loyalty to him, his daughter had discovered that the chapel butcher invariably charged for a few ounces more than the actual weight when he sent meat to them. Now, Mr. Drake was a man of such honesty that all kinds of cheating, even the most respectable, were abominable to him. That the man was a teacher of religion and a member of his own congregation made his conduct unpardonable. So after taking pains to satisfy himself of the fact, he stopped dealing with him any further and told him plainly enough why. The man was far too dishonest to profit by the minister's rebuke and was revengeful in proportion to the justice of the accusation. And of course, he brought his substantial influence to bear upon the votes of the rest of the church members when it came to a decision regarding the pastorate.

Had there been another butcher in Cowlane Chapel, Mr. Drake would have turned to him. But as there was not, he had to take his business instead to Mr. Jones who was a member of the Church of England. Soon afterward his troubles with his own people began, and before many weeks were over he saw plainly that he must either make some attempt to retire gracefully and accept the pittance they offered him, or else resign altogether and go out into the world in search of some pastorless flock. To retire would be to remove himself from the forefront of the battle and take an undistinguished place in the crowd of mere campfollowers. But for the sake of honesty, and with the hope that it might be only for a brief time, he had chosen the first of the two alternatives.

And truly it was a great relief not to have to grind out of his poor, weary, groaning mill the two inevitable weekly sermons. For his people thought themselves intellectual, and certainly were critical. Mere edification in holiness was not enough for them. Their ambition was not to grow in grace but in social influence—to glorify the doctrine of their dissent against the Church of England, not the communion of saints. Upon the chief cornerstone they would build their stubble of paltry religionism; they would set up their ragged tent in the midst of the eternal temple, not caring if it blocked up window and stair.

But now, just last week, because of the sudden cutback in his income and with some anxiety, Mr. Drake had asked his new butcher to send a current bill. When he saw it he was horrified. He was always feeding some of his flock, and at this time two sickly nursing mothers drew their mortal life from his kitchen. Besides, the doctor had some time ago ordered a larger amount of meat for little Amanda. The result was that the sum at the bottom of that long slip of paper, small as the amount would have seemed at one time in his history, was now greater than he could possibly pay. Therefore, if he went to the church, he would imagine the eye of the butcher and not that of the curate upon him all the time. It was a horror to him to have an account which he could not settle—especially from his new butcher after he had so severely rebuked the old one. What was the difference between his honesty and the offender's? The one billed for meat he had not sold, the other ordered meat for which he could not pay! Would not Mr. Jones imagine he had left the chapel butcher and come to him because he had run up a bill he could not pay?

It was over these painful circumstances that Mr. Drake now brooded, looking almost lovingly upon the fast-flowing river because it was a symbol of death.

He had chosen preaching as a "profession"—unfortunately, just as so many others had done. Yet he had striven to convince himself that he trusted in the merits of the Redeemer. He left his father's shop in his native country town for a dissenting college in the neighborhood of London. There he worked well and became a good scholar. His character was sound and his conscience firm. But he was injured both spiritually and morally by some of the instructions given there. For one of the highest priorities of the place was in teaching the would-be pastors how to make themselves *acceptable* to a congregation.

Most of the students were ready to treat this as their foremost duty. Therefore, much was said about the plan and composition of sermons, about style and utterance and elocution—all with a view to *success* in the pulpit, the lowest of all successes and the most worldly.

Walter Drake accepted these instructions on composition as high wisdom. He labored to form his style on the best models, so before beginning to write a sermon, he always heated the furnace of production with fuel from some exciting author. Even after some years when at last he did begin to develop some individuality, he could not shake himself free of those weary models. Thus his thoughts always seemed to have a certain stiffness and unreality, which blunted their impression.

Determined to *succeed*, he cultivated eloquence also—what he supposed was eloquence, that is. To attain the right gestures he looked far more into his landlady's mirror than he did into his own soul for any reflection of spiritual action. He had his reward in the success he sought. In a few years he was a popular preacher in one of London's suburbs— a good deal sought after and greatly lauded. He lived in comfort, indulged in some amount of show, married a wealthy widow whose life-annuity they spent completely between them. One might say he gazed out on the social landscape far oftener than he lifted his eyes to the hills.

After some ten or twelve years, a change began. They had three children; the two boys, healthy and beautiful, took scarlet fever and died; the poor sickly girl lived on. His wife, who had always been more devoted to her children than to her husband, pined away and died also. Her money was gone and his spirits began to fail him, and his small, pale daughter did not comfort him much. He was capable of true, but not yet of pure love. Little Dora—a small Dorothy—had always been a better child than either of her brothers. But he had loved them the more because others had admired them, and her the less because others pitied her. He did try to love her, but there was still much for him to unlearn.

Further change followed—gradual but rapid. His congregation began to discover that he was not the man he had once been. They complained of lack of variety in his preaching: he took it too easy, did not study his sermons sufficiently, often spoke extempore. A few in the church had not been favorable to him from the first, and this party was now gaining influence. Their leaders went so far as to request a detailed report of certain charitable funds administered by the pastor. Not only had the money been spent with complete uprightness, such as few of his accusers exercised in their own business affairs, but in making the payments he had actually exceeded the contributions which had been given him— the balance coming from his own pocket. Confident in his position and occupied with other thoughts, he had not been careful to set down the particulars of every expenditure. Therefore, his enemies seized upon the opportunity, hinting at a connection between the loss of his wife's annuity and the lack of details available regarding the whereabouts of the church's charitable monies. Tongues began to wag. And as gossip always does, the cancerous doubt about him grew worse. Mistrust of another, especially one in spiritual leadership, always heightens one's own feeling of righteousness and therefore remains one of the most insidious and ever-present cancers within the Church. Inevitably, doubts of his orthodoxy began to be expressed, and were believed without examination.

All at once he became aware of the general disloyalty of his flock and resigned. Scarcely had he done so when he was invited to Glaston and received with open arms. There he would heal his wounds, he thought, and spend the rest of his days in peace. The fall was painful, but he soon began to find the valley of humiliation that wholesome place all true pilgrims have declared it. He gradually sensed the futility of all for which he had spent his strength, and a waking desire for the God in whom he had only vaguely believed. These two questions favored the birth in his mind: had he ever entered in at the straight gate himself at all, or had he merely been standing by its side calling others to enter in?

He grew humble before the Master, sought his presence, and found him. He began to think less of books and rabbis, and even for a time of Paul and Apollos and Peter. Instead, he pored over the living tale of the New Covenant in the Gospels. He began to feel that the Lord meant what he said, and that his apostles also meant what he said. He forgot Calvin a good deal, outgrew the influences of Jonathan Edwards, and began to understand Jesus Christ.

That had been many years before, and he had grown much toward true life since. But from where he sat at this moment, even his previous humiliation seemed mild. Suddenly he had fallen still further: first from his handsome London house to a slightly above-average cottage, from comparative wealth to a hundred fifty pounds a year, and from a congregation of educated people to one in which there was not a person of higher standing than a tradesman. Yet now, even that congregation had rejected him as not up to their mark, and had turned him out to do his best on a scanty fifty pounds a year. From London he had fallen in humiliation; but this was pure shame. Now for the first time he knew what true poverty was. Had God forgotten him? Was this what God had brought him nearer to himself for? Was this the end of a ministry in which, in recent years at least, he had tried to serve God?

If only he could pay Mr. Jones's bill! That was what made the whole thing intolerable. Even that he could have borne had he been anything but a so-called man of God—one whose failure must certainly brand him as a hypocrite. What a reproach to the *the cause*!—the Congregational minister had run up a bill with the Church of England butcher which he was unable to pay! It was a shame he could not bear.

A humbler and better mood slowly dawned with unconscious change, and he began to ponder within himself whether he had been misusing the money God had given him. But he could only think of the poor he had fed and little Amanda whom he adopted, and surely God would overlook those points of extravagance. Yet if he had not the means, he had no right to do even those things. His only excuse was that he could not have foreseen how soon his income was going to shrink to a third. In the future he would have to withhold his generosity. But surely he could keep the child. At least there could be no doubt about that. God had money enough and certainly he would enable him to do that!—Only why did he bring him to such poverty?

So round and round he went in his thoughts, coming back again to his same old doubts. He rose at last with a tear trickling down his cheek, and walked back and forth along the riverbank.

Things went on nevertheless as if all were right with the world. The Lythe still flowed to the sea. The sun still shone gracious over all his kingdom. The primroses were shining about in every garden. The sound of the great organ pealed from the grand old church, and the sound of many voices issued from the humble chapel. Only where was the heart of it all?

8 / An Impromptu Transfusion

Meanwhile Faber was making his rounds, with the village of Owlkirk at the end of them. Before he was halfway there, his groom was tearing after him on Niger with a message from Mrs. Puckridge. But the groom never did catch him. When the doctor returned to the cottage, opened the door and walked upstairs, he expected to find the patient weak but on the way toward recovery. He was horrified instead to see her landlady weeping over the bed, the lady lying motionless with pale white lips and distended nostrils—to all appearances dead. Pillows, sheets and blankets were all a mass of red. The bandage had come off as she had slept, and all night long her blood had softly flowed from her. She was one of those from whom the blood, once set flowing, will flow on and on, and the tiniest wound is hard to make heal over.

Was the lovely creature gone? In dismay Faber reached for her wrist but could discern no pulse. He folded back the bedclothes and laid his ear on her heart. His whole soul listened.

Yes! Certainly there was the faintest flutter. He watched for a moment. Yes, he could just see the faintest movement of her lungs.

"Run!" he cried. "For God's sake run and bring me a jug of hot water and two or three basins. There is still a chance! We may save her. Bring me a syringe. If you don't have one, run from house to house till you get one. Her life depends on it!" By this time he was shouting after the scurrying landlady.

In a minute or two she returned.

"Have you got the syringe?" he cried, the moment he heard her step.

To his great relief she had. He told her to wash it out thoroughly with the hot water, unscrew the top, and take out the piston. While giving his directions he unwrapped the arm, enlarged the wound in the vein, and rebound the arm tight below the elbow. Then quickly he opened a vein of his own and held the syringe to catch the spout that followed. When it was full, he replaced the piston, telling Mrs. Puckridge to put her thumb on his wound. He turned the point of the syringe up and forced a little of the blood out to get rid of the air, then, with the help of a probe, inserted the nozzle in the wound, and gently forced the blood into her arm.

That done, he placed his own thumbs on the two wounds and made the woman wash out the syringe in clean hot water. Then he filled it as before, and again forced its contents into the lady's arm. This process he went through repeatedly.

Listening, he found her heart beating quite perceptibly, though irregularly. Her breath was faintly coming and going. Several times more he repeated the strange operation, then stopped. As he was occupied in binding up her arm, suddenly she gave a great shuddering sigh. By the time he had finished, the pulse was perceptible at her wrist. Last of all he bound up his own wound, from which had escaped a good deal more than what he had used. As he was doing so, he began to go faint and lay down on the floor. After a few moments' rest he was able to crawl from the room, and down into the garden at the back of the house, where he walked slowly to the little arbor at the end of it, and there sat down as if in a dream.

But in the dream his soul felt wondrously awake. He had been tasting death from the same cup with the beautiful woman who lay there, now coming alive with his life. If she had died, he would have believed all his life long that he had sent one of the loveliest of nature's living dreams back to the darkness long before her time. But in feeling her reviving pulse a terrible weight was lifted from him. Yet even in this blissful thought, a horror seized him at the presumption he had taken. What if the beautiful creature would rather have died than have the blood of a man she neither knew nor loved coursing through her veins?

"I am glad she never has to know it," he said to himself.

But Faber had little time to examine his feelings further, even had he been so inclined. With that big wound in the lady's arm, he would have to watch it almost constantly. Therefore he did not leave the village all day. He went to see another patient in it, and one on its outskirts, then had his dinner at the little inn where he put up Ruber. Returning, he sat all night long by the bedside of his patient.

There the lovely white face, blind like a statue, and the perfect arm which he had to watch as the very gate of death, grew into his heart. He dreaded the moment when she would open her eyes and his could no longer wander at will over her countenance. Again and again in the night he put a hand under her head and held a cooling drink to her lips. But not even when she drank did her eyes open. Like a child too weak to trust itself, therefore free of all anxiety and fear, she took whatever came and questioned nothing. He was at the foot of the bed where he could see the slightest movement perfectly through the opening of the curtain.

As the night wore on, by some change of position he had unknowingly drawn one of the curtains back a little from between them as he sat thinking about her. The candle shone full upon his face. Suddenly she opened her eyes.

Fever from loss of blood, remnants of sleep and dream, the bewilderment of sudden waking—all combined to paralyze her judgment and gave her imagination full swing. When she opened her eyes, she saw a beautiful face and nothing else. And it seemed to her as if it was itself the source of the light by which she saw. Her dream had combined fear and trouble, and when she beheld the shining countenance, she thought it was the face of the Savior: he was looking down upon her heart and reading all that was written there.

The tears rushed to her eyes and the next moment Faber saw two fountains of light and weeping in the face which had been only loveliest marble. The curtain fell between them, and the lady thought the vision had vanished. The doctor came softly through the dusk to her bedside. He felt her pulse, examined the bandage on her arm, gave her something to drink, and left the room.

Presently Mrs. Puckridge brought her some beef broth.

9 / Father and Daughter

The poor minister paced up and down, stung by gadflies of doubt. If he were in London he could sell his watch to raise some money. He had a ring somewhere too—an antique worth what now seemed a good deal. Mr. Drew would undoubtedly lend him what he needed, but he could not bring himself to ask. If he sold his watch and ring in Glaston, they would soon appear in the watchmaker's window, and that would cause a scandal—and with the Baptists growing so rapidly on the other side of town! For despite the heartless way in which the Congregationalists had treated him, theirs was no doubt the cause of scriptural Christianity, and it made him shudder to think of bringing even the smallest discredit upon his own denomination.

As he thought, Mr. Drake began to look back with something like horror upon the sermons he had preached on honesty. How would his inability to pay his debts appear in the eyes of those who had heard them? Oh, why hadn't he paid for everything when he had the money!

When Miss Drake returned from the chapel, she found her father leaning on the sun-dial where she had left him that morning. To all appearance he had not moved.

"Father," she said.

"It is a hard thing, my child," he responded, still without moving, "when the valley of humiliation comes before the river of death, and there is no land of Beulah in between. I had my good things in my youth, and now there are only bitter disappointments ahead."

She laid her hand on his shoulder lovingly, tenderly, worshipfully, but did not speak.

"As you see me now, Dorothy, my gift from God, you would hardly believe your father was once a young and popular preacher. Fool that I was! I thought they prized my preaching, and loved me for what I taught them. I thought I was somebody! With shame I confess it! Who were they, or what was their judgment to fool me in my own estimation of myself! Their praise was indeed a fit rock for me to build my shame upon."

"But, Father, what is even a sin when it is repented of?"

"A shame forever, my child. Our Lord did not protect even an apostle for his conceit and self-sufficiency, but he let him fall."

"He has not let you fall, Father."

"He is bringing my gray hairs to the grave with sorrow and shame, my child."

"Why, Father!" cried the girl, shocked at his words, "what have I done to make you say that?"

"Done, my darling! *You* done? You have done nothing but good ever since you could do anything. You have been like a mother to your old father. It is that *bill*, that horrid butcher's bill!"

Dorothy burst out laughing through her dismay, and wept and laughed at the same time for more than a minute before she could recover herself.

"Father! you dear father! You're too good to live. Why, there are forks and spoons enough in the house to pay that paltry bill!—not to mention the silver cream jug. Why didn't you tell me what was troubling you, Father?"

"I never could bear to owe money. I asked the man for his bill some time ago. The moment I looked at it I felt as if the Lord had forsaken me. It is easy for you to bear it because you are not the one accountable. And to find myself in such a miserable condition, with next to nothing between us and the workhouse, makes me doubt whether I have been a true servant of the Lord. During these last days the enemy has even dared tempt me with the question whether, after all, the unbelievers may indeed be right."

"I wouldn't think that unless I was driven to it, Father," said Dorothy, hardly knowing what she said, for his doubt shot a poisoned arrow of despair into her very heart.

Never doubting the security of his child's faith, he had not the slightest suspicion into what a sore spot his words had just carried torture. He did not know that doubt—shall I call him an angel or a demon?—had knocked at her door, that words dropped by Faber had conjured up in her heart hollow fears and stinging questions. Ready to trust and incapable of arrogance, it was hard for her to imagine how an upright, kind, and self-denying man like Mr. Faber could say such things if he did not *know* them to be true. The very word *science* appeared to carry overwhelming authority. But nothing she had learned from her father either provided her with reply or argument against her doubts. And nothing that went on at chapel or church seemed to have anything to do with the questions that presented themselves to her.

Such a rough shaking of so-called faith has been of endless service to many by exposing the insecurity of all foundations of belief except that which is discovered by digging with the spade of obedience. It is good for all honest souls to be thus shaken. That shaking should be for those who have been building upon doctrines, upon faith, upon experiences, upon anything but Christ himself, as revealed by himself and his spirit to all who obey him, and so revealing the Father.

Dorothy was a gift from God, and the trouble that gnawed at her heart she would not let out to gnaw at her father's.

"There's Ducky come to call us to dinner," she announced, glad for the intrusion.

"Dinner!" groaned Mr. Drake, and would have remained where he was. But for Dorothy's sake he rose and followed, feeling like a repentant thief who had stolen the meal.

On the next day, Monday morning, Mr. Bevis's groom came to the rectory with a note for the curate, inviting him and Mrs. Wingfold to dine at Nestley the same day if possible.

> I know that Monday ought to be an idle day for you, but I want to see you as soon as possible. I would come to you except I have reasons for wishing to see you here rather than at Glaston. The earlier you can come and the longer you can stay the better, but you shall go as soon after an early dinner as you please. God bless you.
>
> John Bevis

The curate took the note to his wife. An affirmative answer was given to the groom, and Helen's pony carriage was ordered out.

The curate called everything Helen's. He had a great contempt for the spirit of men who marry rich wives and then lord it over their money as if they had done a fine thing in getting hold of it, and the wife had all along been but keeping it from its rightful owner. But Helen did not like his habit, especially when he would ask her if he might have this or that, and do so and so. Any common man who heard him would have thought him afraid of his wife; but a large-hearted woman would at once have understood, as did Helen, that it all came of his fine sense of truth, reality and obligation.

"Your ponies are splendid today, Helen," he said admiringly.

They were the tiniest, daintiest things, the smallest ever seen in harness but with all the ways of big horses, therefore amusing in their very grace.

"Why *will* you call them *my* ponies, Thomas?" returned his wife, just sufficiently vexed to find it easy to pretend to be cross. "I don't see what good has come to me by marrying you if everything is to be mine just like it always was!"

"Don't be unreasonable, Helen," entreated the curate. "Don't you see it is my way of showing myself how much they are mine? If I had bought them with my own money, I should hardly care for them. Thank God they are *not* mine. *You* are mine, my life, and they are yours. They *are* mine therefore because they are part of you like your clothes or your watch. If a thing is yours, it is ten times more mine than if I had bought it. For, just because it is yours, I am able to possess it as the meek who inherit the earth rather than the landowners. It makes *having things* such a deep and high—indeed, a perfect—gift!"

"But people will think I am like the lady we heard the other day, who told her husband the sideboard was hers, not his. Thomas, I hate to look like the rich one, when *you* gave me all that makes life worth living."

"No, no, my darling! Don't say that. I was only the postman that brought you the good news."

"Just don't make me look in public as if I did not behave like a lady to my own husband, Thomas."

"Well, my beautiful, I'll make up for all my wrongs by ordering you about like a king if you like."

"I wish you would. You don't order me about half as much as you should."

"I'll try to do better," he said agreeably, and the look that passed between them was full of love and humor and goodwill.

Nestley was a lovely place. The house was quite old—one of those houses with a history and a growth which are getting rarer every day as the ugly, modern, overdone temples of mammon usurp their place. It was dusky, cool, and somber—a little rundown, actually, which harmonized with its peculiar charm and, indeed, added to it. A lawn, not immaculate, sank slowly to a babbling little brook of the Lythe, and beyond were fern-covered slopes and heather and pine woods. The rector was a sensible Englishman who loved grass like a village poet and would have no flower beds cut in his lawn. Neither would he have any flowers planted in the summer to be taken up again before the winter. The result was that for half the show he had twice the loveliness.

As soon as his visitors arrived, he and his curate went away together, and Mrs. Wingfold was shown into the drawing room where Mrs. Bevis sat with her knitting. It would be difficult to imagine a greater contrast between the two ladies seated together in that long, low, dusky room. I am greatly puzzled to think what conscious good in life Mrs. Bevis enjoyed. She had no special friends to whom she unburdened herself. She had no pet, had never been seen hugging a child, never read poetry or novels or history, never questioned anything, never doubted. Certainly she had her virtues. Her servants stayed with her for years and years. When her husband asked her to go out with him, she was always ready. She never kept a tradesman waiting for a bill, never refused a reasonable request, and never humiliated one of lower standing. In fact, she was a stuffed bag of virtues. But what puzzles me is how she contrived to live with herself, never questioning the comfort of the arrangement or wondering about any of life's deeper questions.

As for Helen, she had since her marriage changed considerably in the right direction. She used to be a little dry, a little stiff, and a little stately. Now her step was lighter, her voice more flexible, her laugh much merrier and more frequent, for now her heart was full of joy. Her husband praised God when he heard her laugh, for the laugh in itself suggested praise. She would pull up her ponies in the middle of the street, and at a word or sign the carriage would suddenly be full of children. At the least rudeness by one of them, the offender would be deposited on the sidewalk to watch her drive two or three times up and down the street with her load. Then she would let everyone out, and take another load, and another, until as many of the village children as she judged fit had a taste of the pleasure.

She was overbearing in one thing, and that was submission. This occasionally made her husband just as uncomfortable as his references to *her* possessions did her. In truth, they were submissive to one another, out of the depths of their mutual love and respect. Their spirits were so one that that quality which is often mistaken for the *necessary* opposite to submission, authority—by which is erroneously at times thought to be the kingly setting down of instructions for strict obedience—was scarcely, if ever, seen between them. True authority is born in a heart of submission. And because Helen and Thomas were submitted in love to one another, the authority of Christ flowed in and through them both, without so much as a thought given to the *words* themselves by either of them.

I have said enough to show there was a great contrast between the two ladies. As to what passed in the way of talk, I dare not attempt to report, for I was not present. I did hear them talk once, and they laughed too, but not one significant point could I afterward recall. But Mrs. Wingfold had developed a great aptitude for liking people. Surely more people would allow themselves to be thus changed if they realized how greatly the coming of the kingdom of God is slowed by a simple lack of courtesy. So many by their very look imply dislike. Whether such a feeling is actually in their heart, I do not know. But true courtesy, putting those we meet at ease by our look and tone, is a most lovely and indispensable grace—one that nobody but a Christian can thoroughly develop. A year before, Helen could hardly endure Mrs. Bevis. But now she had found something to like in her, and there was confidence and faith between them. So there they sat, the elder lady meandering on, and Helen, who had taken care to bring some work with her, every now and then giving her a bright glance, or saying two or three words with a smile, or asking some simple question. Mrs. Bevis talked chiefly of the supposed illness of Miss Meredith, which she had heard strange reports about.

In the meantime the two gentlemen were walking through the park in earnest conversation. They crossed the little brook and climbed to the heath on the other side. There the rector stood, and turning to his companion, admitted: "It's rather late in the day for a fellow to wake up, isn't it, Wingfold? I never was much of a theologian, and was brought up to hate fanaticism. But it may have blinded me to some things. It's not for me to start up and teach the people, though I ought to have been doing it all this time. I've got nothing to teach them. God only knows whether I haven't been breaking every one of the commandments I used to read to them every Sunday."

"But God *does* know," declared the curate, with even more than usual respect in his tone. "And that is well, for otherwise we might go on breaking them forever."

The rector gave him a sudden look, but said nothing. Then he fell deep in thought, and for some time was silent.

"There's one thing that's clear," he resumed. "I've been taking my pay and doing no work. I used to think I was at least doing no harm—that I was merely using one of the privileges of my position: I not only paid a curate but saw to the repair of the place. But now for the first time I am beginning to see that the money was not given me merely for that. And there's all this property my wife has given me. What have I done with it? The kingdom of heaven has not come a hairsbreadth nearer because of my being a rector and parson of the Church of England. Neither are the people of England a shade the better because I am one of her landowners. It is surely time I did something worth doing, Wing-fold!"

"I think it is, sir," agreed the curate.

"Then in God's name, what am I to do?" he pleaded.

"Nobody can answer that question but yourself, sir," replied Wing-fold.

"It would be of no use my trying to preach. I could not write a sermon if I worked at it a month. If it were a paper on the management of the stable, now I think I could write respectably about that. I know what I'm doing there. But that's not what the church pays me for. There is one thing that comes over me now and then; I would like to read prayers in the old place again." He paused and gazed reflectively at Wingfold.

"I tell you what," he resumed. "We won't make any fuss about it—what's in a name anyway!—but from now on you shall be incumbent* and I will be curate. You shall preach—or what you please, and I shall read the prayers or not, just as you wish. Can you make me into something, Wingfold? Don't ask me to do what I can't, but help me to do

---

*Smaller parishes unable to maintain a full-time *vicar* were presided over by a *curate*— a clergyman who was appointed to preach and perform the duties and services of the vicar but who did not hold that office himself. The curate's position, which Wingfold held, was less substantial and represented the bottom rung of the ecclesiastical ladder. A curate's pay was less, and he could be removed at any time with no reason given. The *rector*, Mr. Bevis in this instance, held responsibility for overseeing the business affairs of the parish on behalf of the Church of England. In offering to make Wingfold *incumbent*, Mr. Bevis was proposing to advance him into the permanent position of *vicar*.

what I can. Here's another thing I've been thinking: it came to me last night as I was walking about here after returning to Owlkirk from Glaston. Here in this corner of the parish we are a long way from the church. In this village there is no place of worship except a little Methodist one. They preach, and they mean it, and it's fine so far as it goes. But it isn't for everyone, you know. Now, why shouldn't I build a little place here on my own ground and get the bishop to consecrate it? I would read prayers for you in the abbey church in the morning, and then you would not be too tired to come and preach here in the evening. I would read the prayers here, too, if you liked."

"I think your plan is delightful," answered the curate after a moment's pause. "I would only suggest one improvement—that you should not have your chapel consecrated. You would find it much more useful then. It will be dedicated to the God of the whole earth instead of the God of the Church of England."

"Why! aren't they the same?" cried the rector, half aghast.

"Yes," answered Wingfold, "and all will be well when the Church of England really recognizes the fact. Meantime, its idea of God will not at all fit the God of the whole earth. And that is why our church is in bondage. Unless she bursts the bonds of her own selfishness, she will burst her heart and go to pieces."

"I don't understand you," exclaimed the rector. "What does all that have to do with the consecration of my chapel?"

"If you don't consecrate it," answered Wingfold, "it will remain a thoroughfare for all divine influences, not just those deemed appropriate by the Church of England. It will be open to every wind of the Spirit that blows. Consecration—"

Here the curate checked himself, realizing what an insensitive thing it would be, merely for the satisfaction of speaking his own mind, to disturb his rector as he was thinking about a good work.

"But," Wingfold concluded, "there will be plenty of time to think of all that later. The idea is a delightful one. Apart from it altogether, however, if you would but read prayers in the church here, it would wonderfully strengthen my hands. Only I am afraid if you were in attendance regularly, I might shock you sometimes."

"I will take my chances. If you do, I will tell you of it. And if I do what you don't like, you must tell me of it. I trust neither of us will find that we are incapable of understanding each other's position."

They walked to the spot which the rector already had in mind for the proposed chapel. It was on a bit of gently rising ground, near the whole village of Owlkirk. One of the nearest cottages was that of Mrs. Puckridge. They saw the doctor ride in at the other end of the street, stop there, fasten his horse to the fence, and go in.

11 / The Garden at Owlkirk_____

No sooner had Faber left the cottage Monday morning than foolish Mrs. Puckridge proceeded to tell the patient, still upset and weak, all the terrible danger she had been in and the marvelous way the doctor had brought her back from the door of death. What little blood there was in her body rushed to her face, then back to her heart. She turned faint and it was with great difficulty that her landlady brought her out of it. When Faber came in and saw his patient, he perceived at once that something had overly excited her. He strongly suspected that, for all her promises to keep quiet, Mrs. Puckridge had betrayed what he had done.

When Miss Meredith saw him approach her bedside, a look reminding him of the ripple of a sudden cold gust passing over still water swept across her face. She closed her eyes and turned a little from him. Cursing in his heart the faithlessness of Mrs. Puckridge, he felt her pulse with a gentle yet rather distant professional manner, gave her attendant some authoritative directions, and left, saying he would call again in the afternoon.

As much as she might detest him for what he had done, he said to himself, he had had no choice. Without the bold and hasty operation he had contrived, she would surely have died. She might well despise him for putting his blood into her veins. But she would be no worse for knowing it. And at least she was alive.

During the next seven days he visited her twice a day. He still had good cause to be anxious, for her recovery was very slow. During all these visits hardly a word passed between them. After a week the visits were reduced to one a day. But even as the lady grew stronger she seemed to become more reserved, cool, and her manner grew more withdrawn. After two weeks he reduced his visits to every other day—very unwillingly. By that time she had come to occupy nearly as much of his thoughts as all the rest of his patients together. Because his visits seemed less than welcome to her, except for the physical help they brought her, she was so restrained toward him that he could gain no insight whatever into her personality or character. He was haunted with her form, to which he had given a renewal of life, as a murderer is haunted with the form of a man he has killed. But always her face wore a look of aversion, as if she regarded him as some vile magician who had first cast her into the grave and then brought her back by some hellish art. She did fascinate him. But he would not admit that he was in love with her. A man may be fascinated and hate. A man is not necessarily in love with the woman whose form haunts his thoughts. So said Faber to himself. And, indeed, who knows at what exact moment love begins to be love. But he must have been a good way toward that point to have begun such denials.

He had long come to believe that she was in some dire straits. She appeared to be a lady, and the daintiness of some of her garments confirmed this. And yet other factors indicated poverty. What reason could a lady have for being alone in a poor country lodging, without a maid, with little luggage, and near death with illness? Could it be the peculiarity of her strange position, and no dislike to him, that made her treat him with such coldness? Perhaps she dreaded being misunderstood.

She would want to pay him for his services. And what was he to do? He must let her pay something or she would consider her position all the more awkward. And yet how could he take the money from her hand?

One day Mrs. Puckridge met him at the door, looking mysterious. She pointed with her thumb over her shoulder to indicate that the lady was in the garden, but at the same time nudged him with her elbow, confident that what she had to say would justify the liberty. Then she led the way into the little parlor.

"Please, sir," she whispered, turning and closing the door. "I need you to tell me what to do. She says she's got no money to pay neither me nor the doctor, so she's done given me this and wants me to sell it. I daren't show it to anyone! They'd say I stole it! She declares if I mention to a living soul where I got it, she'd never speak to me again. 'Course she don't mean you, sir, seein' as doctors and clergymen ain't nobody—leastways nobody to be spreadin' secrets. My meanin' is they ain't them as ain't to be told things. I declare I'm 'most terrified to set eyes on the thing!"

She handed the doctor a little morocco leather case. He opened it and saw a ring, plainly of great value. It was old-fashioned—a round mass of small diamonds with a good-sized one in the center.

"You are quite right," he acknowledged. "The ring is far too valuable for you to dispose of. Bring it to my house at four o'clock, and I will take care of selling it for you."

Mrs. Puckridge was greatly relieved and ended the interview by leading Faber to the back door. When she opened it, he saw his patient sitting in the little arbor. She rose and came to meet him.

"You see I am quite well now," she declared, holding out her hand.

Her tone was guarded, but surely the ice was melting a little. She stooped to pick a daisy and spoke again while she was still stooped down.

"When you come again," she added, "will you kindly let me know how much I am in your debt?"

As she ended she rose and stood before him. Ashamed to speak of her indebtedness, the whiteness of her cheek grew warm, which was all her complexion ever revealed of a blush. It showed plainer in the deepened darkness of her eyes and the tremulous increase of light in them.

"I will," he replied. "You will be careful?" he added. "Indeed you must, or you will never recover your strength."

She answered only with a little sigh, as if weakness was such a weariness, then looked away across the garden and beyond.

"And of all things," he advised, "wear shoes whenever you come outside, not mere slippers like those."

"Is this a healthy place, Dr. Faber?" she asked, plainly a little trouble in her eyes.

"Yes," he answered. "And when you are able to walk on the fields of heath, you will find the air invigorating. Only remember what I say about your shoes. May I ask if you intend to remain here some length of time?"

"I have already remained so much longer than I intended that I am afraid to say."

"Excuse me—I know I am presuming—but in our profession we must do so now and then. Could you not have some friend with you till you are perfectly strong again? After what you have come through, it may be years before you are quite what you were. I don't want to frighten you—only to make you careful."

"There is no one," she answered, her voice low and trembling.

"No one—?" repeated Faber, as if waiting for the end of the sentence. But his heart gave a great bound.

"No one to come to me. I am alone in the world. My mother died when I was a child and my father two years ago. He was a military officer. I was his only child and used to go about with him. I have no friends."

Her voice faltered more and more. When it stopped she seemed to be choking back the tears.

"Since then," she resumed resolutely, "I have been a governess. My last job was in Yorkshire, in a cold part of the county, and my health began to fail me. I heard that Glaston was a warm place, and one where I would likely get employment. But I became ill on my way there and was forced to stop. A lady on the train told me that this was such a sweet, quiet little place and so when we got to the station I came here."

Faber found himself unable to speak. The thought of a lady like her traveling about alone looking for work was frightful!

"I have papers to show," she added quietly, as if thinking that he might be taking her for an imposter.

All this time she had never looked him in the face. She had fixed her gaze on the far horizon, but a smile, half pitiful, half proud, flickered about her upper lip.

"I am glad you have told me," he assured her. "I may be able to serve you if you will permit me. I know a great many of the families about here."

"Oh, thank you!" she cried, looking up at him with an expression of dawning hope. It was the first time he had ever seen her face light up, and she appeared more beautiful than ever. Then she turned from him, apparently lost in relief, and walked away toward the arbor. He followed a little behind her, for the path was narrow. All at once she grew pale, shuddered, put her hand to her head, and sat down on the bench just inside the arbor. Faber was alarmed and took her cold hand. She would have drawn it away, but he insisted on feeling her pulse.

"You must come in at once," he insisted.

She rose, visibly trembling. He supported her into the house, made her lie down, got a hot water bottle for her feet, and covered her with blankets.

"You are quite unfit for any exertion yet," he said, seating himself near her. "You must consent to be an invalid for a while. Don't worry. By the time you find the job you are seeking, you should have regained a good deal of your strength. I promise to look around for you. Keep your mind at rest."

She answered with a look that dazzled him, her eyes radiating with thankfulness. His gaze sank before the look and he felt himself catching his breath. When he raised them again he saw tears in her eyes. He rose, said he would call again in the evening, and left the room.

During the rest of his rounds he did not find it easy to give sufficient attention to his other patients. His custom was to think about them as he rode, but the last look he had seen on her face, and the tears in her eyes, pushed everything else from his thoughts.

Before long the shadow of love, whose name is Human Kindness, began to resume its earlier tyranny over him. Oh, the bliss of knowing oneself the protector of such a woman! What a glory to be the object of such looks of thankfulness! Thinking he was growing to love her, his true mental condition was nothing but the blossom of his childhood dream: to be the benefactor of his race, of being loved and worshiped for his kindness.

But the poison of the dream had since grown more lethal. Since then, the credit for his goodness had fallen upon himself and had gathered sway over his spirit. He had become proud of his kindness, and pride in goodness is far worse than delight in the thanks of our fellows. He had become a slave to his own ideal. He had taken several steps backward in time, though forward in his real history. It would be long before he learned to love true Goodness. For to him who *is* good, goodness has ceased to be either an object or an abstraction; it is *in* him—a thirst to give, a solemn quiet passion to bless others, a delight in witnessing well-being. Ah, how we dream and talk of love, until the holy fire of the true divine love, the love that God kindles in a man toward his fellows, burns the shadow out of our shallow ideals!

In the afternoon Mrs. Puckridge appeared with the ring. He took it, told her to wait, and went out. In a few minutes he returned, and to the woman's astonishment, gave her fifty pounds in bills. He did not tell her he had been to nobody but his own banker. The ring he had carefully put away, with no definite plans of what to do with it, but with the great hope that it should one day be returned. In the meantime, no one would know he had simply borrowed the money.

The idea shot across the heaven of his thoughts about what a lovely wedding present it would make! and the meteor drew a long train of shining fancies after it.

12 / The Parlor at Owlkirk

When Faber called in the evening, his patient looked much better. There was even a touch of playfulness in her manner. Assessing the look on her face, he hoped some crisis had passed, and he assumed the money she had received for the ring had something to do with it. As he was thinking these things, suddenly she looked up and said, "I can never repay you for what you have done for me, Dr. Faber."

"You can repay me," he returned, "simply by never again thinking of yourself as under obligation to me."

"That would not be right," she rejoined.

"Then I shall be content," he replied, "if you will say nothing about it until you are well settled. After that, I promise to send you a long bill if you like."

She smiled, looked up brightly, and added, "You promise?"

"I do."

"If you don't keep your promise, I shall have to take severe measures. Don't fancy me without money. I could pay you now; at least I think so."

It was a good sign that she could talk about money so openly. Only a clean soul can talk frankly about money. Most people treat it like a hidden sin: they follow it earnestly, but do not talk about it in the society of other people. What had become all at once of her constraint and stateliness?

Some books were lying on the table which could hardly belong to Mrs. Puckridge. He took one up.

"Do you like Tennyson?" she asked.

"That is a hard question to answer," he replied. "I like Tennyson better than I like this particular book of his."

"Ah! You do not understand it. I didn't until after my father died. Then I began to know what it meant, and now I think it is the most beautiful poem I ever read."

"You are fond of poetry then?"

"I don't read much. But I think there is more in some poetry than in most of the prose in the world."

"That is saying a great deal."

"Too much, probably, when I think of how few good books I have actually read in my life. You don't like poetry?"

"I can't say I do much. I like the men that give you things just as they are. I don't like poets that mix themselves up with what they see, and then rave about Nature. I confess myself a lover of truth beyond all other things."

"But are you sure," she inquired, looking him straight in the eyes, "that in your anxiety not to make more of things than they are, you do not make less of them than they are?"

"There is hardly fear of that, Miss Meredith. I only dislike humbug when it rears its head in our sentimental poets."

"But surely, Mr. Faber, if there be a God—"

"Ah!" interrupted the doctor, "but suppose there should be no God, what then?"

"Then I grant you, there could be no poetry. Somebody says poetry is the speech of hope; and certainly if there were no God there could be no hope."

Faber was struck with what she said. Not from any feeling that there was truth in it, but from its indication of a logical mind. He was on the point of further reply, but he was afraid of disturbing his bird by scattering his crumbs too roughly. He honestly believed that to deliver one from such superstitions as she seemed to hold was the greatest gift one human being could offer to another. But at the same time he could not bear to think of her recoiling from a statement of his unbelief. And he realized too that he had already misrepresented himself by giving her the impression that he was incapable of enjoying imaginative poetry. He had indeed in his youth been fond of such verse.

And who would wish for a lady to be scientific in her ways of regarding things? He would not have a lady indifferent to poetry. That would argue a lack of poetry in herself, and such a lady would be like a scentless rose. Was not womanhood itself the live concentration, the perfect outcome, of the vast poetic show of Nature? Was she not the sublimation, the essence of sunsets, and fading roses, and butterflies, and snows, and running waters, and changing clouds, and cold shadowy moonlight? He argued this now in sorrow; for what was woman but a bubble on the sand of the infinite soulless sea—a bubble of a hundred lovely hues, that must shine because it could not help it, and for the same reason break? She was not to blame. Let her shine and glow and sparkle and vanish. For him, he cared for nothing but science. To him science stood for truth, and for truth in the inward parts stood obedience to the laws of Nature. If he was one of a poor race he would rise above his fellows by being good to them in their misery. Let the laws of nature work, eyeless and heartless as the whirlwind, he would live his life and depart without a murmur. He would do his endeavor and die and return to nothing. Such had been for years his stern philosophy, and why should it now trouble him that a woman thought differently?

Yet as he sat gazing in the broad light of day through the cottage window, across whose panes waved the little red bells of the common fuchsia, something that had nothing to do with science, and yet *was*, seemed to linger and hover over the little garden—something from the very depths of loveliest folly. Was it the refrain of an old song? or the smell of withered rose-leaves? or was there indeed a kind of light such as never was on sea or shore?

"I did not mean," said the doctor at length, "that I could not enjoy the kind of verse you spoke of. It's just that I have a weakness for honesty."

"There is something not right about that, Mr. Faber," asserted Miss Meredith. "You cannot mean that you enjoy something you do not believe in?"

"Surely there are many things one can enjoy without believing in them?"

"On the contrary, it seems to me that enjoying a thing is only another word for believing in it. Surely the thing that ought to be is the thing that must be."

"How can we tell that?" he returned. "What evidence do we find for it in nature? Destruction is the very center and framework of the world. I will not call Nature cruel; what right have I to complain? Nature cannot help it. She is no more to blame for bringing me forth than I am to blame for being brought forth. We are the slaves of our circumstances, and therefore we resort to dreams of *what ought to be*."

Miss Meredith sat silently for a time.

"I don't know how to answer you," she admitted at length. "But you do not disturb my hope of seeing my father again."

Faber suppressed the smile that was ready to break forth on his lips, and she went on.

"And I could hardly fall into doubt today, whatever you said, and you will agree with me when I tell you something wonderful. This morning I had not enough money to buy myself the pair of strong shoes you said I should wear. I had nothing left but a few trinkets of my mother's—one of them a ring I thought worth about ten pounds. I gave it to my landlady to sell for me, hoping she would get five for it. She brought me fifty, and I am rich!"

Her last words rang with triumph. Faber realized that he himself had been responsible for building up her foolish faith. He consoled himself by thinking how with a single word he could destroy her phantom house. It was he, the unbeliever, and no God, in or out of her Bible, that had helped her! It did not occur to him that she might then see him as only a reed blown by a divine wind.

"I am glad to hear of your good fortune," he answered. "Yet I cannot see how it has anything to do with the 'hope' you spoke of. You simply had in your possession more than you realized."

"In all nature and history," she replied, "God likes to see things grow. If that ring was given to my mother against the time when the last child of her race should find herself otherwise helpless, does the fact that the provision was made when she was so young turn it all into mere chance? Must I call every good I receive a chance unless an angel comes visibly out of the sky and gives it to me? That would be to believe in a God who could not work his will by his own natural laws. Here I am, free and hopeful—all I needed is provided. Yesterday all was dark and troubled; today the sun has risen."

"There is a tide in the affairs of men that comes and goes," declared the doctor, "but I hardly think Providence is behind every little wave."

"How would I have got through till now had I not believed there was one caring for me all the time, even when I was most alone?"

"Do you never lose that faith?"

"Yes, many times. But it always comes back."

"It comes and goes with your health."

"No, it is strongest sometimes when I am least well."

"When you are most feverish, no doubt," judged the doctor. *What a fool I am to go on contradicting her!* he added to himself.

"I think I know you better than you imagine, Mr. Faber. You are one of those men who like to represent things worse than they really believe. One who lives for other people as you do cannot be so far from the truth as your words would indicate."

Though he honestly denied the praise, nevertheless he found it sounded sweet from her lips, sweeter still from her eyes and from the warmer white of her cheek. And as he rode slowly home, the doctor thought, *If it were not for sickness, age, and death, this world of ours would be no bad place to live in. Surely mine is the most needful and noblest of callings—to fight for youth and health and love, against age and sickness and decay. To fight death to the last, even knowing he will win in the end!*

Faber's materialism did not come from a defect in his imagination or powers of thought. But I cannot determine how much honesty, pride, and the desire to be satisfied with himself had to do with it. It is not that he had an unusual amount of pride; he was less easily satisfied with himself than most are. Most people will make excuses for themselves which they would neither make nor accept for their neighbor. Their own failures and idiosyncrasies trouble them little. But Faber was of another sort. As ready as any other man to discover what could be said in his favor, he was not so ready to completely accept it. He required a good deal of himself. But then he unconsciously compared himself with his acquaintances, and judged himself by their lives.

It is hard to understand how a man can prefer being the slave of blind helpless law to being the child of living Wisdom; why, he would believe in nothing rather than a perfect Will. Yet it is not unintelligible because he cannot see the Wisdom or the Will unless he draws near to it.

But for those who have lost a "faith" they once adhered to in their youth, for my part I would rather disbelieve with them than have what they have lost. For I would rather have no God than the God whom they suppose me to believe in, and therefore must be the God in whom they imagined they believed in the days of their ignorance. That those were the days of their ignorance, I do not doubt; but are these the days of their knowledge? The time will come when they will see deeper into their own hearts than now, and will be humbled, like many other men, by what they see.

13 / Mr. Drake's New Outlook

About four years previous to this time, while Mr. Drake was still in good standing with the people of Cowlane Chapel, he traveled to London to visit an old friend—a woman who was very benevolent toward orphans. At the time of his visit her thoughts and feelings were largely occupied with a lovely little girl whose history had been severed and lost completely.

A poor woman in Southwark had established two rooms of her house where mothers who had to work away from home could bring their children in the morning and leave them till night. This she did partly out of compassion for children and their mothers, and partly to earn her own bread. This particular child had been committed to her charge day after day for some weeks. One morning when she brought her, the mother seemed ill, and she did not appear at night to take her home. The next day the woman heard she was in a smallpox hospital. For a week or so the money to pay for the child continued to come regularly, and then ceased altogether. After that the woman heard nothing more, either from or about the mother. After two weeks she went to the hospital to ask about her. No patient corresponding to her description was in the place. The surname was a common one, and several patients with it had lately died and been buried, while others had recovered and were gone. Her inquiries in the neighborhood had no better success: no one knew the mother, and she was unable even to discover where the woman had lived.

She could not bear the thought of taking the child to the workhouse, and kept her for another six or eight weeks. But she had a sickly son and a grown lad also to support. So she had asked the counsel of the lady I have mentioned. When Mr. Drake arrived, his friend had been searching in vain to find a home for the little girl.

Since his boys had been taken from him, and the unprized girl left behind had grown so precious, Mr. Drake had learned to love children as God's little ones. No doubt like many people, he had a dread of children with unknown parents, for who could tell what roots of bitterness, beyond man's common inheritance, might spring up in them? But what little was known of this child's mother was unusually favorable; and when his friend took him to see the child, his heart went out to her. He took her home to Dorothy. Now she was growing up, as we have seen her, a somewhat wild, roguish, sweet, forgetful, but not disobedient child—very dear to both Drakes, who called her their duckling.

In his adversity Mr. Drake had grown fearful, and had begun to doubt whether he had a right to keep her. His was an impetuous nature, and would not give even God time to do the thing that needed time to be done well. He saw that a crisis was at hand. Perhaps, however, God saw a spiritual crisis where he could see only a material one.

Dorothy had a small sum, saved by her mother and so invested to bring her about twenty pounds a year. Of the last payment she had two pounds left, with the next payment not due for another two months. Her father had nothing. This was their state of affairs as they sat down at breakfast Monday morning after the saddest Sunday either of them had ever spent. And all Mr. Drake could think of now was his butcher's bill. The moment breakfast was over he rose hastily and left the room. Dorothy quickly followed him. He was already opening the front door of the house, his hat in his hand.

"Where are you going in such a hurry, Father?" she inquired. "Wait a moment and I'll go with you."

"My child, we must be as honest as we can. I must go see Mr. Jones."

"But we may be able to borrow the money—who knows what may happen?"

"That's just it, my dear! Who knows what? We can be sure of nothing in this world."

"And what about the next world then, Father?"

The minister was silent. If God was anywhere, he must be here as much as there! But that was not the problem at hand now. He owed the money; the man had sent him a bill, and he was bound to let him know that he could not pay it by the end of the week. Without another word, he walked from the house, a man afraid of cowardice, and went straight toward the butcher's. He was out of the lane and well into Pine Street before he remembered to put on his hat.

While still a good distance off, he saw the butcher standing in front of his shop—a tall, thin man in blue. His steel glittered by his side and a red cap colorfully adorned the curls of his gray hair. He was discussing, over a small joint of mutton, some point of economic interest with a country customer in a checkered shawl. To the minister's annoyance the woman was one of his former congregation, and he would gladly have passed the shop without being seen. But he could not leave his mission. When he came near, the butcher turned from the woman and removed his hat momentarily as he greeted Mr. Drake.

"At your service, sir," he said.

His courtesy added to the minister's awkwardness; clearly the man imagined he had brought him his money. Times were indeed changed since his wife used to drive out in her carriage and pay the bills! Was this what came of working in God's vineyard for the better part of a lifetime? The poverty was not the worst of it; but the shame! Who ever heard of St. Paul not being able to pay a butcher's bill? No doubt St. Paul was one of God's generals and he was a mere private, but in the service there was no respect of persons. On the other hand, who ever heard of St. Paul having any bills to pay?—or for that matter, of his marrying a rich wife and getting into expensive habits through popularity! Who ever heard of his being dependent on a congregation! Paul had accepted help sometimes but always had his tentmaking to fall back upon.

Much more of this sort of thing went through his mind in a flash. The country woman had again drawn the attention of the butcher with a parting word.

"You don't want a chicken today, do you, Mr. Drake?" she said, as she turned to go.

"No, thank you, Mrs. Thompson. How is your husband?"

"Better, thank you, sir. Good morning, sir."

"Mr. Jones," began the minister—and as he spoke he stepped inside the shop, removed his hat, and wiped his forehead—"I come to you in shame. I do not have enough money to pay your bill. Indeed, I cannot even pay a portion of it for two months."

"Don't mention it, Mr. Drake, sir."

"But the bill you just sent, Mr. Jones."

"Oh! never mind. I shall do very well, I dare say. There are many that owe me a good deal more than you do, sir, and I'm obliged to you for letting me know at once how things stand."

"It is all very disgraceful, but I simply can't help it."

"Disgraceful, sir!" exclaimed Mr. Jones. "I wish everyone thought as you do that has ten times more to be ashamed of."

"I have a request to make," the pastor went on, heedless of the butcher's remark, and he pulled out a large and handsome gold watch. "Would you oblige me by taking this watch as security until I do pay you? It is worth a great deal more than your bill. If I should die before paying you your bill, you will be at liberty to sell it; and what is left over after deducting interest, you can give to my daughter."

Mr. Jones stared at him with his mouth open.

"What do you make of me, sir?" he gasped. "You want to trust me with a watch like that but don't think I will trust you with a little bill that ain't yet three months old? Now you just never mention the bill again to me. If I have to, I'll ask for it in good time. Now, can I serve you with anything today?"

"No. I thank you. I must at least avoid adding to my debt."

"I hope what you do buy, you'll buy from me, sir. I don't mind waiting for my money, but what cuts me to the heart is to see one who owes me money goin' over the way as if he hadn't found my meat good enough. That does rile me, sir.''

"Take my word for it, Mr. Jones, all the meat we have we shall have from you. But you see, I am not quite so—so—''

Here he stopped with a grim smile.

"Look ye here, Mr. Drake!" broke in the butcher. "You parsons ain't proper brought up. You ain't learned to take care of yourselves. Us others, we've learned from the first to look out for number one. But you parsons now—you'll excuse me, sir; I don't mean no offense—you ain't brought up to it. An' it ain't expected of you, but it's a great neglect in your education, sir. An' I can't say I think much o' them dissenters; they don't stick by their own. But you're an honest man, sir, if ever there was one. An' ask for that money I never will, because I know when you can pay, pay you will. Keep your mind easy, sir. I won't come to grief for lack of what you owe. Only don't go starving yourself, Mr. Drake. Have a bit of meat when you want it, an' don't think twice about it.''

The minister was just able to thank his new friend and no more. He held out his hand to the butcher, forgetful of the grease that came with his work. The butcher gave it a squeeze that nearly shot it out of his lubricated grasp, and they parted, both better men as a result of the interview.

When Mr. Drake reached home, he met his daughter coming out to find him. He took her hand, led her into the house, and up to his study where he closed the door.

"Dorothy," he said, "it is sweet to be humbled. The Spirit can bring water from the rock and grace from a hard heart—I mean mine, not the butcher's. He has behaved to me as I don't see how any but a Christian could. He reminds me of the son in the parable who said, 'I won't go,' but went; while I fear I am like the other who said, 'I will go,' but didn't. I have always found it hard to be grateful. But from the bottom of my heart I thank Mr. Jones.

"Dorothy, I am beginning to doubt the ways of our church. It may make the good better. But if a bad person comes in, how does it help him become better? I doubt that it does. And I am beginning to think that a minister should be financially independent of his flock. He ought to have some trade or profession. Still, if I had the money to pay that bill, I would now be where I am glad I am not—up on my castle top instead of down at the gate. Our God has made me poor that he might send me humility, and that is a good thing. Perhaps he intends us to live more simply—on vegetables, perhaps. Beans are now proved to be as full of nourishment as meat itself, and to many constitutions even more wholesome.''

"We will begin this very day," agreed Dorothy, delighted to see her

father calm again. "I will go and see about a dinner of beans and vegetables and herbs. We shall enjoy it with love, Father!" she added,
kissing him.

That day the minister, who in his earlier days had been a little particular about his food and had been a connisseur in wines, found more
pleasure at his table, from lightness of heart and a joy of a new inde-
pendence, than he had had for many a day. It added much to his satisfaction with the experiment, that, instead of sleeping as his custom had
usually been after dinner, he was able to read without a trace of drow-
siness.

14 / Growing Intimacy _____

Faber had never made any effort to believe in a divine order of things; indeed, he had never made a strenuous effort to believe in anything. It never occurred to him that it might be a duty to believe. He was a kindly man, but his whole outlook tended toward doubt. And there must be something basically wrong when a man's sense of duty urges him mainly to denial. Man's existence is a positive thing; therefore his chief outlook ought to be positive.

To Faber it seemed the true and therefore right thing to deny the existence of any such being called God. Yet such a denial might be a better condition for a man to be in than if he says he believes in what he calls a deity, but then does not seek to follow God's will. At the same time, Faber's conclusion that he was not bound to believe in any God seemed to lift a certain weight off the heart of the doctor. He had almost freed himself from the knowledge of having done wrong things and from the consciousness of not being altogether right.

But this was not the only source of relief his unbelief gave him. For through it the doctor also got rid of the horrible notion of a cruel, uncaring being at the head of the universe. This common notion is mainly the fault of the so-called religious people, for they seem to believe in and certainly proclaim such a God. They can only partially be excused from the fact that they tell the story as it was told to them. But their main fault lies with themselves. With the gospel in their hands, they yet live in ignorance and disregard of its precepts. They have never discovered that their wrong representation of God is such that the more honest a man is, the less he can accept it.

The honest man's refusal to see whether there might not be a true God—despite the believer's distortions—arises from a mental and spiritual condition for which the man will one day discover himself to blame. In whatever way the gospel may be distorted by those who claim to believe it, the so-called honest man who rejects it because of others' hypocrisy is not such a lover of the truth as he would think.

Faber was of the class who, accepting things at their worst, alleviate their sorrows in the strenuous effort to make the best of them. There was no God, in his opinion, and people would be more comfortable to know it. In any case, they *ought* to know it. As to his certainty of there being none, Faber felt no desire to find one, had met with no proof that there was one, and had reasons for supposing that there was none. He had not searched very long or very wide, or with any eager desire to discover him, if indeed there should be a God who hid himself.

Faber's genial nature delighted in sympathy, in agreement, and therefore he plied his views of unbelief among others that he might feel the joy of victory and the personal success of persuasion. It was sympathy that he was now bent on bringing about in Juliet Meredith. He wanted to get nearer to her. Something pushed, something drew him toward the lovely bud of nature's accidental making. He would have her trust him, believe him, love him. And if in the process of finding a home for truth in her heart he should cause her pain, would not the tenderness born of their lonely need for each other be far more consoling than any mere yearning after imaginary comfort?

As far as her father was concerned, Juliet had been religiously brought up. No doubt Captain Meredith had been more fervid than he was reasonable, but he was a true man. In his regiment, on which he brought all his influence to bear, he had been regarded with respect, even where not heartily loved. But her mother was one of those weakest of women who can never forget the beauty they once possessed, or quite believe they have lost it. Even after every trace of it has vanished, they remain as greedy as ever of admiration. But she died when Juliet was only five years old, and the child grew to be more than a daughter to her father. She became familiar with the forms of a religious belief as narrow as its followers. She never discovered what a beggarly thing the system was and how incapable of satisfying any childlike soul. Never did she question the truth of what she heard, and she became skilled in its arguments and forms of thought. But the more familiar one becomes with any religious system, while the conscience and will remain unawakened and obedience has not yet begun, the harder it is to enter into the kingdom of heaven. Such familiarity is a soul-killing experience, and some of those sons and daughters of religious parents are less guilty than many born and bred thieves and sinners.

When Juliet first understood that her new friend actually did mean thorough unbelief—the rejection of all the doctrines she had been taught by the father she revered—she was altogether shocked. But her horror was mainly a reflection of the reaction with which her father would have regarded him. All that was needed to moderate horror to mere disapproval was a growing familiarity with Faber's doctrines in the light of his agreeable presence and undeniable good qualities. As thoroughly acquainted as she believed herself with "the plan of salvation," Jesus of Nazareth was to her but the vague shadow of an excellent man, yet no man at all. Her religion was dusky and uncertain because its object was obscure and unrealized. Since her father's death, though she had read and thought a good deal, her religion had lain as before in a state of dull inactivity. But the experience with the heirloom ring made her realize the special care which she needed so much and awoke in her a sense of gratitude.

The next day, as Juliet sat thinking about what they had discussed, she was suddenly seized with the same ambition as his—of converting him to *her* beliefs. The purpose justified an interest in him beyond the professional, and explains in part why she did not grow alarmed at the rapid growth of their friendship. But only they who love the truth simply and completely can really know what they are about.

I do not care to follow the intellectual duel between them. But nothing could have suited Faber's desires better. They debated the same difficulties wise men have been pondering from the dawn of human thought, and will in new shapes keep returning to so long as human understanding yearns to grasp its origin. Faber brought up an array of arguments utterly destructive of the wretched forms of religion which were all she had to bring into the field. Before his common sense, Juliet's arguments went down like toy soldiers. Without consciously yielding at first, she soon came to realize that her arguments were worse than worthless—weapons whose handles were sharper than their blades. She had no others, nor metal of which to make any. And with Faber's persuasion and the pleasure in the mere exercise of her thought-processes and understanding, she became more and more interested in his side of the discussion, especially as she saw the drift of his arguments and perceived the weight of what truth lay on his side. For the most powerful lie of all is the lie which contains a likeness to the truth. It would not have mattered that she was driven from her defense, line after line, if only she had not lost sight of that for which she was striving.

It added much to Faber's influence on Juliet that a tone of pathos and an element of poetry generally pervaded the forms of his denial. The tone was more penetrating because it veiled the pride behind it all, the pride of an unhealthy conscious individuality. This pride of *self* as self makes a man the center of his own universe and a mockery to all the demons of the real universe. Only the man who rises above the mighty influence of his own pride, who sets the self of his own consciousness behind his back and sets his eyes only on the Father is a free and noble being; only he breathes the air of the infinite.

The nature of Juliet Meredith was true and trusting. But because of her mother's early influence she had begun in weakness, and she was not yet raised in strength. But from her father Juliet had learned a certain strength of honest purpose, which would stand her in good stead, even as it had for him.

Late one evening in the early summer, Juliet and Paul sat together in the dusky parlor of the cottage, with the window to the garden open. The sweetest of western airs came in with a faint scent of damp earth, moss, and primroses. Their free imaginations found the faded yellow of the sunset in the scent, too.

"I am sorry to say we must shut the window, Miss Meredith,"

advised the doctor in a professional tone. "You must always be watchful of the night air. It will never be friendly to you."

"What enemies we have all about us," she returned with a shudder. "How strange it is that all things should conspire against us."

"Clearly, we are not at home among the elements—not genuinely so at least."

"And yet you say we are sprung from them," challenged Juliet.

"We have lifted ourselves above them," explained the doctor, "and must conquer them next."

"And until we conquer them," suggested Juliet, "our lifting above them is in vain?"

"For we return to them in the end," assented Faber, and silence fell. "Yes," he resumed, "it is sad. The upper air is sweet, and the heart of man loves the sun—"

"Then why would you have me so willing to go down to the darkness where, as you say, all is meaningless?"

"I would not have you willing. I would have you love the light as you do. We cannot help but love the light, for it is good; and the sorrow that we must leave it only makes it dearer. The sense of coming loss ought to be the strongest of all bonds between us. The sweetest, saddest, most entrancing songs that love can sing must be but variations on this one theme: 'The morning is clear; the dew mounts heavenward; the odor spreads; the hill looks over the sea; the world breaks into laughter: let us love one another! The sun grows hot, the shadows lie deep; let us sit in it, and remember; the sun lies flashing in green, dulled with purple; all is mute but the rush of the stream; the soft evening draws nigh; the dew is coming down again; the air is cool, dusky, and thin; it is sweeter than the morning; other worlds of death gleam out of the deepening sky; the birds close their wings and hide their heads, for death is near: let us love one another! The night is come, and there is no tomorrow; it is dark; the end is nigh; it grows cold; in the darkness and the cold we tremble, we sink: a moment more and we are no more; ah! ah, beloved! let us love, let us cleave to one another, for we die!' "

He was moved in his soul by the sound of his own words. Yet he was the harp upon which the fingers of a mightier nature than he knew were playing a prelude to a grander fantasy than he could comprehend. Faber caught the hand of Juliet where it gleamed white in the gathering gloom. But she withdrew it, saying in a tone which through the darkness seemed to him to come from afar, "You ought to have been a poet, not a doctor, Mr. Faber!"

The jar of her apparent coolness brought him back with a shock to the commonplace, like a gust of icy wind piercing a summer night.

"I trust the doctor can rule the poet," he replied, recovering his self-possession with effort.

"The doctor ought at least to keep the poet from falsehood. Is false poetry any better than false religion?" returned Juliet. "Your day is not a true picture of life such as you would make it. Let me see! I will give you one. Give me a moment.—'The morning is dark; the mist hangs heavy and will not rise; the sodden leaves sink under foot; overhead the boughs are bare; the cold creeps into the bone and marrow; the sun is buried in miles of vapor; the wood will not burn in the grate; there is but a crust in the larder, no wine in the cellar: let us love one another!' "

"Yes!" cried Faber, again seizing her hand, "let us love one another and I will be content."

Again she withdrew it.

"No, you must hear my song out," she insisted, turning her face toward the window. In the fading light he saw a look of pain, which vanished in a strange, bitter smile as she resumed: " 'The ashes of life's volcano are falling; my forehead is wrinkled, my cheeks are furrowed, my brow is sullen; I am weary and discontented and unlovely; my heart is sick; the wheels of time grind on; I care not for myself, and you are no longer lovely to me; I cannot recall how I desired you once; death alone has charms; love is now a mockery too bitter to be felt; even sadness is withered; no more can it make me sorrowful to brood over the days that are gone or remember the song that would have once made my heart a fountain of tears.

" 'Ah! ah! The folly to think we could love to the end. There is only a grave for you and me—part or together, I care not. You need love me no more. I care not for your love. I hardly care for the blessed darkness itself. Give me no sweet antidote, no precious poison such as I once prayed for when I feared the loss of love, that it might open me to the gate of forgetfulness, take me softly in unseen arms and sink with me into the everlasting darkness. All is an acrid mist. I do not love thee.'— And do you still say in the face of such a life as that, 'Let us love one another' "?

She broke into a dreadful laugh, all horribly unnatural. She rose, and in the deepening twilight seemed to draw herself up far beyond her height, then turned, and looked out on the shadowy remnants of the sunset. Faber rose also. He felt her shiver, though she was not within two arms' length of him, and he sprang to her side.

"Miss Meredith—Juliet—you have suffered! The world has been too hard for you! Let me do all I can to make up for it! I too know what suffering is, and my heart is bleeding for you."

"What! Are you not a part of the world? Are you not born of her, the product of all this heartlessness and meaninglessness you attribute to her? And will *you* act as my consolation? Isn't that the last stroke of eternal mockery?"

"Juliet!" he cried, and once more took her hand. "I love you."

"No," she rejoined and pulled her hand from his grasp. "Such love as you can give is too poor even for me. If you speak to me so again, you will drive me away. Talk to me as you will of your void and empty world; tell me of the darkness. But do not talk to me of love. For in such a world as you preach, there can be no love."

Faber made a gentle apology and withdrew—abashed and hurt, vexed with himself and annoyed at his failure.

The moment he was gone she threw herself down on the sofa and sobbed, but no tears would come. Life had been poor and arid; now there was not even left the luxury of grief! Where all was loss, no loss was worth a tear.

But the doctor came again and again, and though he never spoke of love, he did show his devotion. He also avoided for a time any further pressing of his opinions and talked instead of poetry, science, and nature—all he said tinged with the same sad glow. And when by degrees denial came up again, Juliet scarcely attempted opposition. Gradually she became quite used to his doctrine; and as she grew accustomed to it, it seemed less dreadful and somewhat less sad. She began to see for herself that it must draw closer the bonds between human beings to learn that there was no great power to hurt them *or* aid them or to claim lordship over them and enslave them to his will. For Juliet had never glimpsed the idea that in oneness with the love-creating Will alone lies freedom for the love-created. And on his part, when Faber perceived that his words had begun to influence her, he grew more kindly disposed toward her superstitions. For certainly until we see God as he is, and are changed into his likeness, all our beliefs must partake more or less of superstition. But if there be a God, the greatest superstition of all will be found to have consisted in denying him.

"Do not think me incapable," he said one day, after they had moved back into their former freedom with each other, "of seeing much that is lovely and gracious in some aspects of religion. Much depends, of course, upon the person who holds a given view. No belief could be beautiful in a mind that is unlovely. For instance, a sonnet of Shakespeare's would be no better than a burnt cinder in such a mind as Mrs. Ramshorn's. But there is Mr. Wingfold, the curate of the abbey church. He is a true and honest man who will even give an infidel like me fair play. Nothing that finds acceptance with him could not be noble, whether it be true or not. I am afraid he expects me someday to come over to his way of thinking about God. I am sorry he will be disappointed, for he is a fellow quite free from the humbug of his profession. For my part, I do not see why two friends should not respect one another's opinions, letting the one do his best with his belief and the other his best without a God to hinder him."

Juliet answered nothing. She had not yet decided to abandon the faith of her father. But she did not see why a man and a woman, the one denying like Faber, the other believing such as she, could not live together and love and help each other. Of all useless things, a merely speculative theology is of the least value. To her, God had never been much more than a name—hardly as much her Father as was the first forgotten ancestor of her line. Under the growing fascination of the handsome, noble-minded doctor, she was fast losing what little shadow of faith she might have possessed. The theology she had attempted to defend was so faulty, so unfair to God, that Faber's atheism had a great advantage over it, and her faith—which in reality was no faith at all— was swept away like the uprooted weed it was.

"If God is as has been described to me," he declared, "I do him a favor in denying his existence, for his very being would be a disgrace to himself. At times, when I see all the horrors of misery and suffering about me, I think there must be an evil supreme being over it all. But then I realize that there could be no such being who actually created for the very joy of inflicting agony on those he made. No, I merely labor in a region of immovable law, blind as Justice herself—law that works often for the good, but which is careless of individual suffering. And so I work, even in harmony with nature herself, to alleviate the pains and try to restore the ills that result from breaking her laws. And the best the man who would help his fellows can do is to search after and find other laws which will make life longer and more endurable, even more desirable."

"But you can do nothing about death," argued Juliet.

"Nothing, yet—alas!"

"Is death a law, or a breach of law then?" she asked.

"That is a question I cannot answer."

"In either case, would it not be better to let the race die out, instead of laboriously piecing and patching at too old a garment, and thereby make room for a new race to come up? Perhaps the fruit of experience, both sweet and bitter, left behind in books, might enable the new race to avoid a similar ruin."

"Ages before they learned to read our books, they would have broken the same laws, found the same evils, and be as far gone as we are now."

"Then would not the kindest thing be to poison the race—as men on the prairie meet fire with fire—and so with death foil Death and have done with dying."

"It seems to me better to live on in the hope that someone may yet— in some far-off age—discover the law of death, learn how to meet it, and thus banish disease, decay, and death from the world. Would you crush the dragonfly, the moth, or the bee because its days are so few? Rather, would you not pitifully rescue them, that they might enjoy to their natural end the wild intoxication of being?"

"Ah, but they are happy while they live."

"So are men—for parts of their lives, at least. How many of my patients would thank me for offering them poison?"

Talk after talk of this kind took place between them until at length Juliet became silent and pensive. All the time, that mysterious force which draws the individual man and woman together was mightily at work between them—a force which, terrible as is the array of its attendant shadows, will at length appear to have been one of the most powerful in the redemption of the world. But Juliet did nothing, said nothing, to encourage Faber. Something in her carriage prevented him from throwing himself at her feet. At one time he read it as an unforgotten grief, at another as a cherished love in her past, and he trembled at the thought of the agonies that might be in store for him.

Weeks passed and he had made no inquiries about a situation for her. He did not want to prolong the present arrangement, but he found it almost impossible to talk about her. If she would only accept him, he thought! But he dared not urge her, mainly from fear of failure rather than from any modesty, for he soberly believed a love and devotion such as his to be worth the acceptance of any woman. At the same time he believed that to be loved of a true woman was the only thing which could make up for the enormous swindle of life.

Why did she repel him? he asked himself over and over. If he could but persuade her that the love offered in the fire of meaninglessness must be a nobler love than that which whispered from a bed of roses, then perhaps she would hold out to him the chalice of her heart, and the one pearl of the world would yet be his—a woman all his own, pure as a flower, sad as the night, and deep as nature unfathomable.

He had a grand idea of woman. He had been built with a goddess-niche in his soul and would worship the woman that could fill it. There was a time when he could not imagine having a woman whose radiant mirror had ever reflected any man but him alone. But now he would be content if for him she would simply obliterate her past. To make the woman who had loved before forget utterly would be a greater victory, he said, than to wake love in the heart of a girl, and would yield him a finer treasure, a richer conquest.

Only she must be pure as the snow—pure as the sun himself! Paul Faber was absolutely tyrannous in his notions as to feminine purity. She must be like the diamond shield of Prince Arthur. Only perfect purity would satisfy this lord of the race who could live without a God. Was he then such a master of purity himself? one so immaculate that such an aspiration was no presumption? Was he such an ideal mate to justify that unspotted ideal?

The notion men have of their own worth is amazing. But most amazing of all is the standard a man will set up for the woman he will marry.

What standard the woman may have a right to never enters his thoughts. He does not doubt the righteousness of aspiring to wed a woman between whose nature and his lies an immense gulf. Never a twinge of conscience pricks the leprous soul as he stretches forth his arms to enfold the clean woman. Such men have—what is it?—virtue? pride? or cruel insolence? For they shrink with rudest abhorrence from any woman who would, in nature and history and character, be their fitting and proper mates.

What turning of things upside down there will be one day! What a setting of lasts first, and firsts last!

15 / The Dedication at Nestley_____

Just inside the park was a mossy knoll, a little way from the ancient wrought-iron gate that opened near the only street of Owlkirk. On this knoll the rector dug the foundation of his chapel. In his wife's eyes Mr. Bevis was now an absolute saint, for not only had he begun to build a chapel on his own grounds but to read prayers in his own church! She was not the only one, however, who noticed how devoutly he read them, and his presence was a great boost to Wingfold. The rector often objected to what his curate preached—but always to his face and seldom when they were not alone. And even in such discussions as they had, he saw that he probably would have to give in—that his curate would most likely convince him that he was right. The relationship between them truly was marvelous and lovely.

The rector's was a quiet awakening, a gentle second birth almost in old age—not nearly so laden with emotion as the curate's own spiritual awakening of the previous year. But then Mr. Bevis had been but a boy all the time, and a very good sort of boy. He had acted in no small measure according to the light he had, and time was of course given him to grow in.

The foundation stone of the chapel was to be laid with a short and simple ceremony, at which no clergy but themselves were to be present. The rector had not consented and the curate had not urged that it remain unconsecrated. Wingfold was therefore uncertain whether it was to be a chapel or a lecture hall. In either case it was for the use and benefit of the villagers, and they were all invited to be present. A few of the neighbors who were friends of the rector and his wife were also invited, among them Miss Meredith.

Mr. and Mrs. Bevis had long before now called upon her and found her, as Mrs. Bevis said, fit for any society. She had lunched several times with them and was all the readier to accept the present invitation now that her health was greatly restored, and she was becoming anxious again about employment.

Almost everyone was taken with her sweet manner, shaded with sadness. She and Mrs. Puckridge had gone to the ceremony together, and when he called soon after, Faber found the door locked. He saw the gathering in the park, however, had heard something about the new chapel, and therefore rode in that direction. Tying his horse to the gate, he approached the little assembly, but before he reached it, he saw them kneel. He stopped and waited behind a tree, for he would not willingly seem rude and he refused to be hypocritical. From where he stood he saw Juliet kneeling with the rest and could not help being rather annoyed. Neither could he help being a little struck with the unusual kind of prayer the curate was making; for he spoke as to the God of workmen, the God of invention and creation, who made the hearts of his creatures so like his own that they must build and create.

When the observance was over and the people were scattering in groups, Mr. Bevis caught sight of the doctor and went to him.

"Faber!" he cried, holding out his hand, "this *is* kind of you! I should hardly have expected you to be present on such an occasion."

"I hope my presence does not offend you," answered the doctor. "I did not presume to come closer than just within earshot of your devotions. Please don't think me unfriendly for keeping aloof."

"Certainly not. I would not have you guilty of irreverence."

"That could hardly be if I recognized no presence."

"But your not recognizing a presence," said Wingfold, who had come up as they talked, "might have its root in some fault of your own of which you are not yet aware."

"If I am not aware of it, then I am not to blame," stated Faber quietly.

"But you might still be terribly the loser by it."

"You mean if there should in fact be such a one to whom reverence is due?"

"Yes."

"Would that be fair then—in an all-wise being, to hold me accountable for something I was unaware of?"

"I think not. So I look for something to reveal his presence to you. I dare not say you are to blame, because that would be to take upon myself the office of a judge, which is God's only since he only can give fair play. I would yet have you search yourself and see whether you may not come upon something which keeps you from giving full and honest attention to what some people, as honest as yourself, believe they see as true. What if you were to discover that you do not really and absolutely disbelieve in a God? That the human nature is not capable of such a disbelief? That your unbelief has been only indifference and irreverence—and that to a being grander and nobler and fairer than human heart can conceive?"

"If it be so, let him punish me," declared the doctor gravely.

"If it be so, he will," affirmed the curate solemnly, "and you will thank him for it—after a while. The God of my belief is too good not to make himself known to a man who loves what is fair and honest as you do."

The doctor was silent.

While they were talking, Helen Wingfold and Juliet Meredith had left the others and approached them. They had heard the last few sentences, and seeing two clergymen against one infidel, now hurried with the generosity and sympathy of women to help him.

"I am sure Mr. Faber is honest," said Helen.

"That is to say a great deal for any man," returned the curate.

"If any man *is* honest," added Juliet.

"That is a great *if*," rejoined Wingfold. Then turning to his wife he added, "Are *you* honest, Helen?"

"No," she answered, "but I am more honest than I was a year ago."

"So am I," added her husband, "and I hope to be even more honest yet before another year is over. It is a serious thing to say, *I am honest*."

Juliet was silent, and Helen, who was very concerned about her, turned to see how she was taking it. Her lips were as white as her face. Helen attributed the change to anger and was silent also. The rector moved toward the place where the luncheon tables were, and they all accompanied him, Helen still walking, a little anxiously by Juliet's side. It was some minutes before the color came back to her lips; but when Helen talked to her, she answered as gently and sweetly as if the silence had been nothing but an ordinary one.

"You will stay and lunch with us, Mr. Faber?" suggested the rector. "There can be no hypocrisy in that—eh?"

"Thank you," returned the doctor heartily; "but my work is waiting for me, and we all agree that *must* be done, whatever our opinions as to the basis of the obligation."

"And no man can say you don't do it," rejoined the curate kindly. "That's one thing we do agree on, as you say: let us hold by it, Faber, and stay as good friends as we can till we grow better ones."

Faber could not quite match the curate in plain speaking; the pupil was not up with his master yet.

"Thank you, Wingfold," he returned, his voice not quite free of emotion, though Juliet alone felt the tremble of the one vibrating thread in it. "Miss Meredith," he went on, turning to her, "I have heard of a position that may suit you. Will you allow me to call in the evening and discuss it with you?"

"Please do," responded Juliet eagerly. "Come before post time in case it is necessary to write."

"I will. Good morning."

He made a general low bow to the company and walked away, cutting off the heads of the dandelions with his whip as he went. All eyes followed his firm, graceful figure as he strode over the grass in his riding boots and spurs.

"He's a fine fellow!" said the rector heartily. "—But bless me!" he added, turning to the curate, "how things have changed! If you had told me the day would come when I should call an atheist a fine fellow,

I should almost have thought you were one yourself! Yet here I am saying it—and never in my life so much in earnest to be a Christian! How is that, Wingfold, my boy?"

"He who has the spirit of his master will speak the truth even of his master's enemies," answered the curate. "To this he is driven if he does not go willingly, for he knows his master loves his enemies. If you see Faber as a fine fellow, say so, just as the Lord would, and try all the more to save him. A man who loves and serves his neighbor may speak many words against the Son of man, but eventually the greatest servant of all will get his attention. He is still open to the holy influence—the virtue which is ever going from God to heal. It is the man who in the name of religion opposes that which he sees to be good who is in danger of eternal damnation."

"But tell me," said the rector, "are not the atheists of the present day a better sort—more honest—than those we used to hear about when we were young?"

"I do think so. But whether they are or not, I am convinced of this, time and continued unbelief will bring them down from whatever height. They will either repent or fall back into worse things. But atheists do not concern me half so much as the worse dishonesty and greater injustice found in the great defenders—lay and cleric—of religious opinions. If God were like many of those who would fancy themselves his apostles, the universe would be but a vast hell. Their tongues roar with the fires of hell against their brothers."

"I imagine," the rector added, "that they would withhold the name 'brother' from those they speak against."

"No doubt. And such treatment of one toward another is often to blame for unbelief. It is the vile falsehood and miserable unreality of Christians, their faithlessness to their Master, their love of their own wretched sects, their worldliness and unchristianity, their placing doctrines above obedience, their talking and not doing, that has to answer, I suspect, for the greater portion of atheism's existence."

"I have seen Mr. Faber often lately," Juliet said, a slight tremor in her voice, "and he seems to me incapable of falling into those vile conditions I used to hear attributed to atheists."

"Many have conveniently attributed to atheists all the world's evils without looking deeper," agreed Wingfold. "In reality the atheism of some men is nobler than the 'Christianity' of some of the foremost of the so-called Christians, and I do not doubt they will fare better at the last."

The rector looked a little blank at this, but said nothing. Lately, he had more than once found that what seemed outlandish in his curate was indeed scriptural, and he now was in the habit of suspending judgment.

Miss Meredith's face glowed with pleasure at hearing justice rendered the man in whom she was so much interested, and she looked all the more beautiful. She left soon after luncheon was over, leaving a favorable impression behind her. Some of the ladies said she was much too taken with the doctor; but the gentlemen admired her spirit in standing up for him. Some objected to her paleness; others said it was not paleness but fairness; others again, that it was certainly not fairness, for her eyes and hair were dark as the night. All agreed that, whatever it was to be called, her complexion was peculiar. Some for that very reason admired it, and others not. Some said she was too stately, and attributed her carriage to a pride to which, in her position, she had no right. Others judged that she needed such a bearing all the more for self-defense, especially if she had come down in social class. Her dress, it was generally allowed, was a little too harsh—in defiance of the fashion. No one disputed that she had been accustomed to good society, and none could say that she had been at all presumptuous or had made the slightest intrusive movement toward their circle.

Still, when all was said and thought, nobody really knew anything about her.

16 / With the Wingfolds _____

The curate and his wife talked a good deal about Juliet as they drove home from Nestley. From their hostess they had learned all she knew of Juliet's history and were all the more interested. They agreed that a situation must be found where she would feel at home. In the meantime they would let her understand that she was welcome with them if she wanted to see what might present itself in Glaston, the town being large enough for the possibility of her finding a good position.

Before they had left Nestley, Helen had told Mrs. Bevis she would like to ask Miss Meredith to visit them for a few days.

"No one knows much about her," remarked Mrs. Bevis.

"She can't be poison," returned Helen. "And if she were, she couldn't hurt us. That is the good of being husband and wife; so long as you are of one mind, you can do anything."

When Faber called on Juliet in the evening, nothing was said about the situation at which he had hinted. When he entered she was seated as usual in the corner of the dingy little couch under the small window, looking into the garden. She did not rise, but held out her hand to him. He went hastily up to her, took the hand she offered, sat down beside her, and at once broke into a full declaration of his love. Whatever the man's conceit or his estimate of the person he would have her accept, it was in all honesty and modesty that he offered her the surrender of the very citadel of his being.

Juliet kept her head turned from him, and he felt her hand tremble every now and then and make a faint struggle to escape from his. But he did not see that her emotion was beyond either pleasure at the welcome words, or sorrow that her reply must cause pain.

He ceased at length and with longing eyes sought her face. Her expression frightened him. It was pallid like an old sunset, and her breath came and went stormily. Three times, in a growing agony of effort, she failed to speak. Suddenly she turned her head sideways in despair, her mouth opened, and she threw a pitiful glance into his face. Then she burst into a tumult of sobs and fell back on the couch. Not a tear came to her eyes. But such was the trouble of her inner torment that she did not even try to lift her hand to her face to hide the movements of its rebellious muscles.

Faber sat bewildered, but was the master of himself from the habits of his profession. He instantly prepared something to calm her, which she took obediently. As soon as she was quiet, he mounted and rode away. Two things were clear: one, she could not be indifferent to him; the other, whatever caused her emotion, she would, for the present, be better without him. He was both too kind and too proud to persist.

The next morning the Wingfolds arrived at Mrs. Puckridge's door, and Helen went in to call on Miss Meredith.

Juliet had spent a sleepless night and greatly dreaded the next meeting with Faber. Therefore Helen's invitation to pay them a few days' visit came to her like a redemption. In their house she would have protection from Faber and from herself. Heartily and with a few tears gathering in her eyes, she accepted it, and her cordial and grateful readiness placed her yet a step higher in the eyes of her new friends. Quickly she put a few things in a bag, and with a sad, sweet smile of gentle apology, took the curate's place beside his wife while he got into the seat behind.

Having been so much confined to the house lately, Juliet could not keep back the tears called forth by the pleasure of the rapid motion through the air, the constant change of scene. A sense of human story haunts the mind in passing unknown houses and farms and villages. An old thatched barn can work as directly on the social feeling as the ancient castle or venerable manor-seat. Many a simple house will move one's heart like a poem; many a cottage like a melody. When at last she caught sight of the great church tower, she was delighted. *There is a place in which to wander and hide!* she thought—*in which to find refuge and rest, coolness and shadow!* Even for Faber's own sake she would not believe that the faith which had built such a structure as that was mere folly! Surely there was some way of arguing against the terrible things he said—if only she could find it!

"Are you very particular, Miss Meredith, or willing to do anything that is honest?" the curate asked abruptly, leaning forward from the back seat.

"If ever I was particular," she answered, "I think I am pretty nearly cured. I certainly would like my work to be something I'm capable of doing—and not too unpleasant."

"Then we need not worry," answered the curate. "The people who don't succeed are those that pick and choose upon false principles. They generally attempt what they are unfit for and deserve their failures.— Are you willing to teach little ones?"

"Certainly."

After lunch Helen found to her delight that Juliet could both sing and play the piano with expression. When the curate came home from the afternoon visits to the sick in his flock, he was delighted to hear his wife's report of Juliet's gifts.

In the course of a day or two, they had discovered most of the strengths and weaknesses in her teaching and set about to help her bolster those areas in which she was lacking. But nothing was more satisfactory than the way in which she set herself to learn. Wingfold, who had been a tutor in his day, was well qualified to assist her, and she learned very rapidly.

The point that most perplexed Wingfold was that, while very capable of perceiving and admiring the good, she was at the same time capable of admiring things altogether inferior. He could not tell what it meant. He could also clearly see Faber's influence upon her. Often when the talk between the curate and his wife would turn on some point connected with the unbelief of the land, she would make a remark in which the curate heard the doctor as plainly as if the words had come directly from his lips. But she listened well, and seemed to understand what they said.

When Faber called on Juliet the morning after their last conversation and found where she had gone, he did not doubt that she had taken refuge from his persistence with her new friends. This at once confirmed the idea he had been thinking through the whole wakeful night that the cause of her agitation was the conflict between her heart—which loved him—and the false sense of duty arising out of prejudice and superstition. She was not yet willing to send him away, and yet she dared not accept him. Her behavior had certainly revealed anything but indifference to him. At the same time, what chance had he of seeing her alone at the rectory? The thought upset him so greatly that for a moment he imagined his friend, Wingfold, had played him false.

"I suppose he thinks everything's fair in religion as well as in love and war!" he said to himself. "It's a mighty stake, no doubt—a soul like Juliet's!"

His lip curled scornfully. It was but a momentary yielding to the temptation of injustice, however, for his conscience told him at once that the curate was incapable of anything either overbearing or underhanded. He would call on Juliet in the morning as his patient, and satisfy himself how things were between them. At best their relationship had taken a bad turn.

On further reflection, however, he judged it better to let a day or two pass. When he did call he was shown into the drawing room where he found Helen at the piano and Juliet having a singing lesson from her. Till then he had never heard her sing. Never in his life had he been so overwhelmed by a piece of music. It was as if some potent element, undreamed of before, came rushing into his brain to undo him. Her voice was a full contralto, pathos at the very heart of it, and it seemed to wrap itself around his heart like a serpent of sad splendor. The ladies were too much occupied to notice his entrance, and he stood by the door, absorbed, entranced.

"Ah! Mr. Faber," acknowledged Helen presently, "I did not know you were there. We were so busy we never heard you."

"Please, don't apologize," he said. "I could have listened forever."

"I don't wonder. It is not often one hears notes like those. Were you aware of what a voice you had saved for the world?"

"Not in the least. Miss Meredith leaves her gifts to be discovered."

"All good things wait the seeker," declared Helen, who, according to some of her half-friends, had taken to preaching since she married the curate. In truth life had grown to her so gracious, so happy, so serious, that she would often speak a thing worth hearing.

In the course of this little talk, Juliet and Faber had shaken hands and murmured a conventional word or two.

"I suppose this is a professional visit?" asked Helen. "Shall I leave you with your patient?"

As she put the question, however, she turned to Juliet.

"There is no occasion for that," Juliet replied a little eagerly. "I am quite well and have dismissed my doctor."

Faber was in a frame of mind to imagine more than what met his ear, and the words seemed to him of cruel significance. A flush of anger rose to his forehead, though he said nothing. But Juliet saw and understood. Instantly she held out her hand to him again, and supplemented the offending speech with, "—but I hope I have retained my friend?"

The light rushed again into Faber's eyes and Juliet repented again, for the words had gone too far in the other direction.

"That is," she amended lightly, "if Mr. Faber will condescend to friendship after having played the tyrant so long."

The words were commonplace enough that Helen Wingfold imagined nothing more to them. So she did not leave the room, and presently the curate entered, with a newspaper in hand.

"They're still at it, Faber," he remarked, "with their experiments, trying to prove where we all came from."

"I need not ask which side you take," stated the doctor, not much inclined at the time to enter upon any discussion.

"I take neither," answered the curate.

"To which side then do you lean?" Faber asked, intrigued in spite of himself. "How do you view the weight of the evidence in their heated-liquid experiments?"

"I take the evidence," answered the curate, "to be in favor of what they so absurdly call 'spontaneous generation.' "

"I am surprised to hear you say so," returned Faber. "The conclusions necessary for a belief in that theory are opposed to all your theology."

"Because I believe in a living Truth must I then be an unjust judge?" asked the curate. "But, indeed, the conclusions thus far—as inconclusive as they are—are opposed to no theology I have any acquaintance with. And if they were, it would still give me no concern. God, not *theology*, is my origin. If I were to shirk an argument or refuse to look a fact in the face, I should be ashamed to look *him* in the face. What he requires of his friends is pure, open-eyed truth."

"But how can you grant spontaneous generation, and believe in a creator?"

"I said the term was an absurd one."

"Never mind the term then: you admit the fact?" quizzed Faber.

"I admit nothing of the sort. I only admit that insofar as the incomplete experiments which have been made are concerned, the evidence *seems* to favor that. But nothing in life can exist only of and by itself. *Spontaneity* is out of the question. Whatever exists, whatever comes into existence, must in some way—whether man can see it in a test tube or not—spring from the true, the original, the self-existent life."

"There you are, begging the question," objected the doctor.

"Not really," persisted the curate, "for I fancy even you will admit there is some driving law behind the phenomenon."

"If I accept your premise that there is nothing spontaneous, then, yes, from all eternity a blind, unconscious law has been at work, producing."

"I say an awesome, living Love and Truth and Right, creating children of its own," explained the curate, "—and there is our difference."

"Yes," assented Faber slowly.

"Anyhow, then," continued Wingfold, "as far as the matter of our discussion, all we can say is that under such and such circumstances, life does appear—from whence, you and I believe differently. I can't talk in scientific terms like you, Faber, but truth is not tied to any form of words."

It was rather hard on Faber to have to argue when out of practice, and with a lady listening to whom he was longing to pour out his soul, and his antagonist a man who never counted a sufficing victory gained unless his adversary had had light and wind both in his back. Trifling as was the occasion of the present skirmish, he had taken his stand on the lower ground. Faber imagined he read both triumph and pity in Juliet's face, and could scarcely endure the situation a moment longer.

The curate followed the doctor to the door. When he returned he said, "I wonder what it is in that man that won't let him believe?"

"Perhaps he will yet someday," speculated Juliet softly.

"He will. He must," answered the curate. "He always reminds me of the young man who had kept the law, and whom our Lord loved. Surely he must have been one of the first who came and laid his wealth at the apostle's feet. Perhaps that half of the law which Faber tries to keep will be schoolmaster enough to lead him to Christ.—But come, Miss Meredith, now for our mathematics."

Every two or three days thereafter the doctor called to see his former patient. She needed looking after, he said, but not once did he see her alone. He could not tell from their behavior whether she or her hostess was to blame for his recurring disappointment. But the fact was, his ring at the doorbell was the signal to Juliet not to be alone.

17 / Juliet's New Situation

Happening to hear that the Wingfolds were expecting visitors, despite the assurances of her hostess that there was plenty of room for her, Juliet insisted on finding lodgings and taking more direct measures for obtaining employment. But the curate had already arranged for her to care for some small children; only he had not arranged for it to begin just yet. And now, consulting with Helen, he began to look into a new idea on the matter of a place for her to stay.

A day or two before, Mr. Jones the butcher had been talking to Wingfold about Mr. Drake, saying how badly his congregation had behaved to him, and in what trouble he had come to because he could not pay his bill.

"We don't know all the circumstances, however, Mr. Jones," the curate replied, "and perhaps Mr. Drake does not think as badly of it as you do. He is a most worthy man. Be sure you let him have whatever meat he wants. I'll see to you. Don't mention it to a soul."

"Bless your heart and liver, sir!" exclaimed the butcher. "He's ten times too much a gentleman to take no charity. What he do live on now, I can't nohow make out. He's doin' his best to live on nothin' at all! Leastways so they tell me—turned a—what's it they call it?—a vegetablarian! Why don't he come to me for a bit o' wholesome meat? Them peas an' beans an' cabbages an' porridges an' carrots an' turmits—why, sir, they ain't nothin' but water an' wind. I don't say as they mightn't keep a body alive for a year or two, but, bless you, there's nothin' in them, an' the man'll be a skeliton afore long."

Mr. Jones the butcher never sold bad meat, never charged for an ounce more than he delivered, and when he sold to the poor he usually slashed his price without their knowledge. A local preacher once asked him if he knew what the plan of salvation was. He answered with the utmost innocence, while cutting him a great leg of beef for a family the preacher had just told him was starving, that he hadn't the least idea what it was, but no Christian could doubt it was a good thing.

Pondering over what Mr. Jones had told him about Mr. Drake, the curate decided to attempt an arrangement for Juliet with the Drakes. What she would be able to pay them would ease their situation a little and it would provide her a place from which to teach. Juliet was willing to do anything they thought best.

Therefore Wingfold called on the minister and was shown up to his study. The walls from top to bottom were entirely hidden with books.

Mr. Drake received him with a touching mixture of sadness and cordiality and listened in silence to his proposal.

"It is very kind of you to think of us, Mr. Wingfold," he replied after a moment's pause. "But I am afraid the thing is impossible. Indeed, it is out of the question. Circumstances are changed with us. Things are not as they once were."

There had always been a certain negative virtue in Mr. Drake. He never attempted to gain credit for what he didn't have. If in his time of plenty he liked men to be aware of what he had, he now, in the time of his poverty, preferred that men should be aware of the bonds in which he lived. His nature was simple, and loved to be in the daylight. Concealment was absolutely alien to him. His openness may have sprung from too great a desire for sympathy—I cannot tell. But I will admit that if his faith had been as a grain of mustard seed, he would not have been so haunted with a sense of his poverty as to be morbidly anxious to confess it. He would have known that his affairs were in a high charge, and that in the full flow of the fountain of prosperity, as well as in the scanty, gravelly driblets from the pump of poverty, the supply all came from the throne of God, and he would not have *felt* poor. A man ought never to feel rich because of riches, nor poor because of poverty. The perfect man must always feel rich, because God is rich.

"The fact is," Mr. Drake went on, "we are very poor—absolutely poor, Mr. Wingfold—so poor that I cannot even refuse the trifling annuity my former congregation will dole out to me."

"I am sorry to hear it," said the curate.

"But I think they treated me so, imagining that I had private means. Now I fear that even with what your friend would contribute to the household, we would not be able to provide a table fit for her. But Dorothy ought to have the pleasure of hearing your kind proposition: I will call her if you will allow me."

Dorothy was in the kitchen making bread to go with the rare treat of a couple of chickens, a present from Mrs. Thompson. Not knowing anyone was with her father when he called her from the top of the stairs, she hurried up with her bare arms covered with flour.

She recoiled half a step when she saw Mr. Wingfold, then stepped forward to welcome him, wiping her hands on her white apron.

"It's only flour," she said smiling.

"It is a rare pleasure nowadays to catch a lady at work," asserted Wingfold. "My wife always dusts my study for me. I told her I didn't want anyone else to do it, just for the pleasure of seeing her at it. My conviction is that only a lady can become a thorough servant."

"Why don't you have a lady helper then?" questioned Dorothy.

"Because I don't know where to find one. Servants are plentiful;

ladies are scarce. And anything would be better than a houseful of half-ladies."

"I think I understand," acknowledged Dorothy thoughtfully.

Her father now stated Mr. Wingfold's proposal—in the tone of one sorry not to be able to take advantage of it.

"I see perfectly why you think we must say no, Papa," admitted Dorothy. "But why should not Miss Meredith lodge with us in the same way as with Mrs. Puckridge? She could have the drawing room and my bedroom, and eat her meals by herself."

"Miss Meredith would hardly relish the idea of turning you out of your drawing room," declared Wingfold.

"Tell her it may save us from being turned out of the house. Tell her she will be a great help to us," returned Dorothy eagerly.

"My child," said her father, the tears standing in his eyes, "your willingness sinks into my soul. Mr. Wingfold," he went on, turning to the curate, "I try hard to put my trust in the Lord, but my faith is weak. It ought by this time to have been strong. I always want to see the way he is leading me, to understand something of what he is doing with me or teaching me, before I can accept his will or stop my heart from complaining. It makes me very unhappy. I begin to fear that I have never known even the beginning of confidence, and that my faith has been but a thing of the understanding and the lips, not of my deeds."

He bowed his head on his hands. Dorothy went up to him and laid a hand on his shoulder, looking unspeakably sad. A sudden impulse moved the curate.

He rose, went to the minister's side, and knelt down. It was an unlikely thing to do, but he was an unlikely man, and did it. The others knelt also.

"Oh, God," he prayed, "you know how hard it is for us, and you will be fair with us. We have seen no visions; we have never heard the audible voice of your Son; we have to fight on in much darkness of spirit and mind, both from the ignorance we cannot help and from the fault we could have helped. We inherit blindness from the error of our fathers; and when fear or the dread of shame or the pains of death come upon us, we are ready to despair and cry out that there is no God, or that if there be he has forgotten his children. There are times when the darkness closes about us like a wall and we can see you nowhere, either in our hearts or in the outer universe. We cry aloud and we listen for any sound of your voice, but we hear nothing. You who know that for which we groan, you whom Jesus called Father, we appeal to you, not as we imagine you but as you see yourself, as Jesus knows you. To your very self we cry—help us! Be our Father!

"We beg for no signs and wonders, but only for your breath upon our souls, your Spirit in our hearts. We pray for no tongues of fire, for no rousing of brain or imagination or emotion. But we do, with all our power of prayer, pray for your Spirit. We do not even pray to know that he is given us. Let us, if so it pleases you, remain in doubt of the gift for years to come; but still lead us by your Spirit. Aware only of ordinary movements of mind and soul, may we yet be possessed by the Spirit of God, led by your will in ours. For all things in a man, even those that seem the most common and least spiritual, are the creation of your heart, and by the doors of our wavering judgment, dull imagination, lukewarm love, and palsied will, you can enter and glorify all. Give us patience, because our hope is in you, not ourselves. Work your will in us and our prayers are answered. Amen."

They rose. The curate said he would call again in the evening, bade them good-bye, and went. Mr. Drake turned to his daughter and said, "That's not the way I have been used to praying or hearing people pray. The young man seemed to speak straight to God. It appears to me there was another Spirit there with his. I will humble myself before the Lord, and see what will come."

Dorothy was a rather little woman, with light auburn hair, small well-fashioned features, and a fair complexion. Their poverty did not weigh on her. She was proud to share in her father's lot and was indeed a trifle happier since it had come upon them. Even so, inwardly she was troubled. The impossibility of regarding her father's church with reverence laid her mind open to the kind of spiritual doubts that had been suggesting themselves to her long before any of Faber's words reached her. The more her devout nature longed to worship, the more she found it impossible to worship that Being which the church presented her. She believed entirely in her father, but she knew he could never dissolve her doubts, for many things made it plain that he had never had such questions himself. An ordinary mind that has had doubts and has encountered and overcome them will be profoundly helpful and comforting to any mind struggling with its own doubts. But no knowledge of books, no amount of logic, and especially no dogmatically pat answers of rote theology can enable a man who has not encountered skepticism in his own mind to offer the smallest measure of help to those caught in the net of doubt. For one thing, most who have not had similar doubts themselves will criticize the doubter rather than encourage the healthy flow of their God-created active brain. Thus they will be incapable of perceiving that the net of doubt may be the net of the Fisher of men.

Therefore, Dorothy had been sorely oppressed of spirit for some time. And now that her father was fainting on the steep path of life, she had no spiritual water to offer him. She had never heard the curate preach, but had heard of his oddity from men and women no more capable of judging him than the caterpillar of judging the butterfly—which it yet must become. And now for the very first time she had heard him speak out of the abundance of his heart, and he had left behind a faint ray of hope in hers. It seemed very peculiar of him to break out in prayer in such an abrupt fashion, especially in the presence of an older minister than himself—and praying for him too! But he had such a simplicity in his look, such a directness in his requests, and such an active hope in his tone—without a trace of the religiosity she had grown accustomed to. His thought and speech did not seem to come from some separate sacred *mood* that might be put on and taken off at will, but seemed instead to come from the daily point of his life. His prayer was an immediate appeal to a hearing and understanding and caring God, whose breath was the very air his creatures breathed. Such was the shining of the curate's light, and it created a spark of hope in Dorothy.

In the evening Thomas came again, as he had said, and brought Juliet. Dorothy and she recognized suffering in each other, and in a very few minutes everything was arranged between them. Juliet was charmed with the simplicity and intentness of Dorothy. And in Juliet's manner and carriage, Dorothy at once recognized a breeding superior to her own. In a moment she made Juliet understand how things were, and Juliet saw as quickly that she must agree to the arrangement proposed. But she had not been with them two days before Dorothy found the drawing room as open to her as before, and far more pleasant.

While the girls were talking below, the two clergymen sat again in the study.

"I have taken the liberty," said the curate, "of bringing an old book I should like you to look at if you don't mind. I brought it chiefly for the sake of some verses that pleased me much when I read them first, and now please me more when I read them for the tenth time. If you will allow me, I will read them to you."

Mr. Drake liked good poetry, but did not much relish being called upon to admire, as he imagined he was now. He assented, of course, graciously enough, and soon found his mistake.

This is the poem Wingfold read:

CONSIDER THE RAVENS

Lord, according to thy words,
I have considered thy birds;
And I find their life good,
And better the better understood:
Sowing neither corn nor wheat,
They have all that they can eat;
Reaping no more than they can sow,
They have all that they can stow;
Having neither barn nor store,
Hungry again, they eat more.

Considering, I see too that they
Have a busy life, and plenty of play;
In the earth they dig their bills deep,
And work well though they do not heap;
Then to play in the air they are not loath;
And their nests between are better than both.

But this is when there blow no storms;
When berries are plenty in winter, and worms;
When their feathers are thick and oil is enough
To keep the cold out and the rain off.
If there should come a long hard frost,
Then it looks as thy birds were lost.

The bird has pain, but has no fear,
Which is the worse of any gear;
When cold and hunger and harm betide him,
He gathers them not, to stuff inside him;
Content with the day's ill he has got,
He just waits, nor haggles with his lot;
Neither jumbles God's will
With driblets from his own still.

But next I see in my endeavor,
Thy birds here do not live forever;
That cold or hunger, sickness or age,
Finishes their earthly stage;
The rook drops without a stroke,
And never gives another croak;
Birds lie here, and birds lie there,
With little feathers all astare;
And in thy own sermon, thou
That the sparrow falls dost allow.

It shall not cause me any alarm,
For neither so comes the bird to harm,
Seeing our Father, thou hast said,
Is by the sparrow's dying bed;
Therefore it is a blessed place,
And the sparrow in high grace.

It cometh therefore to this, Lord:
I have now considered thy word,
And henceforth I will be thy bird.

By the time Wingfold had ceased, the tears were running down the old man's face. The curate rose at once, laid the book on the table, shook hands with him, and went away. The minister laid his head on the table and wept.

Juliet soon had almost as much teaching as she could manage. People liked her and children came to love her not a little, and a good report of her spread. The work was hard, mainly because it included more walking than she had been accustomed to, getting to and from the houses of her pupils. But generally Dorothy walked with her, and to the places farthest off Helen frequently took her with her ponies, and she got through the day's work pretty well. The fees were small, but they sufficed and made life a little easier for her host and his family. Amanda grew very fond of her, and without pretending to teach her, Juliet taught her a good deal. On Sundays she went to church. Dorothy went regularly with her, although she had to struggle against the imagined resentment by which the chapel people would necessarily interpret the change. But Dorothy found this outweighed by the growing hope of receiving light from the curate. Her father, not unfrequently, also accompanied her.

18 / The Will

All this time poor Faber had received no further answer to his offer of himself but a swoon. Every attempt he made to see Juliet alone at the rectory had been foiled, and he had almost arrived at the conclusion that the curate and his wife had set themselves to prejudice Juliet against him. His uneasiness increased when as he soon discovered, she went regularly to church with them. He knew the power and persuasion of Wingfold and looked upon his influence as antagonistic to his own hopes. Pride, anger, and fear were all at work in him; but he went on calling and did his best to appear untroubled. Juliet perceived no change in his feelings, and her behavior to him was not such as to prevent them from deepening still.

Every time he visited her, it was with a desperate resolution of laying his hand on the veil in which she had wrapped herself, but every time he found it impossible to make a single movement toward withdrawing it. Again and again he tried to write her, but the suspicion that she would show his letter to her new friends always made him throw down his pen in smothering indignation.

When he first learned she had gone to live with the Drakes, he felt relieved. Although he knew the retired minister was far more personal in his hostility to agnostic ideas than Wingfold, he was confident his influence over her would not be as great. Thus he thought he would have a better chance of seeing her alone. In the meantime he took satisfaction in knowing he did not neglect any of his patients. He pitied himself just a little as a martyr to the truth, a martyr the more meritorious since the truth to which he sacrificed himself gave him no hope for the future. It remained a question, however, whether there was not a supreme being putting forth claims of obedience. And even though he considered such imaginary, it remained for him an uncomfortable sort of phantom to have brooding above him, continually coming between him and the freedom of an otherwise empty universe. To the human soul as I have learned to know it, an empty universe would be as an exhausted airbag to the lungs that thirst for air. But Faber liked the idea: how he would have liked the *reality* remains another thing. I suspect that even what we call damnation can never exist; for even the damned live by God's life.

The summer at length reigned lordly in the land. The roses were in bloom, from the black purple to the warm white. Ah, those roses! He must indeed be a God who invented the roses. They sank into the red hearts of men and women, caused old men to sigh, young men to long, and women to weep with strange ecstatic sadness. But their scent made Faber lonely and poor, for the single rose-heart he yearned for would not open its leaves to him.

The winds were soft and fragrant. The wide meadows through which the river flowed seemed to smite the eye with their greenness. Along the banks, here with nets, there with rod and line, they caught the gleaming salmon, silver armor flashing useless in the sun. The old pastor sat often in his little summerhouse and paced his green walk on the border of the Lythe. But in all the gold of the sunlight, in all the glow and plenty around him, his heart was oppressed with the sense of his poverty. It was not that he could not do the thing he would, but that he could not meet and rectify the thing he had done. And worst of all, he could not get rid of a sense of wrong—of rebellious heavings of heart, of resentments, of doubts that came thick upon him—not of the existence of God, nor of his goodness toward men in general, but of his kindness to himself. Logically, of course, they were all bound up in one, and the being that could be unfair to a beetle could not be God. But our feelings, especially where a wretched self is concerned, are notably illogical.

The morning of a glorious day came in with saffron, gold, and crimson. The color sobered, but the glow grew. The azure sky, the white clouds, and the yellow fire remained. The larks dropped down to their breakfast and everything that could move was in motion, and what could not move was shining, and what could not shine was feeling warm.

But the pastor was restless. He had had a troubled night. The rent on his house fell due at the same time as the miserable pittance allowed him by the church. The hard thing was not that he had to pay nearly all of it to meet his rent, but that he had to take it at all. Yet he had no choice. The thought of it burned in his veins. It was hard that he who all his life had been urging people to have faith should have his own turned into such a mockery!

His heart and conscience together smote him. Well might his faith be mocked, for what better was it than a mockery itself? Where was this thing called his faith? Was he not talking just like an unbeliever? Was he not telling God he did not trust in him? But why then did God leave him like this without faith? Why did God not make him able to trust? He had prayed quite as much for faith as for money.

His conscience replied, "That is your part. If God put faith into your heart without your stirring up your heart to believe, the faith would be God's and not yours."

"But I have tried hard to trust in him," said the little self.

"Yes, and then fainted and ceased," said the great self, the conscience.

So it went on in the poor man's soul. Over and over he repeated to himself the words of Job, "Though he slay me, yet will I trust in him." And over and over his heart sickened afresh, and he said to himself, "I shall go down to the grave with shame, and my memorial will be debts unpaid, for the Lord hath forsaken me." All night he had lain wrestling with fear and doubt: fear was hard on him, but doubt was much harder. "If I could but trust," he concluded, "I could endure anything."

In the splendor of the dawn he had fallen into a troubled sleep, only to give way to a more troubled dream which woke him again to misery. Outside his room the world was rich in light, in song, in warmth, in smell, in growth, in color, in space. Inside, all to him was gloomy, cold, musty, dingy, and confined. Yet there he was more at ease, shrinking from the light, and in the glorious morning that shone through the chinks of his shutters he saw but an alien common day, not the coach of his Father come to carry him yet another mile toward his home.

His daughter always came into his room the first thing in the morning. It was plain to her that he had been more restless than usual, and at the sight of his reddened eyes and gray face her heart sank within her. For a moment she was half angry with him, but with his faith she would have done just the same as he. How the poor girl sighed for the freedom of a God to trust in! She could content herself with the husks the swine ate if only she knew that a father sat at the home-heart of the universe. Faithful in her faithlessness, she did her best to comfort her father. But he did not listen to a word she said, and she left him at last with a sigh, and went to get him his breakfast. When she returned she brought him his letters with his tea and toast. He told her to take them away. She might open them herself if she liked, but they could be nothing but bills. She might take the tray too. He did not want any breakfast, for what right had he to eat what he had no money to pay for? There would be a long bill at the baker's next! Dorothy told him she paid for every loaf of bread as it came and that there was no bill at the baker's. Mr. Drake stretched out his arms, drew her to him and said she was his only comfort. Then pushing her away, he turned his face to the wall and wept.

She saw it would be better to leave him, and knowing in this mood he would eat nothing, she carried the tray with her. A few moments later she came rushing back up the stairs, her face white as a sheet.

That afternoon a message came to Wingfold in which Dorothy begged him to come see her father. The curate rose and went at once. When he reached the house, Dorothy opened the door even before he knocked.

"What's the matter?" he asked in some alarm.

"Nothing much, I hope," she replied. There was a strange light on her face. "But I am a little alarmed about him. He has suffered much lately. He wants very much to see you. He thinks you may be able to help him. I'm sure if you can't, nobody can. But please don't heed much what he says about himself. He is feverish and excited. There is such a thing—isn't there?—as a morbid humility? I don't mean a false humility, but one that passes over into a kind of self-disgust?"

"I know what you mean," affirmed the curate as Dorothy led the way up the narrow, creaking stairs.

It was a lowly little room in which the once-loved preacher lay. As the curate stepped in, a grizzled head turned a haggard face toward him. The eyes were dry and bloodshot, and he extended a long hand from the bed to greet his friend.

"Ah, Mr. Wingfold!" cried the minister. "God has forsaken me. He has ceased to work his own way and will with me, and has given me my own way instead, my own will. Sit down, Mr. Wingfold. You cannot comfort me, but you are a true servant of God, and I will tell you my sorrow. I am no friend to the church, as you know, but—"

"As long as you are a friend of its Head, that goes a long way with me," assured the curate.

"Ah, Mr. Wingfold," continued the minister, not to be diverted from the fullness of his misery, "I have been serving mammon; diligently have I been serving him. I served him not a little in my time of prosperity, with confidence and show, and then in my adversity with fears and complaints. Our Lord tells us expressly that we are to take no thought for the morrow, because we cannot serve God and mammon. I have been taking thought for a hundred morrows, and not patiently, but grumbling in my heart at his dealings with me. Therefore, now he has cast me off."

"How do you know he has cast you off?" asked the curate.

"Because he has given me my own way with a vengeance. I have been pulling my hand out of his, and he has let me go and I lie in the dirt."

"But you have not told me your grounds for thinking such to be the case."

"Suppose a child had been crying and fretting to his mother for a spoonful of jam," said the minister, quite gravely, "and at last she put a whole potful in front of him. What would you say to that?"

"I would say she meant him to learn a sharp lesson, perhaps a reproof as well—certainly not that she meant to cast him off," answered Wingfold, laughing. "But I still do not understand you."

"Have you not heard, then? Didn't Dorothy tell you?"

"She has told me nothing."

"Not that my old uncle has left me a hundred thousand pounds?"

The curate was on the point of saying, "I am very glad to hear it," when the warning Dorothy had given him returned to his mind, and with it the fear that the pastor was under a delusion.

"Oh," he returned lightly and soothingly. "Perhaps it is not so bad as that. You may have been misinformed. There may be some mistake."

"No, no!" returned the minister. "It is true, every word of it. You shall see the lawyer's letter. Dorothy has it, I think. My uncle was an ironmonger in a country town, got on, and bought a little bit of land in which he found iron. I knew he was flourishing, but he was a churchman and a terrible tory, and I never dreamed he would remember me. There has been no communication between our family and his for many years. He must have fancied me still a flourishing London minister with a rich wife. If he had a suspicion of how sorely I needed a few pounds, I cannot believe he would have left me a farthing. 'I did not save my money to waste it on bread and cheese,' I can hear him saying."

Although a look almost of despair kept coming and going upon his face, he lay so still and spoke so quietly that Wingfold began to wonder whether there might not be fact in his statement after all. He hardly knew what to say.

"When I heard the news from Dorothy—she read the letter first you see—old fool that I was, I was filled with such delight. I jumped out of bed and hurried on with my clothes, but by the time I came to kneel at my bedside, God was away. I could not speak to him. I had lost the trouble that kept me crying after him. The bond was broken and he was out of sight. I tried to be thankful, but my heart was so full of the money. But I dared not go even to my study until I had prayed. I tramped up and down this little room, thinking more about paying my butcher's bill than anything. Then all at once I saw how it was: he had heard my prayers in anger. Mr. Wingfold, the Lord has sent me this money as he sent the quails to the Israelites, and has at the same time smitten me with hardness of heart. O my God! how shall I live in the world with a hundred thousand pounds instead of my Father in heaven! If it were only that he has hidden his face, I would be able to pray somehow. But he has given me over to the mammon I was worshiping. Hypocrite that I am! He has taken from me the light of his countenance."

He looked the curate in the face with wild eyes.

"Then you would willingly give up this large fortune," Thomas concluded, "and return to your former condition?"

"Rather than not be able to pray—I would! I would!" he cried; then paused, and added, "If only he would give me enough to pay my debts and not have to beg from other people."

Then, with tone suddenly changed to one of agonized effort, with clenched hands and eyes shut tight as if in the face of a lingering un-willingness to encounter again the miseries through which he had been passing, he cried vehemently, "No, no, Lord! Forgive me. I will not think of conditions. Thy will be done! *Take* my money, and let me be a debtor and a begger if thou wilt, only let me pray to thee; and do thou make it up to my creditors."

Wingfold's spirit was greatly moved. Here was a victory indeed! Whether the fortune was fact or fancy made no difference now. He thanked God. The same instant the door opened and Dorothy came in, hesitating and looking anxious. He threw her a look of questioning. She gently bowed her head and gave him a letter with a broad black border which she held in her hand.

He read it. No room for doubt was left. He folded it softly, gave it back to her, knelt down by the bedside, and said, "Father, I thank you that you have set my brother's heel on the neck of his enemy. But the suddenness of your relief has so shaken his heart and brain, or rather perhaps has made him think so keenly of his lack of faith in his Father in heaven, that he fears you have thrown him the gift in disdain. Father, let your Spirit come with the gift, or take it again, and make him poor and able to pray."

Here an *amen* groaned out as from the bottom of a dungeon—"Pardon him, Father," the curate prayed on, "all his past discontent and the smallness of his faith. You are our Father and you know us ten times better than we know ourselves. We will try to be better children. We will go on climbing the mount of God through all the cloudy darkness that surrounds it, even in the face of the worst of terrors."—Here Dorothy burst into sobs.—"Father, take pity on your children," said Wingfold further. "You will not give them a stone in place of a piece of bread. We are yours, and you are ours; in us do your will! Amen!"

As he rose from his knees, he saw that the minister had turned his face to the wall and lay perfectly still. Therefore he ventured to now try a more authoritative mode of address.

"And now, Mr. Drake, you have got to spend this money," he advised, "and the sooner you set about it the better."

The sad-hearted man rolled over and stared at the curate.

"How is a man whom God has forsaken to do anything?" he asked.

"If he had forsaken you, as dreary as it would be, you would still have to do your duty. But he has not forsaken you. He has given you a very sharp lesson, I grant, and you must receive it. But that is the very opposite of forsaking you. He has let you know what it is not to trust him, and what it would be like to have money that did not come from his hand. You did not conquer in the fight against mammon when you were poor, and God has given you another chance: he expects you to get the better of your tempter now that you are rich. If God had forsaken you, you would now be strutting about and glorying over your imagined enemies."

"Do you really think that is the mind of God toward me?" cried the poor man, starting half up in bed. "Do you think so?"

"I do," avowed Wingfold. "And it will be a bad job indeed if you fail in both trials. But I am sure you will not. It is your business now to get this money and proceed to spend it as God would have you."

"Someone may dispute the will. They do sometimes," cautioned Dorothy.

"They do very often," answered Wingfold. "It does not look likely in the present case. But our trust must not be in the will or in the fortune, but in the living God. You have to get all the good out of this money you can. If you will walk over to the rectory with me, we will tell my wife the good news."

Dorothy ran to put on her bonnet. The curate went back to the bedside where Mr. Drake had again turned his face to the wall.

"Mr. Drake," said Wingfold, "so long as you bury yourself with the centipedes in your own cellar instead of going out into God's world, you are tempting Satan and mammon together to come and oppress you. Worship the God who made the heaven and the earth and the sea and the mines of iron by doing his will. Be strong in him who is your strength, and all strength. Help him in his work with his own. Give life to this gold. Rub the canker off it by sending it from hand to hand. Get up. Rise and bestir yourself. I will come and see you again tomorrow. Good-bye for the present."

He turned away and walked from the room. But his hand had scarcely left the knob when he heard the minister alight from his bed unto the floor.

"He'll do!" declared the curate to himself, and walked down the stairs.

19 / A Nighttime Meeting

After tea that evening Mr. Drake and Dorothy went out for a walk together—a thing they had not once done since the church meeting of acrid memory in which had been decreed the close of the minister's activity in Glaston. It was a lovely June twilight.

Juliet, left all but alone in the house—for little Amanda was in bed—sat at her window reading. As the twilight deepened, the words began to play hide and seek on the page before her. She closed the book and was soon thinking about Paul Faber. Within another five minutes she had fallen asleep where she sat in her chair. Her last thoughts had been, *Why should I not give myself to him? Why should he not love me? If it is all but a vision that flits before us, why should we not be sad together?*

She slept for some time. The house was very still, for Mr. Drake and Dorothy were in no hurry to return. Suddenly Juliet awoke with a great start. Arms were around her from behind, lifting her from her half-prone position of rest. With a terrifed cry she tried to free herself.

"Juliet, my love! Be still, and let me speak," hushed Faber, his voice trembling. "I can bear this no longer. I shall cease to live when I know for certain that you have turned from me."

"Pray leave me, Mr. Faber!" she cried, half terrified, half bewildered as she rose and turned toward him. But while she pushed him away with one hand, she unconsciously clasped his arm tight with the other. "Do go away. I will come to you."

"Pardon, pardon, my angel! Do not speak so loudly," he warned, falling on his knees.

"Do go away," persisted Juliet. "What will they think if they find us—you here? They know I am perfectly well."

"You drive me to liberties that make me tremble, Juliet. Everywhere you avoid me. You are never to be seen without some hateful protector. Ages ago I put up a prayer to you—and you, like the God you believe in, have left it unanswered. You have no pity on the sufferings you cause me! Is not one tormentor enough in your universe? If there be a future, let us go on together to find it. If there be none, let us enjoy what we can in life. My past is a sad one—"

Juliet shuddered.

"Ah, my beautiful, you too have suffered," he went on. "Let us be angels of mercy to each other, each helping the other to forget. My griefs I should count worthless if I might but erase yours. Whatever your sorrows have been, my highest ambition shall be to make you forget them. We will love like beings whose only eternity is the moment. Juliet, my brain is deserting me. I mistake symptoms, forget cases, my hand trembles. You are ruining me."

He saved my life, thought Juliet. *He has a claim on me; I must be his property. He found me a castaway on the shore of Death, and gave me* his *life to live with.* She was just on the point of yielding when she heard a step in the lane approaching the door.

"If you love me, do go now, dear Mr. Faber," she begged. "I will see you again. Do not urge me further tonight. Go into the drawing room."

He obeyed. The steps came up to the door. There came a knock and Juliet heard the door open.

Faber had hardly been a moment in the drawing room when Wingfold entered it also. Expecting his friends back momentarily, he had let himself in. It was almost dark, but the doctor stood against the window and the curate recognized him.

"Ah, Faber," he said, "it is a long time since I saw you. But we have each been about our work, I suppose, and there could not be a better reason for missing each other."

"Under different masters certainly," returned Faber, a little out of temper.

"I don't exactly think so. All good work is done under the same master."

"I disagree!" He certainly was in no mood for an argument, but too stubborn to keep silent.

"Who is your master, then?"

"My conscience. Who is yours?"

"The author of my conscience."

"A legendary personage!"

"One who is every day making my conscience harder upon me. Until I believed in him my conscience was dull and stupid, not even half awake."

"Oh, I see!" Faber said. "You mean my conscience is dull and stupid."

"Not at all. But if you were once lighted up with the light of the world, you would pass that judgment on yourself. I don't think you are so different from myself that this shouldn't be the case; though most heartily I grant that you do your work ten times better than I did before my awakening. And all the time I thought myself an honest man. I wasn't. A man may honestly think himself honest, and a new week's experience makes him doubt it altogether. I sorely needed God to make me honest."

Here Juliet entered the room, greeted Mr. Wingfold, and then shook hands with Faber. He was glad the room was dark.

"What do you think, Miss Meredith—is a man's conscience enough for his guidance?" asked the curate.

"I don't know anything about a man's conscience," answered Juliet.

"A woman's then?" prodded the curate.

"What else does she have?" returned Juliet.

The doctor was inwardly cursing the curate for continuing this confounded theological discussion.

"Of course she has nothing else," answered the curate, "and if she had, she must follow her conscience all the same."

"There you are, Wingfold!—always talking paradoxes!" blurted Faber.

"Why, man! You may have only a blundering boy to guide you, but if he is your only guide, you must follow him. You don't therefore call him a sufficient guide."

"You're playing with words!"

"Suppose the boy's father knew all about the country, but you never thought it worthwhile to send the lad to him for instructions?"

"Suppose I didn't believe the lad had a father? Suppose he told me he hadn't?"

"Some men would call out to ask if there was anybody in the house to give the boy a useful hint."

"Oh, bother! I am quite content with my conscience—boy or not."

"Well, even if it were ten times better than it is, I should count my conscience poor company on any journey. That's the joy of God's Spirit, Miss Meredith. He is the living Truth.—What if you should find one day, Faber, that above all other facts, the thing you had been so coolly refusing was the most precious?"

That was more than enough for Faber. There was but one thing precious to him: Juliet was the perfect flower of nature, the apex of law, the summit exhibition of evolution, the final reason of things. The very soul of the world stood there in the dusk, and there also stood the foolish curate, whirling his little vortex of dust and ashes between him and her!

"It comes to this," stated Faber, with great effort controlling his voice: "what you say moves nothing in me. I am aware of no need, no want of that being of whom you speak. Surely if in him I did live and move and have my being, as some old heathen taught your St. Paul, I should in one way or another be aware of him."

While he spoke, Mr. Drake and Dorothy had come into the room and lighted a lamp. They stood silent, listening with Juliet to one, then the other.

"That is a weighty word," concluded Wingfold. "But what if you do feel his presence every moment, only do not recognize it as such?"

"What would be the good of it to me then?"

"What if any further revelation to one who does not seek it would but obstruct the knowledge of God he already has? Truly revealed, the word would be read *untruly*—even as the Word has been read by many in all ages. Only the pure in heart, we are told, shall see him. The man who, though made by him, does not desire him, how should he know him?"

"Why don't I desire him then? I don't."

"That is for *you* to find out."

"I do what I know to be right. On your theory, I ought to get on well," declared Faber, turning from him with a forced laugh.

"I think so too," replied Wingfold. "Go on and prosper. Only what if there be untruth in you alongside the truth? It might be, and you are not aware of it. It is amazing what can coexist in the human mind."

"In that case, why should not your God help me?"

"I think he will. But it may have to be in a way you will not like."

"Well, well! Good night. Talk is but talk, whatever be the subject of it.—I beg your pardon," he added, turning to shake hands with the minister and his daughter. "I hardly noticed you come in. Good night." He gave a slight bow to Juliet as he passed but was too emotionally charged to look her in the face.

"I won't agree that talk is only talk, Faber," Wingfold called after him with a friendly laugh. Then turning to Mr. Drake, "Pardon me," he said, "for ignoring you. I saw you come in, but believed you would rather have us end our discussion naturally than break it off in the middle."

"Certainly. But I can't help thinking you grant him too much, Mr. Wingfold," admonished the minister seriously.

"I never find I lose by giving, even in argument," responded the curate. "Faber rides his hobbyhorse well. But the brute is a sorry jade. He will find one day she has not a sound joint in her whole body."

The man who is anxious to argue every point will speedily bring a conversation to a mere dispute about trifles, leaving the deeper matter out in the cold. Such a man, having gained his paltry point, will crow like a bantam, while the other, who may be the greater man though maybe even in the wrong, is embittered by his smallness and turns away with increased prejudice. Few men do more harm than those who are on the right side but argue for personal victory. And even genuine argument for the truth is not preaching the gospel. He whose unbelief is attacked by argument will never be brought into a mood fit for receiving the truth. Argument should be kept to books. Preachers ought to have nothing to do with it—in the pulpit at any event. Let them hold forth the light, and let him who will receive it do so, and him who will not wait. God alone can convince, and till the full time is come for the birth of the truth in a soul, the words even of the Lord himself can have little potency.

"The man irritates me, I confess," admitted Mr. Drake. "I do not say he is self-satisfied, but he is very self-sufficient."

"He is such a good fellow," maintained Wingfold, "that I think God will not let him go on like this very long. I think we shall live to see a change about him. But as much as I esteem and love the man, I cannot help a suspicion that he has a great lump of pride somewhere about him, which has much to do with all his denials."

Juliet's blood grew hot in her veins to hear her beloved thus talked about; and with this came the first rift of a threatened breach between her heart and the friends who had been so good to her. Faber had done far more for her than any of them, she reasoned, and mere loyalty seemed to call upon her to defend him. But she did not know how, and, satisfied with herself as well as indignant with them, she brooded in angry silence.

20 / Osterfield Park

Dorothy would now have been as a mother to her father had she but a good hope of finding her Father in heaven. But she was not at peace enough to mother anybody. She saw none of her father's faults. And they had never been very serious in comparison with his virtues. I do not mean that every fault is not so serious that a man must be willing to die twenty deaths to get rid of it, but relative to the getting rid of it, a fault is serious or not in proportion to the depths of its roots, rather than the amount of its foliage.

It had been a long time since Mr. Drake and Dorothy had spent such a pleasant evening as when they walked into Osterfield Park to be alone with the knowledge of their changed fortunes. The anxiety of each differed greatly from that of the other and tended to shut each away in loneliness beyond the hearing of the other, even though there was never any breach in their love. But this evening their souls rushed together.

Silently they walked out together—for the good news had made them shy—through the lane, into the cross street, and out westward into Pine Street, meeting the gaze of the low sun which wrapped around them in a veil of light and dark.

"This fading sunlight is like life," remarked the pastor: "Our eyes can best see from under the shadow of afflictions."

"I would rather it were from under the shadow of God's wings," replied Dorothy timidly.

"So it is! So it is! Afflictions are but the shadow of his wings," said her father eagerly. "Stay there, my child, and you will never need the afflictions I have needed. I have been a hard one for him to save."

Little more passed between them in the street. All the way to the entrance of the park they were silent. There they exchanged a few words with the sweet-faced little dwarf-woman who opened the gate for them, and whose few words set their thoughts singing yet more sweetly. They entered the great park through the trees bordering it, and when they reached the wide expanse of grass, with its clumps of trees and thickets, simultaneously they breathed a deep breath of the sweet wind. The evening was lovely and they wandered about in delight. It was getting dark before they thought of returning.

The father had been confessing to the daughter how he had mourned and wept when his boys were taken from him, never thinking at all of the girl who was left him.

"And now," he said, "I would not part with you, Dorothy, to have them back as the finest boys in the world. What would my old age be without you, my darling?"

Dorothy's heart beat high, and she tucked her hand in the crook of his arm. They walked a while in silence again, for the heart of each was full. All the time hardly an allusion had been made to the money.

As they returned they passed the new house some distance away, on the highest point in the park. It stood unfinished, all its windows boarded up.

"The walls of that house," reminisced Mr. Drake, "were scarcely above ground when I came to Glaston. And so they had been for twenty years, and so they remained until, as you remember, the building began again some three or four years ago. Now again, it is forsaken and only the wind is at home in it."

"They tell me the estate is for sale," replied Dorothy. "Those lots just where the lane leads into Pine Street must belong to it too."

"I wish," returned her father, "they would sell me that tumble-down place in the hollow they call the Old House of Glaston. What a place it would be to live in! And what a pleasure it would be to make it once more habitable, to watch order dawn out of neglect!"

"It would be delightful," responded Dorothy. "When I was a child I would dream that that house was my papa's—with the wild garden and all the fruit, and the terrible lake, and the ghost of the lady that was drowned.—But would you really buy it, Father, if you could get it?"

"I think I would, Dorothy," answered Mr. Drake.

"Would it not be damp—so much in the hollow? Isn't it the lowest spot in the park?"

"In the park—yes; for the rest of the park drains into it. But the park is high, and as deep as the lake is, it yet drains into the Lythe. For all they say about there being no bottom to it, I am sure that the deepest part of the lake is still higher than the surface of the river. If I am right, then we could empty the lake altogether—but I would not like the place nearly so well without it. The situation is charming—and so sheltered, looking to the south—just the place to hold open house in!"

"That is just like you, Father!" cried Dorothy. "The very day you are out of prison you want to begin to keep an open house!"

"Don't mistake me, my darling. There was a time, long ago, after your mother was good enough to marry me, when—I am ashamed to confess—I did enjoy making a show. I wanted people to see that although I was the minister of a sect looked down upon by the wealthy priests of a worldly establishment, I knew how to live by the world's fashions as well as they. You will hardly remember that time, Dorothy."

"I remember the coachman's buttons," answered Dorothy, and he smiled and patted her hand on his arm.

"I liked to give dinner parties and we returned every invitation we accepted," he went on. "I took much pains to have good wines, and the right wines with the right dishes, and all that kind of thing—though I'm sure I made more blunders than I knew. Your mother had been used to that way of living, so it was not pride for her as it was for me. And I was proud of my library and the rare books in it. I delighted in showing them and talking about the rarity of this edition, the fine binding of another, and such-like foolishness. And it is not surprising, since I served my religion in the same way—with eyes only for the externals rather than the truth of it. I'm sure I had my better times. But how often I insisted on the trivial, 'dill, mint, and cummin,' while I forgot judgment, mercy, and faith. How many sermons I preached merely about the latchets of Christ's shoes when I might have talked about Christ himself! But now I do not want a good house to make a show with anymore. I only want to be hospitable. I would have my house a hiding place from the wind of the world. That would be true hospitality! Ah! If your mother were with us, my child! But you will have to be my little hostess, as you have been for so many years now.—I wonder, does anybody ever preach hospitality as a Christian duty?"

"I hope you won't get a butler, and set us up as gentlefolk, Father," cautioned Dorothy.

"Indeed I will not, my child. I will look to you to keep a warm, comfortable, welcoming house, and we'll hire servants only if we need them and if they shall be hospitable in heart and behavior as well. Perhaps we can now have Lisbeth back to keep house for us. But whomever we have must make no distinction between rich and poor."

"I don't think anyone is poor," said Dorothy after a pause, "except those who can't be sure of God. They are *so* poor!"

"You are right, my child!" returned her father. "It was not my poverty that crushed me; it was not being sure of God. How long has it been since I was poor, Dorothy?"

"Less than two days, Father."

"It seems like two centuries. My mind is at ease, and yet I have not paid a single debt. How unbelieving it was of me to want the money in my own hand and not be content it should be in God's pocket! Alas! I have more faith in my uncle's fortune than I had in my Father's generosity. But in my shame I must not forget gratitude. Come, my child, let us kneel down here on the grass and pray to God."

I will not give the words of the minister's prayer. The words themselves are not the prayer. Mr. Drake's sentences were commonplace, with much of the conventionality and platitude of prayer meetings. He had always objected to the formality of the prayer book, yet his own prayers were just as formal. But the prayer itself was in his heart, not in his lips and was far better than the words. Sadly, poor Dorothy heard only the words, and they did not help her. They seemed to freeze rather than revive her faith, making her feel as if she never could believe. She was too unhappy to reason well, or she might have seen that she was not bound to measure God by the way her father talked to him—that the form of the prayer had more to do with her father than with the character of God.

When they had resumed their walk, their talk again turned to the Old House of Glaston.

"If it is true, as I have heard," said Mr. Drake, "that Lord de Barre intends to tear down the house, and if he is as short of money as they say, then he might perhaps take a few thousand for it. I have wanted for some time to leave our home by the river. The Old House is not nearly so low even as the one we are in now. Besides, if we could buy the property, we would have room to build on an even higher level."

When they reached the park gate on their return, a second dwarfish figure, pigeon-chested, short-necked, asthmatic, gnome-like man came from the lodge to open it. Everybody in Glaston knew Polwarth the gatekeeper.

"How is the asthma tonight, Mr. Polwarth?" inquired the pastor.

"Not very bad, thank you, Mr. Drake. But, bad or not, it is always a friendly devil," answered the little man.

"I am surprised to hear you express yourself so, Mr. Polwarth," said the minister, a hint of rebuke in his voice at the characterization.

The little man laughed a quiet, huskily melodious, merry laugh.

"I am not original in the idea, and scarcely so in my way of expressing it. I found it in the second letter to the Corinthians last night, and my heart has been full of it ever since."

"I am at a loss to understand you, Mr. Polwarth," said the minister, shaking his head.

"I beg your pardon. In the passage I refer to, St. Paul says, 'There was given to me a thorn in the flesh, the messenger of Satan to buffet me, lest I should be exalted above measure.' Am I not right in speaking of such a demon as a friendly one? He was a gift from God."

"I had not noticed the unusual combination of phrases in the passage," answered Mr. Drake. "It is a very remarkable one, certainly. I remember no other in which a messenger of Satan is spoken of as being *given* by God."

"Clearly St. Paul accepted it as something to be grateful for. Therefore, who is to say what may not be a gift of God? It won't do to grumble at anything, will it, sir, when it may so unexpectedly turn out to be given to us by God? I suspect that until we see a thing is plainly from God, we can never be sure that we see it rightly. I am quite certain the most unpleasant things may be such gifts. I would be glad enough to part with this asthma of mine if it pleased God; but I would not yield a fraction of what it has brought me for the best lungs in England."

"You are a happy man, Mr. Polwarth—if you can say that and abide by it."

"I *am* a happy man, sir. I don't know what would come of me sometime for very gladness if I hadn't my good friend, the asthma-devil, to keep me down a bit. Good night, sir," he called, for Mr. Drake was already moving away.

Mr. Drake had long felt superior to this man. Always ready to judge by externals, he would have been shocked to discover how much the deformity of the man prejudiced him against Polwarth. And since the little man seldom was seen in a place of worship, that hardly elevated him in the minister's opinion. The minister had set him down as one of those mystical interpreters of the Word who are always searching for strange things. It is amazing from what a mere fraction of fact concerning him a man will dare judge the whole of another man. In reality, little Polwarth could have carried big Drake to the top of any spiritual hill of difficulty, up which in his pilgrimage with the Lord he had yet to go panting and groaning—and to the top of many another besides, which the minister would never come close to in this world.

"He is a little too ready with his spiritual experience, that little man—too fond of airing it," the minister commented to his daughter. "I don't quite know what to make of him. He is a favorite with Mr. Wingfold, but I have always been doubtful of him."

Now Polwarth was not in the habit of airing his religious views. But all Glaston could see that Mr. Drake was in trouble. Therefore, the dwarf took the first opportunity he had of showing his sympathy for him by offering him a share of the comfort he had just been receiving himself. He smiled at its apparent rejection and closed the gate softly, saying to himself that the good man would think about it in time.

Dorothy took little interest in Polwarth, little therefore in her father's judgment of him. But better even than Wingfold himself, that poor physical failure of a man could have helped her out from under the gravestones that were now crushing the life out of her. He could have helped her even better than Wingfold—not from superiority of intellect or learning, but because he was alive all through, because the life eternal pervaded every atom of his life, every thought and action. No door or window of his being had a lock to it. All of them were always on the swing to the wind that blows where it will. Upon occasions when most people would seek refuge from the dark skies of trouble by hiding from temptation and difficulty in the deepest cellars of their hearts, there to sit grumbling, Polwarth always went out into the open air. If the wind was rough, there was nonetheless life in it: the breath of God. It was rough to blow the faults from him, genial to put fresh energy in him. If the rain fell, it was the water of cleansing and growth. Misfortune he would never call by that name; there was no *mis* but in himself. So long as God was, all was right.

Indeed the minister and Polwarth were poles apart, but Polwarth was right: As Mr. Drake went home he pondered the passage to which the dwarf had referred, wondering whether he was to regard the fortune sent him as a messenger of Satan given to buffet him.

21 / Cowlane Chapel

Juliet no longer tried to conceal from herself that she now loved Faber as she had at one time resolved never to love a man. If her father were alive, Faber's atheism would have stood as an almost insurmountable barrier. But it now appeared likely that life was but a flash across from birth to death, and her father, tenderly as he had loved her, was gone from her forever. Why should not those who loved make the best of it for each other during that one brief moment? All that Faber had ever argued was now blossoming in her thoughts. She had not a doubt that he loved her. A man of men he was—noble, unselfish, independent, a ruler of himself, a benefactor of his race. What right had those *believers* to speak of him as they did!

She felt herself wholly unworthy of him. She believed herself not for a moment comparable to him. But his infinite chivalry, gentleness and compassion would be her refuge. Such a man would bear with her weakness, love her love, and forgive her sins! If he took God from her, he must take his place and be a godlike man to her. Then, if there should be any more truth discoverable, why should they not discover it together, as he himself had said?

She must think about it a little longer though. She could not make up her mind the one way, and would not the other. She dared not yet. If she could only see into the deepest recesses of his heart for one moment.

All this time she had been going to church every Sunday and listening to sermons in which the curate poured out the energy of a faith growing stronger day by day. But not a word he said had as yet laid hold of one root fiber of her being. She judged, she accepted, she admired, she refused, she condemned, but she never *did*. To many souls hell itself seems a less frightful alternative than the agony of resolve, of turning, of being born again. But Juliet had never got so far as that. She had never yet looked the thing required of her in the face. She came to wonder that she had made any stand at all against the arguments of Faber.

But how is it that *anyone* who has been educated in Christianity, yet does not become the disciple of Jesus Christ, avoids becoming an atheist? Does he prefer to keep half-believing the revelation in order to justify himself in refusing it totally? Would it not be better to reject it altogether if it be not fit to be believed with heart and soul? But if he dares not proclaim his intellectual unbelief out of some reverence for father or mother or some desire to keep an open door of escape, what a hideous folly the whole thing has become for him.

I well know how foolish words like these must seem to such as Faber, but for such they are not written. They are written for the men and women who close the lids of half-blinded eyes and think they do God service by not denying that there is a sun in the heavens. But there may be some denying Christ who shall fare better than they, when he comes to judge the world with a judgment which even those whom he sends from him, shall confess to be absolutely fair.

That night Juliet hardly knew what she had said to Faber, and longed to see him again. She slept little and in the morning was weary and exhausted. But he had set her the grand example of placing work before everything else, and she would do as he had taught her. So she rose, and in spite of her headache, set out to do her day's duty. And in the days that came she grew more confident in the doctor, and no longer took pains to avoid him. Indeed, just the opposite.

By degrees Mr. Drake's emotional state grew quiet and he adjusted to the changed circumstances of his life. He found himself again able to pray, and while he bowed his head lower before God, he lifted up his heart higher toward him. He at once decided to be a faithful and wise steward over his uncle's bequest, and that was the primary reason for the return of his peace. Now and then the fear that God had sent him the money in displeasure would clutch at him. He feared falling into the leprosy of a desire to accumulate. Therefore he remained anxious to spend freely and right in order to keep it flowing, lest it should pile up its waves and drown his heart.

That he could hoard now if he pleased gave him the opportunity of burning the very possibility out of his soul. When a man can do a thing, then can he abstain from doing it. Now, with his experience of both poverty and riches, the minister knew that he must make them both follow like hounds at his heel. He must be lord of his wealth; mammon must be the slave, not Walter Drake.

"I am sixty," he told himself, "and am finally beginning to learn to learn." Behind him his public life looked like a mere ancient tale. His faith in the things he had taught had been little better than the mist which hangs about an old legend. He had been in a measure truthful; he had tried to act on what he taught. But how unlike the affairs of the kingdom of heaven did all that church business look to him now! In the whole assembly, including himself, could he honestly say he knew more than one man who sought the kingdom of heaven *first*? And yet he had been tolerably content until his congregation began to turn against him. What better could they have done than get rid of him? But now he would strive to enter in at the narrow gate; he would be humble as the servant of Christ.

Dorothy's heart was relieved a little. She could read her father's feelings better than most wives can their husbands', and she knew he was happier. She would gladly have parted with all the money for a word that could assure her there was a God in heaven who *loved*. But the teaching of the curate had begun to tell upon her. She began to have a faint perception that if the story of Jesus Christ was true, there might be a Father to be loved. The poorest glimmer of Christ's loveliness gives a dawn to our belief in a God, and even a small amount of genuine knowledge of him will neutralize the most confident declaration against him. Nothing can be known except what is true. A negative may be a *fact*, but it cannot be *known* except by the knowledge of its opposite. Nothing can really be *believed*, except it be true. But people think they believe many things which they do not and *cannot*, in the real sense, believe.

However, in trying to help her father to do the best with their money, she began to reap a little genuine comfort. For the more a man occupies himself in doing the works of the Father—the sort of thing the Father does—the easier will he find it to believe that such a Father is at work in the world.

In the curate Mr. Drake had found not only a man he could trust, but one to whom, young as he was, he could look up to. And it was nothing short of noble in the minister that he did look up to the curate—perhaps without knowing it. Mr. Drake was able to give the curate much also. For Wingfold soon discovered that the minister knew a great deal more about Old Testament criticism, church history, and theology than he did. They often disagreed. But as long as each held the will and law of Christ to be the very foundation of the world, and obedience to him as the way to possess it, how could they fail to know they were brothers? They were gentle with each other, for they loved him whom in eager obedience they called Lord.

The moment the money actually came into his hands, the minister went straight to the curate.

"Now," he said—for he too had the gift of going straight to the point—"Now, Mr. Wingfold, tell me plainly what you think is the first thing I ought to do with this money toward making it a true gift of God."

"Are you telling me you want to set right what is wrong wherever it is possible to you?"

"That is what I mean. What do you think is the first thing I should try to set right?"

"I should say justice. My soul revolts against talk about kindness to the poor when such a great part of their misery comes from the injustice and greed of the rich."

"And in the specific? What could I actually *do*?"

"I will give you a special instance which has stirred about in my mind a long time. Last spring the floods brought misery upon every family down by the river. How some of them get through any wet season, I cannot imagine. Faber will tell you what a multitude of sore throats, croup, scarlet fever, and diphtheria he has to attend to in those houses every spring and autumn. They are crowded with laborers and their families. And since the railway came, they have no choice but to live there and pay a much higher rent in proportion than you or I do. Men are their brothers' keepers indeed, but it is in chains of wretchedness that they keep them. I am told that the owner of these cottages, who makes a considerable amount every year from them, ignores all the pleas of his tenants for seriously needful repairs and gives them nothing but promises. He is one of the most influential attendants of a chapel you know well, where Sunday after Sunday the gospel is preached. If all this is true, then here is a sad wrong. What can those people think of religion when it is so misrepresented to them?"

"I am a sinful man!" exclaimed the pastor. "That Barwood is one of the deacons. He is the owner of the chapel as well as the cottages. I ought to have spoken to him years ago. But," he cried, starting to his feet, "the property is for sale! I saw it in the paper this very morning! Thank God!" He grabbed his hat. "I shall have no choice but buy the chapel, too," he added with a strange smile. "It is all part of the same property. Come with me, my dear sir. We must see to it directly. But you must speak. I would rather not appear in the affair until the property is my own. But I will buy those houses, please God, and make them such as his poor sons and daughters may live in without fear or shame."

They went out together, got all the information required, and set things in motion so that within a month all the title deeds would be in Mr. Drake's possession.

When the rumor reached the members of his former congregation that he had come into a large bequest (but before it was public knowledge as to his use of it), many called to congratulate him, and such congratulations are pretty sure to be sincere. But he was both annoyed and amused when Dorothy came and told him that a committee from the church in Cowlane had come and was waiting below.

"We've taken the liberty of calling in the name of the church to congratulate you, Mr. Drake," their leader announced as the minister entered the dining room.

"Thank you," said the minister quietly.

"I fancy," added another—Barwood himself—with a smile such as paves the way for the facetious, "you will hardly condescend to receive our little gratuity now?"

"I shall not require it, gentlemen."

"Of course we should never have offered you such a small sum, except we were sure you had independent means."

"Why did you offer it then?"

"As a token of our regard."

"The regard could not have been very great when you made no inquiry as to our circumstances. My daughter had twenty pounds a year; I had nothing. We were in no small peril of simple starvation."

"Bless my soul! We hadn't an idea of such a thing, sir! Why didn't you tell us?"

Mr. Drake smiled and made no other reply.

"Well, sir," resumed Barwood after a very brief pause, "it's all turned out so well; you'll let bygones be bygones and give us a hand?"

"I am obliged to you for calling," said Mr. Drake, "especially to you, Mr. Barwood, because it gives me an opportunity of confessing a fault of omission on my part toward you."

"Don't mention it, please," implored Mr. Barwood. "This is a time to forget everything."

"I ought to have pointed out to you, Mr. Barwood," pursued the minister, "both for your own sake and that of those poor families, your tenants, that your property in this lower part of town was quite unfit for the habitation of human beings."

"Don't let your conscience trouble you because of that neglect," answered the deacon, his face flushing with anger while he tried to force a smile. "My firm opinion has always been that a minister's duty is to preach the gospel and not meddle in the private affairs of the members of his church. Besides, I am selling the property.—But that's neither here nor there, for we've come on other business. Mr. Drake, it's clear to everyone that the cause of the gospel will never prosper so long as that's the chapel we've got. We did think perhaps a younger man might do something, but there doesn't seem to be any sign of betterment yet. In fact, things look worse. No, sir! It's the chapel that's the stumbling block. What can religion have to do with a place that's ugly and dirty, a place that any lady or gentleman might turn up their noses from? I say what we need is a new place of worship. Cowlane is behind the times."

The former pastor ventured no word, and his face looked stern in the silence.

"At least you'll admit, sir," persisted Barwood, "that the house of God ought to be as good as the houses of his people. He won't give us any success until we give him a decent house. Depend upon it. What are we to dwell in, houses of cedar, and the ark of the Lord in a tent?"

"You think God loves newness and finery better than the old walls where generations have worshiped?" admonished the pastor, his spiritual anger finally rising at this paganism in a Pharisee's robe.

"What's generations to him?" answered Barwood. "He wants the people drawn to his house, and as it is, there's nothing to draw them into Cowlane."

"I understand from the paper you wish to sell the chapel," said Mr.

Drake. "Is it not rather imprudent to bring down the value of your property by removing its tenant before you have got rid of it? Without the church paying rent, it wouldn't be worth half the price."

Barwood smiled a superior smile. He considered the bargain safe, confident that the anonymous purchaser was certain to tear the chapel down anyway.

"I know who the intending purchaser is," said Mr. Drake, "and—"

"You would never do such an unneighborly thing!" he cried, "as—"

"As conspire to bring down the value of a property the moment it had passed out of my hands?—I would not, Mr. Barwood; and this very day the intending purchaser shall know of your scheme."

Barwood looked at him in rage. He jumped to his feet, took up his hat, and rushed out of the house. Mr. Drake smiled, looked around calmly on the rest of the deacons, and held his peace. It was a most awkward moment for them. At length one of them, a small tradesman, ventured to speak, daring to make no allusion to the catastrophe that had occurred. It would take much reflection to get hold of the true weight and bearing of what they had just heard and seen, for Barwood was a mighty man among them.

"What we was thinking, sir," he explained—"and you will remember that I was always on your side, and it's better to come to the point—there's a strong party of us in the church, sir, that would like to have you back. And we was thinking if you would condescend to help us, now as you're so well able to, sir, toward building a new chapel, now as you have the means as well as the will to do God's service, sir, what with the chapel-building society and every man among us setting our shoulder to the wheel, and we should all do our very best, we should get a nice, new, I won't say 'showy,' but attractive—that's the word, attractive place—a place to which the people would be drawn by the look of it outside, and kept by the look of it inside—a place as would make the people of Glaston say, 'Come, and let us go up to the house of the Lord.' If, with your help, sir, we had such a place, then perhaps you would condescend to take the reins again, sir, and we would then pay Mr. Rudd as your assistant, leaving the whole management in your hands—to preach when you pleased, and not when you didn't. There, sir! I think that's the whole thing in a nutshell."

"And will you tell me what results you would look for under such an arrangement?"

"We would look for the blessing of a little success. It's many years since we was favored with any."

"And by success you mean—?"

"A large attendance of regular hearers in the morning—not a seat left empty—and the people of Glaston crowding to hear the Word in the evening! That's the success I would like to see."

"What! Would you have all Glaston such as yourselves!" exclaimed the pastor. "Gentlemen, this is the crowning humiliation of my life! Yet I deserve it, and it will help to make and keep me humble. I see in you the wood and hay and stubble with which, alas! I have been building all these years! I have been preaching dissent against the Church of England instead of preaching Christ. I cannot aid your plans with a single penny in the hope of taking one inhabitant of Glaston away from the preaching of Mr. Wingfold, a man who speaks the truth and fears nobody. I would be doing the body of Christ a grievous wrong." He passed a trembling hand over his brow.

"I have all these years been as one beating the air," he continued. "I have taken to pieces and put together for you the plan of salvation, when I ought to have spoken of him who is the way and the truth and the life. Go to the abbey church, my friends, and there a man will stir you up to lay hold of God and will teach you to know Christ. Shut the doors of your chapel and go to the abbey church and there be filled with the finest of the life-giving wheat. Do not mistake me: I believe as strongly as I ever did that the constitution of the Church of England is all wrong; that the arrogance of her priesthood is essentially opposed to the very idea of the kingdom of heaven; that the Athanasian Creed is unintelligible, and where unintelligible, cruel. But where I find my Lord preached as only one who understands him can preach him—and as I never could preach him and never heard him preached before—even such faults with the church system as these shall pale into insignificance to me.

"Gentlemen, everything is pure loss—chapel and creeds and churches—all is loss that comes between us and Christ individually— no matter how religious. One of the most unchristian things is to dispute and separate in the name of him whose one object was, and whose one victory will be, unity. Gentlemen, if you should ever ask me to preach to you, I will do so with pleasure. But I will not build you a new chapel."

They rose as one man, bade him an embarrassed good morning, and walked from the room, some with their heads thrown back, others hanging them in shame. The former spread the rumor that the old minister had gone crazy, the latter began to now and then visit Wingfold's church.

I should here mention that a new chapel was not built, that the young pastor soon left the old one, and that the deacons declared themselves unable to pay the rent. Mr. Drake then took the place into his own hands, cleaned and repaired the building, and preached there every Sunday evening, but went always in the morning to hear Mr. Wingfold.

There was a kindly human work of many kinds done by the two of them together, and each felt the other a true support. Whenever they met, even in some lowly cottage where they both chanced to call at the same time, it was never with embarrassment but always with hearty and glad greetings. And they always went away together.

I doubt if wickedness does half as much harm as sectarianism in the church—sectarianism which is full both of condescension and pride. Division has done more to hide Christ from the view of man than all the infidelity that has ever been spoken. I believe the half-Christian clergy of every denomination is the main cause of the so-called failure of the church of Christ. Thank God, it has not failed so miserably as to succeed to the satisfaction of any party in it.

But it was not merely in relation to forms of church government that the heart of the pastor now in his old age began to widen. It is foolish to say that after a certain age a man cannot change. That some men cannot—or will not (God alone can draw the line between those two *nots*), I will grant. But the cause of a lack of growth is not age, and it is not universal. The man who does not care and ceases to grow becomes dormant, stiffens, and in a sense is dead. But he who has been growing all the time needs never stop. And where growth is, there is always capability of change: growth itself is a succession of slow, melodious, ascending changes.

The very next Sunday after the visit of their deputation to him, the church in Cowlane asked their old minister to preach to them.

22 / Progressions

Juliet took advantage of the holidays of summer to escape what had become a bondage to her—daily interaction with people who disapproved of the man she loved. She had no suspicion what an awful swamp lay around the prison of the self-content (or self-discontent!) in which she was chained. To her the one good and desirable thing had become the love and company of Paul Faber. He was her savior, she said to herself, and the woman who could not love and trust and lean upon such a heart of devotion and unselfishness as his was unworthy of the smallest of his thoughts. He was nobility, generosity, justice itself. If she sought to lay her faults bare to him, he would but fold her to his heart and shut them out. He was better than the God the Wingfolds and Drakes believed in, she decided, because their God demanded humiliation as a condition of acceptance.

She told the Drakes that in order to breathe the fresh air of Owlkirk again, she was going to occupy her old quarters with Mrs. Puckridge during the holidays. They were not much surprised, for they had noticed a change in her manner. And it did not remain unexplained long, for walking from the Old House together rather late one evening, they met her with the doctor in a secluded part of the park. When she left them, they knew she would not be returning to their home again. And her tears betrayed that she knew it also.

In the meantime the negotiation for the purchase of the Old House of Glaston was progressing very slowly through tangled legalities. Mr. Drake had offered the full value of the property, and yet his heart and mind were far more occupied with the humbler purchase he had already made in the town that was now to be fortified against the river. A survey of the ground had satisfied him that a wall at a certain point would divert a great portion of the water in case of another flood, and this wall he began at once to build. There were many other changes which were imperative too, but they could not all be coped with at once. The worst of the cottages would have to be pulled down. As they all were too full already, he would have to build new ones first. And not until that was completely done could he set about making the best of them fit for human habitation.

The other chapel, the one in Nestley Park at Owlkirk, had also been advancing, for the rector was no dawdler by nature. And at length on a certain Sunday evening in the autumn, the people of the neighborhood were invited to attend and the rector read prayers in it, and the curate preached a sermon. At the close of the service the congregation was informed that prayers would be read there every Sunday evening, and then they were dismissed. Mrs. Bevis, honest soul, though rather shallow, was the only one to grumble at the total absence of ceremonial pomp.

It was about this same time that Juliet went to Owlkirk, knowing full well that she went to meet her fate. Faber came to see her every day, and both Ruber and Niger began to show signs of neglect. In an apathetic sort of way, Juliet allowed the course of affairs between them to drift and let Faber gradually begin to speak to her as though her consent had been explicitly given. They had long ceased to talk about God or no God, about life and death, truth and superstition, and spoke only of love and the days at hand. Before much time had passed Juliet found herself as firmly engaged to be Paul's wife as if she had granted every one of the promises he had wanted from her, but which she had avoided. She had imagined that she was thus keeping herself free. It was perfectly understood in all the neighborhood that the doctor and Miss Meredith were engaged.

"She may well be ashamed of such an unequal yoking," Helen said to her husband, troubled by the relationship but not sure why.

"I see nothing unequal in it," he returned. "In the matter of faith, I hardly see a difference between them. Between *don't believe* and *don't care* I don't want to choose. Let them marry and God bless them. It will be good for them for this one reason if for no other: it is sure to bring trouble to both."

"Indeed, Mr. Wingfold!" responded Helen playfully. "So that is how you regard marriage!—Sure to bring trouble?" In contrast to her words, she laid her head on his shoulder.

"Trouble to everyone, my Helen, like the gospel itself. It has brought more trouble to you, I'm afraid, than to me, but only what will serve to bring us closer to each other. But about those two—well, I am both doubtful and hopeful. I think it will be for both of them a step nearer to the truth. The trouble that will inevitably come will perhaps drive them to find God. I must confess to you that with all her frankness, all her charming ways, all the fullness of the gaze of her black eyes, there is something about Juliet that puzzles me. At times I have thought she must be in some kind of trouble and that she was on the point of asking me to help her. At other times I have imagined she was trying to be nice against her inclination and did not altogether approve of me. Sometimes the doubting question crosses me but then vanishes the moment she smiles. I wish she could have been open with me. I am pretty sure I could have helped her. As it is, I have not gotten one step nearer the real woman than when I first met her."

"I know," affirmed Helen. "Don't you think she has never come to know anything about herself and her own nature? If she is a stranger to herself, how can she reveal herself to those around her? She is just what I was, Thomas, before I met you—a dull, sleepy-hearted, self-centered thing waiting to be awakened. But now that you have said your mind about Juliet, allow me to say that I trust her more than I do Faber. I do not for a moment imagine him consciously dishonest, but he makes too much of a show of his self-perceived honesty for me. I cannot help feeling that he is selfish; and can a selfish man be altogether honest?"

"Not thoroughly. I know that only too well, Helen, for I am selfish."

"I don't see it. But if you are, you know it, hate it, and strive against it. I do not think he knows it, even when he says that everybody is selfish. I think that down inside, he still thinks he is less so than anyone else. But what better way to get rid of selfishness than to love and marry?"

"Or to confirm it," said Wingfold thoughtfully.

"I wonder if they're married already," mused Helen.

She was not far wrong, although not quite right. Already Faber had more than hinted at a hurried marriage, as private as could be arranged. It was impossible, of course, to be married at church. That would be to cast mockery on the marriage itself, as well as on what Faber called his beliefs—or lack of them. The objection was entirely on Faber's side, but Juliet did not hint at the least difference of opinion in the matter. She was letting everything take its own way now.

At length Faber arranged all the necessary preliminaries in a neighboring town. He got one of the other doctors in Glaston to attend to his practice for three weeks and went away to take a holiday. Juliet left Owlkirk the same day. They met, were lawfully married, and at the end of the three weeks returned to Glaston to the doctor's house.

This sort of thing did not please Glaston society, and although Faber was too popular as a doctor to lose status by it, the people of the town were slow in acknowledging that it knew there was a lady at the head of his house. Mrs. Wingfold and Miss Drake, however, set their neighbors a good example, and by degrees there came about a dribbling sort of recognition. Faber's social superiors remained aloof the longest—mainly because the lady had behaved so much like one of themselves while still a governess. They thought it only proper to teach her a lesson. Most of them, however, not willing to offend the leading doctor in the place, yielded and made the proper social calls. Mrs. Ramshorn (who declared she did not believe they were married) and two elder spinsters did not. General agreement was that they were the handsomest couple ever seen in the area.

Juliet returned the calls at the proper intervals, and gradually her life settled into a routine. The doctor went out every day and was out most of the day, while she sat at home and worked or read. Sometimes she found life more dull than when she had earned her bread and might meet Paul unexpectedly upon Ruber or Niger as she went from place to place. Already the weary weed of *commonplace* began to show itself in the marriage garden. This weed, like all weeds, requires only neglect for perfect development. As it grows it will drive the undisciplined wife who has never made her life worth *living* to ask whether life be worth *having*. She was not a great reader. No book had ever yet been to her a well-spring of life. If only Paul would buy a yellow gig, she thought, like his friend Dr. May, and take her about with him on his rounds! Or if she had a friend or two to go and see when he was out—friends like what Dorothy and Helen might have been. But she certainly was not going to be hand-in-glove with anyone who didn't like her Paul! She missed church too—not the prayers too much, but she did like what she considered a "good sermon"—that is, a lively one.

23 / Two Conversations _____

One Saturday morning the doctor was called to a home many miles distant, and Juliet was left with the prospect of being alone longer than usual. Though late summer, it had been hot and sultry lately. She pretended to herself that she had some shopping to do, but it was a longing for air and motion that sent her out. Also, certain thoughts which she did not like had recently been coming more and more frequently, and she found it easier to avoid them in the street. These troubled thoughts were not the kind that were hard to think out. Properly speaking, she *thought* less now than ever. She often said nice things, but they were merely the gracious responses of a sweet nature.

As she turned the corner by Mr. Drew's shop, the house door opened and a woman stepped out. Juliet knew nothing about her, but as their eyes met Juliet felt something like a physical pain shoot through her heart. She began to suspect, and gradually became quite certain, that she had seen her face before, though she could not tell where. The shock of seeing the woman indicated some painful association which she had to recall before she could rest. She turned in the other direction and walked straight from the town.

Scene after scene of her life came back as she searched for some circumstance associated with that face. Several times she seemed almost on the point of laying hold of something, when the face and the near-memory vanished altogether. In the process many painful memories arose, some connected with her mother, others connected with her father. Then gradually her thoughts took another direction and began to settle back into the erratic circles which had sent her from the house in the first place.

Could it be that already the glamor of marriage had begun to disperse, the roses of love to wither, the magic to lose its force, the common look of things to return? Paul was as kind, as courteous, as considerate as ever, and yet there was a difference. Her heart did not grow wild, her blood did not rush to her face when she heard the sounds of his horse's hooves in the street. Sadder and sadder grew her thoughts as she walked along, hardly caring where she went.

Had she begun to cease loving? No. But the first glow was gone—already. She had thought it would not go, and so she was miserable. She recalled that even her honeymoon had disappointed her a little. Juliet was proud of her Paul, and loved him as much as she was yet capable of loving. But she had thought they were enough for each other, and already, though she was far from admitting it to herself, in the twilight of her thinking she had begun to doubt it. And she can hardly be blamed for the doubt. No man and woman have ever succeeded in being all in all to each other.

She was suddenly roused from her painful reverie by the pulling up of Helen's ponies, with much clatter, close beside her.

"Will you jump in, Juliet?" called Helen. She was one of the few who understand that no being can afford to let the smallest love-germ die. Therefore, her voice contained determined cheerfulness. She was resolved that no stiffness on her part should deposit a grain to the silting up of the channel of their former affection.

Juliet hesitated. She was a little bewildered with the sudden interruption of her thoughts and the demand for immediate action. She answered uncertainly, trying to think what was involved.

"I know your husband is not waiting for you at home," pursued Helen. "I saw him on Ruber, three fields off, riding away from Glaston. Jump in, dear. You can make up your mind in the carriage just as well as on the road. I will let you out wherever you please. My husband is out too, so I have all morning."

Juliet could not resist. She had little reason to do so anyway, so she yielded without another word, and took her seat beside Helen. She felt a little shy of being alone with her and yet glad of her company. Away went the ponies, and as soon as she had got them settled to their work, Helen turned toward Juliet.

"I *am* so glad to see you!" she exclaimed.

Juliet's heart spoke too loud for her throat. It was a relief to her that Helen had to keep an eye on the horses.

"Have you returned Mrs. Bevis's call yet?" asked Helen.

"No," murmured Juliet. "I haven't been able to yet."

"Well, here is a good chance. Sit where you are and you will be at Nestley in half an hour and I will be all the more welcomed for having brought you. You are a great favorite there!"

"How kind you are!" said Juliet, the tears beginning to rise. "Indeed, Mrs. Wingfold—"

"You used to call me Helen!" remonstrated Helen, pulling up her ponies as they shied from a bit of paper on the road, nearly putting them in the ditch.

"May I still?"

"Surely! What else?"

"You are too good to me," Juliet murmured, and wept outright.

"My dear Juliet," returned Helen, "I will be quite plain with you, and that will set things straight in a moment. Your friends understand perfectly why you have avoided seeing them lately. We know it is from no unkindness. But neither must you imagine we think badly of you for marrying Mr. Faber. While we think very highly of him, we are very concerned about his opinions. We feel sure that if you saw a little further into them, neither of you would hold them.''

"I don't know—that is, I—''

"You don't know whether you hold them or not; I understand quite well. My husband says in your case it does not matter much. For if you had ever really believed in Jesus Christ, you could not have done it. In any event, the thing is done, there is no question about it left. Dear Juliet, think of us as your friends still, who will always be glad to see you and ready to help you when we can.''

Juliet was weeping for genuine gladness now. But even as the tears flowed, suddenly it flashed upon her where she had seen the lady that came from Mr. Drew's. Her heart sank within her, for the place was associated with that portion of her history which she was so desperately trying to hide. During the rest of the drive she was so silent that Helen at last gave up trying to talk to her. The clouds now had risen on all sides and the air had grown more still and sultry than ever.

Just as they got within the gate at Nestley, a flash of lightning followed almost immediately by a loud thunderclap, shot from overhead. The ponies plunged, reared, swayed, nearly fell, and then recovered themselves only to dart off in wild terror. Juliet screamed.

"Don't be frightened, child,'' Helen called to her as she held firmly to the reins. "There is no danger here. The road is straight and there is nothing on it. I will soon pull them up. Only don't cry out; the ponies will like that as little as the lightning.''

Juliet snatched frantically at the reins.

"In the name of heaven don't do that!'' cried Helen. "You will kill us both!''

Juliet sank back in her seat as the ponies charged at full speed along the road. The danger was small, for the park was level with the drive on both sides of them. Helen, perfectly calm, gradually tightened her pull on the reins. Before they had reached the house, she had entirely regained command of them. When she drew up at the door, they stood quite steady but panting as if their little sides would burst. By this time Helen was as rosy as a flower in bloom, her eyes were flashing with adventure, and a smile was playing about her mouth. But Juliet was like a lily on which the rain has been falling all night. Her very lips were bloodless. When Helen turned and saw her, she realized Juliet was far more frightened than the ponies could make her.

"Why, Juliet, my dear!'' she gasped, "I had no idea you were so terrified! What would your husband say to me for frightening you so! But you are safe now.''

A servant came to take the ponies. Helen got out first, and gave her hand to Juliet.

"Don't think me a coward, Helen," she whispered through stiff lips. "It was the thunder. I never could stand thunder."

"I would be far more of a coward than you are, Juliet," answered Helen, "if I believed just one false step of one of my ponies here might wipe me out from the world and I would never more see the face of my husband."

She spoke eagerly, believingly, lovingly. Juliet shivered, stopped, and laid hold of the baluster rail. Things had been too much for her that day. She looked so pale and ill that Helen was again alarmed, but Juliet eventually came to herself a little, and went on to Mrs. Bevis's room. She received them most kindly, made Mrs. Faber lie on the sofa, covered her with a blanket, for she was still trembling, and got her a glass of wine. But she could not drink it and lay sobbing in a vain effort to control herself.

In the meantime the clouds gathered thicker and thicker. The thunder that had frightened the ponies had been but the herald of the storm, and it now came on in earnest. The rain fell in torrents upon the earth, and as soon as she heard its comforting sounds, Juliet ceased to sob. Presently Mr. Bevis came running in from the stable, drenched in only crossing to the house. As he passed to his room, he looked in and saw the visitors.

"I am glad to see you safely housed, ladies," he greeted them warmly. "You must make up your minds to stay where you are. It will not be clear before the moon rises, and that will be about midnight. I will send John to tell your husbands that you are not cowering under a hedge and will not be home tonight."

He was a good weather prophet, for the rain continued relentlessly. In the evening the two husbands appeared, dripping. They had come on horseback together. The doctor would have to return home after dinner for some calls and be out the greater part of Sunday. He gladly agreed to leave his wife in such good quarters. The curate would have his services Sunday morning in Glaston, preaching Sunday evening at Nestley, and then drive home with Helen early Monday, taking Juliet if she were up to accompanying them.

After dinner, when the ladies had retired to another room, a lengthy conversation arose between the two clergymen and the doctor. I will take it up at an advanced point.

"Now tell me," said Faber in the tone of one sure he stands in the right, "which is the nobler—to serve your neighbor with hope of a future reward from God, or to serve him in the dark, obeying your conscience, with no hope except that those who come after you will be better for it?"

"I readily allow," answered the curate, "that it is admirable and grand to live for the sake of your neighbor and generations to come. But

I will not say that there is anything grand in having no hope, since it is the hopeless man who can do *least* for his fellows. All he can offer them is hopelessness for them and their families. If there be *no* God, it may be noble to be able to live without one. But if there *be* a God, it must be far nobler not to be able to live without him. We would both agree that the man who serves his fellow in order that he himself may be noble misses the mark altogether. Only he who follows the truth, not he who desires to be noble, shall in the end attain the noble."

"I dispute nothing of all that," concurred Faber, while good Mr. Bevis sat listening hard, not quite able to follow the discussion. "But I know you will admit that to do right with hope of a reward hardly amounts to doing right in and of itself."

"I doubt if any man could ever do anything worth calling good merely for the sake of a reward," rejoined the curate. "But a man may well be strengthened and encouraged by the hope of being made a better and truer man, and capable of greater self-forgetfulness and devotion. There is nothing low in that, even if you choose to call it a reward for having done good, now is there?"

"It seems to me better," persisted the doctor, "to do right for the sake of duty rather than for the sake of any goodness that might come to you as a result—again I say, goodness merely for goodness' sake, with the thought of nothing more."

"But *is* there such a thing as goodness for goodness' sake alone?" asked the curate. "You would say yes, but I would doubt it. The duty you speak of is only a stage toward something better. It is but the God-given impulse toward a far more vital contact with the truth. We shall one day forget all about duty, and do everything from the love of the loveliness of it, the satisfaction of the rightness of it. What would you say to a man who supported his wife and family only from duty? Of course better from duty than to neglect them altogether. But the strongest sense of duty would hardly be satisfying between a husband and wife. There must be something more. There are depths within depths of righteousness. Duty is the only path to freedom. But that freedom is the love that goes beyond duty."

"I have heard you say," said Faber, "that to take from you your belief in a God would be to render you incapable of action. Now, isn't the man who acts, who does his duty without the strength of that belief, the stronger man?"

"While the need of help might indicate a weaker nature, the capacity for receiving it must indicate a higher. The mere fact of being able to live and act without spiritual awareness in itself proves nothing. It is not the highest nature that has the fewest needs. The highest nature is the one that has the most necessities, but the fewest of its own making. He is not the greatest man who is most independent, but he who thirsts most after a conscious harmony with every element and portion of the mighty whole, and who demands from every region its influences to perfect his individuality. For such a man his greatest treasure, the highest freedom he can attain, is not to hold but to give. His self is the one thing he can devote and sacrifice. By dying thus, ever losing his soul, he lives like God, and God knows him, and he knows God."

"Such a way of life is too good to be grasped, but not too good to be true," Thomas continued. "The highest is that which needs the highest, the largest that which needs the most. The finest and strongest is that which to live must breathe essential life, self-willed life, God himself. It follows then that it is the largest or strongest nature which will feel a loss the most. An ant will not gather a grain of wheat any less because its mother is dead. But a boy will turn from his books and his play and his dinner because his dog is dead. But is the ant therefore the stronger nature? No. It is not the weak who seek dependence on God, but the stronger and higher natures."

"Is it not weak to be miserable?" argued the doctor. "Would you not be a weak man to be so miserable learning there was no God?"

"Without good cause misery may indicate weakness," answered the curate. "But you do not know what it would be to me to lose my God. The emptiness would be total—the conviction that I should never myself become good, never have anything to love absolutely, never be able to love perfectly, never be able to make amends for the wrongs I had done. Call such a feeling selfish if you will; I cannot help it. I cannot count one fit for existence to whom such things would be no grief. The worthy existence must hunger after good. The largest nature must have the mightiest hunger. Who calls a man selfish because he is hungry? It cannot be selfishness to hunger and thirst after righteousness when righteousness is just your duty to God and your neighbor. If there be any selfishness in it, the very answer to your prayer will destroy it."

"There you are again—out of my region," said Faber. "But answer me one thing: Is it not weak to desire happiness?"

"Yes, if the happiness is poor and low," rejoined Wingfold. "But the man who would choose even the grandeur of duty before the bliss of truth must be a lover of himself. If there be a God, truth must be joy. But honestly, I do not know a single advanced Christian who tries to obey for the hope of heaven or the fear of hell. Such ideas have long since vanished from a mature man. He loves God; he loves truth; he loves his fellows and he knows he must love them more. You have fallen into the fatal—and if you will pardon me, Faber—the short-sighted trap of judging Christianity either by those who are not true representatives of it and are indeed less of Christians than you yourself; or by others who are true, yet intellectually inferior, perhaps even stupid, and insult Christ with their dull theories about him. Yet even they may have a noble seed in them, urging them toward heights that are at present inconceivable to you."

"There is always weight as well as force in what you say, Wingfold," returned Faber, admiring in spite of it all. "Still it looks to me like a cunningly devised fable of the human mind, deceiving itself with its own hopes and desires."

"It may well look that way to those who are outside of it. But if, as you profess, you are *doing* the truth you see, I fully believe that you will eventually come to see the truth you do not now see."

The doctor laughed.

"Well, only time will tell whether your words are prophetic. But I wouldn't watch too intently for it if I were you," advised Faber. Then he made his departure and left the clergymen together.

What a morning dawned after the storm! All night the lightning had been flashing itself into peace, and gliding farther and farther away. Bellowing and growling, the thunder had crept with it; but long after it could no more be heard, the lightning kept gleaming up, as if from a sea of flame behind the horizon. The sun brought a glorious day, and seemed larger and mightier than before. To Helen, as she gazed eastward from her window, he seemed ascending his lofty pulpit to preach the story of the day named after him—the story of the Son-day. He testified to the rising again in splendor of the buried Son of the universe, with whom all the worlds and all their hearts and suns arose. A light steam was floating up from the grass and the raindrops were sparkling everywhere.

As Helen looked out on the fresh reviving of nature's universal law of birth, she was conscious that her own life, her own self, had risen from the dead, had been newborn also. She did not have to look back far to the time when all was dull and dead in her own being. Then came the earthquake, and the storm, and the fire, and after them the still small voice breathing new life and hope and strength. Now her whole world was radiant with expectation. It was through her husband that the change had come, but he was not the rock on which she built. For his sake she could go willingly to hell—even cease to exist; but there was one whom she loved more than he—the one whose love had sent forth her husband and herself to love one another; whose heart was the nest of their birth, the cradle of their growth, the rest of their being. In him, the perfect love, she hoped for a perfect love toward her husband, and a perfect nature in herself.

On such a morning, so full of resurrection, Helen was only slightly troubled not to be one of her husband's congregation. She would take her New Testament and spend the sunny day in the open air. In the evening he was coming and would preach in the little chapel. If only Juliet might hear him too! But she could hardly ask her to go.

Juliet was better, for fatigue had brought sleep. The morning brought *her* little hope, however, no sense of resurrection. A certain dead thing had begun to move in its coffin; she was utterly alone with it, and it made the world feel like a tomb around her. Not all resurrections are the resurrection of life, though in the end they will be found to have contributed to it. She did not get up for breakfast. Helen persuaded her to rest instead and took breakfast to her. But she rose soon thereafter, and said she was quite well.

The rector and the curate drove to Glaston to read prayers and preach the sermon. Helen went into the park with her New Testament and poet, George Herbert. Poor Juliet was left with Mrs. Bevis. By the time the two ministers returned, she was bored almost beyond endurance. She had not yet such a love of wisdom as to be able to bear with folly. The foolish and weak are the most easily disgusted with folly and weakness which is not of their sort, and are the last to make allowances for them. The softly smiling old woman refused to go across the grass to the chapel after such a rain the night before. Juliet would not even think of spending the evening alone with her. Therefore, she borrowed a pair of galoshes, and insisted on going to the chapel. In vain the rector and his wife tried to dissuade her on the grounds of her health.

Neither Helen nor her husband said a word.

24 / Conscience

The chapel in the park at Nestley, without paint, organ, or choir, was a cold, uninteresting little place. It was neat, but not particularly beautiful, and had as yet no history. Even so, in the hearts of two or three of the congregation, a feeling of quiet sacredness already had begun to gather about it. Some soft airs of the Spirit-wind had been wandering through their souls as they sat there and listened. And a gentle awe, from old associations, stole like a soft twilight over Juliet as she entered. Even the dusk of an old reverence may help to form the fitting mood through which the still small voice shall slide that makes appeal to what of God is yet awake in the soul. There were about twenty villagers attending as well as the party from the house.

With his New Testament in his hand, Wingfold rose to speak. He read: "Beware ye of the leaven of the Pharisees, which is hypocrisy. For there is nothing covered that shall not be revealed; neither hid, that shall not be known."

Then he began to show them that the hypocrite was one who pretended to be what he was not; who tried to look different than what he was. It made no difference, he said, that a man might be only semiconsciously assenting to the false appearance. If he was unwilling to look carefully at the truth concerning himself, he was still guilty of the crime.

"Is it not strange," asked the curate, "that we are so prone to hide behind the veil of what is not? to seek refuge in lies? to run from the daylight for safety deeper into the cave? In the cave live the creatures of night, while in the light are true men and women and clear-eyed angels. But the reason is clear. They are more comfortable with the beasts of darkness than with the angels of light. They dread the peering of eyes into their hearts. They feel themselves ashamed and therefore put the garment of hypocrisy around themselves, hiding their true selves and trying to appear other than they really are.

"But God hides nothing. His work from the very beginning has been *revelation*—a throwing aside of veil after veil, a showing to men of truth after deeper truth. On and on, from fact to fact, he advances, until at length in his Son Jesus he unveils his very face and character. When he is fully known, we shall know the Father also. The whole of creation, its growth, its history, the gathering of all human existence, is an unveiling of the Father.

"He loves light and not darkness. Therefore he shines, reveals. There are infinite gulfs in him into which our small vision cannot see. But they are gulfs of light, and the truths there are only invisible through excess of their own clarity.

"But see how different we are—until we learn of him! See the tendency of man to conceal his treasures, to claim even *truth* as his own by discovery, to hide it and be proud of it, gloating over that which he thinks he has in himself. We would be forever heaping together possessions, dragging things into the cave of our finitude, our individual *self*, not perceiving that the things which pass that dreariest of doors come to nothing inside. When a man tries to bring a truth in there, as if it were of private interpretation, he drags in only the bag which the truth, remaining outside, has burst and left."

With this the curate's voice softened, as he drew the undivided attention of each one there. "If then, brother or sister, you have that which would hide, make haste and drag the thing from its hiding place into the presence of your God, your light, your Savior. If it be good, he can cleanse it. If evil, it can be stung through and through with the burning arrows of truth and perish in glad relief. For the one bliss of an evil thing is to perish and pass out of existence. If we have such things within ourselves, we must confess them to ourselves and to God. And if there be anyone else who has need to know it, to that one also we must confess, casting out the vile thing that we may be clean. Let us hurry to open the doors of our lips and the windows of our humility, to let out the demon of darkness and in the angels of light.

"If we do not thus open our house, the day will come when a roaring blast of his wind, or the flame of his keen lightning will destroy every defense of darkness and set us shivering before the universe in our nakedness. For there is nothing covered that shall not be revealed, neither hid that shall not be known! It is good that we cannot hide! Some of our souls would grow great vaults of uncleanness. But for every one of them, just as for the universe, the day of cleansing is coming. Happy are they who hasten it, who open wide the doors, take the broom in hand, and begin to sweep! It may be painful, but the result will be a clean house, with the light and wind of heaven shining and blowing clear and fresh through all its chambers. Better to choose such cleansing than to have a hurricane from God burst in door and window and sweep clean with his broom of destruction to every lie."

Every listener thought at this point that the curate was speaking only to him. Several shifted in discomfort. "Brothers and sisters, let us be clean. Let us open ourselves to the light. Let us hide nothing in our souls. The light and air around us are God's purifying furnace; let us cast all hypocrisy into it. Let us be open-hearted, and speak every man the truth to his neighbor. Amen."

The faces of the little congregation had been staring all the time at the speaker's as the flowers of a little garden stare at the sun. Juliet's had drawn the eyes of the curate. But it had drawn his heart also. *Have her troubles already begun, poor girl?* he thought. Had the sweet book of marriage already begun to give out its bitterness?

It was dark, and Juliet took the offered arm of the rector and walked with him toward the house. Both were silent, for both had been touched. The rector was busy tumbling over the contents, old chests and cabinets in the lumber room of his memory, seeking for things to get rid of by holy confession. He was finding little yet beyond boyish escapades, and faults and sins which he had given up long ago and almost forgotten. His great sin, which he had already repented of, was undertaking holy service for the sake of earning a living, then, in natural sequence, taking the living but doing no service in return. When at length the heavy lids of his honest, sleepy-eyed nature had arisen and he had seen the truth of his condition, his dull, sturdy soul had gathered itself like an old wrestler to the struggle, hardly knowing what was required of it or what it had to overthrow till it stood panting over its adversary.

Juliet also was occupied, but with no such search as the rector's, hardly with what could be called thought, but with something that must soon either cause thought or spiritual callousness. Somewhere in her was a motion. It would cease, then begin again, like a creature trying to sleep but which was ever being startled awake.

"You are feeling cold, Mrs. Faber," observed the rector, and with the fatherly familiarity of an old man, drew her cloak closer around her.

"It is not cold," she faltered, "but the night air always makes me shiver."

The rector pulled a muffler from his coat pocket and laid it like a scarf on her shoulders.

"How kind you are!" she murmured. "I don't deserve it."

"Who deserves anything?" said the rector. "I less, I am sure, than anyone I know. Yet if you believe my curate, you have but to ask and I will have whatever I need."

"I wasn't the first to say that, sir," Wingfold interjected over his shoulder.

"I know that, my boy," answered Mr. Bevis, turning to him, "but you were the first to make me want to find it true.—I say, Mrs. Faber, what if it should turn out after all that a grand treasure hides in your field and mine, but we never got the good of it because we didn't believe it was there and dig for it? What if this scatterbrained curate of mine should be right when he talks so strangely about our living in the midst of heavenly voices, cleansing fires, baptizing dews, and godly winds of unveiling while we won't listen, won't be clean, and won't give up our sleep and our dreams to receive the very bliss for which we cry out in them?"

The old man had stopped and turned back to her. His voice carried such a strange solemnity that those who knew him only as a judge of horses could hardly have believed it his.

"I would call it very hard," returned Juliet, "to come so near and yet miss it altogether."

When they reached home, Juliet went straight to bed—or at least to her room for the night.

"I say, Wingfold," remarked the rector as they sat alone after supper, "that sermon of yours was above your congregation."

"I am afraid you are right. I am sorry. But if you had seen their faces, as I did, perhaps you might think it was worthwhile nonetheless."

"I am very glad I heard it at least," added the rector.

In the morning, as soon as breakfast was over, Helen's ponies were brought to the door, she and Juliet got into the carriage, Wingfold jumped up behind, and they returned to Glaston. Little was said on the way, and Juliet seemed strangely depressed. They left her at her own door.

"What did that look mean?" Wingfold asked his wife the moment they were down the road and alone.

"You saw it then too?" returned Helen.

"I saw what I could not help taking for relief when the maid told her that her husband was not home."

They said no more until they reached the rectory, where Helen followed her husband to his study.

"He can't have turned into a tyrant already," she asserted, resuming the subject of Juliet's look. "But she almost seems afraid of him."

"It did look like it," rejoined her husband. "What a hideous thing it must be for a woman to fear her husband, and then have to spend her nights close by his side! I do wonder how so many women dare to marry."

"If ever I come to be afraid of you, it will be because I have done something very wrong indeed."

"Don't be too sure of that, Helen," returned Wingfold. "There are very decent husbands as husbands go, who are yet unjust, exacting, and selfish. The most devoted of wives are sometimes afraid of the same men they consider the very models of husbands. It is a brutal shame that a woman should feel afraid, or even uneasy, instead of safe, beside her husband."

"You are always on the side of the woman, Thomas," said his wife with a smile, "and I love you for it, somehow—I can't tell why."

"You make a mistake to begin with, my dear. You don't love me because I am on the side of women, but because I am on the side of the wronged. If the man happened to be the injured party, and I took the side of the woman, you would be down on me like an avalanche."

"I dare say. But there is something more in it. I don't think I am altogether mistaken. You don't talk like most men. They have such an ugly way of asserting superiority and sneering at women that you never do and as a woman I am grateful for it."

That same afternoon Dorothy Drake visited Mrs. Faber. She was hardly seated before the feeling that something was wrong arose in her. Plainly Juliet was suffering, from some cause she wished to conceal. Several times she drew a deep breath, and once she rose hastily and went to the window, as if struggling with some oppression.

"What is the matter, dear?" asked Dorothy.

"Nothing," answered Juliet, trying to smile. "Perhaps I took a little cold last night," she added with a shiver.

"Have you told your husband?"

"I haven't seen him since Saturday," she replied quietly, but a pallor almost deathly spread over her face as she said the words.

"I hope he will soon be home," stated Dorothy. "Mind you, tell him how you feel the instant he comes in," she encouraged.

Juliet answered with a smile, but such a smile as Dorothy never forgot. It haunted her all the way home. When she entered her room she sat down and thought. Could it be that Juliet, just like herself, had begun to find there could be no peace without the knowledge of an absolute peace? If it were so, and Juliet would but let her know it, then they would be sisters, at least in sorrow and search. Her heart was heavy all day, thinking of that sad face. Juliet was in trouble, like herself, thought Dorothy, because she had no God.

Her conclusion shows that Dorothy was not far from truth. She harbored a hope there might be a God to be found. For herself, if she could but find him, she felt there would be nothing but happiness evermore. Dorothy then was more hopeful than she herself knew. I doubt if there is ever absolute hopelessness. Hope springs within us from God himself, and however down-beaten, however sick and depressed, hope will always lift its head again.

She could say nothing to her father. She loved him—oh, how dearly!—and trusted him. But she had no confidence in his understanding her in her present state. The main cause of this insufficiency in him and her lack of trust was that his faith in God was not yet independent of narrow thought-forms, word shapes, dogmas, and creeds.

How few there are whose faith is simple and mighty in the Father of Jesus Christ, waiting to believe all he will reveal to them! How few of those who talk of faith as the one necessary thing will accept as sufficient a simple declaration of belief in him. How few will demolish the walls of doctrinal partition simply by saying that with the whole might of their natures, they will obey him.

And indeed, *your* temptation is the same—to exclude from your love and sympathy the brethren (weak or boisterous though they may be) who exclude you and put no confidence in your truth and insight. If perhaps you know more of Christ than they, then the heavier obligation lies upon you to be true to them. I imitate Paul who encouraged the Judaizing Christians whom these so much resemble.

In Christ we must forget Paul and Apollos and Cephas, pope and bishop and pastor and elder and evangelist, creed and doctrine and interpretation and theory. Whether careless of their opinions, we must be careful to love the people themselves—careful that we have salt in ourselves, and that the salt not lose its savor. We must be careful that the old man, dead through Christ, shall not, vampire-like, creep from his grave and suck the blood of the saints, by whatever name they be called or however little they may yet have entered into the freedom of the gospel, that God is light and in him is no darkness at all.

Dorothy went to sleep thinking how she was to get nearer to Juliet, find out her trouble, and comfort her.

25 / The Old House of Glaston_____

The next evening Dorothy and her father walked to the Old House.

Already the place looked very much changed. The very day the deeds were signed, Mr. Drake had set men at work upon the substantial necessary repairs. The house was originally so well built that these were not so heavy as were expected, and when complete they made little show of change. The garden, however, was quite another thing. The old bushes were well trimmed and the weeds removed. The hedges and borders, of yew and holly and box, tall and broad, looked very bare and broken and patchy. Now that the shears had removed the gathered shade, after so many seasons of neglect, the naked stems and branches would again send out the young shoots of the spring. A new birth would begin everywhere, and the old garden would dawn anew. For all his lack of sympathy with the older forms of religion in the country, the minister yet loved the past and felt its mystery.

Dorothy would have hurried along the lighter repairs inside the house as well. But her father very wisely argued against it. He said it would be a pity to get the house in good condition only to find out later how it could have been altered better to suit their tastes and necessities. His plan, therefore, was to leave the house for the winter, now that it was weathertight. With the first of the summer they would partly occupy it as it was, find out its faults and capabilities, and have it gradually repaired and altered to their minds and requirements. In this way there would be plenty of time to talk about everything, even to the smallest whim, and discover what they would really like.

Ever since the place had been theirs, Dorothy had been in the habit of going almost daily to the house. With her book and needlework, she sat now in this, now in that empty room, undisturbed by the noises of the workmen outside. She had taken a strange fancy to those empty rooms. Perhaps she felt them like her own heart, waiting for something to come and fill them with life. So even after the renovation was at a standstill for a time, she continued to go there still, as often as she pleased, and she would remain there for hours, sometimes nearly the whole day. In her present condition of mind and heart, she desired and needed solitude. She was one of those who when troubled rush away from companionship, and urged by the human instinct after the divine, seek refuge in loneliness—the cave on Horeb, the top of Mount Sinai, the closet with shut door—any lonely place where, unseen, the heart may call aloud to God.

How different, yet how fit to merge in a mutual sympathy, were the thoughts of the father and daughter as they wandered about the place that evening. Dorothy was thinking her commonest thoughts—how happy she would be if only she knew there was a central will in the universe— a Will she might love and thank for *all* things. He would be to her not a God whom she could thank only when he sent her what was pleasant. She must be able to thank him for everything or she could thank him for nothing.

Her father was questioning how the lifting from his soul of such a gravestone of debt could have made so little difference to his happiness. He fancied honest Jones the butcher had more pleasure from the silver snuffbox he had given him than he himself had from his fortune. Relieved he certainly was, but the relief was not happiness. His debt had been the stone that blocked up the gate of Paradise; the stone was rolled away, but the gate was still unopened. He seemed for the first time beginning to understand that God himself, and not any of his gifts, is the life of a man. He had rid himself of the dread thought that God had given him the money in anger, nor did he now find that the possession formed any barrier between him and God. But in learning to derive his *life* from God, and only God himself, he was still but a beginner. Yet making the beginning is the most important thing of all.

"You and I ought to be very happy, my love," he remarked as they were now walking home.

"Why, Papa?"

"Because we are lifted above the anxiety that was crushing us into the very mud," he answered, a little surprised at her question.

"It never troubled me so much as all that," she answered. "But it is a great relief to see you free from it, Father. Otherwise I cannot say it has made much difference to me."

"My dear Dorothy," said the minister, "it is time we understand each other. Your unrest has for a long time troubled me. But I was so hopelessly caught up in my own troubles that I could not venture outside my own doubts. But now why should there not be perfect openness between a father and daughter who belong to each other, alone in the world? Tell me what it is that oppresses you. What prevents you from opening your heart to me? You cannot doubt my love."

"Never for a moment, Father," she answered, pressing to her heart the arm on which she leaned. "I know I am safe with you because I am yours, and yet somehow I cannot get so close to you as I would. Something comes between us and prevents me."

"What is it, my child? I will do all and everything I can to remove it."

"You dear Father! I don't believe ever a child had such a father."

"Oh yes, my dear! Many have had better fathers, but none better than I hope to be to you one day by the grace of God. I am but a poor creature, Dorothy, but I love you as my own soul. To see you happy would fill my heart with gladness."

For a time neither said anything more. Silent tears were falling from Dorothy's eyes. At length she spoke. "I wonder if I could tell you what it is without hurting you, Father," she whispered.

"I can hear anything from you, my child," he answered.

"Then I will try." Here she paused, wiped her eyes, and said as calmly as she could, "I do not think I shall ever quite know my father on earth, or quite be able to open my heart to him, until I have found my Father in heaven."

"Ah, child! Is it so with you? Do you fear you have not yet given yourself to the Savior? His arms are ever open to receive you." He always spoke, though quite unconsciously, with a little of the *ministerial* tone.

"That is hardly the point, Father.—Will you let me ask you any question I please?"

"Assuredly, my child."

"Then tell me, Father, are you just as sure of God as you are of me standing here before you?"

She had stopped and turned and stood looking him full in the face with wide, troubled eyes.

Mr. Drake was silent. He was a true man, and as he could not say *yes,* neither would he hide his *no* in a multitude of words—at least to his own daughter, with those eyes looking straight into his. Could it be that he had never believed in God at all? The thought went through him like a knife blade. He stood before his child like one whose hypocrisy had been proclaimed from the housetop.

"Are you vexed with me, Father?" asked Dorothy sadly.

"No, my child," answered the minister in a voice of unnatural composure. "But you stand before me there like the very thought sprung out of my own soul, alive and visible. That doubt, embodied in my own child, has been haunting me, dogging me, ever since I began to teach others," he said, as if talking in his sleep. "Now it looks me in the face. Am I myself to be a castaway?—Dorothy, I am *not* sure of God, not as I am sure of you, my darling."

He stood silent. His ear expected a shocked, sorrowful reply. He was surprised at the tone of gladness in which Dorothy cried, "Then, Father, there is no cloud between us, for we are in the same cloud together! It does not divide us. It only brings us closer to each other. Help me, Father. I am trying hard to find God. And yet at the same time, I confess I would rather not find him than find him as I have sometimes heard you talk about him in the past."

"It may well be," returned her father. The ministerial, professional tone vanished utterly for the time. He spoke with the voice of a humble, true man. "It may well be that I have done him wrong. For if now at my age I am compelled to admit that I am not sure of him, it is likely that I may have been holding many wrong ideas about him and so not looking in the right direction for finding him."

"Where did you get your ideas of God, Father? Those you took with you into the pulpit?"

If he had been asked that question even a year ago he would at once have answered, "From the Word of God." But now he hesitated and several minutes passed before he began a reply. For now he saw that even if they originally had come from the Bible, that was certainly not where *he* had gathered them. He pondered and searched and it seemed plain that the real answer began in a time beyond his earliest memory. The sources where he first began to draw those notions, right or wrong, must have been the talk and behavior of his father and mother. Next came the teachings and sermons he heard on Sundays and the books given him to read. Then followed the books recommended at college, this author and that, and the lectures he heard there upon the attributes of God and the plan of salvation and every other doctrine imaginable. Certainly the Bible had been given him to read, too, but he had read it not with the idea of pulling truth out of it for himself and then putting that truth into practice; instead he interpreted it through the notions with which his mind was already vaguely filled, and through the eyes of his superiors around him.

He opened his mouth and bravely answered her question as well as he could, not giving the Bible as the source from which he had taken any one of the notions of God he had been in the habit of preaching.

"But mind," he added, "that does not necessarily mean all my ideas are incorrect. They may be secondhand and still true. But where they have continued to be only secondhand, they can surely be of little value to me."

"You have taken none of your ideas directly from God himself or the Bible itself?"

"I am afraid I must confess just that, my child—with this added, I have thought many of them over a good deal, and altered some of them to make them fit the molds of truth in my own mind."

"I am so glad, Father!" cried Dorothy. "I was positively certain from what I knew of you that some of the things you said about God could never have risen in your own mind."

"They might be in the Bible despite that," said the minister.

"But still have been incorrectly interpreted by men," asserted Dorothy.

"Go on, my child," urged her father. "Let me understand clearly your drift."

"I have heard Mr. Wingfold say," continued Dorothy, "that however men may have been driven to form their ideas of God before Christ came, no man can, with thorough honesty, take the name of Christian whose ideas of the Father of men are gathered from any other field than the life, thought, words, and deeds of the only Son of that Father. He says it is not from the Bible as a book that we are to draw our ideas of God, but from the living Man into whose presence that book brings us, who is alive now, and gives his Spirit that they who read about him may understand what kind of being he is."

"I suspect," returned the minister, "that I have been far off the mark. But after this we will seek our Father together, in his Son, Jesus Christ."

This talk proved to be the initiation of a daily lesson together in the New Testament. While it drew their hearts to each other, it drew them gradually nearer and nearer to the ideal of humanity, Jesus Christ, in whom *is* the fullness of the Father.

A man may look another in the face for a hundred years and not know him. Men *have* looked Jesus Christ in the face, and not known either him or his father. It was necessary that he should appear, to begin the knowing of him, but his visible presence was quickly taken away so that it would not become a veil to hide men from the Father of their spirits. Many long for some sensible sign or intellectual proof. But such would only delay and impair that better, that best, vision—a contact with the heart of God himself, a perception of his being imparted by his spirit. For the sake of the vision God longs to give you, you are denied the vision you want. The Father of our spirits is not content that we should know him as we now know each other. There is a better, closer, and nearer way than any human way of knowing, and he is guiding us to that across all the swamps of our unteachableness, the seas of our faithlessness, the deserts of our ignorance.

Is it so very hard to wait for that which we cannot yet receive? Shall we complain of the shadows cast upon the mirrors of our souls by the hand and the polishing cloth, to receive more excellent glory? Have patience, children of the Father. Pray always, and do not faint. The mists and the storms and the cold will pass; the sun and the sky are forever. The most loving of you cannot imagine how one day the love of the Father will make you love. Even your own.

Much intimate talk passed between father and daughter as they walked home. They were now nearer to each other than ever in their lives before.

"You don't mind my coming out here alone, Papa?" questioned Dorothy, as they left the park after a little chat with the gatekeeper. "Lately I have found it so good to be alone. I think I am beginning to learn to think!"

"Do whatever pleases you, my child," said her father. "I will have no objection to what you see good. Only don't be so late that I will worry about you."

"I like coming early," said Dorothy. "These lovely mornings make me feel as if the struggles of life were over, and only a quiet old age left."

The father looked down at the daughter. It cut him to the quick that he had done so little to make her life a blessed one. He had not guided her steps into the way of peace. He had not led her to the house of wisdom and rest. And with good reason; he himself had not yet found that home! But from this moment on, for her sake as well as his own, he would pray that God would do what he had failed to do.

A man needs many fresh starts in the spiritual life as he climbs to the heavenly gates. The opening of his heart in confession to his daughter was just such a dawning for the minister.

26 / The Confession

Faber did not reach home till a few minutes before the dinner hour. He rode into the stable yard, entered the house by the surgery room, and went straight to his dressing room. The roads had been muddy; he was a mess and also respectful of his wife's carpet. Waiting for him in the drawing room, her heart lurched within her when she heard his steps pass the door and go up the stairs, for generally he came to greet her the moment he entered the house. It was ten dreadful minutes before he came down, but he entered cheerily—with the gathered warmth of two days of pent-up affection. She did her best to meet him as if nothing had happened. For indeed what had happened—except her going to church? And hearing the curate's message? Was marriage a slavery of the very soul in which a wife was bound to confess everything to her husband? Was a husband lord not only over the present and future of his wife, but over her past also?

The existence of such questions reveals that already there was a gap showing between them. Juliet was too bewildered with misery to tell whether it was a rift of a hairsbreadth, or a gulf across which no cry could reach. The secret which caused the division had troubled her while he sought her love, had troubled her on to the very moment of her surrender. The deeper her love for him grew, the more fiercely she wrestled with the evil fact in her memory, and at length she believed she had finally put it down for good. And besides, according to Faber's view of the world, such a thing in one's past could not possibly make any difference. It would be as nothing to him. And even if she were mistaken in this conclusion, it would be to wrong his large nature, his generous love, his unselfish regard, his tender pitifulness not to put her silent trust in him. After all these arguments, something remained unsatisfied in her thinking. She strove to strangle it, and thought—hoped—she had succeeded. She had made up her mind to marry him despite her past, had yielded to Paul's solicitations, and had put the whole painful thing from her.

The step was taken, the marriage had taken place, thus nothing now could alter either fact. But unfortunately for the satisfaction and repose she had desired and expected, her love to her husband had gone on growing after they were married and she had already begun to long after a total union—spiritual and emotional as well as physical—with him. But this growth of her love, and longing after its perfection was all the time bringing the past closer to her consciousness—out of the far toward

152

the near. And now suddenly, that shape lying in the bottom of the darkest pool of the stagnant past, had been stung into life by a chance meeting and by wind of words that swept through Nestley Chapel, had stretched up a hideous neck and threatening head from the deep, and was staring at her with sodden eyes. She knew that the hideous fact had now claimed its appointed place between her and her beautiful Paul. The demon of the large gulf had parted them.

The moment she spoke in reply to his greeting, her husband also felt something dividing them. But he had no idea of its being anything important.

"You're tired, my love," he said gently, taking her hand and feeling her pulse. It was feeble and rapid.

"What have they been doing to you, my darling?" he asked. "Those little demons of ponies running away again?"

"No," she answered, scarcely audible.

"Something is wrong with you?" he persisted. "Have you caught a cold? None of the old symptoms, I hope."

"None, Paul. There is nothing the matter," she answered, laying her head lightly on his shoulder, yet afraid of taking such liberty. His arm went round her waist.

"What is it then, my wife," he asked tenderly.

"Which would you rather have, Paul—have me die, or do something wicked?"

"Juliet, this will never do!" he returned, quietly but almost severely. "You have been letting your morbid imagination go again. Weakness and folly are the only things that can come of that. It is nothing but hysteria."

"No, but tell me, dear Paul," she persisted pleadingly. "Please, answer my question."

"There is no question to be answered," he returned. "You are not going to die, and I am even more certain you are not going to do anything wicked. Are you now?"

"No, Paul. Indeed, I am not. But—"

"I know what it is!" he exclaimed. "You went to church last night at Nestley! Confound them all with their humbug! You have been letting their infernal nonsense get a hold of you again. It has upset you, and you have gone so long without dinner too. What *can* be keeping it?" He left her hurriedly and rang the bell. "You must speak to the cook, my love. She is getting out of the good habits I had so much trouble to teach her. But no—you shall not be troubled with my servants. I will speak to her myself. After dinner I will read to you some of my favorite passages in Montaigne. No, you shall read to me: your French is so much better than mine."

Dinner was announced, and nothing more was said. Paul ate well,

Juliet scarcely at all, but she managed to hide the fact from him. They rose together and returned to the drawing room.

The moment Faber shut the door Juliet turned in the middle of the room and as he came up to her, she began to speak in a voice very different than her own. "Paul, if I *were* to do anything very bad, as bad as could be, would you forgive me?"

"Come, my love," remonstrated Faber, speaking more gently than he had before, for he had had his dinner. "Surely you are not going to spoil our evening with any more such nonsense."

"Answer me, Paul, or I will think you do not love me," she said, her tone not to be argued with. "Would you forgive me if I had done something *very* bad?"

"Of course I would," he answered with almost irritated haste. "If I could ever bring myself to think of anything you did as wrong, that is. Only you could bewitch me into admitting any opinion and everything else with but two words from your dear lips."

"Should I, Paul?" she asked, and lifting her face from his shoulder, she looked up at him from the depths of two dark fountains of tears. Faber kissed eyes and lips and neck in a glow of delight. She was the vision of a most blessed dream, and she was his, altogether his!

A summons for the doctor interrupted them. When he returned, Juliet lay in bed, pretending to be sleeping.

The next morning at the breakfast table she appeared so pale, so worn, so troubled that her husband was quite worried about her. All she would say was that she had not slept well and had a headache. Attributing her condition to nerves, he gave her some medicine, took her to the drawing room, and prescribed the new piano he had bought for her, which he had already found the best of sedatives for her. But she loathed the very thought of it. She watched from the window while he mounted his horse, and the moment the last red gleam of Ruber had vanished, she flung herself with a stifled cry on a couch and sobbed.

It was a terrible day. After she returned to her room she did not go out of it again. Her mood changed a hundred times. The resolve to confess alternated with wild mockery and laughter at the very thought, but always the resolve returned. She would struggle to persuade herself that her whole condition was one of foolish exaggeration about nothing. Yet the next instant she would turn cold with horror at a fresh glimpse of the awful fact. What could the wretched matter be to him now—or to her? Who was the worse, or had ever been the worse but herself? What claim had anyone, what claim could even a God, if there were such a being, have upon the past which was now gone? Was it not as if it had never been? Was the woman to live in misery because of what she had done as a girl? It was all nonsense. If only she had died. She would never have thought of it again but for that horrid woman that lived over the draper's shop! All would have been well if she had kept from thinking about it! Nobody would have been a hair the worse. But poor Paul—to be married to such a woman as she!

Would it not be foolish to let him know? How would it strike him? Ought she not to be sure before she said anything, before she uttered the irrevocable words? Would it seem a mere trifle to him, or would he be ready to kill her? Did he have a *right* to know? But even if he didn't, how horrible that there should be such a thing between them. That was the worst of all. For she would never belong to him utterly until he had a right to know *everything* about her! She *would* tell him all! She would! She would! She had no choice!

But she need not tell him now. She was not strong enough to utter the necessary words. But if she could not utter the words, then the thing must be dreadful indeed! She *could* not tell him! She would faint in the mere telling. Or fall dead at his feet!

Yes, that would be good. She would take a wineglass of laudanum just before she told him. Then if he was kind she would confess about the opium and he could save her from its effects. If he was hard, she would say nothing and die at his feet.

Worn out with thought and agony, she often fell asleep—only to snap awake in renewed misery and go over and over the same torturing questions in her mind. Long before her husband appeared, she was in a burning fever. When he came he put her to bed, soothed her to sleep, and then went and ate some dinner.

On his return, she still slept as he expected. He sat down by her bedside and watched. Her slumber was broken now and then with a deep sigh, now and then with a moan. Faber was ready enough to attribute everything human to a physical origin, but as he sat there pondering her condition, he recalled her strange, emotional words of the night before. Watching the state she was now in, a vague uneasiness began to gather in him—undefined, but from a different origin than her health. Something must be wrong somewhere. He kept constantly assuring himself that at worst it could be some molehill that her sensitive nature had made into a mountain under the influence of foolish preaching. Still, it concerned him; he well knew how to the mental eye a tiny speck can grow and grow until it absorbed the whole universe. And the further disquieting thought kept coming to him that as thoroughly as he believed he knew her mind, he in fact knew very little of her history. He had never met one person who knew anything about her family, or had the slightest acquaintance with her earlier than his own. What he dreaded most was that the shadow of some old love had returned, and that she had heaped blame upon herself that she had not absolutely forgotten it.

He flung from him every slightest temptation of blame. He must get her to say what the matter was—for her sake. He must help her to reveal her trouble, whatever it might be. He would love her out of her guilt. She would find how kind and generous he could be!

Thus thinking, he sat patiently by her bedside. Hour after hour he sat, and still she slept. Morning had begun to peep gray through the window curtains when she woke suddenly with a cry.

She had been dreaming. In the little chapel in Nestley Park, she once again sat listening to the curate's denouncement of hypocrisy, when all at once the scene changed. The pulpit had grown into a mighty cloud, upon which stood an archangel with a trumpet in his hand. He cried that the hour of the great doom had come for all who bore knowledge of any evil thing neither bemoaned before God nor confessed to man. Then he lifted the great, gleaming silver trumpet to his lips, and every fiber of her flesh quivered in expectation of the tearing blast that was to follow. Instead, only sweet words came. They were soft as a breath of spring from a bank of primroses, uttered in the gentlest of sorrowful voices, and the voice seemed to be that of her unbelieving Paul, saying, "I will arise and go to my Father."

It was no wonder, therefore, that she awoke with a cry. It was one of indescribable emotion. When she saw his face bending over her in anxious love, she threw her arms round his neck, burst into a storm of weeping, and sobbed. "Oh, Paul! Husband! Forgive me. I have sinned against you terribly—the worst sin a woman can commit. Oh, Paul! Paul! make me clean or I am lost."

"Juliet, you are raving," he answered, bewildered and a little angry, and not a little alarmed at her condition. As for the confession, it was preposterous; they had been married only a few weeks! "Calm yourself," he urged. But then he changed his tone when he saw the pale despair that spread over her face and eyes. "Be still, my precious," he soothed. "All is well. You have been dreaming and are not yet quite awake. It is the medicine you had last night. Don't look so frightened. It is only your husband."

He sought to reassure her with a tender smile and tried to release himself from the agonized clasp of her arms about his neck. He wanted to go and get her something but she tightened her hold.

"Don't leave me, Paul!" she cried. "I was dreaming, but I am wide awake now and know only too well what I have done."

"Dreams are nothing," he admonished her.

But the thought of his sweet wife even dreaming a thing to be repented of so despairingly tore his heart. For he was one of those who cherish an ideal of woman which—although in actuality is poverty-stricken—is in their minds that of loftiest excellence, snowy white in essential innocence. Faber prided himself on the severity of his requirements of woman, and saw his own image reflected in the polish of his ideal. And now all of a sudden, from out of nowhere, a fear whose presence he would not acknowledge began to gnaw at his heart. A vague suggestion's horrid image flitted once across his brain before he crushed it.

"Would to God it were a dream, Paul!" answered the stricken wife.

"You foolish child!" returned her husband, now nearly trembling. "How can you expect me to believe that you, married but a few days, have already become tired of me?"

"Tired of you, Paul! Never. Eternal paradise would be to lie in your arms forever."

"Then for my sake, darling wife, banish these follies, this absurd fancy that has laid such a hold on you. It will turn into something serious if you do not resist it. There can be no truth in it." But even as he spoke to her, in his own soul he was fighting off the demons of doubt. "Tell me what the matter is," he went on, "that I may assure you it is nothing—that I may swear to you that I love you the more for the weakness you have to confess."

"But you will not be able to forgive me," returned Juliet. "I have read somewhere that men never forgive—that their honor is more important than anything to them, even more than their wives. Paul, if you should not be able to forgive me, you must help me to die and not be cruel to me!"

"Juliet, I will not listen to any more such foolish words. Either tell me plainly what you mean, that I may convince you what a goose you are, or be quiet and go to sleep again."

"*Could* it be that it is not really so much?" she wondered aloud to herself, meditating in the light of a little flicker of hope. "Oh, if only it could be so! And what is it really? I have not murdered anybody! I *will* tell you, Paul!"

She drew his head closer down, laid her lips to his ear, gave a great gasp, and whispered two or three words.

He jerked up, breaking at once the bonds of her clasped hands. He threw one brief stare at her, turned, and walked with great quick stride to his own dressing room and closed the door.

As if with one rush of a cruel wind, they were ages, deserts, empty galaxies apart! She was outside the universe, in the cold of infinite loneliness. The wolves of despair howled at her.

But Paul was only in the next room! Only the door stood between them. She sprang from her bed and ran to a closet to fetch a certain object. Then she hastened out of the room, and the next moment appeared in her husband's dressing room.

Paul sat slumped in his chair, his head hanging, his teeth set, his whole shape carrying the show of profound injury. He jumped to his feet when she entered. She did not once lift her eyes to his face, but sank on her knees before him, and over her head held up to him a riding whip.

They were baleful stares that looked down on the helpless woman beneath them.

An evil word rushed to the man's lips, but died there in a strangled murmur.

"Paul!" moaned Juliet, in a voice whose soul had left. "Take it— take it. Strike me."

He made no reply, but stood utterly motionless, his teeth clenched so hard that he could not have spoken without grinding them. She waited motionless, her face bowed to the floor, still holding the whip over her head.

"Paul!" she cried once again, "you saved my life once; save my soul now. Whip me, and take me back."

He answered with only a strange unnatural laugh through his teeth.

"Whip me and let me die then," she begged.

He spoke no word. Despair gave her both insight and utterance— despair and great love, and the truth of God that underlies even despair.

"You insisted I marry you," she said. "What was I to do? How could I tell you? And I loved you so. I persuaded myself I was safe with you. You were so generous. You would protect me from everything, even my own past. In your name I sent it away and would not think of it again. I said to myself you would not wish me to tell you the evil that had befallen. I persuaded myself that you loved me enough even for that. I held my peace, trusting you. Oh, my husband! My Paul! My heart is broken. The dreadful thing has returned. I thought it was gone from me, and now it will not leave me. I am horrified with myself. There is no one to punish me and forgive me but you. Forgive me, husband. You are the god to whom I pray. If you pardon me, I shall be content even with myself. Please, Paul, make me clean that I may look other women in the face. Take the whip and strike me. Comfort me with the sting of it. I am waiting for the pain to know that you have forgiven me. Oh, my husband!"—here her voice rose to an agony of pleading— "I was but a girl—hardly more than a child in knowledge. I did not know what I was doing. He was much older than I was, and I trusted him! Oh, my God!—I hardly know what I knew and what I did not know. Only when it was too late I awoke and understood. I hate myself. I scorn myself. But am I to be wretched forever because of that one fault, Paul? To lose you, Paul? Will you not be my savior and forgive my sin? Oh, do not drive me mad. Whip me and I shall be well. Take me back again, Paul. I will not, if you like, even consider myself your wife anymore. I will be your slave. You can do with me whatever you will. Only beat me and let me go."

She sank onto the floor, and grabbed and kissed his feet.

He took the whip from her hand.

Of course a man cannot strike a woman! He may drag her through the mud; he may hold her one minute and scorn her the next; he may kiss her and then throw her from him; he may insult her with his looks and words, but he must not strike her—that would be *unmanly*! If only Faber had not then been so full of his own precious self; had he even stooped so low as to yield to her prayer or his own wrath, how many hours of agony would have been saved them both.

Do you object, dear reader? "What!" do you say; "would you have had him really *strike* her?"

I would have had him do *anything* rather than choose *himself* and reject his wife: make of it what you will. Even if he had struck once, and had then seen the purple streak rise in the snow of her back, that instant his pride-frozen heart would have melted into a torrent of grief. He would have flung himself on the floor beside her and, in an agony of pity over her and horror at his own sacrilege, would have drawn her to himself and baptized her in the tears of remorse and repentance. And from that moment they would have been married indeed.

When she felt him take the whip, the poor lady's heart gave a great heave of hope. Then her flesh quivered with fear. She closed her teeth hard in order to welcome the blow without a cry.

A brief delay—long to her! Then the hiss, as it seemed, of the coming blow. But instead of the pain she awaited, the sharp ring of glass followed. He had thrown the whip through the window into the garden. The same moment he dragged his feet rudely from her embrace, and left the room.

The devil had conquered. He had spared her—not in love, but in scorn. She gave one great cry of utter loss, and fainted where she lay.

27 / The Bottomless Pool

Juliet came to herself in the gray dawn. She was cold as ice—cold to the heart; her very being was frozen. The man who had given her life had thrown her from him. She was a defiled and miserable outcast. This was what came of speaking the truth—of making confession. The cruel scripture had mocked her and ruined her husband. How foolish she had been! What was left to her? What would her husband have her do? Oh, misery! He cared no more what she did nor did not do. She was alone—utterly alone! But she need not live.

Dimly, vaguely, the vapor of such thoughts passed through her as she lifted herself from the floor and tottered back to her room. Yet even then, in the very midst of her freezing misery, there was a tender, dawning comfort in that she had spoken and confessed. And although the torture was greater, yet it was more endurable than what she had been suffering before. But what a deception was that dream of the trumpet and the voice! A poor trick to entrap a helpless sinner!

Slowly she took off her nightgown and dressed herself. The bed before her she would lie in no more, for she had wronged her husband. To have ever called him husband was wrong. She had defiled him; he had cast her off, and she could not blame him. She saw nothing contemptible in his conduct and did not cast him down from his pedestal in her thoughts.

But is such a man the ideal of a woman's soul? Can he be a champion of humanity who would only help another within the limits of his pride? who, when a despairing soul cried in agony for help, thought first and only of his own honor? The notion men call their honor is the shadow of their flawed righteousness. It is a devil that dresses as nearly in angel clothes as he can, but is nonetheless a sneak and a coward.

She put on her coat and hat. The house was his, not hers. He and she had never truly been one. She must go out to meet her fate. There is one powerful liberty that the weakest as well as the strongest hold the key to: she could die. Ah! How welcome death would be now. In the meantime, her only anxiety was to get out of the house. Away from Paul she would understand better what she had to do. Within the power of his angry presence she could not think. Yet how she loved him!

She was leaving the room when a glitter on her hand caught her eye—the antique diamond ring which he had bought for her. She took it off; he must have it again. With it she drew off also her wedding ring. Together she laid them on the dressing table. With noiseless foot and

160

empty heart she went through the house, opened the door, and stole into the street. A thin mist was waiting for her. A lean cat, gray as the mist, stood on the steps of the door across the street. No other living thing was to be seen. The air was chill. The autumn rains were at hand. In her heart was only desolation.

Already she knew where she was going.

Shortly before, she had gone with Dorothy, for the first time, to see the Old House. Walking down by the edge of the garden she had almost slipped into the pond, which all the children of Glaston knew was bottomless. She had been frightened of the deep, black gulf and had quickly stepped back up the bank to safety.

Today, however, the thought of its dark unknown mysteriously drew her; and she was now on the road to this place of terror. When she had regained consciousness on the floor of her husband's dressing room, with it came the thought of the awful pool. She seemed standing on its side watching herself slowly sinking into the bosom of the earth, down and down, and still down, through the one and only door out of her misery.

She followed the same way into the park Dorothy had showed her, through a little-used door that did not go by the lodge. The light was growing fast, but the sun was not yet up. With feeble steps but feverish haste she hurried over the grass. Her feet were wet through her thin shoes. Her dress was fringed with dew. But there was no need to take care of herself now. She felt herself already beyond the reach of sickness. The still pond would soon wash off the dirt and dampness.

"Oh, thank you, Paul!" she said as she hurried along. "You taught me of the darkness and made me brave to seek its refuge. Think of me sometimes, Paul. I will come back to you if I can—but, no, there is no coming back, no more greeting. I shall be the one that does not dream. Where I am going there is nothing—not even the darkness. Make haste, Paul, and you come into the darkness too."

While she was hurrying toward the awful pool, her husband sat in his study, sunk in a cold fury of conscious disgrace—not because of his cruelty, not because he was about to cast a woman into hell—but because his honor, his self-satisfaction in his own fate, was destroyed. Had he known the man of the gospel, he could not have left her. He would have taken her in his arms, wept with her, forgotten himself in pitiful grief over the spot upon her whiteness. He would have washed her clean with love. He would have welcomed his shame as his part of her burden, and helped lift it, with all its misery and loss, from her heart forever.

His pride was indeed great, but it was not grand. Nothing whose object is self has in it the poorest element of grandeur. Our selves are ours that we may lay them on the altar of love. Lying there, bound and bleeding and burning, they are grand indeed, for they are in their noble place, rejoicing in their fate. But this man was miserable. Thinking himself the possessor of a priceless jewel, he had found it marred. He sat there an injured husband, a wronged, woman-cheated, mocked, proud, and self-centered man.

Let me not be supposed to make little of Juliet's sin. But its disgrace let Juliet feel herself. For me, I read and I hope I understand the words of the perfect Man: "Neither do I condemn thee; go and sin no more."

That same morning there was another awake and up early. When Juliet was about halfway across the park hurrying to the water, Dorothy was already opening the door of the empty Old House, seeking the one who is more easily found in solitude. She went straight to one of the upper rooms looking out upon the garden, kneeled down, and prayed to her Unknown God. As she knelt the first rays of the sunrise shone on her face. This was not the sunrise Dorothy was looking for, but she smiled when the warm rays touched her: they too came from the home of answers.

The God to whom we pray is nearer to us than the very prayer itself before it leaves the heart. Hence his answers may well come to us through the channel of our own thoughts. But the world is also one of his thoughts, and therefore he may also make the least likely of his creatures an angel of his will to us. Even the blind, if God be with him— that is, if he knows he is blind and does not think he sees—may become a leader of the blind up to the narrow gate. It is the blind who says *I see* that leads his fellow into the ditch.

Dorothy instinctively knelt facing a window, for her soul yearned for light. The window looked down on the garden, at the foot of which the greater part of the pond's edge was visible. But Dorothy, with her eyes closed and busy with her prayers, did not see her sister soul in agony as she approached the water. All of a sudden, a great bitter cry, as from a heart in the grip of a fierce terror, pierced her ears. She had been so absorbed, and it so startled and shook her, that she was never certain whether the cry she heard was of this world or not. In an instant Dorothy was on her feet and looking out the window. Something was lying on the grass beyond the garden wall, close to the pond: It looked like a woman. She darted from the house, out of the garden, and down to the other side of the wall. When she came nearer she saw that it was indeed a woman, evidently in a faint. Her bonnet was floating on the pond; the wind had blown it almost to the middle of it. Her face was turned toward the water. One hand was in it. The bank overhung the pond and with a single step more she would probably have been beyond help from Dorothy.

Dorothy took her by the arm and dragged her away from the edge before she ever looked in her face. Then to her amazement she saw it was Juliet. She opened her eyes, and it was as if a lost soul looked out of them upon Dorothy, a being far away. It hung attached to the world by only a single thread of brain and nerve.

"Juliet!" cried Dorothy, her voice trembling with the love which only souls that know trouble can feel for the troubled; "come with me. I will take care of you."

At the sound of her voice, Juliet shuddered. Then a better light came into her eyes and feebly she tried to get up. With Dorothy's help she succeeded, but stood as if about to collapse again. She threw her cloak about herself, turned and stared at the water, turned and stared at Dorothy, and at last threw herself into her arms with a wail of grief beyond description. For a few moments Dorothy held her in a close embrace. Then she turned to lead her to the empty house, and Juliet yielded at once. She took her into one of the lower rooms, got her some water, and made her sit down on the window seat. It seemed a measureless time before she again made the attempt to speak; again and again she opened her mouth to try but failed.

At length, interrupted with choking gasps, low cries of despair, and long intervals of sobbing, she said something like this: "I was going to drown myself. When I came within sight of the water I fell down in a half faint. All the time I lay I felt as if someone was dragging me nearer and nearer to the pool. Then something came and drew me back—and it was you, Dorothy.—But you ought to have left me. I am a wretch! There is no room for me in this world anymore." She stopped for a moment, then fixing wide eyes on Dorothy's face, said, "Oh, Dorothy, dear! There are awful things in the world! As awful as you ever read in a book!"

"I know that, my dear. And I am sorry if any of them has come your way. Tell me what is the matter. I *will* help you if I can."

"I dare not; I dare not! I should go raving mad if I said a word about it."

"Then don't tell me. But come upstairs with me. There is a warmer room there—full of sunshine. I came there this morning to be alone and to pray to God. Come upstairs!"

With Dorothy's arm around her waist, Juliet climbed trembling to the warmer room. On a rickety wooden chair she had found, Dorothy made her sit in the sunshine while she went and gathered chips and shavings and bits of wood left in the garden by the workmen. With these she soon kindled a fire in the rusty grate. She spread her cloak on a sunny spot on the bare floor, made Juliet lie down upon it, covered her with her own cloak, and was about to leave the room.

"Where are you going, Dorothy?" cried Juliet, seeming all at once to wake up.

"I am going to fetch your husband," answered Dorothy.

She gave a great cry, rose to her knees, and clasped Dorothy around hers.

"No, no, no!" she screamed. "You must not. If you do, I swear I will run straight to the pond."

Despite the look of wildness in her eyes, there was an evident determination in her voice.

"I will do nothing you don't like," promised Dorothy. "I thought that would be the best thing I could do for you."

"No, no! Anything but that!"

"Then of course I won't. But I must go and get you something to eat."

"I could not swallow so much as a mouthful; it would choke me. And what would be the good of it anyway when life is over?"

"Don't talk like that. Life can't be over till it is taken from us."

"You would see it just as I do if you knew all."

"Then tell me all."

"What is the use when there is no help?"

"No help!" echoed Dorothy. She had said the words so often to herself, but when they came from another it sounded like an incredible contradiction. Could God make the world so there was no help? "Juliet," she went on after a little pause, "I have often said the same thing to myself, but—"

"You!" interrupted Juliet, "you who always professed to believe!"

"You never heard me profess anything, Juliet. If my surroundings made it seem as though I believed, I could not help it. I never dared say I believed anything. But I hope—and perhaps," she went on with a smile, "since Hope is a sister to Faith, maybe it will bring me to know her someday. Paul says—"

Dorothy had been brought up a dissenter and never used the title *saint* this or that.

At the sound of the name, Juliet burst into tears. She threw herself down again and wept as if her heart would break. Dorothy knelt beside her and laid a hand on her shoulder.

"You see," she said at last, for the weeping went on and on, "nothing will do you any good but your husband."

"No, no! He has cast me from him forever!" she cried in a strange wail that rose to a shriek.

"The wretch!" exclaimed Dorothy, clenching a fist whose little bones looked fierce through the whitened skin.

"No," returned Juliet, suddenly calmed; "it is I who am the wretch. He has done nothing but what is right."

"I don't believe it."

"I deserved it."

"I am sure you did not. I would believe a thousand things against him before I would believe one against you!" cried Dorothy, kissing her hand.

Juliet snatched it away and covered her face with both hands.

"I would only need to tell you one thing to convince you," she sobbed from behind them.

"Then tell it to me that I may not be unjust to him."

"I cannot."

"I won't take your word against yourself," returned Dorothy determinedly. "You will have to tell me, or leave me to think the worst of him." She was not moved by any form of curiosity, but how is one to help without knowing? "Tell me all about it, and in the name of the God in whom I hope to believe, I promise to give myself to help you."

Thus besought, Juliet found herself compelled. But it was with heart-tearing groans and sobs and intervals of silence in which the truth seemed unutterable for despair and shame. Then followed hurried wild confessions, and at length the sad tale found its way into Dorothy's aching heart. It entered at the wide-open eternal doors of sympathy. If Juliet had lost a husband, she had gained a friend; and that was no little thing—for the friend was truer, more complete than the husband. When a final burst of tears had ended the story of loss and despair, a silence fell.

"Oh, those men! those men!" said Dorothy, in a low, bitter voice, as if she knew them and their ways well, though no kiss of man except her father had lighted on her cheek. "My poor friend!" she said after another pause, "and he cast you from him! Well, I suppose a woman's heart can never make up for the loss of a man's; but here is mine for you to go into the very middle of and lie down in."

As she told her story, Juliet had risen to her knees. Dorothy was on hers too, and as she spoke she opened her arms wide and clasped the discarded wife to her. None but the arms of her husband, Juliet believed, could make her alive with forgiveness, yet she felt a strange comfort in that embrace. It worked upon her as if she had heard a far-off whisper of the words: *Thy sins be forgiven thee*. And no wonder: she was resting on the bosom of one of the Lord's clean ones! It was her first lesson in the mighty truth that sin, of all things, is mortal and will someday die, but purity alone can *live* forever.

28 / Dorothy and Juliet

Nothing makes a man or a woman more strong than the call for help. A hen-like mother becomes bold as a tigress for her periled offspring. A stranger will even fight on behalf of one who puts his trust in him. The weak but lovely, the doubting yet living, faith of Dorothy arose, stretched out its crippled wings, and began to arrange and straighten their disordered feathers—feeble, ruffled, bent, and crushed. But Juliet's were full of mud, paralyzed with disuse, and grievously singed in the smoldering fire of her secret.

"There must be some way out of it," concluded Dorothy, "or there is no saving God in the universe. And don't begin to say there isn't, because, you see, it is your only chance. It would be a pity to make a fool of yourself by being over-wise, to lose everything by taking for granted there is no God. If after all there is a God, it would be the saddest thing of all to perish never finding him. I won't say I am as miserable as you, for I haven't a husband to trample on my heart. But I am miserable enough, and I want dreadfully to be saved. I cannot help thinking if we could only get up there—I mean into a life of which I can at least dream—if I could get my head and heart into the kingdom of heaven, I would find that everything else would come right. I believe it is God himself I want: nothing but himself in me."

"But why did he make us," demanded Juliet bitterly, "if we were only to be so miserable? Or why didn't he make us good? I'm sure I don't know what was the use of his making me!"

"Mr. Wingfold would say that he hasn't finished with you yet. He is in the process of making you, and you don't like it."

"No, I don't!—if you call this making. Why does he do it? He could have avoided all the trouble by leaving us alone."

"I once asked Mr. Wingfold something like that," answered Dorothy. "He said it was impossible to show anyone the truths of the kingdom of heaven; he must learn them for himself, 'If God has not made you good,' he said, 'he has made you with the feeling that you *ought* to be good and with at least a half-conviction that he is the one you have to go to to become good. When he is finished making you, then you will know why he did not make you good in the first place, and you will be perfectly satisfied with the reason. But until that time, any answer he gives you would be beyond your understanding. You will never get a thoroughly satisfactory answer to any question till you go to him for it—and then it may take years to make you fit to receive and understand the answer.' Oh, Juliet, I almost feel sorry for God sometimes, because he has such a troublesome nursery of children that will not or cannot understand him, and will not do what he tells them, even though all the while he is doing the very best for them that he can.''

"It may be all very true, or all great nonsense, Dorothy. But I don't care a bit about it. All I care for is—well, I don't know what I care for. I love my husband with a heart that is breaking. But he hates and despises me, and I dare not wish that he wouldn't. I don't care about a God. If there were a God, what would he be to me if I didn't have my Paul?''

"You may yet come to say, 'What would my Paul be to me without my God?' I doubt that you and I have any more idea than that lonely fly on the window what it would really be like *to have a God*.''

"I don't care. I would rather go to hell with my Paul than go to heaven without him," moaned Juliet.

"But what if the only place to truly find your Paul is in God?" said Dorothy. "What if the gulf that separates you is just the very gulf of a God not believed in—a universe which neither of you can cross to meet the other, just because you do not believe it is there at all?''

Juliet made no answer. The fact was, the words conveyed no more meaning to Juliet than they will to some of my readers. But there are some who will understand them at once, and others who will grow to understand them, and therefore they are words worth writing. Dorothy was astonished to find herself saying them. The demands of her new office of comforter gave shape to many half-formed thoughts, substance to many shadowy perceptions, something like music to not a few dim feelings moving within her. But what she said hardly seemed her own at all.

Had it not been for Wingfold's help, Dorothy might not have learned these things in this world. But had it not been for Juliet, they would have taken years more to blossom in her being and become clearly her own. Whether or not she was saying things that Juliet could grasp mattered little at the moment. As Juliet lay there in misery, she would have taken hold of nothing. But love is the first comforter, and where love and truth speak, the love will be understood even where truth is not. Love indeed is the highest in all truth; and the pressure of hand, a kiss, the caress of a child, will do more to save, sometimes, than the wisest argument, even rightly understood. Love alone is wisdom, love alone is power. And where love seems to fail, it is where self has stepped between and dulled the potency of its rays.

"Juliet," said Dorothy, "suppose you were to drown yourself, and then your husband were to repent?''

"That is the only hope left me. You can see yourself I have no choice.''

"You have no pity then, Juliet, for what would become of him?

What if he should come to himself in bitter sorrow, in wild longing for your forgiveness, but you had taken your forgiveness with you where he had never hope of finding it? Do you want to punish him? to make him as miserable as yourself? to add to the wrong you have done him by going where no word, no message, no letter can pass, no cry can cross? No, Juliet—death cannot set things right. But if there be a God, then nothing can go wrong that he can't set right again, and set it right better than it was before."

"He could not make it better than it was."

"What! Is that your ideal of love, a love that fails in the first test? If he could not do better than that, then indeed he could not be God."

"Why, then, did he make us such—make such a world that is always going wrong?"

"Mr. Wingfold says it is always going righter the same time it is going wrong. And what if he is turning our problems into blessings? How wonderful it should be so, Juliet! It *may* be so. I do not know. I have not found him yet. Help me to find him. Let us seek him together."

"I don't care a straw for life. If I could but find my husband, I would gladly die forever in his arms. It is not true that a soul longs for immortality. I don't. I long only for love—for forgiveness from my husband."

"But would you die so long as there was the poorest chance of regaining your place in his heart?"

"No. Give me the feeblest chance of that and I will live. I could live on forever in the mere hope of it."

"I can't give you any, but I have hope of it in my heart."

"Oh, if only I had been ugly, then Paul would never have thought of me. Oh! hide me; hide me," she pleaded. "Let me stay here. Let me die in peace. I am disgraced. I cannot show my face again. Nobody would ever think I was here in this empty house."

"It is a strange old place: you could hide here for months and nobody know."

"But I shouldn't live long. I couldn't, you know."

"I will be a sister to you if you will only let me," replied Dorothy. "Only then you must do what I tell you—and begin at once by promising me not to leave this house till I come back to you."

As she spoke she rose.

"But someone might come!" cried Juliet, half rising, as if she would run after her.

"No one will. But in case anyone should come here, I will show you a place where no one would find you."

She helped her to her feet and led her from the room to a door in a rather dark hallway. She opened it and, striking a match, led the way into an ordinary closet with pegs for hanging clothes on. The sides of the closet were paneled and in one of them, not immediately seen, was another door. It opened into a room lighted only by a little window high in a wall. Through the window's dusty, cobwebbed panes crept a bit of secondhand light from a stair.

"There!" said Dorothy. "If you should hear any sound before I come back, run in here. See, there is a bolt there for the door. You can close the shutter over the window too if you like, but you don't need to. Nobody can look in at it without getting a ladder, and there isn't one about the place. I don't believe anyone knows of this room but me."

Juliet was too miserable to be frightened at the appearance of the strange room. She promised not to leave the house, and Dorothy went. Many times before she returned, Juliet had fled from the sounds of imagined approach and taken refuge in the musty dusk of the hidden room. When at last Dorothy came, she found her in it, trembling.

She came bringing a basket with everything necessary for breakfast. She had not told her father anything. He was too open to keep a secret. And she was still unclear about what ought to be done. Her only plan was to wait. With difficulty she got Juliet to take some tea and a little bread and butter, feeding her like a child and trying to comfort her with hope. Juliet sat on the floor, leaning against the wall, the very picture of despair. Her look was of utter lostness.

"We'll let the fire go out now," said Dorothy, "for the sun is shining in warm and there had better be no smoke. The wood is rather scarce too. I will get you some more, and here are matches. You can light it again when you please."

She then made Juliet a bed on the floor with a quantity of wood shavings and some shawls she had brought, and when Juliet had lain down upon it, Dorothy knelt beside her, and covering her face with her hands, tried to pray. But it seemed as if all the misery of humanity was pressing upon her and not a sound would come from her throat, till she too burst into tears and sobs.

It struck a strange chord in the soul of the wife to hear the maiden weeping over her. The great need common to all men had opened the fountain of her tears. It was hunger after the light that slays the darkness. It was one of the groanings of the spirit that cannot be uttered in articulate words, or even formed into defined thoughts. But Juliet was filled only with the thought of herself and her husband, and the tears of her friend only left dew on the leaves of her bitterness, and did not reach the dry roots of her misery.

Dorothy's spirits revived when she found herself on the way home a second time. *She must be stronger*, she said to herself. Struggling in the slough of despond, she had come upon one worse mired than she, for whose sake she must now search all the more vigorously for the hidden steppingstones—the peaks whose bases are the center of the world.

"God help me!" she cried time and again as she went, and every time she said it she quickened her pace and ran.

It was just breakfast time when she reached the house. Her father was coming down the stairs.

"Would you mind, Father," she said as they sat down, "if I were to make a room at the Old House a little comfortable?"

"I don't mind anything you want to do, Dorothy," he answered. "But you must not become a recluse. In your search for God, you must not forsake your neighbor."

"If only I could find my neighbor," she returned with a rather sad smile, "I shall never be able to even look for him, I think, till I have found one nearer first."

"You have surely found your neighbor when you have found his wounds and your hand holds the ointment with which to heal them," said her father, who well knew her capacity for ministration, for serving.

"I don't feel that way," she answered. "When I am doing things for people my arms seem to be miles long."

As soon as her father left the table, she got her basket again, filling it from the larder and storeroom. She laid a book or two on the top and then set out on her third journey of the day. To her delight she found Juliet fast asleep. Her great fear was that Juliet would become ill, and then what was to be done? But she remembered that the Lord had said she was to take no thought for the morrow, and she began to understand the word, for she could *do* nothing in tomorrow, only in today. One thing seemed clear—so long as it was Juliet's desire to remain concealed from her husband, she had no right to act against that desire. Whether Juliet was right or wrong, a sense of security was absolutely necessary for the present to quiet her mind. It seemed, then, that the first thing she had to do was to make the concealed room habitable for her. It was dreadful to think of her being there alone at night. But her trouble was too great to leave much room for fear. Anyhow, there was no choice.

So while Juliet slept, Dorothy set about cleaning it, and found it tiring work. Her hard work continued as piece by piece, at night or in the early morning, she carried there everything necessary to make the place clean and warm and comfortable.

The labor of love is its own reward, but Dorothy received much more. For in the fresh impulse and freedom which resulted from this service, she soon found not only that she thought better and more clearly on the things that troubled her, but that, by giving herself, she grew more and more able to believe in one whose glory is perfect ministration. She was not finding an atom of what is called proof. But when the longing heart finds that the truth is alive, it can go on without such evidence that belongs to the lower stratum of things.

When we rise into the mountain air, we require no other testimony than our lungs that we are in a healthful atmosphere. We do not find it necessary to submit it to a quantitative analysis; we are content that we breathe with joy. Truth is a very different thing from fact; it is the loving contact of the soul with spiritual fact, vital and potent. It does its work in the soul independent of the soul's ability to explain it. Truth in the inward parts is a power, not an opinion.

How can it be otherwise? If God be so near as the very idea of him necessitates, what other proof of his existence can there be than such *awareness* as must come of the developing relation between him and us? The most satisfying of all intellectual proofs would be of no value. God would be no nearer us for them all. They would bring about no blossoming of the mighty fact.

Peace is for those who *do* the truth, not those who believe it intellectually. The true man troubled by doubts is so troubled into further health and growth. Let him be alive and hopeful, above all obedient, and he will be able to wait for the deeper contentedness which must follow with more complete insight. Men such as Faber may say such as Wingfold deceive themselves. But this is at least worth reflecting on— that while the man who aspires to higher regions of life sometimes does fear he deceives himself, it is the man who aspires for nothing more whose eyes are not looking for truth from whatever quarter it pleases to come. The former has eyes open, the latter eyes closed. And so, as more and more truth is revealed, one day the former may be sure, and the latter begin to doubt in earnest!

29 / A Reckless Ride

Paul Faber's condition as he sat through the rest of that night in his study was as near absolute misery as a man's could be. The woman he had left in a swoon he did not go near again. How could he? Had he not been duped, sold, married to— His pride was bitterly wounded. If only it had been mortally! But pride in some natures seems to thrive on wounds. Faber's pride grew and grew as he sat and brooded, or rather, was brooded upon.

He, Paul Faber, who knew his own worth, his truth, his love, his devotion—with his grand ideas of woman and purity and unity, whose love any woman might be proud to call hers—he to be so deceived! To have taken to his heart a woman who had before taken another to hers, and yet thought it good enough for him!

It would not even bear thinking about! Indignation almost crazed him. Forevermore he must be a hypocrite, for he now knew something about himself which he would not want others to know. This was how the woman whom he had brought back from death with his own blood had served him! Years ago she had sacrificed her bloom to some sneaking wretch, and then she enticed and bewitched and married *him*!

In all this thinking there was no thought but for himself. He forgot how she had avoided him, resisted him, refused to confess the love which his goodness, his persistence, his besieging love had compelled in her heart. It is true she ought either to have refused him absolutely and left him, or confessed and left the matter with him. But he ought to remember the hardness of some duties, and what duty could be more difficult to a delicate-minded woman than either of those?

We do our brother, our sister, grievous wrong every time we ignore the excuse that would ease the blame. Such a thing God never does, for it would be to disregard the truth. As he will never admit a false excuse, so will he never neglect a true one. It may be he makes excuses which the sinner dares not think of; while the most empty of false ones shrivel into ashes before him. A man is bound to think of all just excuse for his offender, for we are called to imitate God.

I would not set Faber down as heartless. His life showed the contrary. But his pride was now roused to such furious self-assertion that his heart lay beaten down under its cyclone. Fortunately, the heart is always there; rage is not. The heart can bide its time. And even now it did not lay quite still. For the thought of his wife lying prostrate on the floor haunted him, so that every now and then he had to rouse an evil will to restrain himself from rushing to gather her into his arms.

Why had she now told him all? Was it from love to him, or simply reviving honesty to herself? From neither, he said. Superstition alone was at the root of it. She had been to church and the preaching of that honest idiotic enthusiast, Wingfold, had terrified her.

Before morning he had made up his mind what he would do. He would not make known his shame, but neither would he leave the smallest doubt in her mind as to what he thought of her, or what he felt toward her. All would be completely changed between them. He would behave to her with marked politeness. He would pay her every courtesy. But her friend, her husband, he would be no more. His thoughts of vengeance took many turns, some of them childish. He would always call her *Mrs. Faber*. Unless they had friends at the house, he would never sit in the same room with her. He would eat with her if he could not help being at home, but when he rose from the table he would go to his study. Never once would he cross the threshold of her bedroom. She should have plenty of money. He would refuse her nothing she asked of him— except it had anything to do with himself. As soon as his old aunt died he would get her a brougham, but never would he sit in it at her side.

Such, he thought, would be the vengeance of a gentleman. Thus he fumed and raved and trifled in an agony of selfish suffering. And all the time the object of his vengeful indignation was lying insensible on the spot where she had prayed to him.

In the morning he went to his dressing room, had his bath, and went down to breakfast. He was half desiring his wife's appearance that he might begin his vindictive torture at once. He could not eat, and was just rising when the door opened and the parlormaid, who was Juliet's attendant, appeared.

"I can't find mis'ess nowhere, sir," she said.

Faber realized at once that she had left him. A terror, neither vague nor ill-founded, possessed him. He knew in an instant this would throw the scandal wide open to the public and bruise his reputation.

He sprang from his seat and darted up the stairs to her room. Little more than a glance was necessary to insure him that she had gone deliberately, intending it should be forever. The diamond ring lay on her dressing table; the wedding ring lay beside it, and the sparkle of diamonds stung his heart like fiendish laughter, the more horrible that it was so silent and so lovely. Only three days earlier he had been justifying suicide in his wife's presence with every argument he could think of. There could be no doubt that ending her life was foremost in Juliet's mind. It was just the sort of mad thing she would do!

He rushed to the stable, saddled Ruber, and galloped wildly away. But at the end of the street he suddenly realized he had not a single idea to guide him how to find her. She was no doubt already lying dead somewhere. In complete dismay, he was ready in a moment or two to blow his brains out. If the Christians were right, that was his only chance of overtaking her. What a laughingstock he would be to them all! The strangest, wildest, maddest thoughts came and went in his brain. When at last he found himself still seated on Ruber in the middle of the street, an hour seemed to have passed. It was but a few moments, and this thought finally roused him: she had probably gone to her old lodging at Owlkirk. He would ride there and see.

"They will say I murdered her," he fumed to himself as he rode—so little did he expect to see her again. "I don't care. Let them prove it if they can and hang me. I shall make no defense. It will be but a fitting end to the farce of life."

He laughed bitterly, struck his spurs in Ruber's flanks and rode wildly. He was desperate. He did not know what he felt, or what he desired. If he had found her alive, I do not doubt he would have behaved cruelly to her. His life had fallen in a heap around him: he was ruined, and she had done it, he said, he thought, he believed.

He did not realize how much of his misery was brought on by the growing dread of the judgments of people he despised. His reputation, his pride in his own *goodness*, was all to him. It had been the thing which had kept him from needing anyone else, or needing the God of the weak. It had been his own form of salvation. And he despised the judgments they would all make against him at this, the collapse—as they viewed it—of his ideal life. Had he known how much the opinions of these he looked down on mattered to him, he would have been all the more miserable and would have scorned himself for it. But he was not aware of the cause of his misery.

Before arriving at Owlkirk he made up his mind that if she were not there, he would ride on to the town of Broughill, where lived the only professional friend he had in the neighborhood—one who sympathized with his views of things and would not close his heart against him. Owlkirk did not harbor Juliet, and so he rode on, a conscious being with a heart set on his own pride. Faber's one idea was to satisfy the justice of his outraged dignity by the torture of the sinner. If she should have destroyed herself, he said more than once as he rode, was it more than a just sacrifice to his wronged honor? He would accept it as such if she had. It would be best—best for her and best for him! But what did it even matter! He and she would soon be wrapped up in the great primal darkness anyway!—no, not together; not even in the dark of nothingness could they lie together again! Hot tears forced their way into his eyes and rolled down, the lava of the soul scorching his cheeks. He struck his spurs into Ruber fiercely and rode madly on.

At length he neared the outskirts of Broughill. He had ridden at a fearful pace across country, leaving all to his horse, who had carried him wisely as well as bravely. But Ruber was not as strong as he had once been, and was by now all but exhausted with his wild morning. For all the way his master, unconscious of everything else, had been immediately aware of the slightest slackening of the great muscles under him, the least slowing of the pace. The moment Ruber flagged, Faber drove the cruel spurs into his flanks, and the grand unresenting creature would rush forward again with all the straining speed left in his weary body.

They were now approaching the high road in their dash through the fields. Close to the road, a rail fence had just been put up to enclose a small piece of ground. The owner wished to rent the land for building and was about to erect a great signboard announcing the fact. At the close of the previous day he had dug the hole for the signpost and had then gone to his dinner. The enclosed land lay between Faber and the road, in the direct line he was taking. On went Ruber blindly—more blindly than his master knew, for with the prolonged running and the sweat pouring down his hairy face, he had partially lost his vision, so that he was close to the fence before he saw it. But he rose boldly and cleared it—to land, alas! on the other side with his right foreleg in the hole. Down he came with a terrible crash, pitched his master onto the road on his head, and lay groaning with a broken leg. Faber neither spoke nor moved but lay as he fell.

A peasant woman ran to his assistance, and finding she could do nothing for him, hurried to the town for help. His friend, who was the leading surgeon in the place, flew to the spot, and had him carried to his house. It was a severe brain concussion.

Poor old Ruber was speedily helped to another world, better than this one for horses, I trust.

In the meantime, Glaston was in a commotion. The servants had now spread the frightful news that their mistress had vanished, and that their master had ridden off like a madman. "But he won't find her alive, poor lady!" was the general concensus of their communications, accompanied by a would-be wise and sympathetic shake of the head. Most agreed with this conclusion, for there was a general impression of something strange about her, added to by the mysterious way in which Mrs. Puckridge had spoken concerning her illness and the marvelous thing the doctor had done to save her life. People now supposed that she had gone suddenly mad, or rather that the latent madness so plain to read in those splendid eyes had suddenly surfaced, and that under its influence she had rushed away and probably drowned herself. And there were others among the discontented women of Glaston who regarded the event as judgment upon Faber for marrying a woman nobody knew anything about.

Hundreds went out to look for the body along the river. Many hurried to an old quarry, half full of water, on the road to Broughill. They peered horror-stricken over the edge, but of course discovered nothing. The boys of Glaston agreed that the pond at the Old House was the most likely place to attract a suicide, for they were well acquainted with the fascination of its horrors. To it they sped, and soon Glaston received its expected second shock in the news that a lady's bonnet had been found floating in the frightful pool. The boys brought the wet mass back with them, and some of her acquaintances recognized with certainty a bonnet they had seen Mrs. Faber wear.

There was no more room for doubt; the body of the poor lady was lying at the bottom of the pool! A multitude rushed at once to the spot, although they knew it was impossible to drag the pool because it was so deep. Neither would she ever come to the surface, they said, for the pikes and eels would soon leave nothing but a skeleton. So Glaston took the whole matter as ended and began to settle down again to its affairs, condoling greatly with the poor gentleman, such a favorite. So young and after so brief an experience of marriage, he had lost in a tragic way such a beautiful and clever wife.

But some said a doctor ought to have known better than to marry such a person, however beautiful, and they hoped it would be a lesson to him. On the whole, Glaston was so sorry for him that if the doctor could have gone about the town invisibly, he would have found he had more friends and fewer enemies than he supposed.

For the first two or three days no one was surprised that he did not make his appearance. They thought he was upon some false trail. But when four days had elapsed and no news was heard of him, some began to hint that he must have had a hand in his wife's disappearance. Dr. May, knowing nothing of what had happened, had written to Mrs. Faber, and the letter lay unopened. It began to be doubted that Faber would ever be seen in Glaston again. On the morning of the fifth day, however, his accident became known, along with the fact that he was lying insensible at the house of his friend, Dr. May. Sympathy for him became even greater than what it was before. The other medical men immediately took his practice upon themselves to keep it together for him until he returned, though few believed he would ever come back to the scene of such dark memories.

For weeks his recovery was doubtful. During the entire time no one dared to tell him about what all believed was the certainty of his loss. But when at length he awoke and began to desire information, his friend was compelled to answer his every question. He closed his lips, bowed his head on his chest, gave a great sigh, and said nothing.

Everyone saw that he was terribly stricken.

30 / The Mind of Juliet

One person in Glaston was somewhat relieved at the news of what had happened to Faber. As much as she would not have wished harm to come to him, Dorothy greatly dreaded meeting him. She knew she could never tell a lie, and she was afraid that the first time she saw Faber, he would instantly know everything from one look in her face. How much she had hoped that their first encounter might be in the presence of Helen or some other ignorant friend, behind whose innocent front she might shelter her secrecy. No wonder then that she felt relief at the news that she would not have to meet him, at least for some time to come. But she did feel up to the task of withholding from Juliet the knowledge of her husband's condition. For the present, any further emotional shocks could damage her sensitive constitution even more.

In the meantime, she had to beware of any feeling of security and continue to be cautious. And so successful was she that weeks passed and not a single doubt associated Dorothy with anything concerning Juliet. Not even her father had a suspicion. She knew he would one day approve what she had done. To tell him now, thoroughly as he was to be trusted, would only increase the risk.

It was a satisfaction, however, despite her dread of meeting him, to hear at length that Faber had returned to Glaston. For if he had gone away for good, how could they have ever known what to do?

Her father frequently accompanied her to the Old House, but Juliet and she had arranged signals so that the simple man saw nothing, heard nothing, felt nothing. Now and then a little pang would quaver through Dorothy when she caught sight of him peering down into the terrible dusk of the pool, or heard him speak some sympathetic hope for the future of poor Faber. But she knew he would be glad when she was able to tell him all, and how he would chuckle at the story of their precautions even against him.

Her chief anxiety was for Juliet's health. When the nights were warm she would sometimes take her out into the park, and every day at one time or another she would make her walk in the garden while she kept watch on the top of the steep slope. Her father would sometimes remark to a friend how Dorothy's love of solitude seemed to have grown upon her, but the remark suggested nothing, and slowly Juliet was being forgotten at Glaston.

It seemed strange to Dorothy that Juliet did not fall ill. For the first few days she was restless and miserable as any human could be. She had only one change of mood: either she would talk rapidly or sit in the gloomiest silence, now and then varied with a fit of weeping. Every time Dorothy came from town she was overwhelmed with questions. At first Dorothy could easily meet these, for she spoke only fact when she said she knew nothing of her husband. When at length the cause of his absence was understood, she told Juliet he was with his friend, Dr. May, at Broughill. Knowing the universal belief that she had committed suicide, nothing could seem more natural.

But when day after day she heard the same thing for weeks, Juliet began to fear he would never be able to resume his practice in Glaston, and she wept bitterly at the thought of the evil she had brought upon the man who had given her her very life, and love as well.

After the first day she paid increasingly less attention to anything of a religious nature. When Dorothy ventured onto such ground to try to console her, which grew more and more seldom, she would sit listless, with a far-away look. Sometimes when Dorothy thought she had been listening a little, her next words would show that her thoughts had been only with her husband. Eventually, after her initial agony had begun to subside, any hint at supernatural consolation made her angry, and she rejected everything Dorothy said almost with indignation. To accept such comfort, she would have regarded as traitorous to her husband. Not even Dorothy's utter devotion could make her listen with patience. So absorbed was she in her trouble that she had no idea of what Dorothy had done for her.

There was much latent love for Dorothy in her heart. I may go further and say there was much latent love to God in her heart, only the latter was *very* latent as yet. When her heart was a little freer from the grief and agony of loss, she would love Dorothy. But God must wait with his own patience—wait long for the child of his love to learn that her very sorrow came of his dearest affection.

Dorothy, who had within her the chill of her own doubt, soon yielded to Juliet's coldness and ceased to say anything that could be called religious. She saw that it was not the time to speak and that she must content herself with being. Nor had it ever been anything very definite she could say beyond the expression of her own hope, and the desire that her friend would look up. She saw that her part was not instruction, but humble serving in obedience to Jesus in whom she hoped to believe. Dorothy dared not say she was a disciple herself; she dared only say that right gladly would she become one if only she could.

There is great power in quiet, for God is in it. When the hand of God is laid on a man, it may be followed at first with an indignant outcry, struggle, and complaint. But when, weary at last, he yields and is still, and listens to the quiet, then the God at the heart of him begins to grow.

Juliet had not yet reached this point. The quiet was all about her, but she could not hear its voice. So her trouble went on. She saw no light, no possible outlet. Her cries, her longings, and her agonies could not reach the ears or the heart of the man who had cast her off. Believing her dead, he might go and marry another, and what would be left her then? Nothing but the death from which she now restrained herself. As Dorothy had begged, she would not deny him the opportunity of softening his heart, but the moment she heard that he sought another woman, she would seek death, leaving but one letter behind her. He would see and understand that the woman he despised was yet capable of the noblest act of a wife; she would die that he might live. Having settled this idea in her mind, she became quieter.

I have said that Dorothy wondered why she did not become ill. There was a secret hope in Juliet's mind which may have had a part in her physical endurance. It was simply this: that the sight of his baby, which she now knew was stirring inside her, might move the heart of her husband to pardon her!

But the time grew very dreary. Juliet had had little consciousness of her own being. She had never reflected upon it. Joy and sorrow had come and gone as rambling troubadours; she had never brooded or thought about them. Never until now had she known any very deep love. Even the love she bore her father had not ripened into a grand love. She forgot quickly; she hoped easily; she had some courage, and naturally much activity. She faced necessity by instinct, and took almost no thought for the morrow—but in much the same way as the birds, not in the way required of those who can consider the birds. It is one thing to take no thought when you are incapable of thought, and altogether another to take no thought when you are filled with thoughts. The one way is the lovely way of God in the birds; the other, his lovelier way in his men and women.

Juliet had in her the making of a noble woman. But that is true of every woman. Yet without God, she would never in any worthy sense be a woman at all. Up till now her past had always turned into a dream as it glided away from her. But now the tide rose from the infinite sea to which her river ran, and all her past was crashing back upon her—even long past childish quarrels with her mother and the disobedience she had too often been guilty of toward her father. And the center of her memory was the hot coal of that one secret. Around that everything else burned and hissed. She was a slave to her own history, to her own deeds, to her own concealments.

All the time Dorothy gave great thought to what might possibly bring husband and wife together again. But it was not as if any misunderstanding had arisen between them. The thing that divided them was the misunderstanding which lies deep and black between every soul and the soul next to it, where self and not God is the final thought. But she was ignorant of Faber's mood. Did he mourn over his harshness, or did he justify himself in resentment? Dorothy could only wait. So, she turned herself again to think of what could be done for the consolation of her friend.

Though it would be some time before either woman would recognize the fact—poor Juliet, and indeed Dorothy too, would never have begun to learn anything worth learning if they had not been brought into genuine, miserable trouble. Indeed, I would guess that of those who seem so good and at peace with themselves, and without any trouble, have peace now because they have already been most severely tried.

31 / Joseph Polwarth

But while the two ladies lived free from any suspicion of danger, and indeed were quite safe, they were not alone in their secret. There was another who for some time had been on the track of it, and had by now traced it with certainty. Although he was known to his friends as a great talker, those outside that circle generally regarded him as a somewhat silent man. His outward insignificance was so great that he scarcely attracted any attention to himself. But the ones who knew Wingfold heard him commend Mr. Polwarth the gatekeeper more often than anyone else. And from what she had heard the curate say, Dorothy had come to have a great respect for the dwarf, although she knew him very little.

In returning from Nestley with Juliet by her side, two days before her flight, Helen had taken the road through Osterfield Park. When they reached Polwarth's gate, she had pulled up so that they might have a chat with the keeper. On the few occasions during which he had caught a glimpse of Miss Meredith, Polwarth had been struck with a something in her that distracted from her beauty—that look of strangeness which everyone felt, but did not understand which held her back from bending with the human wave. So while the carriage had stood, he had glanced often at her face.

From long observation, much silence and gentle pondering; from constant illness and frequent suffering and loving acceptance of it; from an overflowing sympathy with every form of humanity; from deep acquaintance with the motions of his own spirit; and from his dwelling in the secret place of the Most High—from all these things had been developed in Polwarth an insight into the natures of people. He was usually able to read a face and know what was turning in the mind. From the wise use of this power of God within him, he had learned to sometimes make contact with the inner workings of another's spirit. At times this revealed to him not only the character and prevailing drift, but even the main points of a past moral history.

When Polwarth had such an opportunity of reading Juliet's countenance, the curate's sermon had intensified the strangeness of it. And so it arrested him to such an extent that when the ponies had darted away, he stood for a whole minute in the spot and exact posture in which they had left him.

"I never saw Polwarth look so unusual before," observed the curate. But Polwarth had gotten no sudden insight into Juliet's condition.

All he had seen was that there was some battle raging within her spirit. Almost the moment she vanished from his sight, it dawned upon him that she had a secret. As one knows by the signs of the heavens that the ingredients of a storm are in them and must break out, so Polwarth had read in Juliet's sky the inward throes of a pent-up convulsion.

He knew something of the doctor, for he had met him again and again where he himself was trying to serve. But they had never had a conversation together. Faber had not the slightest idea what was in this creature who represented to him one of nature's failures at man-making. Polwarth, on the other hand, from what he heard and saw of the doctor, knew him better than he knew himself. And although the moment when he could serve him had not begun to appear, the dwarf looked for such a time to come. There was so much good in the man that his heart longed to give him something worth having.

How Faber would have laughed at the notion! But Polwarth felt confident that one day the friendly doctor would be led out of the miserable desert where he harvested nothing but thistles and sage and yet fancied himself a hero. And now in the drawn look of his wife's face, in the broken lights of her eyes, Polwarth thought he knew the direction from which unwelcome deliverance might be on its way. And with the observation he resolved to keep himself alert for what help he might offer.

In his inmost being he knew that the mission of man is to help his neighbor. But as much as he was ready to help, he recoiled from meddling. Meddlesomeness is the very opposite of helpfulness, for it consists of forcing yourself into another self instead of opening yourself as a refuge to the other. They are opposite extremes, and like all extremes, touch. It is not correct that extremes meet; they lean back to back.

To Polwarth, a human self was a shrine to be approached with reverence, even when he held deliverance in his hand. He could worship God with the outstretched arms of love anywhere, but in helping his fellow he not only worshiped but served God—ministered to the wants of God by helping the least of his.

He never doubted that his work, just as much as his daily bread, would be given to him. He never rushed out wildly snatching at something to do for God, never helped a lazy man to break stones, never preached to foxes. What the Father gave him, that he cared to do. And that only. It was the man next to him that he helped—the neighbor in need of the help he had. He did not trouble himself greatly about people's so-called happiness. But when the opportunity arrived to aid in the struggling birth of eternal joy, the whole of his strength and being responded to the call. And now, having felt a thread of need vibrate, he waited and watched.

In proportion as the love is pure, and only in proportion to that, can such be a pure and real calling. The least speck of self will defile it. A little more may ruin its most hopeful effort.

Two days later, from some of the boys hurrying to the pond, he heard that Mrs. Faber was missing. He followed them and watched their proceedings. He saw them find her bonnet—a result which left him room to doubt. Almost the next moment a waving film of blue smoke rising from the Old House caught his eye. It did not surprise him, for he knew Dorothy Drake was in the habit of going there—knew also by her face why she had been going. Accustomed to seek solitude himself, he understood. Very little conversation had passed between them. Sometimes two persons are like two drops running alongside each other down a windowpane: one marvels how it is they can escape running together for so long. Persons who could become the best of friends will meet and part throughout the days and weeks, for years, and never say much beyond "good day" to one another.

Polwarth thought to himself that he had never known Dorothy to light a fire, and the day was certainly not a cold one. And how could it be that, with the cries of the boys in her very ears, searching for sight of the body in her very garden, she had never come out of the house to see what the commotion was about, or even looked out a window? Then it came to his mind what a place for concealment the Old House was. He knew every corner of it, and so he arrived at the conviction that Mrs. Faber was there. When a day or two had passed he was satisfied that, for some unknown reason, she was there for the sake of refuge. The reason must be a good one or else Dorothy would not be aiding her. And it must of course have to do with her husband.

He next noted how for some time Dorothy never went through his gate, although she seemed to go to the Old House every day. Then after a while, she began going through it again as before. They always exchanged a few words as she passed, and he saw plainly enough that she carried a secret. By and by he began to see the hover of unspoken words about her mouth. She wished to speak about something, but could not quite make up her mind about it. He would sometimes meet her look with the corresponding look of "Well, what is it?" But then she would invariably change her mind, bid him good morning, and pass on.

32 / Dorothy and Polwarth

When Faber at length returned to Glaston, his friends were shocked at his appearance. Either the hand of the Lord or the crushing hand of chance had been heavy upon him. He looked pale and haggard, appearing to the townspeople as Job must have seemed to his friends. All Glaston was tender to him. He walked feebly and seldom smiled. When he did it was only from kindness, never from pleasure. His face was now as white as his lost Juliet's.

At first he visited only his patients in the town, for he was unable to ride; and his grand old Ruber was gone! For weeks he looked like a man of fifty. And although by degrees the restorative influences of work began to show, he never recovered the look of his actual years. Nobody tried to comfort him. Few even dared to speak to the man who carried within him such an awful sorrow. Who would be so heartless as to counsel him to forget it? And yet what other counsel was there for one like him?

Few men would consent to be comforted in accordance with their professed theories of life. And more than most, at this period of his life, Faber would have scorned his "truth" as comfort. As it was, men gave him a squeeze of the hand, and women a tearful look. But from their sympathy he derived not the faintest comfort, for he knew he deserved nothing that came from a heart of tenderness.

Not that he had begun to condemn himself for his hardness. He was sorry for Juliet, but she and not he was to blame. She had ruined his life as well as lost her own, and his was the harder case, for he had to live on.

Alas for life! It was all so dull. But he would bear on till its winter came. The years would be tedious. But he would not willingly fail in his work. He would work life out that he might die in peace. But he felt nothing, cared for nothing, only ached with a dull aching through body and soul. He was still kind to his fellows, but the glow of the kindness had vanished.

He very seldom saw Wingfold now, and less than ever was inclined toward anything he might say. For had it not been through him this misery had come upon him? Had Wingfold not with confidence uttered the merest dreams as eternal truths? How could poor Juliet have helped supposing he knew the things he asserted, and thus take them for facts? The human heart was the one unreasonable thing—always longing after what is not. Sprung from nothing, it yet desired a creator! At least some hearts did so. He did not; he knew better!

Of course his thoughts contained no reason now. Was it not a fact that she had confessed? And was he not a worshiper of facts? Did he not even dignify facts with the name of truth? And could he wish that his wife had kept the miserable fact to herself, leaving him to his fool's paradise of ignorance? But the thing was out of the realm of logic in his mind by this time.

Sometimes he grew fierce, and determined to face every possible agony, endure all, and dominate his misery. But time after time it returned with its own disabling sickness, bringing the sense of the unendurable. He studied hard, even to weariness, contrived strange experiments, and founded theories as wild as they were daring. By degrees a little composure returned, and the old keen look began to revive. But there were wrinkles on the forehead that had before been smooth. Furrows, the dry water course of sorrow, appeared on his cheeks and a few silvery threads glinted in his hair. His step was heavy and his voice had lost its ring; the cheer was out of it. He slackened none of his opinions, but held to them as firm as ever. He would not be driven from the truth by suffering!

When Dorothy knew of his return and his ways began to show that he intended living just as before his marriage, the time seemed come for telling Juliet of Paul's accident and his recovery. She went into violent hysterics, and the moment she could speak blamed Dorothy for not having told her before.

"It's all your lying religion!" she accused.

"I could not trust you with knowing it before," explained Dorothy. "Had I told you, you would have rushed to him and been anything but welcome. He would not even have known you. You would have made everything public, and when your husband came to himself would probably have been the death of him after all."

"He may have begun to think more kindly of me by that time," said Juliet, humbled a little.

"We must not act on *may-haves*," answered Dorothy.

"You say he looks wretched now?"

"And well he may, after your confession, the severe fall and a concussion of the brain," declared Dorothy.

She had come to see that Juliet required very plain speaking. Juliet had so long practiced the art of deceiving herself that she was skillful at it. One cannot help sometimes feeling that the only chance for certain persons is to commit some fault sufficient to shame them out of their self-satisfaction. A fault great and plain enough to exceed their powers of self-justification may be of God's mercy. It will work not as an angel of mercy to draw them, but a demon of darkness to terrify them out of themselves. For the powers of darkness are God's servants also, though incapable of knowing it.

"You must not expect him to get over such a shock all at once," advised Dorothy. "It may be that you were wrong in running away from him. I do not pretend to judge between you. But by taking it in your own hands and running away, you may have only added to the wrong."

"And who helped me run?" returned Juliet in a tone of reproach.

"Helped you to run from him, Juliet! You forget the facts. Far from helping you run from him, I stopped you from running so far that he could never find you again. But now we must make the best of things by waiting. We must find out whether he wants you again or whether your absence is a relief to him."

Dorothy had seen some signs that self-abhorrence (which can be a cleansing thing) was waning in her patient, and self-pity (which never can be!) was reviving. Therefore she would permit no unreality in her patient. Juliet was one person when bowed to the earth in misery and shame, and quite another if thinking of herself as abused on all sides and therefore to be pitied.

It was a strange position for a young woman such as Dorothy to be in—watcher over the marriage relations of two persons, yet a friend close to neither of them under any other circumstances. Day after day she heard or saw that Faber continued to be sunk in himself, and how things were going there she could not tell. Was he thinking about the wife he had lost, or brooding over the wrong she had done him?

That was the question—and yet who was to answer it? At the same time, even if a reconciliation were to take place, the root of bitterness would no doubt raise itself and trouble them again. If but one of them had begun the task of self-conquest, there would be hope for both. But as of yet, there was not the slightest sign of such a change in Juliet.

What was Dorothy to do? To whom could she turn for help? Naturally she thought first of Mr. Wingfold. But she did not know if it would be right to confide another's secret with him when he might feel bound to reveal it. And if he kept the secret, it could result in serious consequences for a man in the curate's position.

While she thus reflected, she remembered with what enthusiasm the curate had spoken of Mr. Polwarth, attributing to him the beginnings of his own enlightenment. Ought she to tell him? Would he keep the secret? Could he help if he would? Was he indeed as wise as they said?

In the meantime, though she didn't realize it, Polwarth had been waiting for a word from her. But the question whose presence was so visible in her whole bearing neither died nor bore fruit. He therefore began to wonder if he might not help her to speak. Therefore, the next time he opened the gate for her, he held in his hand a little bud which he had just broken from a rose. It was small and hard, and its tiny green leaves clung as if choking it.

"What is the matter with this bud, do you think, Miss Drake?" he asked.

"That you have plucked it," she answered, glancing at him with a hint of suspicion.

"That cannot be it," he replied, "for it has been just like this for three days. I only plucked it the moment I saw you coming."

"Then the frost has got it."

"The frost no doubt locked it shut," he agreed, "but I think the struggle of the life in it to unfold itself was the cause of its death."

"But the frost was the cause of its not being able to unfold itself," argued Dorothy.

"That I admit," said Polwarth, "and perhaps I carried the analogy a bit too far. I was only seeking to establish the similarity between it and the human heart in which repression is all the more dangerous. Many a heart has withered like my poor little bud because it did not know its friend when it saw him."

Dorothy was frightened! He knew something! Or at least he was guessing.

"No doubt you are right, Mr. Polwarth," she admitted carefully, "but there are some things it would not be right to speak about."

"Quite true," he answered. "I did not think it wise to say anything sooner, but now I venture to ask how the poor lady is."

"What lady?" returned Dorothy, dreadfully startled and turning white.

"Mrs. Faber," answered Polwarth with complete calmness. "Is she not still at the Old House?"

"Is it known then?" faltered Dorothy.

"To nobody but myself, so far as I am aware," replied the gate-keeper.

"And how long have you known it?"

"From the very day of her disappearance, I may say."

"Why didn't you let me know sooner?" asked Dorothy, aggrieved.

"For more reasons than one," answered Polwarth, "but one will be enough: you did not trust me. It was best, therefore, to let you understand that I could keep a secret. I let you know now only because I see you are troubled about her."

Dorothy stood silent, gazing down with big frightened eyes at the strange creature who looked so calmly up at her from under what seemed a huge hat—for his head was as large as a tall man's. He seemed to be reading her very thoughts.

"I can trust you, Miss Drake," he resumed. "If I did not I should at once have acquainted the authorities with my suspicions; for you are hiding from the community a fact it has a right to know. But I have faith enough in you to believe that you are only waiting a fit time, and have good reason for what you do. If I can give you any help, I am at your service."

He doffed his big hat and turned away into the house.

Dorothy stood still for a moment or two longer, then walked away slowly with her eyes on the ground. Before she had reached the Old House she had made up her mind to tell Polwarth as much as she could without betraying Juliet's secret. She would ask him to talk to her, and would look for an opportunity.

For some time she had been growing more anxious every day. No sign of helpful change showed itself from any direction. Difficulties were now greatly added to by the likelihood that another life was on the way into the midst of them. What was to be done? She had two lives on her hands; did she indeed want counsel? The man who knew their secret already—the minor prophet, she had heard the curate call him—might at least help her to the next step she must take.

Juliet's mental condition was not at all encouraging. She was often ailing and peevish, behaving as if she owed Dorothy grudge instead of gratitude. She found it more and more difficult to interest her in anything. She could not get her to read. Nothing pleased her but to talk about her husband. If Dorothy had seen him, Juliet had endless questions to ask about him. And when she had answered as many of them as she could, Juliet began them all over again. One time she went into hysterics when Dorothy could not say she believed he was thinking about his wife. She was growing so unmanageable that Dorothy almost thought of giving her up altogether. The charge was wearing her out; her strength was giving way, and her temper growing so irritable that she was ashamed of herself—and all without doing Juliet any good.

Twice after Juliet had been talking as if Dorothy alone was preventing her from returning to him, Dorothy hinted at letting her husband know where she was. Juliet had fallen down on her knees in wild distress, begging her to bear with her. As soon as the idea approached her, the recollection rushed back of how she had humbled herself soul and body before him and how he had turned from her with loathing, would not put out a hand to lift her from destruction, and had left her lying prostrate on the floor. She shrank with agony from any thought of putting herself through such torture again.

Soon another difficulty began to assert itself. Mr. Drake had made up his mind about the remodeling he would do and was saying there was no reason to put it off till the spring. He began to talk about starting the work most any day. So Dorothy proposed to Juliet that as soon as it became impossible to conceal her there any longer, she should go to some distant part of the country, where Dorothy would arrange to follow her. But the thought of moving farther away from her husband was frightful to Juliet. His nearness, though she dared not seek him, seemed her only safety. The dreadful anxiety she was causing Dorothy did not occur to her.

Sorrow is not selfish in itself. But many persons who are in sorrow are entirely selfish. It makes them so important in their own eyes that they seem to have a claim upon all that people can do for them.

Therefore, Dorothy was driven to her wit's end and resolved to open the matter to the gatekeeper, without telling the substance of Juliet's confession itself. Accordingly, one evening on her way home, she called at the lodge. Dorothy told Polwarth where and in what condition she had found Mrs. Faber, and what she had done with her. She said that she did not think it was her part to advise her to return to her husband at present, and that Juliet would not hear of returning anyway. The lady had no comfort and her life was a burden to her. But she could not possibly keep her concealed much longer, and she did not know what to do next.

Polwarth's only answer was that he must make the acquaintance of Mrs. Faber. If that could somehow be arranged, he believed he would be able to help them. Between them, then, they must arrange a plan for his meeting her.

33 / The Old Garden

The next morning Juliet went walking in the garden. As she listlessly turned the corner of a hedge, she suddenly came upon a figure that might have been a gnome from the old legends. He was digging slowly but steadily, and crooning a strange song.

She started back in dismay, but the gnome did not raise his head. He showed no other sign than the ceasing of his song that he was aware of her presence. Slowly and steadily he went on with his work. He was trenching the ground deep, throwing earth from the bottom to the top. Concluding that he was deaf and that the ceasing of the song had been accidental, Juliet turned softly and began to retreat. But far from being deaf, Polwarth heard better than most people. Indeed, his senses had been sharpened by his infirmities—except for taste and smell which came and went in fits. At the first movement with which she broke the stillness, he spoke.

"Can you guess what I am doing, Mrs. Faber?" he asked, throwing up a shovelful of dirt and a glance toward her at the same time.

Juliet could not answer him. She felt much like a ghost who had suddenly been addressed by the name she had had in the old days when she was still alive. Could this man live as close as he did to Glaston and see so many people at the gate, and yet not have heard that she had passed away? Or could it be that Dorothy had betrayed her?

She stood trembling. The situation was strange. In front of her was a man who did not seem to know that what he knew about her was a secret from the whole rest of the world!

And with that realization came a sudden insight into what would happen when her husband discovered that she was not even dead. Would it not add to his contempt and scorn? Would he not conclude that she had been contriving to work on his feelings, trying to make him repent, counting on a return of his old love to make him forget all her faults?— But she must answer the creature! She could hardly afford to offend him. What could she say? She had completely forgotten what he had even said to her?

She stood staring at him, unable to speak. It was just for a few moments, but they were long as minutes. As she gazed it seemed like the strange being in the trench had dug his way up from the lower parts of the earth, bringing her secret with him, and come to ask her questions. What an earthy yet unearthly look he had! For a moment she almost believed the ancient rumor of other races than mankind that shared the earth with them, but led such differently conditioned lives that, in the course of the ages, only a scanty few of the unblending natures crossed each other's path, to stand staring in mutual astonishment.

Polwarth went on digging, not once looking up. After a little while he resumed, speaking as if he had known her well.

"Mr. Drake and I were talking some weeks ago about a curious old-fashioned flower in my garden at the back of the lodge. He asked me if he could have a root of it. I told him he could have any flower in my garden, roots and all, if he would let me dig three yards square in his garden at the Old House, and have all that came up of itself for a year."

He paused again. Juliet neither spoke nor moved. He dug rather feebly, with panting, asthmatic breath.

"Perhaps you are not aware, ma'am," he began again, and ceasing his labor stood up, leaning on the spade, which was nearly as tall as he was himself, "that many of the seeds which fall upon the ground and do not grow, strange to say, retain the power of growth. I suspect myself that they fall in their pods or shells and that before these are sufficiently decayed to allow the sun and moisture and air to reach them, they get covered up in the soil too deep for those influences to get at them. They say fish trapped alive and imbedded in ice for a long time will come to life again. I cannot tell about that. But it is well known that if you dig deep in any old garden, such as this one, ancient—perhaps forgotten—flowers will appear. The fashion has changed, they have been neglected or uprooted, but all the time their life is hid below."

By this time she was far more composed, though she had not yet made up her mind what to say or how to treat the dilemma in which she found herself.

After a brief pause, he continued.

"Just think how the fierce digging of the great Husbandman, plunging a nation into crisis every now and then, brings back to the surface old, forgotten flowers of its past virtues."

What a peculiar goblin this is! thought Juliet, beginning to forget herself a little in watching and listening to the strange creature.

"I have sometimes wondered," Polwarth again resumed, "about the troubles without end that some people seem born to—not the ones they bring on themselves. Are they ploughs, tearing deep into the family mold, that the seeds of the lost virtues of their race may be once more brought within reach of sun and air and dew? It is a pleasant, hopeful thought, is it not?"

"It is indeed,"' answered Juliet with a sigh, thinking that if some hidden virtue would come up in her, it would certainly be welcome.

How many people would like to be good without taking any trouble about it! They do not like goodness well enough to hunger and thirst after it, or enough to sell all they have that they may buy it. They will not batter at the gate of the kingdom of heaven, but they look with daydreaming pleasure on this or that aerial castle of righteousness. They do not know that it is goodness all the time that their very being is longing for, and that they are starving their nature of its necessary food.

Then Polwarth's idea turned itself around in Juliet's mind, and grew clearer, but only in reference to weeds and not flowers. She thought how that fault of hers had been buried for years, unknown to anyone alive and almost forgotten by herself; and now here it was again in all its horror and old reality!—But she must speak, if possible, and prevent the odd creature from going and telling all Glaston that he had seen Mrs. Faber at the Old House.

"How did you know I was here?" she asked abruptly.

"How do you know that I knew?" returned Polwarth gently.

"You were not in the least surprised to see me," she answered.

"A man who keeps his eyes open," returned the dwarf, "may almost stop being surprised at anything. I have seen so much that is wonderful in my life that I hardly expect to be surprised anymore."

He said this, trying to instigate conversation. But Juliet took the answer for an evasive one and it strengthened her suspicion of Dorothy. She was getting tired of her. But the minor prophet had resumed his work, delving deeper and deeper, and throwing spadeful after spadeful to the surface.

"Miss Drake told you I was here!" accused Juliet.

"No, indeed, Mrs. Faber. No one told me," answered Polwarth. "I learned it for myself. I could hardly help finding out."

"Then—then—does everybody know it?" she faltered, her heart sinking within her at the thought.

"Indeed, ma'am, as far as I know, not a single person is aware you are alive except Miss Drake and myself. I have not even told my niece who lives with me and can keep a secret as well as myself."

Juliet breathed a great sigh of relief.

"Will you tell me why you have kept it so secret?" she asked.

"Because it was your secret, not mine."

"But you were under no obligation to keep my secret."

"How do you justify such a frightful statement as that, ma'am?"

"Why, what could it matter to you?"

"Everything."

"I do not understand. You have no interest in me."

"On the contrary. I have the strongest of motives. I saw that an opportunity might come to serve you."

"But that is just what I don't understand. There is no reason why you should wish to serve me!" declared Juliet, thinking to get to the bottom of some scheme.

"There you are mistaken. I am under the most absolute and imperative obligation to serve you."

What a ridiculous, crooked little monster! Juliet thought. But almost the same instant she began to wonder if she could turn the creature's devotion to the best interest. She might at least insure his silence.

"Would you be kind enough to explain yourself?" she asked, now also interested in continuing the conversation.

"I would be happy to," replied Polwarth, "if I had sufficient ground for thinking you could understand my explanation."

"I don't think I am so stupid that I could not understand you," she returned with a wan smile.

"On the contrary," said Polwarth, "I have heard you are quite intelligent. Yet I cannot help doubting if you will understand what I am going to tell you. I am one of those, Mrs. Faber, who believe there is a Master of men—even though perhaps our senses tell us otherwise. He is a perfect Master who demands of them that they also shall be right and true men—true brothers to their brothers and sisters of mankind. Therefore, because I serve him and love him, I am bound to help you, Mrs. Faber."

Juliet's heart turned sick at the thought of such an ill-shapen creature claiming brotherhood with her.

In her countenance Polwarth read at once that he had blundered, and a sad, noble, humble smile spread over his face. It had its effect on Juliet. She would be generous and forgive his presumption: she knew dwarfs were always conceited—that wise nature had provided them with high thoughts to substitute for the missing cubit to their stature. *What repulsive things Christianity teaches!* Juliet sputtered inwardly.

"I trust you are satisfied," the gnome added, "that your secret is safe with me."

"I am," answered Juliet with a condescending motion of her stately neck.

The moment she had thus yielded, she began to wish to speak of her husband. Perhaps he could tell her something of this man. At least he could talk about him.

"But I do not see," she went on, "how you, Mr. Polwarth—I think that is your name—how you can, consistently with your principles—"

"Excuse me, ma'am, I cannot admit that you know anything whatever of my principles."

"Oh!" she returned with a smile of generous confessions. "I was brought up to believe as you do."

"That but confirms to me that for the present you are incapable of knowing anything of my principles."

"I'm not surprised that you think so," she returned with the condescension of what she supposed to be superior education. The man with wheezing chest went on throwing up the deep, damp fresh earth, to him smelling of marvelous things. "Still," Juliet went on, "supposing your judgment of me correct, that only makes it all the stranger you should think that to serve me is to please him you call your Master. He says whoever denies him before men he will deny before the angels of God."

"What my Lord says he will do, he will do. What he tells me to do, I try to understand and do. Now he has told me most clearly not to say that good comes from evil. He condemned that in the Pharisees as the greatest of crimes. Therefore, when I see a man like your husband, helping his neighbors far and near, and being kind and loving to all men"—here a great sigh came from the heart of the wife—"I am bound to say that such a man cannot be working totally against his Master, even though he opposes him in words. If I am mistaken in this, then to my own Master I stand or fall."

"How can he be his Master if he does not acknowledge him?"

"Because the very tongue with which he denies him is yet God's. I am master of the flowers that will one day grow here by my labor, though not one of them will know me. How much more must God be the Master of the men he has created, whether they acknowledge him or not? If the gospel story be true, then Jesus of Nazareth is Lord and Master even of Mr. Faber, and for him not to acknowledge it is to fall from the highest potential of his being. To deny one's master is to be a slave."

"You are very polite!" snapped Juliet and turned away. She immediately recalled her imaginary danger, however, and turning again, said, "But though I differ from your opinion, Mr. Polwarth, I quite recognize you as no common man, and put you upon your honor about my secret."

"Had you entrusted me with your secret, ma'am, the phrase would have had more significance. But, obeying my Master, I do not require to think of my own honor."

Turning away without a word of farewell, Juliet marched straight into the house. She instantly accused Dorothy of treachery. Dorothy repressed her indignation and begged Juliet to return with her and talk to Polwarth. But when they reached the spot, the gnome had vanished.

He had been digging only for the sake of the flowers buried in Juliet, and had gone home to lie down, his bodily strength exhausted.

Dorothy turned to Juliet.

"You might have asked Mr. Polwarth, Juliet, whether I had betrayed you," she said.

"Now that I think of it, he did say you had not told him. But how was I to take the word of a creature like that?"

"Juliet!" cried Dorothy, very angry. "I am beginning to doubt you were worth taking the trouble for!"

She turned from her and walked toward the house. Juliet rushed after her and embraced her.

"Forgive me, Dorothy," she pleaded. "I was not in my right mind. But what *is* to be done now that this man knows it?"

"Things are no worse than they were before," asserted Dorothy, as quickly appeased as angered. "On the contrary, the one we now have to help us is the only one able to do it. Why, Juliet, what am I supposed to do with you when my father sends the carpenters and bricklayers to the house? They will be into every corner. He talks of starting next week, and I am at my wit's end."

"Oh, don't give up on me, Dorothy, after all you have done for me," begged Juliet. "If you turn me out, there will never have been a creature as miserable as I will be—absolutely helpless, Dorothy!"

"I will do all I can for you, my poor Juliet. But if Mr. Polwarth cannot think of some way, I don't know what is to be done. You don't know what you are guilty of in despising him. Mr. Wingfold speaks of him as the first man in Glaston."

Mr. Wingfold, Mr. Drew, and some others of the best men in the place did think him the greatest in the kingdom of heaven of those they knew. But Glaston was altogether of a different opinion. Which was the right opinion must be left to the measuring rod that shall be applied to the statures of men on the last day.

The history of the kingdom of heaven—need I say how very different a thing that is from what is called *church history*?—is the only history which will ever be able to be thoroughly written. It will not only explain itself, while doing so it will explain all other attempted histories as well. Many of those who will then be found first in this eternal record may have been insignificant in the eyes of their contemporaries—even their religious contemporaries. They may have been absolutely unknown to the generations that came after them, and yet were the real men and women of potency, who worked as light and as salt in the world.

When the real worth of things is the measuring rod of their esteem, then will the kingdom of our God and his Christ be at hand.

34 / The Pottery

It had been a very dry autumn, for the rains had been long delayed. Thus the minister had been able to do much for the poor houses he had bought in the area called the Pottery. There had been just enough rain to reveal how much help the wall he had built would provide. It was impossible to make the houses thoroughly dry and healthy, at least for the present. Yet it is one thing to have water all about the place outside, and another to be up to the knees in it. But he had done what he could wherever water might enter in against his poor colony. He had used stone and brick and cement liberally. One or two of the people about Glaston began to have a glimmering idea of the use of money in a gospel fashion—that is, for thorough work where it is needed.

But to some the whole thing was highly displeasing. Those more well-to-do farther down the street feared their houses would suffer even more as a result of the diverted water. Several of these were forced to add to the defenses of their property, and this of course was felt to be a grievance. Personal inconvenience blinded their hearts to the evils their neighbors were being delivered from in the process. But why, they felt, should not the poor neighbors continue miserable; they had been miserable all their lives and were used to it? Persons who unconsciously reason like this could do well to read with a little attention the parable of the Rich Man and Lazarus.

In the present case the person who found himself the most wronged was the dishonest butcher. A piece of brick wall which the minister had built in contact with the wall of the butcher's yard was likely to cause a rise in the water as it approached his own cellar. Protecting his cellar would require the addition of two or three rows of bricks to his present wall. It was but a matter of a few shillings at most. He ought to have known that if he would only let the minister know of the difficulty, he would himself set the thing right at once, for the minister did not realize the implications of his actions.

But the minister had shamed him by changing butchers. Therefore he much preferred the possession of his grievance to its removal. To his friends he expressed his regret that a minister of the gospel should be so corrupted by the mammon of unrighteousness as to use it against members of his own church. But on the pretense of a Christian spirit, he showed Mr. Drake no visible resentment. He restricted himself to grumbling and brooding some counterplot to get even with the minister. What right had Mr. Drake to injure him for the sake of the poor? Was it not written in the Bible, *Thou shalt not favor the poor man in his cause*? Was it not also written, *For every man shall bear his own burden*? That was common sense! He did his share to help support the poor who were church members, but was he to suffer for improvements for the sake of a pack of rogues?

Already Mr. Drake had accomplished much. Several new cottages had been built and one impossible old one pulled down. He had begun to realize, however, that in this area a cottage was the worst form of dwelling that could be built. For when the soil was wet with rain like a sponge, every cottage upon it was little better than a hollow in a cloud. A house with many stories, out of contact with the soil, must be the proper kind of building for such a situation. He had already prepared for the construction of such a building, that is, he had dug the foundation. But before he could progress further, the rains began and filled the great hole with water.

The weather cleared again, but after a short dry spell, it came down once more in terrible earnest. Day after day the clouds condensed and poured like a squeezed sponge. A wet November it was—wet overhead, wet underfoot, wet all round, and the rivers rose rapidly.

When the Lythe rose beyond a certain point, it overflowed into a hollow, and thereby descended almost straight to Glaston. So it came that in a flood the town was invaded both by the rise of the river from below and by this current from above, and the streets were soon turned into canals. The currents of the slowly swelling river and of its temporary branch then met in Pine Street, and formed a heavy, though not rapid, run at low tide. For Glaston was not far from the sea. Indeed the sea was visible across the green flats, a silvery line on the horizon. Inland high ground rose on all sides, and so it was that the floods came down so deep upon Glaston.

On a certain Saturday, it rained heavily all morning, but toward the afternoon cleared a little, so that many thought the climax had been reached, while the more experienced looked for worse. After sunset the clouds gathered thicker than before, and the rain of the day was nothing compared to the torrent which descended steadily all night. When the slow, dull morning came, Glaston stood in the middle of a brown lake. The prospect was very disturbing. Most cellars were full and the water was rising on the ground floors too. Many people that morning stepped out of bed up to their knees in muddy water.

With the first of the dawn the curate stood peering from the window of his room through the water that ran down the pane. All was gray mist, brown water, and sheeting rain. Only two things were clear: not a soul would be at church that morning, and though he could do nothing to give their souls bread, he might do something for some of their bodies. It was a good thing it was Sunday, for most of the people would have stocked up on bread the day before and would not be dependent on the bakers, half of whose ovens must be now full of water. But most of the kitchens must be flooded too, the firewood soaking, the coal inaccessible, and the matches useless. And even if the rain were to cease at once, the water would still keep rising for many hours.

He turned from the window and went to wake his wife. She was one of those rare, blessed people who always open their eyes smiling. Her husband never spared her when anything was to be done. She could lose a night's sleep without harm, and stand fatigue better than most men. And in the requirements facing them on this day, there would be mingled a great deal of adventure besides.

"Come, Helen, my help—Glaston needs you," he whispered softly in her ear.

"What is it, Thomas?"

"Nothing to frighten you, darling," he answered, "but plenty to be done. The river is out of its banks and the people are all asleep. We shall have no church service this morning."

"But plenty of divine service," rejoined Helen with a smile, as she got up and grabbed some of her clothes.

"Take time for your bath, dear," said her husband.

"There will be plenty of time for that afterward," she replied. "What shall I do first?"

"Wake the servants and tell them to light the kitchen fire and make all the tea and coffee they can. But tell them to make it well. We shall get more of everything as soon as it is light. I'll go and bring the boat. I had it drawn up and moored in the ruins ready to float yesterday. I wish I hadn't put on my shirt though. I imagine I shall have to swim for it."

"I'll have one aired before you come back," said Helen.

"Aired!" returned her husband. "You had better say watered. In five minutes neither of us will have a dry stitch on."

He hurried out into the rain. Happily there was no wind.

Helen waked the servants. Before they appeared she had the fire lighted. When Wingfold returned he found her in the midst of preparing every kind of food and drink they could lay hands on.

He had brought his boat to the churchyard and moored it between two headstones. They would have their breakfast first, for there was no saying when they might get any lunch. Besides, there was little to be gained by rousing people out of a good sleep. There was no danger yet.

"It is a great thing," stated the curate as he drank his coffee, "to see how Drake goes in heart and soul for his tenants. His project is the simplest act of Christianity of a public kind I have ever seen."

"He seems to me so much humbler in his carriage since he had his money and simpler in his manners than before."

"It is quite true," replied her husband. "But it is mortifying to think how many of our clergy would look down on that man with a beggarly pride from their supposedly superior rank."

"It is not quite so bad as that, surely!" disputed Helen.

"If it is not worldly pride, what is it? I do not think it is spiritual pride. Few get far enough to be in much danger of that worst of all vices. It must then be church pride, and that is the worst form of worldly pride. The churchman's pride is utterly disgusting, so discordant is it with human harmony. He is the Pharisee—maybe the good Pharisee— of the kingdom of heaven. But if the proud churchman be in the kingdom at all, it must be as one of the least. I don't believe one in ten who is guilty of this pride is even aware of the sin of it. Those who look down on other churches and denominations are the moth holes in the garments of the church, the dry rot in its floors, the scaling and crumbling of its beams. They do more to ruin what such men call the church than any of the outward attacks on it from the skeptical and unbelieving. He who, in the name of Christ, pushes his neighbor from him is a schismatic of the worst and most dangerous type!—But we had better be going. It's of no use telling you to bring your raincoat; you'd only be giving it to the first poor woman we picked up."

"I may as well have the good of it till then," said Helen, "and she afterward." She ran to fetch it, while the curate went to bring the boat to the house.

When he opened the door there was no longer a spot of earth or sky to be seen—only water and the gray sponge filling the upper air. Dressed in a pair of old trousers and a shirt, he went wading, and where the ground dipped, swimming, to the western gate of the churchyard. In a few minutes he was at the kitchen window holding the boat, for the water, although up to the rectory walls, was not yet deep enough there to float the boat with anybody in it. The servants handed out the great cans full of hot coffee and tea and baskets of bread, and he placed them in the boat and covered them with a tarpaulin. Then Helen appeared at the door in her raincoat holding a great cloak. It was to throw over him, she said, when she took the oars, for she meant to have her share of the fun: it was so seldom there was anything to do on a Sunday!—How she would have shocked her aunt!

"Today," declared the curate, "we shall praise God with the joy of the good old hundreth psalm."

As he spoke he bent to his oars, and through a narrow lane the boat soon shot into Pine Street—now a wide canal. It was banked with houses dreary and dead, except where a sleepy, dismayed countenance peered out now and then from an upper window. In silence, except for the sounds of the oars and the dull rush of water everywhere, they slipped along.

"This *is* fun!" said Helen, where she sat and steered.

"Very quiet fun as yet," answered the curate. "But it will get busier by and by."

Here they were all big houses and he rowed swiftly past them, for his business lay not where there were servants and well-stocked larders, but where there were mothers with children and old people, and little but water besides. They had not left Pine Street by many houses before they came to where help was more than welcome. Around the first turn a miserable cottage stood three feet deep in the water. Out jumped the curate with the rope in his hand and opened the door.

Water was lapping over the edge of the bed on which sat a sickly young woman in her nightgown, holding a baby. She stared for a moment with big eyes, then looked down and said nothing. But the rose of a blush crept into her pale cheeks at the condition in which the curate had found her.

"Good morning, Martha," greeted Wingfold cheerily. "Rather damp, isn't it? Where's your husband?"

"Away looking for work, sir," answered Martha in a hopeless tone.

"Then he won't miss you. Come along. Give me the baby."

"I can't come like this, sir. I ain't got no clothes on."

"Bring them with you. You can't put them on; they're all wet. Mrs. Wingfold is in the boat; she'll see to everything you need. The door's not wide enough to let the boat through, or I'd pull it close up to the bed for you to get in."

She hesitated.

"Come along," he encouraged. "I won't look at you. Or wait—I'll take the baby, and come back for you. Then you won't get so wet."

He took the baby from her arms and turned to the door.

"It ain't you as I mind, sir," said Martha, getting into the water at once and following him, "—no more'n my own family; but all the town'll be at the windows lookin' out by this time."

"Never mind; we'll take care of you," he returned.

In half a minute more she was in the boat, the cloak wrapped around her and the baby, drinking the first cup of the hot tea.

"We must take her home at once," said the curate.

"You said we would have fun!" assented Helen, the tears rushing to her eyes.

When they reached the rectory, all the servants might have been grandmothers the way they received the woman and her child.

"Give them a warm bath together," instructed Helen, "as quickly as possible. And let me out, Thomas. I must go and get Martha some clothes. I shan't be a minute."

The next time they returned, Wingfold could hardly believe that the sweet face he saw by the fire, so refined in comforted sadness, could be Martha's.

Their next catch was a boatload of children and an old grandmother. Most of the houses had a higher story, and they took only those who had no refuge. Many more, however, drank their tea and coffee and ate their bread. The whole of the morning they spent like this, calling out as they passed back and forth through the town, asking for more help and accommodations. By noon twenty boats were out rendering similar help. The water was higher than it had been for many years and was still rising.

Faber had laid hands on an old salmon boat and was the first out after the curate. But there was no fun in the doctor's boat. Once the curate's and his met in the middle of Pine Street—both as full of people as they could carry. Wingfold and Helen greeted Faber kindly. He returned their greeting with solemn courtesy, rowing heavily past.

By lunchtime Helen had her home almost full and did not want to go out again; there was so much to be done! But her husband persuaded her to give him one hour more. The servants were doing so well, he said, and she yielded.

He rowed her up to the church. The crypts and vaults were full of water, but the floor was above it. He landed Helen in the porch and led her to the organ loft. Now the organ was one of great power. Large as the church was, seldom did they use its full force. He now requested her to pull out every stop and send the mighty voice in full blast into every corner of Glaston. He would come back for her in half an hour and take her home.

He had just laid hold of his oars again, when from out of the church rushed a roar of harmony that seemed to seize his boat and blow it away on its mission. As he rowed, it came after him and wafted him mightily along. Over the brown waters it went rolling. He thought of the spirit of God that moved on the face of the primeval waters, and out of a chaos wrought a cosmos.

"If only," he said to himself, "from every church door went forth such a spirit of harmony and healing, of life and peace! But alas! The church's foes are they of its own household. With the axes and hammers of pride and exclusiveness they break down her chapels and build walls from floor to roof, subdividing nave and choir and chancel and aisles into numberless sections. Rather than opening doors outward, they close up and wall off and seek to separate themselves."

But his thoughts did not continue long in that direction. His wife's music was too uplifting. And there remained work to be done!

35 / The Gate Lodge

Polwarth and his niece Rachel rose late, for neither had slept well. They sat down to breakfast and then read together from the Bible. Afterward they chatted a long time by the kitchen fire.

"I am afraid your asthma was bad last night, Uncle," said Rachel. "I heard your breathing every time I woke."

"It was," answered the little man, "but I took my revenge in a little poem at first light."

"May I hear it?"

He slowly climbed the stairs to his room and returned with a half-sheet of paper, from which he read the following lines:

> Satan, be welcome to thy nest,
>> Though it be but in my breast;
> Burrow and dig like a mole;
>> Fill every vein with half-burnt coal;
> Puff the keen dust about,
>> And do your all to choke me out.
>
> Satan, thy might I do defy;
>> Live core of night, I patient lie;
> For Christ's angel, Death, all radiant white,
>> With one cold breath will scare thee quite,
> And give my lungs an air
>> As fresh as answered prayer.
>
> So, Satan, do
>> Thy worst with me,
> Until the True
>> Shall set me free
> And end what he began,
>> By making me a man.

"It is not much of poetry, Rachel!" he confessed, raising his eyes from the paper; "—only but a poor jingle from a very wheezy chest."

"My strength is made perfect in weakness," quoted Rachel solemnly, heedless of his remark. To her the verses were as full of meaning as if she had written them herself.

"I think I like better the older rendition of the Scripture you just quoted—that is, without the *my*," said Polwarth. " 'Strength is made perfect in weakness.' Hearing a grand principle such as that spoken in its widest application, as a fact not just of humanity but of all creation, brings me close to the very heart of the universe. Strength itself—of all kinds—is made perfect in weakness. This is not just a law of Christian growth, but a law of growth itself. Even the Master's strength was thus perfected."

Polwarth slipped from his stool and knelt beside the table; Rachel did likewise.

"O Father of life," he prayed, "we praise you that you will one day take your poor crooked creatures and give them bodies like Christ's, perfect and full of light. Help us to grow faster—as fast as you can help us grow. Help us to keep our eyes on the opening of your hand, that we may know the manna when it comes. We rejoice that we are your making, though your handiwork is not very plain yet in the outer man. We bless you that we feel your hand making us, even if what we feel be pain. Always we hear the voice of the potter above the hum and grind of the wheel. Fashion the clay to your will. You have made us love you and hope in you, and in your love we will be brave and endure. All in good time, O Lord. Amen."

While they thus prayed, kneeling on the stone floor of the little kitchen, dark under the canopy of cloud, the rain went on clashing and murmuring all around. When they rose, it was therefore with astonishment that they saw a woman standing motionless in the doorway. With neither cloak nor hat, her damp garments clung to her form and dripped with rain.

When Juliet woke that morning, she had cared little that the sky was dull and the earth dark. A selfish sorrow, even a selfish love, makes us stupid, and Juliet had been growing more and more dull. Many people, even as Juliet, seem to sink slowly in the scale of existence through sorrow endured without a gracious submission. Juliet's sufferings were working the precise opposite in her character as were Polwarth's and Rachel's. But as the little man had prayed, *All in good time*.

Bad as the weather had been the day before, Dorothy had yet managed to visit her and see that she was provided with every necessity, and Juliet never doubted she would come on Sunday also. She thought of Dorothy's ministrations as we so often do of God's—something automatic, as for which there is no occasion to be thankful.

After Dorothy had left on Saturday, Juliet had sat down by the window, staring out at the pools spreading wider and wider on the gravel walks beneath her. She sat till she grew chilly, then rose and dropped into an easy chair by the fire, falling fast asleep.

She slept a long time, and woke in a terror, seeming to have waked herself with a cry. The fire was out and the hearth cold. She shivered and drew her shawl about her. Then suddenly she remembered the frightful dream she had had.

She dreamed that she had just fled from her husband and made it to the park. The moment she entered it, something seized her from behind and carried her swiftly, as in the arms of a man—only she seemed to hear the rush of wings behind her. She struggled in terror, but in vain; the power bore her swiftly on, and she knew their destination. Her very being recoiled from the horrible depth of the motionless pool, in which, as she now seemed to know, lived a horrible, ageless creature. The pool appeared, but not as she had seen it before, for it boiled and heaved and bubbled. Coil upon coil of the loathsome creature arose out of the water, lifted itself into the air, towering above her, then stretched out a long, writhing, shivering neck to take her from the invisible arms that bore her to her doom. The neck shot out a head, and the head shot out a tongue of a water snake. She shrieked and woke, bathed in terror.

With the memory of the dream, a sizeable portion of its horror returned. She rose to try to shake it off, and went to the window. But what should she see there but that fearsome pool. It had entered the garden and had come halfway to the house! And was plainly rising every moment!

More or less the pool had haunted her ever since she had come to the Old House; she had seldom dared to go nearer to it than halfway down the garden. If it had not been for the dulling influence of her misery, it would have been an unendurable horror to her. And now it was coming to fetch her as she had seen it in her warning dream!

Her brain reeled. For a moment, paralyzed with horror, she gazed at it. With almost the conviction that the fiend of her vision was pursuing her, she turned and fled from the house and across the park, through the sheets of rain, to the gate lodge. She did not stop until she stood at the door of Polwarth's cottage, though she had not thought of him once in her terror.

Rachel was darting toward her with outstretched hands when her uncle stopped her.

"Rachel, my child," he said, "run and light a fire in the parlor. I will welcome our visitor."

She turned instantly and left the room. Then Polwarth went up to Juliet, who stood trembling, unable to utter a word, and he greeted her with perfect old-fashioned courtesy. "You are heartily welcome. I sent Rachel away so that I might first assure you that you are as safe with her as with me. Sit here a moment. You are so wet I dare not place you near the fire.—Rachel!"

She came instantly.

"Rachel," he repeated, "this lady is Mrs. Faber. She has come to visit us. Nobody must know of it.—You need not be at all uneasy, Mrs. Faber. Not a soul will come near us today. But I will lock the door to give us time, in case anyone should.—You will get Mrs. Faber's room ready at once, Rachel. I will come and help you. But a spoonful of brandy in hot water first, please.—Let me move your chair a little, ma'am, out of the draft."

In silence Juliet did everything she was told, received the prescribed antidote from Rachel, and was left alone in the kitchen.

But the moment she was freed from one dread, she was seized by another. Suspicion took the place of terror; and as soon as she heard the toiling of the two up the creaking stair cease, she crept to the foot of it. And with no more compunction than a princess in a fairy tale, she began listening to everything they said.

"I *thought* she wasn't dead!" she heard Rachel exclaim joyfully.

"I could tell you did not seem greatly astonished at the sight of her. But what made you think such an unlikely thing?" rejoined her uncle.

"I could tell *you* did not believe she was dead. That was enough for me."

"You do have extraordinary powers, Rachel! I never said a word one way or the other."

"Which showed me you were thinking, and made me think. You had something in your mind which you did not choose to tell me yet."

"Ah, child!" remarked her uncle, "how difficult it is to hide anything! I don't think God wants anything hidden. The light is his region, his kingdom. It can only be evil, outside or inside, that makes us turn from the fullest light of the universe."

Juliet heard every word and was bewildered. The place in which she had sought refuge was plainly little better than a goblin-cave. Yet merely from listening to the sounds of the goblins without half understanding it, she had begun already to feel a sense of safety stealing over her. She had never felt secure like this even for an instant in the Old House, even with Dorothy right beside her.

They went on talking and she went on listening.

"The poor lady," she heard the man-gnome say, "has had some difference with her husband; but whether she wants to hide from him or from the whole world or from both, she alone can tell. Our business is to take care of her, and do for her what God may put in our hand to do. What she desires to hide is sacred to us. Since we have no secrets of our own, Rachel, we have all the more room for those of other people who are unhappy enough to have any. Let God reveal what he pleases. She needs caring for, poor thing! We will pray to God for her."

"But how shall we make her comfortable in such a poor little house?" returned Rachel.

"We will keep her warm and clean," answered her uncle, "and that is all an angel would require."

"An angel, yes," answered Rachel, "for angels don't eat. But the poor lady is delicate—and I am not much of a cook."

"You are a very good cook, my dear. Few people can have more need than we to be careful what we eat—we have got such a pair of troublesome, cranky little bodies. If you can suit them, I am sure you will be able to suit any invalid.''

"I will do my best,'' Rachel assured him cheerily, comforted by her uncle's confidence.

Juliet retreated noiselessly, and when the tiny woman entered the kitchen, there sat the disconsolate lady where she had been left, still like the outcast princess of a fairy tale. She had walked in at their door and they had immediately begun to arrange for her stay. And the strangest thing to Juliet was that she hardly felt it strange. It was only as if she had come a day sooner than she was expected—which indeed was not far wrong. For Polwarth had been hoping for the possibility of her becoming their guest.

"Your room is ready now,'' beckoned Rachel, approaching her timidly and looking up at her with a woman's childlike face on the body of a child. "Will you come?''

Juliet rose and followed her to the garret room with the dormer window in which Rachel slept.

"Will you please get into bed as fast as you can,'' she advised, "and when you knock on the door I will come and take away your clothes and get them dried. Wrap this new blanket round you so the cold of the sheets won't give you a chill. They are well aired though. I will bring you a hot water bottle and some tea. Dinner will be ready soon.''

So saying, she left the room softly. The creak of the door as she closed it, and the white curtains of the bed and window, reminded Juliet of a certain room she had once stayed in for a time at the house of an old nurse, where she had never been happier. She burst into tears and weeping, undressed and got into bed. There the dryness and warmth and the sense of safety soothed her quickly. And with the comfort crept in the happy thought that here she lay on the very edge of the highroad to Glaston; she would undoubtedly soon be able to see her husband ride past. With that one hope she could sit at a window watching for centuries.

"Oh, Paul! Paul! My Paul!'' she moaned. "If I could but be made clean again for you!''

Gradually the peace of her new surroundings stole into her heart. The fancy grew upon her that she was in a fairy tale, in which she must take everything as it came, for she could not change the story. Fear vanished. No staring eyes or creeping pool could find her in the guardianship of these benevolent little people.

She fell fast asleep. The large clear gray eyes of Rachel came and looked at her as she slept, and their gaze did not rouse her. Softly she went and came again. But although dinner was then ready, Rachel knew better than to wake her. She knew that sleep is the chief nourisher in life's feast, and she would not withdraw the sacred dish. Her uncle said sleep was God's way of giving man the help he could not get into him while he was awake. So the loving uncle and niece had their dinner together, putting aside the best portions until the beautiful lady lying upstairs should wake.

36 / Faber and Amanda

All that same Sunday morning, the minister and Dorothy had of course plenty of work on their hands too, for their closest neighbors were all poor. Although their own house was situated on the very bank of the river, it was in no worse plight than most in the town, for it stood on a raised part of the ground. By late morning, its lower parts were full of water like the rest, but its upper rooms were filled with people from the streets around.

Mr. Drake's heart was anxious for his people in the Pottery. Many of his nearby neighbors had come to his house and he had gone to get what bread, meat, cheese, coffee, and tins of biscuits he could, glad that he was rich and could help them.

When he went out again, this time he went to the Pottery. He took Dorothy with him, and as the cook's hands were more than full with all the people in the house, they agreed it was better to take little Amanda with them. Dorothy was not altogether comfortable at having to leave Juliet alone all day. But they had already talked about the possibility when she left her on Saturday, and she would certainly understand it on a day such as this. Amanda shrieked with delight when she was carried to the boat, and went on shrieking as she floated over flowerbeds and got caught now and then in bushes and overhanging branches. The features of the flat country were all but obliterated. Only trees, houses, and cornstacks stood out of the water, while in the direction of the sea all indication of land had vanished. All was one wide, brown lake with a great, fiercely rushing current in the middle of it. Dorothy held tight to Amanda's frock, afraid the adventurous child would jump overboard. But Mr. Drake poled them along carefully until they reached a certain old shed. They got out of the boat and into it at the door of the loft where a farmer stored his hay and straw. Then they descended into the heart of the Pottery. Its owner was delighted to find that though not dry underfoot, it was free from the worst of the flood.

His satisfaction was short-lived, however, for before he was half through unloading his cargo of food, he caught sight of a bubbling pool. It was from a drain whose covering had burst from the pressure from within and was now threatening to flood the area with water. He shouted for help. Out hurried men, women, and children on all sides. For a few moments he was entirely occupied in giving orders and let Amanda's hand go. Several shovels were soon busily occupied in trying to clear the drain while other men ran to bring clay and stones.

Suddenly there was a great cry and the crowd scattered in all directions. The retaining wall next to the butcher's had given way and a torrent of water was boiling across the Pottery, straight for the spot where the water was rising from the drain. Amanda gazed in wonder at the flight of the people about her, but stood right in the course of the water, neither paying any attention to it nor even seeing it coming. The current caught her, swept her away, and tumbled with her, foaming and roaring, into the deep foundation hole which had recently been dug. Almost the same moment her father realized she wasn't with him. He was looking around anxiously when a shriek of horror and fear burst from the crowd of people and they rushed to the edge of the hole. Without a word spoken he knew Amanda was in it. He darted through them, scattering men and women in all directions, pulling off his coat as he ran.

Though getting old he was far from weak and had been a strong swimmer in his youth. He plunged in recklessly and the falling torrent carried him almost to the bottom of the muddy and foaming little lake. When he came to the top he looked in vain for any sign of the child. The crowd stood breathless on the brink. Not one had seen her, though all eyes were staring into the tumult.

He dived and swam about, groping through the frightful mass, but all in vain.

Then came a shout from above.

He shot to the surface—just in time to see something white vanish. He dived, and at the same moment the recoil of the torrent from below caught her and brought her up, almost into his very arms. He grabbed her and struggled to the edge. Ready hands reached down and pulled him to safety in a moment. Fifty arms were stretched out to take the child, but he would yield her to no one. He blundered through the water, which had now spread over the whole place, and followed by Dorothy was making for the shed. But one of the salmon fishermen interrupted his flight, made him get into his boat, and Mr. Drake dropped exhausted into the bottom of it with the child pressed to his chest. He could not speak.

"To Doctor Faber's!" shouted Dorothy, and the fisherman rowed like a madman.

Faber had just come in from his own mission. He quickly undressed the child with his own hands, rubbed her dry, and did everything to initiate respiration. For a long time all seemed useless. There was no sign of breath in her. But he persisted almost beyond the verge of hope. Mr. Drake and Dorothy stood in mute agony and dismay.

Faber was just on the point of ceasing his efforts in utter despair when he thought he felt a slight motion of her diaphragm. He quickened his pace. She began to breathe. Suddenly she opened her eyes, looked at him for a moment, then with a smile closed them again. To the watchers it seemed as if heaven itself had opened in that smile. But on seeing the radiance break forth momentarily on her lips, Faber abandoned the tiny form, started back from the bed, and stood staring aghast. The next moment he threw some blankets over the child, turned away, and almost staggered from the room. In his office he poured himself out a strong glass of brandy, swallowed it in one gulp, and sat down and held his head in his hands. But only for an instant did he so indulge himself. The next moment he was by the child's side again, feeling her pulse and rubbing her legs and arms under the blankets.

By this time the minister's hands had begun to turn blue and he was shivering, but a smile of delight was on his face.

"God bless me!" cried the doctor. "You've got no coat on! And you are drenched! I didn't notice anyone but the child!"

"He rescued her from the horrible hole," explained Dorothy. "He got her out all by himself, Mr. Faber!—Come home, Father.—I will come back and see to Amanda as soon as I have got him to bed."

"Yes, Dorothy, let us go," agreed the minister, and put his hand on her shoulder. His teeth chattered and his hand shook.

The doctor rang his bell violently.

"Neither of you shall leave this house tonight.—Take a hot bath to the spare bedroom and remove the sheets," he instructed the housekeeper who had answered his summons. "My dear sir," he went on, turning again to the minister, "you must get under the blankets at once. How careless of me! The child's life will be rather expensive to save if it costs yours."

"You have brought back the soul of the child to me, Mr. Faber," said the minister, trembling, "and I can never thank you enough."

"There won't be much to thank me for if you leave us instead. Miss Drake, while I give your father his bath, you must go with Mrs. Roberts and put on dry clothes."

Dorothy was soon dressed in Juliet's clothes, and it was a fair turnabout, for Juliet had been wearing hers for so long. Immediately she went to her father's room. He was already in bed, but it was some time before they could get him warm. Then he grew burning hot and all night was talking in troubled dreams. Yet the morning brought clarity to his feverish brain. How many dawns a morning brings!

His first words were, "How is the child?" Hearing that she had had a good night and was almost well, he turned over and fell fast asleep again. Then Dorothy, who had kept by his bed all night, put her own clothes back on and went to the door.

The rain had stopped and the flood was greatly diminished. She thought it would now be possible to reach the Old House, and after a hasty breakfast she set out, leaving her father and Amanda to Mrs. Robert's care. The flood left her no choice but to go by the highroad to

Polwarth's gate, and even then she often had to wade through mud and water. The moment she saw the gatekeeper, she somehow knew by his face that Juliet was in the lodge. He nodded, smiled and beckoned her inside. When she entered, she could immediately see that Juliet's new circumstances were working upon her for peace.

The spiritual atmosphere, the sense that she *was* not and *would* not be alone, the food they coaxed her to eat, and the whole surrounding of thoughts and things were operating more deeply upon her than she could understand. Juliet still considered herself superior to the dwarfs. Even so she had a feeling that she was in the society of ministering spirits of God, good and safe and true. From the Old House to the cottage was like from the Inferno to Purgatory, across whose borders faint breezes from Paradise now and then strayed. Without knowing it she had already begun to love the strange little woman with the distorted body, the fine head, and the gentle suffering face. Her initial aversion to Polwarth's wheezing breath, great head, and big, still face had begun to pass over into an indescribable awe. It was long, however, before she had ceased to regard him as a power of the nether world, partly human and at once something less and something more. Yet even already she was beginning to feel at home with them.

True, the world in which they lived was above her spiritual vision or intellectual comprehension, yet the air around them was the essential air of *homeness*. The love which enclosed her was far too great for her— as the heaven of the mother's face is beyond the understanding of the newborn child over whom she bends. But that mother's face is nevertheless the child's joy and peace. She did not yet recognize it as love, but it was what she sorely needed. What it cost her hosts she had no idea—she gave them no trouble at all. She never saw the poor quarters to which Rachel for her sake had gone.

And now Dorothy truly had something to say to Juliet about her husband. In telling what had happened, however, she heard many more questions than she was able to answer.

"Does he really believe me dead, Dorothy?"

"I do not believe there is a single person in Glaston who knows what he thinks," answered Dorothy. "I have not heard of his once opening his mouth about it. He is just as silent now as he used to be ready to talk."

"My poor Paul!" murmured Juliet.

Indeed, not a soul in Glaston or anywhere else did know a single one of his thoughts. Certain mysterious advertisements in the county paper were imagined by some to be his, referring to his wife. As the body had never been seen, some began to question whether she was dead. Others hinted that her husband must have done away with her himself, for what could be easier for a doctor, and why else did he make no search for the body? To Dorothy this fact indicated that he believed she was not dead—perhaps a hope that she would sooner reveal herself if he displayed no anxiety to find her. But she said nothing of this to Juliet.

That Dorothy had now warmed to Faber made the news of him all the more welcome to the famished heart of his wife. But when all was told and she was weary of asking questions to which there were no answers, she fell back in her chair with a sigh. Alas, she was still no nearer to him!

Faber too had been up all night, by the bedside of the little Amanda. She scarcely needed such close attendance, for she slept soundly and was hardly feverish at all. Four or five times in the course of the night he turned down the bedcovers to examine her, as if he feared some injury not hitherto apparent. But neither before nor now was there any sign of such.

In his younger days he had been very interested in comparative anatomy and physiology. His instinct for these studies had sharpened his observation, and he noted many characteristics that escaped the eyes even of very perceptive individuals. Among other things, he was very quick to note instances of the strange persistency with which nature perpetuates small peculiarities from one generation to the next. Busy with Amanda, a certain imperfection in one of the curves of the outer ear attracted his attention. It is as rare to see a perfect ear as a perfect form, and the varieties of unfinished curves are many. But this imperfection was somewhat unique. At the same time it was so minor that not even the eye of a lover would have noticed it, unless he was a man of science alert to the smallest details.

The sight of it startled Faber. It was the second instance of the same peculiarity that he had seen, and it gave him something new to think about. When the child suddenly opened her eyes, he saw another face looking at him out of hers. From that moment on the idea haunted him. And whether it was that it drew facts to itself, or that the signs were present, his further search confirmed his initial suspicions.

Despite the state of weakness in which he found Mr. Drake the next morning, the doctor pressed him with question after question, amounting to a thorough cross-examination concerning Amanda's history. He was undeterred that his questioning seemed to annoy his patient. As his love for the child had increased, the subject of her history had grown less and less agreeable to Mr. Drake. She had become so entirely his own that he did not in the least desire to find out anything about her, or to learn a single fact or hear a single conjecture to remind him that she was not in fact his own little daughter.

He was therefore more than a bit annoyed at the persistency of the doctor's questioning, but being a courteous man, and clearly under obligation to him, he told him all he knew. It was not until then that the doctor became able to give his attention to the minister himself, and indeed he could hardly have shown him greater devotion had he been his own son. A whole week passed before he would allow him to go home. Dorothy waited on him, and Amanda ran around the house. The doctor and the little girl had been friends from the first, and now, whenever he was at home, Amanda clung to his side.

The same day the Drakes left him, Faber left on the night train for London, and was gone three days.

Amanda was now perfectly well, but Mr. Drake continued to recover slowly. Dorothy was anxious to get him away from the riverside and suggested getting the workmen started on the Old House at once. To this he readily consented, but he would not listen to her suggestion that in the meantime he should take a short vacation and get away from Glaston. He would be quite well in a day or two, he said, and besides, there was work to be done at the Pottery. He had to make right the work on the retaining wall which had apparently been so badly bungled the first time. He could hardly believe his original plans had been defective and wondered if the job had been done according to the specifications he had laid out. But the builder was an honest man and he too could not account for the collapse of the wall. He offered to put it up again at his own expense; perhaps they might discover the cause of the catastrophe.

A great diversity of opinions were circulated through the neighborhood. At last they were mostly settled into two. The one group stood convinced that the butcher, who was known to have a grudge against the minister, had undermined the wall under cover of his slaughter house. The other group indignantly declared that the idea was nothing but a wicked slander of churchmen against a dissenter. When the rumor reached Mr. Drake's ears, knowing the butcher and believing the builder, he was inclined to think the butcher guilty of the crime. But since any investigation was not likely to lead the butcher to repentance, he decided instead to return good for evil. So before the new wall was built, Drake consulted him as to how his premises might also be included and helped by the defense. The butcher chuckled with delight at his unknown success, but in the end the coals of fire began to scorch, and went on scorching—even more when Mr. Drake soon became his landlord and voluntarily improved the condition of his property as well. But the minister gave Dorothy strict orders that they should do no business with him. It was one thing, he said, to be kind and forgiving to the sinner, and another to pass by his fault without confession, treating it like a mere personal affair which might be forgotten. When the butcher died he left a will assigning all his property to trustees, for the building of a new chapel. But when his finances came to be looked into, there was hardly enough to pay his debts.

The minister was now subject to the comings and goings of a fever to which he paid far too little attention. When Dorothy was not looking after him, he would slip out in any weather and see how things were going in the Pottery. It was little wonder, therefore, that his health did not improve. But he could not be convinced to regard his condition as serious enough for any special thought.

37 / Another Confession

Not long after the flood, Faber was called to the house of the curate because one of Helen's servants was ill. Sadly, Wingfold was not at home. Their communication had lessened since the doctor's marriage, but Helen thought he seemed more distant than ever. He was a troubled man, she told herself, but she had little idea just how troubled he was. For as if the loss of his wife was not enough, he had since the day of the flood been plunged into a fresh mental dilemma. For the time this new emotional quagmire seemed almost sufficient to make him forget about Juliet.

Paul Faber was a man unaccustomed to what would be called personal introspection. He had never allowed his soul within miles of conviction of conscience. Such a thing was foreign to him.

A flood of thoughts that would only flow in the mind of one with the sternest moral scruples was to the doctor like finding within himself a soul that was a stranger. And the introduction was at first a frightful one for him to make. Yet days passed and the duty urged upon him by the ever-present memory of little Amanda's smile grew stronger and stronger.

No observer could know how his personal sufferings and unconscious regrets over his treatment of Juliet had prepared and tilled the subsoil of his conscience since Faber had shared so few of his feelings about his wife with anyone. Suffice it to say that the humiliation of the experience had added greatly to the introspective mood in which he presently found himself.

He had just spent another in a long series of restless nights, and on the morning in question had at length decided what he must do. Consequently, his mind had been otherwise occupied during his call at the Wingfolds. From the curate's door he went directly to the minister's, resolved that morning to make a certain disclosure—one he would gladly have avoided. But honor bound him to make it. The minister grew pale as he listened, but did not utter a syllable until he found himself personally involved in the doctor's tale.

This is what he told Mr. Drake:

Paul Faber had been a medical student of twenty-three when a certain young woman was taken into one of the wards. Her complaint caused her much suffering, but was more tedious than dangerous.

Attracted by her sweet looks, but more by her patience and gratitude, he began to talk to her a little. Then he came to give her books to read, and was often charmed with the straightforward remarks she would make. The day she left the hospital, in the simplicity of her heart and with much timidity, she gave him a chain she had made for him of her hair. On the ground of supplemental medical attention, partly a pretext and yet without any evil motive, he visited her afterward at her lodging. The joy of her face and the light of her eyes when he appeared enchanted him. She pleased his nature; her worship flattered him; her confidence in him was captivating. He did her no end of kindness—taught her much, gave her good advice, still gave her books, went to chapel sometimes with her on a Sunday evening, took her to concerts and the theater, and would have protected her from every enemy, real and imaginary. But all the while he was slowly depriving her of the last line of her self-defense against an enemy neither he nor she could see. For how is an ignorant man to protect even a woman he loves from the hidden god of his idolatry—his own grand, contemptible *self*?

It is not necessary to relate every step of the descending stair. With all his tender feelings and generous love of humanity, Paul Faber had not yet learned the simple lesson of humanity—that a man who would be his brother's keeper, or his sister's, must protect every woman first of all from himself, from everything that calls itself love and yet is but its black shadow: the demon which murmurs *I love* that it may devour.

At length a child was conceived. He put her off with promises for the future—"when my studies are done and I'm earning a decent living." And she heard the words through her own love for him, secure in the hope of one day making a home together with their child. In the meantime, the baby was born. And though the heart of a woman is infinite, her time, her thoughts, and her hands are finite. Thus, occupied with the child, she could not *seem* so much a lover as before. In his enduring selfishness, Faber felt that the child had come between them and he began to grow weary of his bonds. She could see the change in him, and yet continued to love both the child and its father, the more passionately when she saw him receding from her. But once he had confessed the fact to himself, it took only one visit more to reveal to her that she had become a burden to him. He came less often, and when he did visit, the distance between them had noticeably widened.

Hers was a noble nature. She had sacrificed all for him; she would not see him unhappy, nor make demands on him. In her fine generosity, struggling to be strong, she said to herself that he would, after all, leave her richer than she was before. For did she not have the child? He would not want it, and if she went away now, she could be content to live— even if forever—upon the blissful memory of the love they had enjoyed. She would not throw the past from her because the weather of time had changed. She would turn her back upon her sun, before he set altogether, and carry with her into the darkness the last gorgeous glow of his departure. She resolved to go away with a bright and fresh final memory of the way it had once been between them.

Therefore, one evening when he paid her a visit after the absence of a week, he found her charmingly dressed and merry, but in a strange fashion he could not understand. The baby, she said, was downstairs with the landlady, and she was free for her Paul. She read to him, sang to him, and bewitched him anew with all the graces he had helped to develop in her. He said to himself when he left her that surely there had never been a more gracious woman—and she was totally his own!

It was the last flicker of the dying light, the gorgeous sunset she had resolved to carry with her in her memory forever.

When he came again the next evening, he found her landlady in tears. She had vanished, taking with her nothing but her child and her child's clothes. The gown she had worn the night before hung in her bedroom; everything but what she must be wearing then was left behind. The woman spoke of her with genuine affection and said she had paid her everything in full. To his questioning she answered that they had gone away in a cab. The landlady had called it, but remembered neither the man nor his number.

Faber persuaded himself that she had but gone to see some friends, so he settled in her rooms to wait for her return. But a week consumed his hope. The iron entered into his soul, and for a time tortured him. He wept—but consoled himself that he wept, for it proved to himself that he was not heartless. He further comforted himself in the thought that she knew where to find him and that when trouble came upon her, she would remember how good he had been to her. Because he would not give up everything for her, liberty and all, she had chosen to leave him. And in revenge, having so long neglected him for the child, she had at the last roused in her every power of enchantment, had brought her every charm into play, that she might lastingly bewitch him with the old spell and the undying memory of their first bliss—then left him to his lonely misery! She had done what she could to ruin a man of education, a man of family, a man on his way to distinction!—a man of genius, he even said, but he was such only as every man is: a man of latent genius.

Even though our sympathies go with a woman like her, such a man, however little he deserves and however much he would scorn it, is in reality far more to be pitied. She has her love, though he has been false to it, and one day will through suffering find the path to the door of rest. When she left him her soul was endlessly richer than his.

Weeks, months, years passed, but she never sought him. In retrospect, his "service to mankind" was no doubt a subconscious effort to atone for any nagging worry that he might not have done right by the woman and their child. By filling his days with work and by ceasing to think of her, when a chance bubble did rise from the drowned memory, it broke instantly and vanished. As to the child, he had almost forgotten whether it was a boy or a girl.

But since he had discovered her, beyond a doubt, in little Amanda, old memories had been crowding back upon his heart. He had begun to realize how Amanda's mother must have felt when she saw his love decaying visibly before her. And now his character slowly began to reveal itself for the first time to his conscious judgment.

Finally it struck him that twice he had been left by women he loved— at least by women who loved him. Two women had trusted him completely, and he had failed them both. And then came the thought, stinging him to the heart, that the first was the purer of the two. The one he had looked down upon because of her lack of education, and her familiarity with humble things, knew nothing of what men consider evil, while she whom he had worshiped for her refinement, intellect, culture, and beauty was exactly what she had herself confessed to be.

But against all reason and logic, the result of this comparison was that Juliet returned anew to his imagination in all her loveliness. And for the first time he found himself making excuses for her. If she had deceived him, she had done so in love. Whatever her past had been, she had been true to him, and from the moment she loved him, she had been incapable of wrong. But he had cast her from him!

His next thought followed quite naturally: what degree of purity could he demand from any woman? What had he done but destroy the one who had come before Juliet on the altar of his own selfishness? She, not he, had always been the noble one, the bountiful giver, the victim of shameless ingratitude. Having flattered himself that misery would drive her back to him, he had not made a single effort to find her, nor even mourned on learning of her death that he could never make up for the wrongs he had done her.

What room was there to talk of honor? If she had not sunk to the streets it was through her own virtue and none of his care! And now she was dead! And his child, but for the charity of the minister of a despised superstition, would have been left an outcast in the London streets to find her way eventually to a London workhouse!

38 / Faber and Mr. Drake

Faber felt smaller and smaller as he continued his plain-spoken confession of wrong to the man whose life was even now in peril for the sake of Faber's own neglected child. At last he concluded with the conviction that Amanda was his daughter. Then first the old minister spoke. His love had made him guess what was coming, and he was on his guard.

"May I ask what is your object in making this statement to me, Mr. Faber?" he asked rather coldly.

"None but to confess the truth and perform any duty that may be mine," responded the doctor.

"Do you wish this known among the people of Glaston?"

"I do not relish the thought. But I am of course prepared to confess Amanda as my child, and to make what amends may be possible for the trouble and expense she has brought you."

"Trouble! Expense!" cried the minister fiercely. "Do you mean in your cold-blooded heart that because you believe her yours, I who have carried her for years in my heart am going to give her up? Should I hand her over to a man who, all these years, has made not one effort to discover his missing child? In the sight of God, which of us is her true father? But I forget—that is a question you cannot understand. Whether or not you are her father, I do not care. Until you have proved it and the court orders me, I will not yield a hair of her head to you—nor accept a farthing of your money."

He struck his fist on the table, rose, and turned away. Faber rose also, quietly. He stood a moment waiting, silent and pale. At length Mr. Drake turned. Faber bowed without a word and left the room.

The minister was too hard on him. He would not have been so hard but for the doctor's atheism; neither would he have been so hard if he could have seen into the ragged soul. But Faber felt he deserved it, even though it was rather hard on him that, confessing a wrong and desiring to make what reparation he could, he should have the very frankness of his confession thus thrown back in his teeth.

He entered his surgery. There he had been making some experiments with peroxide of manganese, and a solution of it stood in a bottle on the table. A ray of brilliant sunlight was shining upon it, casting its glorious red shadow on a piece of white paper. It caught his eyes. He could never tell what it had to do with the current of his thoughts at that moment, but he could never get rid of the idea that it had had some influence upon it. For as he looked at it, still thinking how hard the minister had been on him, suddenly he found himself in the minister's place with Juliet again before him, making her sad confession. And how had he met that confession? The whole scene returned, and for the first time struck him right in the heart. That was the first he began to be really humbled in his own eyes. What if after all he was but a poor creature? What if, instead of having anything to be proud of, *he* was the one who must hide his head in shame?

Once the question had entered his mind, it never left him. For a time he walked in the midst of a dull cloud, first of dread, then of dismay. A humbler regard of himself had taken the place of his old confidence and satisfaction. An undefined hunger even began to grow within him. Though far from understood by him, he longed to somehow atone for his wrongs and to become a "better man."

The change passed upon him slowly by degrees, with countless alterations of mood and feeling, and yet he began to see plainly that his treatment of his wife—knowing his own guilt—was a far worse shame than any fault Juliet could be guilty of. And with that realization, believing her gone forever, he began to long after the love he had lost until the longing passed over into sickening despair, only to spring back afresh. He longed for Juliet as she had prayed to him—as the only power which could make *him* clean. It seemed somehow as if she could help him even in his repentance for the wrong done to Amanda's mother. The pride of the Pharisee was gone, the conscious dignity of the man had vanished, and his soul longed after the love that covers a multitude of sins.

The rest of the day after Faber's visit, poor Mr. Drake roamed about like one on the verge of insanity. At times he was lost in apprehensive melancholy, at others roused to fierce anger. The following day he had a worse attack of the fever, and Dorothy would have sent for Faber except that her father would not hear of it. He grew worse and worse and did not object to her sending for Dr. Mather, but the man did not do him much good. Mr. Drake was in a very critical state, and Dorothy was miserable about him.

Faber wrote a kind, respectful letter to the minister, saying he was much concerned to hear that he was not well. He felt especially anxious because he feared he himself had been the cause of the relapse. He assured him that he perfectly recognized the absolute superiority of Mr. Drake's claim to the child. He had never dreamed of asserting any right to her, except what was implied in his duty to repay the expense which his wrong and neglect had caused. Beyond that he well knew he could make no restitution except in gratitude. For the sake of his conscience, he asked if he might be permitted to supply the means of the child's education, but he was ready to sign an agreement that all else connected with her should be left entirely to Mr. Drake. He begged to be allowed to see her sometimes, for long before he had a suspicion that she was his, the child had already grown dear to him. He was certain her mother would have preferred Mr. Drake's influence to his own, and for her sake also, he would be careful to disturb nothing. But he hoped Mr. Drake would remember that, however unworthy, he was still her father.

The minister was touched by the letter and it immediately dispelled all his temporary anger. He answered that Faber should be welcome to see the child when he would, and that she could go with him when he pleased. He must promise, however, as the honest man everyone knew him to be, not to teach her there was no God, or lead her to despise the religious instruction she received at home.

The word *honest* was a severe blow to Faber. He had come to the painful conclusion that he was neither an honest man nor a gentleman. He felt he had never been honest before and could never again feel honest.

But what did it matter? What was life worth anymore? What did it matter what he was, just so long as he never hurt anyone again! All of life seemed desolate about him.

To the minister he replied that he had been learning a good deal of late, and among other things that rejecting religious faith did not necessarily do much for the development of the moral nature. Because of this discovery he did not feel bound as before to propagate his negative creed. If his denials of God's existence were true, he no longer believed them necessarily powerful for good. In his own case they seemed to have worked just the opposite. Now he only believed them as facts and did not see that a man was bound to publicize them. Even here, however, he admitted that his personal opinion must count for little, seeing he had ceased to care much for anything, true or false. Life was no longer of any value to him, except where he could be of service to Amanda. Mr. Drake could be assured that she was the last person on whom he would wish to foist any of the opinions so objectionable in the minister's eyes. Would Mr. Drake allow him to say one more thing? He was heartily ashamed of his past history; and if there was one thing to make him wish there was a God (of which he still saw no chance whatever), it was that he might ask of him the power to make up for the wrongs he had done, even if it would require an eternity of atonement. But until he could hope for that, he sincerely must hold that his was the better belief. For if wrong could not be atoned for, what was the good of living? Certainly if there were a God, he had not done very well by his creatures, making them so ignorant and weak that they could not fail to fail. Would Mr. Drake have made his Amanda so?

When Wingfold read this letter—and he did not read it until a long time after, in Polwarth's room—he folded it softly together and said, "When he wrote that letter, Paul Faber was already becoming not merely a man to love, but a man to respect."

It was some time before the minister was able to answer the letter, except by sending Amanda at once to the doctor with a message of kind regards and thanks. But his inability to reply was as much from what the letter gave him to think about as from his weakness and fever. For the first time he saw that to preach the doctrine of forgiveness of sins, as it is commonly understood, to such a man would be useless. He would rather believe in a God who would punish them than in one who would pass them by. To be told he was forgiven would but rouse in him indignation. "What is that to me?" he would return. "I remain what I am."

Then grew in the mind of the minister the realization that divine things can only be shadowed in the human. As the heavens are higher than the earth, so are God's ways higher than ours, and what we call his forgiveness may be, must be, something altogether transcending the understanding of man. It must be overwhelming to a man like Paul Faber, whose soul has begun to hunger after righteousness, and whose hunger must be a hunger that will not easily be satisfied. For a poor nature will for a time be satisfied with a mediocre God; but as the nature grows, the desired ideal of God grows greater too.

Then it came into the minister's mind, thinking over Faber's religion toward his fellows and his lack toward God, how when the young man asked Jesus what commandments he must keep that he might inherit eternal life, Jesus did not say a word concerning his duty toward God. He spoke only of his duty toward man. Then it struck him that our Lord gave him no sketch or summary of a religious system—he only told him what he asked, the practical steps by which he might begin to climb toward eternal life. One thing he lacked—namely, God himself; but as to how God would meet him, Jesus says nothing, but himself meets him on those steps with the offer of God. He treats the secondary duties (service to man) as a stair to the first (love to God)—a stair which, probably by crumbling away in failure beneath his feet as he ascended, would plunge him to such a horror of frustration as would make him stretch forth his hands, like the sinking Peter, to the living God. Only in that final surrender could the life eternal stoop to rescue him.

So, looking out upon truth from the cave of his brother's need, and seeing the direction in which the shadow of his atheism fell, the minister learned in what direction the clouded light lay. Fixing his gaze toward that light he learned much. No one but he who has stopped thinking becomes stupid. Such was not Walter Drake. Certain of his formerly cherished doctrines, he now threw off as rubbish; others he dropped with indifference, of some it was as if the angels picked his pockets without his knowing it or ever missing them. And always he found that whatever so-called doctrine he parted with, that the one glowing truth which had lain at the heart of it—buried, mired, obscured—not only remained with him but shone out fresh. It was restored to itself by the loss of the clay of worldly figures and phrases in which human intellect had enclosed it. His faith was elevated, and so confirmed.

39 / The Borderland

Of all his friends, Mr. Drew, the draper, most frequently visited his old pastor. Though he had been a deacon in the chapel, he had been the first to forsake his ministry there and join the worship of what he believed to be a more godly community. For in the abbey church he heard better news of God and his kingdom. The gospel was everything to him, and this or that church nothing but vanity. It had hurt Mr. Drake considerably at first, but as a result Drew grew even more warmly his personal friend, and since learning to know Wingfold Mr. Drake had come to heartily justify the draper's defection.

Now that he was laid up, hardly a day passed without a visit from the draper. One evening Drew found him doing very poorly, though neither the doctor nor Dorothy could get him to go to bed. He could not rest, but kept walking about, his eye feverish, his pulse fluttering. He welcomed his friend even more warmly than usual and made him sit down by the fire while he paced the room, turning and turning like a caged animal.

"I am sorry to see you so uncomfortable," said Mr. Drew.

"On the contrary, I feel uncommonly well," replied the pastor. "I always measure my health by my power of thinking; and tonight my thoughts are like birds, or like bees rather, that keep flying in delight from one lovely blossom to another. Only, fear keeps coming over me that an hour may be at hand when my soul will be dark and it will seem as if the Lord had forsaken me."

"But is it not just as wrong to distrust God for tomorrow's spiritual food as well as its physical food?"

"You are right, old friend," concurred the minister. "I am still so faithless! But I had been thinking what it would be like if God were to try me with heavenly poverty as he did for a short time with earthly poverty—if he were to withdraw a step and not give me enough of himself to live on. Just suppose that God was nowhere, that life had become dull, and that you had nothing but your own dreary self everywhere."

"It is not a very heartening thought, I admit," agreed the draper.

"Let me tell you how I came into this frame of mind. Don't misunderstand me. I am not obsessed with this idea; I am only trying to understand its nature. Well, I had a strange kind of vision or dream last night. I don't know which—anyhow a very strange experience. I did not say to myself, 'I am dead and now I am coming alive.' I only felt.

I had but one feeling and that feeling was love—the outgoing of a longing heart toward everything. This love made my heart burn, and the burning of my heart was my life—and the burning was the presence of the Absolute. If you can imagine a growing fruit, void of senses yet loving the tree it could neither look at nor hear, knowing it only through the flow of its life from it—that is something like what I felt.

"By degrees there came a change. What seemed the fire in me burned and burned until it began to grow light. With the light, the love kept growing, and I remembered the words of the Lord, 'Let your light so shine before men.' I could no more keep it from shining than I could the sun. Then I began to think of one I loved, then of another, and another—then of all together whom I had ever loved. And the light that went out from me embraced every one of them. But the light did not remain there. It went out beyond them, reaching and enfolding all those on earth I had merely known.

"Such a perfection of bliss arose in me that it seemed as if the fire of the divine had at last seized my very soul and I was dying of absolute glory—which is love and love only. I had all things. I was full and completely content. Yet still the light went flowing out and out from me, and love was life and life was light and light was love. On and on it flowed until at last I beheld before me such a multitude of brothers and sisters whom I loved and who were loving me in return.

"Then suddenly came a whisper. 'Oh, man,' it said, 'what a life is thine! See all these souls, these fires of life regarding and loving thee. It is in the glory of *thy* love their faces shine. Their hearts receive it and send it back in joy. Do you not see that all their eyes are fixed upon thine? Do you not see the light come and go on their faces as the pulses of thy heartbeat? Blessed art thou, oh, man, as no one else in God's universe is blessed!'

"But then, horrible to tell, the glow of the fire began to go out and all the faces before me withered, and the next moment there was darkness—all was black as night. The consciousness of being was intense; in all the universe there was nothing to enter that being and make it other than an absolute loneliness. If before there had been bliss, now was the absolute blackness of darkness. It was a loveless, careless, hopeless monotony of nothing but self-knowing—a hell with but one demon and no fire to make it cry. My self was the hell, my known self the demon of it—a hell of which I could not find the walls, cold and dark and empty, and I longed for a flame that I might know there was a God. But somehow I only remembered God as a word. One time there might have been a God, but there was none now; if ever there was one, he must be dead.

"The blackness grew and grew. I hated life fiercely. Then I felt the blackness begin to go out of me as the light had gone before. Not that

I remembered the light; I had forgotten all about it and only remembered it after I awoke. Then came the words of the Lord to me. 'If therefore the light that is in thee be darkness, how great is that darkness!' And I knew what was coming: oh, horror! In a moment more I should see the faces of those I had once loved, dark with the blackness that went out from my very existence. Then I would hate them, and my being would be a hell to which the hell I was now in would seem a heaven! There was just grace enough left in me for the hideousness of the terror to wake me. I was cold as if I had been dipped in a well. But, oh, how I thanked God that I was what I am, and might yet hope to be!''

The minister's face was pale as the horse that grew gray when Death mounted him, and his eyes shown with a feverous brilliancy. The draper breathed a deep breath and rubbed his white forehead. The minister rose and began again to pace the room, seemingly forgetful of the other's presence.

Drew rose and crept softly from the room, saying to Dorothy as he left the house that she *must* get him to bed as soon as possible. She went to him, and now found no difficulty in persuading him to lie down. But something in his appearance, she could not tell what, alarmed her and she sent for the doctor. He was not at home and had expected to be out all night. She sat by her father's bedside for hours, but at last, as he was quietly sleeping, she herself lay down on the couch in the room. She fell fast asleep and slept undisturbed till morning.

When she went to his bedside, she found him breathing softly and thought he was still asleep. But he opened his eyes, looked at her for a moment intently, and then said, "Dorothy, child of my heart! Things may be very different from what we have been taught, or what we of ourselves may even desire. But every difference will be the step of an ascending stair—each nearer and nearer to the divine perfection which alone can satisfy the children of God and the poorest of their cravings."

She stooped and kissed his hand, then hastened away to get him some food.

When she returned, he was gone up the stair of her future, leaving behind him, like a last message that all was well, the loveliest smile frozen upon a face of peace. The past had laid hold upon his body; he was free in the Eternal.

Dorothy was left standing at the top of the stair of the present.

The desolation that seized Dorothy seemed at first overwhelming. There was no refuge for her. Even Wingfold and Helen could do little for her. Sorrow was her sole companion, her sole *comfort* in her dreariest time of life.

But then a sense of her father's spirit began to steal upon her. Her father's character, especially as developed in his later struggles toward righteousness, began to open itself up to her day by day. She remembered him combatting his faults, dejected by his failures, encouraged by his successes. And he grew even dearer to her for his faults, as she perceived more plainly how he had fought against them. The imperfections he had repudiated made him honorable in her eyes, and sowed seeds of ever-lasting tenderness in her heart. She saw how in those last days he had been overcoming the world with accelerated victory, becoming more of the real father that no man can be until he has attained to the sonship. The marvel is that our children are so tender and trusting to the slow-developing father in us.

The truth and faith which the great Father has put in the heart of the child make him the nurturer of the fatherhood in his own father. And thus in part it is that the children of men will come at last to know the great Father. The family, with all its powers for the development of society, is a family because it is born and rooted in and grows out of the very heart of God.

Few griefs can be so paralyzing as, for a time, that of a true daughter upon the loss of a true parent. But through the rifts of such heartbreaks the light of love shines clearer, and where love is, there is eternity. One day he who is the householder of the universe will begin to bring out of his treasury all the good old things, as well as the better new ones. How true must be the bliss up to which the intense realities of such sorrows are necessary to force the way for the faithless heart and the feeble will! Thou, Lord, art the perfection which every heart sighs toward, yet no mind can attain unto.

Faber came to visit Dorothy—solemn, sad, and kind. He made no attempt at consolation, did not speak a word of comfort. Instead he talked of the old man, revealing a deep respect for him, and her heart was touched and turned itself toward the doctor. Some change, she thought, must have passed upon him. Her father had told her nothing of Faber's relationship to Amanda. It would have to be done someday, but he had shrunk from it. She could not help suspecting there was more between Faber and him than she had at first imagined; but she carried in herself a healthy contentment with ignorance, and she asked no questions. Neither did Faber attempt to find out whether she knew what had passed, or about Amanda and any possible change in her future.

He had never been a man of plans, and had no room for any now under the rubbish of a collapsed life. His days were gloomy and his nights troubled. He dreamed constantly, either of Amanda's mother or of Juliet—sometimes of both together, and of endless perplexity between them. Sometimes he woke weeping. And he did not now despise his tears, for they flowed neither from suffering nor self-pity, but from love and sorrow and repentance.

People said he took the loss of his wife coolly. The truth was that in every quiet way he could, he had been trying to obtain what information about her there might possibly be. But he kept his inquiries quiet and certainly never employed police or newspapers. But Faber had only learned what everybody else had learned, and for a time was haunted by the horrible expectation of further news from the lake. Every knock at the door made him start and turn pale. But the body had not come to the surface, and would not now.

The stinging convictions of conscience burned ever deeper into his soul. He could now see that Juliet had made of him an idol—a god she believed could pardon her. He was the one being in the whole world who, by saying to her, *Let it be forgotten*, could have lifted her into life and hope. She had trusted in him. Had she not confessed to him what he could never have discovered, humbling herself in the very essence of repentance? Was it not an honor to any husband to have been so trusted by his wife? How her fault must have stung and shamed her!

And yet this was his response to her agony, his balm for her pain— to push her from him, to scorn her. He had done all in his power to brand her forever with the stain of her guilt!

Why had he not opened his arms wide and taken her to the heart of his love, which by the very agony of its own grief and its pity over hers would have burned her clean? What was he? What was *his* honor? If he had any, what more fitting honor than to sacrifice it for the redemption of his wife?

Ah, men! Was there ever such a poor, sneaking scarecrow of an idol as that straw-stuffed insanity you worship and call *honor*? It is not honor; it is but *your* honor. It is neither gold nor silver nor honest copper, but worthless straw.

By degrees Faber grew thoroughly disgusted with himself, then heartily ashamed. At last, for the first time in his entire life, he was genuinely brought low. Though it had been slowly dawning on him for some time, he finally saw with clarity the emptiness of what had always been his chief argument against all critics—his own goodness. It had all been a mockery—no goodness at all. He had his lifelong been utterly deceived. Against all the superstitious hypocrites who chastised him for his unbelief, he had always been able to fall back on one defense which they would not shake—he was a better man. That is, he served his neighbor better than most of them. But now, with his pride crumbled around him, he had to bitterly admit that he was not a better man, perhaps a worse man than he had ever met. His so-called goodness had been an illusion. Whether their God existed or not, perhaps what the preachers said about all men being sinners was right after all.

He completely stopped making so much of his denials of God. He had not discarded them, but they no longer held any interest to him. He didn't know what he believed. He didn't care. He grew thinner and paler. He ate little and slept poorly, and the waking hours of the night were hours of torture. He was unhealthy and he knew it, but that did not comfort him. It was the wrong he had done and his misery that had made him ill, not illness that had made him miserable.

Dorothy now sought solitude more than ever. The Wingfolds were like swallows around her, never folding their wings of help, but not pestering her with daily visits. They understood by her bearing that the time had not yet come when their presence would be a comfort to her. The only comfort the heart can take cannot come from itself, but the comfort must come through itself.

Day after day she would go into the park, avoiding the lodge, and walk about, brooding on the memories of her father. And before long she began to feel nearer to him than she had ever felt while he was with her. For where the outward sign has been understood, withdrawing it will bring the inward fact yet nearer. Most people find the first of a bereavement more tolerable than what follows. They find in its fever a support. When the wound in the earth is closed and the wave of life has again rushed over it, when things have returned to their previous ways, then the desert of desolation opens around them, and for a time existence seems almost intolerable. With Dorothy it was different. Alive in herself, she was hungering and thirsting after life; therefore death could not have dominion over her.

To her surprise she found also that since her father's death, many of her doubts had vanished. She had been lifted into a region higher than those questions which had so disturbed her peace. From a point of clearer vision she saw things so differently that the questions she had had were no longer relevant. The truth was being lived out in her that the business of life is to live, not to answer every objection that the mind can raise concerning things spiritual. She had *done* that which was given her to do; therefore she progressed up the stairway of life. It is no matter that a man or woman be unable to explain or understand this or that. It does not matter as long as when they see a truth they do it; to see and not do would at once place them in eternal danger. There is in the man or woman who does the truth, the radiance of life essential—a glory infinitely beyond any that can belong to the intellect.

To know God is to be in the secret place of all knowledge, and to trust him changes the whole outlook surrounding mystery and seeming contradictions and unanswered questions, from one of doubt or fear or bewilderment, to one of hope. The unknown may be some lovely truth in store for us, which we are not yet ready to apprehend. Not to be intellectually certain of a truth does not prevent the heart that loves and obeys that truth from getting the goodness out of it, from drawing life from it because it is loved, not because it is understood.

As yet Dorothy had no plans, except to carry out her father's, and mainly for Juliet's sake to move to the Old House as soon as the work there was completed. But the repairs and alterations were major and took months. Wisely, she was not particularly anxious to shorten Juliet's stay with the Polwarths. The longer that lasted with safety, the better for Juliet, and herself too, she thought.

On Christmas Eve, the curate gave his wife a little poem. Helen showed it to Dorothy, and Dorothy to Juliet. By this time she had gotten some genuine teaching—far more than she recognized—and so the spiritual song was not without its influence on her:

THAT HOLY THING

They all were looking for a king
   To slay their foes and lift them high:
You came a little baby thing
   That made a woman cry:

"O Son of Man, to right my lot
   Nought but your presence can avail;
Yet on the road your wheels are not,
   Nor on the sea your sail.

"My how or when you will not heed,
   But come down your own secret stair,
That you may answer all my need,
   And every little prayer."

The spring was bursting in bud and leaf before the workmen were out of the Old House. The very next day Dorothy began her move. She took every stick of the old furniture with her; every book of her father's she placed on the shelves of the library he had designed. But she took care not to neglect Juliet. She regularly took her a report of her husband whenever she had seen him. It was to Juliet like an odor from Paradise, making her weep when Dorothy said that he looked sad—"so different from his old self!"

But Juliet still did not have any idea what Dorothy had done for her, and if Dorothy even hinted at any sort of mediation between Juliet and her Paul, she would rise in indignation. Yet the next moment she would speak to Dorothy as if she were her only true friend.

"But you *will* be with me in my trouble, won't you, Dorothy?"

"Certainly, Juliet, I will."

"Then promise me, if I can't get through, if I am going to die, that you will bring him to me. I must see my Paul once again before the darkness."

"I will," promised Dorothy, and Juliet was satisfied.

But even though her behavior continued so much the same, a change, unseen by herself, had begun to pass upon Juliet. Every change must begin further back than the observations of man can reach—in regions of which we have no knowledge. However much a person may appear to those around him as the essence of bitterness, other and larger eyes than ours may be watching with delight the germ of righteousness which is swelling within the enclosing husk of evil and which will eventually break its bonds.

The influences now for some time operative upon Juliet were all the more powerful because she neither suspected nor could avoid them. She had a vague notion that she was a help to her host and hostess. She little realized how she interfered with the simple comforts of the two, how many a visit of friends Polwarth avoided because there might be the least danger of her discovery, how often her host left some book un-bought that he might buy instead something to tempt her to eat, how hard Rachel worked cooking for her.

For the sake of Christ hidden in Juliet, that she might be lifted from the dustheap of the life she had ruined for herself into the clear air of a pure will and the divine presence, for this they counted their labor fitly spent. Only in the unfolding of the Christ in every man or woman can the individuality, his or her genuine personality, the flower of his nature, be developed and perfected in its own distinct loveliness.

The main way the influences of the dwarfs reached the princess was their absolute simplicity. They spoke and acted just as they were. Thus their daily, common righteousness slowly revealed itself—their gentleness, their love of all living things, their care of each other, their acceptance of whatever came as the will of God, their general satisfaction with things as they were, their suffering patience. They always spoke as if they felt where their words were going—as if they were hearing them arrive. Pain had taught them not only sensitivity, but delicacy. Their pains had taught them to live in a region unexplored by most, in a deeper, divine center of life. The asthmatic choking which so often made Polwarth's nights a long misery had taught him a sympathy with all prisoners and captives, especially with those bound in the chains of an evil conscience. The two thought little of bearing pain, but to know they had caused it would have been torture. Each, graciously uncomplaining, was tender over the ailing of the other.

Juliet had not been long with them before she realized she had to change her preconceptions. They were not gnomes, goblins, or dwarfs, but a noble prince and princess who loved each other and knew they were presently crushed in the shell of some enchantment. How they served each other! The uncle would just as readily help the niece wash her saucepans as she would help him find a passage in Shakespeare. And to hear them talk!

For some time Juliet did not even try to understand them. She had no idea what they were talking about. But by and by it began to dawn on her that the creatures were speaking of and judging things of this world by quite different laws than those commonly in use. Everything was turned topsy-turvy in their make-believe game of the kingdom of heaven. Their religion was their chief interest, and their work was merely their play. What she counted as their fancies, they seemed to count their business. Things which seemed insignificant to her made them look very grave, and what she would have counted of some importance drew a mere smile from them. She saw all with bewildered eyes.

But she had begun to take note of their sufferings, their lighted eyes, their ready smiles, and their great patience with their own hurts. And she began to wonder whether they might not be in tune with finer issues than she. It was not, however, until she had ministered to them a little on one occasion when they were both disabled for some hours that she began to *feel* that they had a hold upon something unseen.

At first when she found they had no set prayers in the house, she concluded that for all his talk in the garden at their first meeting, they were not really very religious. But by and by she began to discover that one could not tell when they might be praying. One day when she had a bad headache, the little man came into her room and without a word to her, kneeled by the bedside and said, "Father, through your Son you know pain and even now you feel the pain of this your child. Help her to endure until you shall say it is enough. Let it not overmaster her patience; let it not be too much for her. What good it shall work in her, Lord, we do not need to instruct you." With that he rose and left the room.

For some weeks after that Juliet was certain they had some latent intent to convert her to their religion. But she perceived not a single direct approach. Polwarth was an absolute serpent of holy wisdom, and knew that often the most powerful influences are the most hidden. A man's religion, he said, ought never to be held too near his neighbor. It is like violets hidden in the banks, they fill the air with their sweet scent; but if a bunch of them is held to the nose, they immediately cease their own sweetness.

Frequently she heard one of them reading to the other, and eventually she came to join them. Sometimes it would be a passage from the New Testament or from this or that old English book, books she had never heard of in her so-called education. The gatekeeper would often stop the reading to talk, explaining and illustrating what the writer meant in a way that filled Juliet with wonder. "Strange," she would say to herself, "I never thought of that."

A respect for her host and hostess began to spring up in her soul such as she had never felt for God or man. And when this respect was a little established, it naturally went beyond them in the direction of that which they revered. It almost could not be helped that the reverence they showed the name of the Lord and the way they took all he said and did as the fundamental ideal with which to measure their own thoughts and actions began at length to tell on Juliet. She came to feel, not merely as if there had been, but as if there really was, such a person as Jesus Christ. The idea of him ruled so potently in the lives of the two: how could she help but feel a certain awe before it such as she had never felt before?

One detail I will mention here because it sheds light on Polwarth's character. Juliet had come to feel some desire to be useful in the house, and saw not only dust but what she judged to be disorder in her landlord's little library, which to her astonishment in such a mere cottage consisted of many more books than her husband's, and she offered to dust and rearrange them properly.

Polwarth instantly accepted her offer with thanks—which was solely for the kindness of her intent; he could not possibly be grateful for the intended result—and left his books at her mercy. I do not know another man who, loving his books like Polwarth, would have done so. Every book had its own place. He could have laid his hand on any book of at least three hundred of them in the dark. While he used them with perfect freedom, and cared comparatively little for their covers, he handled them with careful respect. He had seen ladies handle books, he said, laughing to Wingfold, in a way that made him afraid to trust them with a child.

It was a year after Juliet left the house before he got them by degrees muddled into order again.

Dorothy's thoughts in the meantime were much occupied with Juliet. Juliet could occupy her old quarters as soon as the workmen were finished. But Amanda could certainly not be trusted with the secret. She would ask Helen to take her for a while.

Juliet was pleased at the prospect of the change. She formally thanked the two rumpled angels, begged them to visit her often, and proceeded to make her very small preparations with a fitful cheerfulness. *Something might come of the change*, she thought to herself. She had always indulged a vague fancy that Dorothy was devising help for her. It was partially the disappointment of nothing yet having happened that made Juliet behave so poorly to her. But for a long time Dorothy had been talking of Paul in a different tone, and that very morning had spoken of him even with some admiration; it might be a prelude to something!

One day Faber was riding at a good round trot along one of the back streets of Glaston. Approaching his own house, he saw Amanda, who still took every opportunity of darting out an open door, running to him with outstretched arms. Unable to trust Niger so well as his dear old Ruber, he stopped and quickly dismounted. Taking her in his arms, he led Niger to his stable. He learned from her that she was staying with the Wingfolds and took her home. After this his visits to the rectory were frequent.

The Wingfolds could not fail to notice the tenderness with which he regarded the child. Indeed it soon became clear that it was for her sake he came to them. But his devotion to her did not make them wonder. Everybody loved little Amanda, and they saw him as only another of the child's conquests and rejoiced in the good the love might do him. Even when they saw him looking intently at her with clear eyes, they set it down to the frustrated affection of the lonely, wifeless, childless man. But by degrees some did come to wonder a little, for his love seemed to grow almost daily.

"I wish," said the curate one morning as they sat at breakfast, "if only for Faber's sake, that something definite was known about poor Juliet. There are rumors accusing him in the town, roving like poisonous fogs. I hardly dare think what would happen should these foolish fancies get rooted among the people. Many of them are capable of brutality. For my part, I don't believe the poor woman is dead yet."

Helen believed that, in her sound mind, Juliet would not have killed herself. But who could tell what state of mind she had been in at the time? There had always been something mysterious about her—something that seemed to want explanation.

Between them they concluded that the next time Faber came, Wingfold should be candid with him. The next day Faber appeared at their door. Wingfold told him that if he could shed any light on his wife's disappearance, it was important that he do so, for reports were circulating against him. Faber answered with a sickly smile that they had had a quarrel the night before for which he was to blame. He had left her, and the next morning she was gone, leaving everything, even her wedding ring, behind her. He had since done all he could to find her, but without success. More he could not say.

The next afternoon he came to the curate in his study. There he told him everything he had told Mr. Drake. The story seemed to explain a good deal more than it actually did. The curate felt confident that this disclosure had caused the quarrel between Faber and his wife. The curate became more doubtful than ever as to Juliet's having committed suicide.

42 / The New Old House_____

It was a lovely moonlit night when the four of them—Dorothy, Juliet and the Polwarths—set out from the gate across the park to the Old House. Like shadows they flitted over the green grass. Scarcely a word was spoken as they went. Suddenly but gently a sense of the wonder of life opened in Juliet's mind. The moon, having labored through a heap of cloud into a lake of blue, seemed to watch her with curious interest as she walked across the field. The air now and then made a soundless sigh about her head, like a waft of invisible wings.

All at once, as if waked from a long sleep, she found herself aware of *herself*—a target for either sorrow or joy, a woman scorned by the man she loved bearing within her another life which would soon become aware of its own joys and sorrows. Was there no one to answer for it all? Surely there must be a heart somewhere in the universe that gave it all meaning. If not, then what an iron net, what a combination of chains and fetters and cages and prisons was this existence—especially to a woman!

Thus meditated Juliet. She was beginning to learn that until we get to the heart of life, we can never be at home. She was hard to teach, but God's circumstances had found her.

When they came near the brow of the hollow, Dorothy ran on ahead to assure that all was safe. Polwarth, who had been walking behind with Rachel, stepped up to Juliet's side and said, "I have been feeling all the way as if another was walking beside us—the same who said, 'I am with you to the end of the world.' "

"It matters little to me," answered Juliet with a sigh. "You know I do not believe in him."

"But I believe in him," affirmed Polwarth, "and Rachel believes in him, and so does Miss Drake. If he be with us, he cannot be far from you."

With that he stepped back to Rachel's side and said no more.

Dorothy opened the door quickly. They entered at once, and she closed it behind them, fearful of some eye in the night. How different was the house from that which Juliet had left! The hall was lighted with a soft lamp, showing soft warm colors on walls and floor. The dining room door stood open; a wood fire was roaring on the hearth, and candles were burning on a snowy table spread for a meal. She showed the Polwarths into the dining room, then turning to Juliet, said, "I will take you to your room, dear."

Dorothy led the way, and as they went up the stairs, she announced, "I have prepared your old quarters for you."

With the words such a memory of mingled dreariness and terror rushed upon Juliet that she could not reply.

But as she opened the door in the closet, Juliet started back in amazement. It was the loveliest room. And, like a marvel in a fairy tale, the great round moon was shining gloriously through an oriel window filled with squares of soft, pale-green glass. Juliet turned in delight, threw her arms around Dorothy, and kissed her.

"I thought I was going into a dungeon!" she exclaimed. "But it is a room for a princess!"

"I sometimes believe, Juliet," returned Dorothy, "that God will give us a greater surprise one day."

A few minutes later the four were seated in the dining room, enjoying the dinner Dorothy had prepared for them. "How your good father will delight to watch you here sometimes, Miss Drake," said Polwarth, "if those who are gone are permitted to see us."

Juliet shuddered. Dorothy's father had not been gone two months!

"Do you really think," queried Dorothy, "that the dead only seem to have left us?" And as she looked at him, her eyes seemed full of holy questions.

"I know so little," he answered, "that I hardly dare say *I think* anything. But our Lord implies that the change we call *death* is nothing at all like what we are thinking of when we use the word. Therefore, as permanent as the separation appears to us, it may not actually be so. And really—I don't care. His will *is* and that is everything. But there can be no harm where I do not know his will, in venturing a *perhaps*. I am sure he likes his little ones to tell their fancies about the nursery fires. Our souls yearning after light of any sort must be a pleasure for him to watch."

Later as the two were walking back to the lodge together, Rachel implored, "Will you come and visit me if you die first, Uncle? You know how lonely I shall be without you."

"If it is within the law of things, if I am at liberty, and if the thing seems good for you, my Rachel, you may be sure I will come to you. But of one thing I am pretty certain: such visions do not appear when people are looking for them. You must do your work, pray your prayers, and be sure I love you. If I am to come I will come. It may be in the hot noon or in the dark night; it may be with no sight and no sound, yet a knowledge of presence; or I may be watching you, helping you perhaps, and you never know it until I come to fetch you at the last—if I may. You have been daughter and sister and mother to me, my Rachel. You have been my one woman in the world. I sometimes think God has planted about you and me, my child, a cactus hedge of ugliness that we might be so near and so lonely as to learn love as few have learned it in this world—love without fear or doubt or pain or anxiety. Ah, Rachel! A bliss beyond speech is waiting us in the presence of the Master, where, seeing him like he is, we shall grow like him and be no more either dwarfed or sickly."

43 / The Coming of the Doctor

Dorothy's faith in Polwarth had been gradually increasing and by now she trusted in him thoroughly. As soon as she had brought breakfast to Juliet the next morning, she went to meet him in the park as they had arranged the night before.

She had already revealed to him the promise she had made Juliet, that she would call her husband the moment she seemed in danger—a possibility which Juliet regarded almost as a certainty when the baby came. Dorothy had asked Polwarth to think of how they might arrange to have Faber within call. He now had a plan to propose which would take care of this need, and another need as well.

"You know, Miss Drake," he said, "that I am well acquainted with every yard of this ground. And there is one thing which, in my opinion, would greatly improve your new home. I have been in the cellars repeatedly, both before and after your father bought the property, and I always found them damp. The cause of it is simple. The foundations are as low as the water level in the pond. The ground at that depth is largely of gravel, and thus the water is getting through to the house. I suggest, then, that from the bank of the Lythe, which is lower, a tunnel be dug, rising at a gentle incline until it pierces the basin of the lake. There would be a strong sluice gate by which you could keep the water at whatever height you please, and at any moment send it into the river."

"Would this be difficult to do?" asked Dorothy.

"I think not," answered Polwarth. "With your permission I will get a friend of mine, an engineer, to look into it."

"I leave it in your hands," consented Dorothy.

The same week all was arranged with the engineer. At an agreed upon day, his men were to be at work on the tunnel.

For a time things went on much the same. Faber had been growing better. He sat more erect on his horse; his eye was keener, his voice more kind, though hardly less sad, and his step was firmer. His love to the child and her delight in his attentions were slowly leading him back to life. Every day, even if only for a moment, he managed to see her, and the Wingfolds took care to remove every obstacle from the way of their meeting. Little did they realize why Dorothy let them keep the child so long. As little as Dorothy know that what she yielded for the sake of the wife, they desired for the sake of the husband.

At length, one morning a change came: Juliet's time was at hand. Shortly after the fact was known, Faber received a note from the gatekeeper, informing him that Miss Drake was having the pond at the foot of her garden emptied into the Lythe by means of a tunnel, the construction of which was already completed. They were now boring for a small charge of gunpowder expected to liberate the water. The process of emptying would probably be rapid, the gatekeeper explained, and he had taken the liberty of informing Mr. Faber, thinking he might choose to be present. No one else but the persons employed would be allowed to enter the grounds.

The news gave him a greater shock than he could have believed possible. At once he arranged with his assistant to be absent the whole day and rode out, followed by his groom. At the gate Polwarth joined him and walked beside him to the Old House, where he said his groom could put up the horses. He accompanied Faber to the mouth of the tunnel and there left him.

Faber sat down on the stump of a fallen tree and covered his face with his hands. Before him the river ran swiftly toward the level country. The wind in the woods rustled through the branches and leaves. But the only sounds he heard were the blows of the hammer on the boring chisel, coming dull and as if from out of the depths of the earth. What strange, awful significance they had to Faber's heart! *What will they find when the lake is empty?*

But the end was delayed hour after hour, and there he sat, now and then a louder noise than usual lifting his white face to stare toward the mouth of the tunnel. But Polwarth had taken good care to delay the explosion until after Juliet's delivery. He would keep Faber there only as long as it seemed necessary. So over and over came the blow of iron upon iron, but no explosion of powder.

Dorothy brought Juliet the news in the labor room that her husband was within a few hundred yards of the house, and Mr. Polwarth would keep him there until all danger to her was over.

Juliet now showed great courage. It seemed as if her husband's nearness gave her strength to do without his actual presence.

At length the infant, a lovely boy, lay asleep in Dorothy's arms. The lovelier mother slept also. Since all seemed well, Polwarth went out to stop the work and let the doctor know that its completion must be postponed a few days. Suddenly he heard the voice of Dorothy's housekeeper behind him, calling while she ran. As he turned to meet her, she told him that Juliet had begun hemorrhaging. He turned back and ran to the doctor as fast as his short legs could carry him.

"Mr. Faber," he cried, "there is a lady up there at the house, a friend of Miss Drake's, taken suddenly ill. You are needed as quickly as possible."

Faber did not answer a word, but ran up the bank and to the house. Polwarth followed as best he could, panting and wheezing.

"Tell my man to saddle my horse and be at the back door immediately," Faber instructed the housekeeper as she let him in.

Polwarth followed him up the stairs to the landing, where Dorothy met Faber and led him to Juliet's room. The dwarf seated himself on the top of the stairs and waited.

44 / Juliet's Chamber_____

When Faber entered, a dim rosy light from the drawn window curtains was the only illumination in the room; he could barely see his way to the bed. Dorothy was in terror lest his discovery of Juliet might so unnerve the husband that the doctor could not do what was required of him. But Juliet's face was turned away from him, and a word from the nurse present let him know at once what was necessary.

He turned to Dorothy and spoke quickly. "I must send my man home to fetch something for me." Then to the nurse he said, "Go on as you are doing." He turned once more to Dorothy, saying, "Come with me, Miss Drake. I need something to write with."

He led the way from the room and Dorothy followed. Scarcely were they in the hallway when the little man rose and approached them. Faber would have pushed past him, but Polwarth held out a little vial to him.

"Perhaps this is what you want, sir," he offered.

The doctor snatched it, almost angrily, from his hand, looked at it, uncorked it, and put it to his nose.

"Thank you," he acknowledged, too intent to be surprised, "this is just what I wanted," and returned instantly to the chamber.

The little man resumed his seat on the stair, breathing heavily. Ten minutes of silence followed. Then Dorothy passed him with a note in her hand and hurried down the stairs to Faber's groom. The next instant Polwarth heard the sound of Niger's hoofs tearing up the slope behind the house.

"I have got some more medicines here, Miss Drake," Polwarth said when she reappeared on the stairs.

Dorothy, however, told him it was not a medicine the doctor wanted just now, but something else. She did not know what. Juliet had lost considerable blood, she said. Dorothy's face was dreadfully white but as calm as an ice field. She went back into the room and closed the door. Polwarth sat down again.

Not more than twenty minutes had passed when he heard again the soft thunder of Niger's hoofs on the turf and in a minute more up came the housekeeper carrying a little morocco leather case.

Then an hour passed, during which he heard nothing. He sat motionless, and his troubled lungs grew quiet.

At Dorothy's step behind him, he rose.

"You had better come downstairs with me," she advised in a voice he scarcely knew, and her face looked almost as if she herself had passed through some terrible illness.

"How is the poor lady?" he asked.

"The immediate danger is over, the doctor says, but he seems in great doubt. He sent me away, muttering that it could never work again. I don't know what he meant."

"Has he recognized her?"

"I don't know. I have seen no sign of it. But we can talk better downstairs. Do you want a glass of wine?"

"I need nothing, my dear," affirmed Polwarth. "I would prefer to stay here, if you will permit me. There is no knowing when I might be of service. I am no stranger to sickrooms."

"Do as you please, Mr. Polwarth," allowed Dorothy, and going down the stairs, went into the garden.

Once more Polwarth resumed his vigil.

Suddenly the noise of a heavy fall shook the floor where he sat. He leaped up and hurried to the door of the chamber, but he heard nothing. Immediately he opened the door and looked in.

All was silent, and the room was so dark he could see nothing at first. As his eyes quickly adjusted, he saw a prostrate figure in the middle of the floor that could only be the doctor, for there was the nurse on her knees beside him. He glanced toward the bed. There all was still.

She is dead! flashed through his mind, *and he has discovered who she was!*

"Have you no brandy?" he asked the nurse.

"On that table," she answered.

"Lay his head down and get it."

Despite Polwarth's unusual appearance, the nurse obeyed. She knew the doctor required brandy, but in the emergency she had lost her presence of mind.

Polwarth took the doctor's hand. The pulse had vanished—and no wonder! Once more the healer had drained his own life-spring of blood to supply what his patient had lost. Yet the doctor knew as little now of what that patient was to him as he knew what she was going to be to him. Indeed, a thrill had shot to his heart at the touch of her hand, scarcely alive as it was, when he first felt her pulse. And what he saw of her turned profile through the folded shadows of pillows and curtains woke wild suggestion. It was fortunate that as he bared her arm, it was too dark to show the scar of his previous lancet.

Always in total possession of himself at critical moments, Faber had insisted to himself that his imagination was playing tricks on him. If he did not banish the fancies that were crowding in upon him, his patient's life, and possibly his own, would be the penalty. Therefore, with obstinate will he kept his eyes turned away from the face of the woman, drawn to it as they were by the terror of what his imagination might show him there. But he held to his duty in spite of growing mental agony and physical weakness. He assured himself that his brain was so fearfully excited he could not trust his senses. Thus he ruled himself until the life within his own veins was exhausted, still not knowing whose life it was he had saved for a second time. His brain, deserted by his heart, gave way, and when he turned from the bed, all but unconscious, he could stagger only a pace or two, and fell like one dead.

Polwarth got some brandy into Faber's mouth with a teaspoon. In about a minute his heart began to beat.

"I must open another vein," the doctor murmured as if in a dream.

When he had swallowed a third spoonful, he lifted his eyelids in a dreary kind of way, saw Polwarth, and remembered that he had something to attend to—a patient probably—he could not tell.

"Tut! Give me a glass of the stuff," he urged.

Polwarth obeyed. The moment he swallowed it, he rose, rubbing his forehead as if trying to remember, and mechanically turned toward the bed. The nurse, afraid he might not yet know what he was about, stepped between, saying softly, "She is asleep, sir, and breathing quietly."

"Thank God!" he whispered with a sigh, and turned to a couch and sank down upon it.

The nurse looked at Polwarth as if to say, *Who is to take the command now?*

"I shall be outside, nurse. Call me if I can be useful to you," he replied in a low voice to the glance, and withdrew to his watch on the top of the stairs.

After about a quarter of an hour, the nurse came out.

"Do you want me?" asked Polwarth, rising hastily.

"No, sir," she answered. "The doctor says all immediate danger is over and he requires nobody with him. I am going to look after the baby. And he says nobody is to go in, sir, for she must not be disturbed. The slightest noise might undo everything. She must sleep now all she can."

"Very well," conceded Polwarth, and sat down again.

The day went on; the sun went down; the shadows deepened; and not a sound came from the room. Again and again Dorothy came and looked up the stairs, but seeing the little man at his post like Zacchaeus in the sycamore, she was satisfied and withdrew. At length Polwarth realized that Rachel would be wondering about him, and he rose reluctantly. The same instant the door opened and Faber appeared. He looked very pale and worn, almost haggard.

"Would you call Miss Drake," he requested.

Polwarth went downstairs and returned with Dorothy.

"She is sleeping beautifully," began Faber, "but I dare not leave her. I must sit up with her tonight. There still exists some danger. Send my man to tell my assistant that I shall not be home. Could you let me have something to eat, Miss Drake, and you take my place. And there is Polwarth! He has earned his dinner if anyone has. I do believe we owe the poor lady's life to him."

Dorothy ran to give the message and her own orders for dinner. Polwarth asked her to tell the groom to inform Rachel as he passed that all was well. When the food was ready, he joined Faber.

The meal was over quickly, however, for the doctor seemed anxious to again join his patient. Then Dorothy came down to Polwarth, and they both had the same question for each other: had Faber recognized his wife or not? Neither had come to a certain conclusion. Polwarth said he had talked strangely during dinner, drinking several glasses of wine in a hurried way.

In reality Faber had not recognized her, but he had been powerfully reminded of her. So it was with a mingling of strange feelings that Faber now returned to sit in the darkened room, watching the woman who with such sweet torture reminded him of the one whom he had lost. She seemed more or less like his Juliet but all the time he could at best see her only partially. Ever since his accident, his sight had been weak, especially in the dark. Twice during his nightlong vigil, he stood over her as she slept and strained his eyes to the utmost, but he could not tell what he saw. Dorothy had hoped to delay the discovery as long as possible, so that when it did come, its way would have been well prepared. She had purposely darkened the room greatly. And now he had no light but a small shaded lamp.

At regular intervals he rose to see how his patient fared. She was still floating in the twilight shadows of death—whether softly drifting on the ebb tide of sleep out into the open sea, or back up the river of life, he could not yet tell.

In his sleepless and bloodless brain strangest thoughts and feelings came and went. The scents of old roses, the stings of past sins awoke and vanished like the pulsing of fireflies. Every time he thought, *What if this should be my own Juliet!* for a moment life seemed as if it would burst into the very madness of delight. Yet ever and again his common sense told him his imagination was fooling him.

He dared not yield to the intoxicating idea. If he did, he would be like a man drinking a delicious-tasting poison. Every sip, in itself a delight, would bring him a step nearer to agony and death. When she woke and the light would fall on her face, he knew—so he said to himself—he *knew* the likeness would vanish and the dream would have been a mockery of the night.

Still the night was checkered with alternating moments of bliss, in the indulgence of the fantasy of what it would be if it *were* she. But fancy always vanished in the rebuke that he must prepare himself for the loss of the dream which morning would certainly bring. Yet like one in a dream who knows it is but a dream, yet hardly dares breathe lest he should break the ecstasy of it, he would not carry the lamp to the bedside. No act of his should disperse the airy flicker of the lovely doubt.

Toward morning Juliet awoke from her long sleep, but her brain was still too empty of life to identify what she saw. Her soul hovered fluttering between two worlds—of her imagination and fact. The only thing she saw was the face of her husband, sadly lighted by the dimmed light, some distance away. It was a more beautiful face than ever before— even than when she first mistook it for the Savior's. Thin and pale with suffering, it was not feeble, but the former self-sufficiency had vanished, and a quiet sorrow had taken its place. In the shadowy and darkened vision of her weakened consciousness, she accepted it as the face of the Son of Man, either sitting beside her so she could not be claimed by death, or waiting just on the other side to welcome her into it.

Faber sat sunk in thought. Suddenly a sound came that shook him as if he were having a seizure. Even then he mastered his emotion and sat still as a stone. He was paralyzed—in mingled delight and awe. He dared not move lest he should break the spell. Was the voice a reality, or was this just another phantom of his imagination? He would not with so much as a sigh break the unfolding of what came next. In the utter stillness of the sleeping house, he sat as stone and listened.

"O Jesus," sighed the voice, as one struggling with weariness, or one who speaks her thoughts in a dream. "O Jesus! You *are* there! They told me you were dead and gone nowhere! They said there never was one such as you. And there you are! O Jesus, what am I to do? Can you do anything with me now? Is it too late? I thought I believed in you. But I never quite did, for all the church of my youth, never loved you as now I see you love me. And there was my Paul! Oh, how I loved my Paul, but he couldn't get rid of my sin. I begged him to make me clean. You could afford to pity a poor girl who hardly knew what she was doing. My heart is very sore, and my whole body is ashamed, and I feel so stupid!

"Do help me, Lord. I denied you, I know. But my husband was the only thing I cared about then. I know you will forgive me for that. Now I see that Paul was wrong, that you *are* real. Forgive me, Lord, and accept me as your child. But, O Christ, please, if you can any way do it, make me fit for Paul. Tell him to forgive me too. And show him that you are real too. O my Savior, do not look at me so or I shall die weeping for joy. O my Lord! . . . Oh—my Paul!"

For Paul had gently risen from his chair and come one step nearer, where he stood looking on her with a smile such as he had never smiled in his life—a smile of unutterable sorrow, love, repentance, hope. She gazed, speechless now, her spirit drinking in the vision of that smile. It was like mountain air, like spring water, like eternal life! It was forgiveness and peace from the Lord of all. And had her brain been as clear as her heart, could she have taken it for less? If the sinner forgave her, then surely the Perfect did also? For working through her yet unbelieving husband, her Lord had revealed his forgiveness as he accepted her, newborn, into the kingdom of his love.

Paul dared not go nearer—partly fearing the consequences of increased emotion. Her lips began to move again, and her voice to murmur, but he could distinguish only a word here and there. Slowly the eyelids fell over the great dark eyes and the sounds vanished. She had slipped away into some silent dream.

At length he approached again on tiptoe. For a few minutes he stood and gazed on the sleeping countenance—then dropped on his knees and cried, *"God, if you be anywhere, I thank you."*

In an hour, Juliet awoke again, vaguely remembering a heavenly dream whose sweet air still lingered and made her happy.

But what a task was Faber's! He must still not go near her. The balance of her life trembled on a knife edge and the slightest touch might incline it toward death.

As soon as he saw that her sleep was about to break, he all but extinguished the light, felt her pulse, listened to her breathing, and, satisfied of her condition, crept from the room. He called the nurse to take his place, saying he would be in the next room or within call in the park.

In the adjoining room, he threw himself on the bed, but he could not rest. He rose, had a bath, listened at Juliet's door, and hearing no sound, sent to the stable. Niger greeted him with a neigh of pleasure. He hastily saddled him, but his hands trembled so he could hardly get the straps into the girth buckles.

"That's Niger!" cried Juliet, hearing his distant whinny from her bedroom. "Has he come?"

"Who, ma'am?" asked the nurse, a stranger to Glaston.

"The doctor; has he come?"

"He's just gone, ma'am. He's been sitting by you all night—would let no one else come near you. Rather peculiar, in my opinion."

A soft flush, all the blood Juliet could show, tinged her cheek—hope's own color.

45 / The Coming of Morning

Faber sprang upon Niger's back and galloped wildly through the park. His soul was like a southern sea under a summer tornado. The slow dawn was gathering under a smoke cloud with an edge of cold yellow; a thin wind was up. Rain had fallen in the night and the grass was wet and cool under Niger's hoofs, sending up a soft, sweet savor from the earth. Through the fine consorting mass of silence and odor, Niger's gallop softly thundered over the turf. His master's joy had overflowed into him.

A deeper, loftier morning was dawning in Faber's world. One dread burden was lifted from his being: his fierce pride, his unmanly cruelty, his spotless selfishness, had not quite sent a woman to the grave. She was given back to him, to tend, to heal, and love as he had never yet dreamed of loving! Endless was the dawn breaking in him. Life was now to be lived, not endured! He would nurse the lily he had bruised and broken. He would shield her from her own remorse. He would be to her a refuge from the wind, a shelter from the storm. Once he laughed aloud as he rode. He found himself actually wondering, prompted by the restoration of Juliet, if the story of the resurrection *might* be true.

Dear reader, forgive my intrusion, but is the idea of God too good or too foolish for your belief? Or is it that you are not great enough or humble enough to hold it? In either case, I will hold it for both of us. Only do not be stubborn when the truth begins to draw you. You will find it hard if truth has to go behind you and drive you—hard to kick against the divine proddings which, no matter how stubborn you may be, will prove too much for you in the end.

But hear me this once more. The God in whom I believe is *not* the God you imagine me to believe in. You do not know him; your idea of him is not mine. If you knew God and Jesus, you *would* believe in them, for to know them is to believe in them. Don't say, "Let him teach me, then," unless you mean it in honest, submissive desire. For he has been teaching you all this time. If you hear and do not heed, then what is the wonder your eyes are not opened to more truth and that the things I tell you sound in your ears as the muttering of a fool? For no one can learn more until he accepts and *obeys* the teaching he is given.

For days Faber took measures not to be seen by Juliet. But he was constantly around the place, and when she woke from a sleep, they often told her that he had stayed by her side all the time she slept. At night he was either in her room or the next. Dorothy told her that if she wanted her husband, all she had to do was go to sleep. She was greatly tempted to pretend just for another glimpse of him, but would not.

At length Faber requested Dorothy to tell Juliet that the doctor said she may send for her husband when she pleased. Much as he longed to hear her voice, he would not come without her permission.

He was by her side the next moment. But for minutes not a word was spoken; a speechless embrace was all.

It does not concern me to relate how by degrees they came to a close understanding. Where love is, everything is easy; or if not easy, yet to be accomplished. Of course Faber made his return confession in full. I won't say that Juliet did not have pangs or retrospective jealousy. Love, although an angel, has much to learn yet, and the demon jealousy may be one of the schoolmasters of her coming perfection. God only knows. There must be a divine way of casting out the demon, however.

Unconfessed to each other, their faults would forever have lain between them to trap them. Confessed, their sins drew them together in sorrow and humility and mutual consolation.

Little Amanda could not tell whether Juliet's house or Dorothy's was home. When at the one, she always talked of the other as *home*. She called her father *Papa* and Juliet *Mama*; Dorothy had always been *Auntie*. She learned to write her name Amanda Duck Faber.

The gossips of Glaston explained everything to their full satisfaction. Obviously, Juliet had left her husband on discovering that he had a child of whom he had never told her. But when she learned that the mother was dead, she agreed to a reconciliation. That was the nearest they ever came to the facts, and they never needed to know more.

There are undoubtedly some who require the shame of a public exposure to make them recognize and face their sin. But such was not Juliet. Her husband knew her fault—that was enough. He knew also that his was immeasurably worse than hers. But when they folded each other to the heart, they left their faults outside, as God does when he casts our sins behind his back in utter annihilation.

Their small son, a sturdy, healthy, happy little fellow, clasped their hearts in each chubby hand and drew them even more closely together and to God.

I will say nothing definite as to the condition of mind at which Faber had arrived when Wingfold and he next had a talk together. He was growing, and that is all we can require of any man. He would not yet say he was a believer in the supernatural, but he believed more than he admitted, and he never again talked against belief.

Also, he went as often as he could to church. Little as that means in general, it did not mean little when the man was Paul Faber and the minister was Thomas Wingfold.

Afterword _____

As you may have discovered in reading *The Lady's Confession*, this book is different than many of MacDonald's. Faber and Juliet are not typical MacDonald heroes. We do not find ourselves drawn to them and endeared to them in quite the way we did when reading of Sir Gibbie or Annie Anderson. Perhaps it is erroneous to use the term "heroes" about them at all. For we cannot help recoiling at what is uncovered in their pasts as the story develops. And yet are they not typical of each one of us? Like Leopold in *The Curate's Awakening,* their sins may be ugly to look at. But they indeed represent the human condition—even yours and mine. Priding ourselves on our goodness, are we not equally separated from God, equally in need of his cleansing forgiveness, equally without wisdom and insight and strength to save ourselves? In ourselves, we cannot even stand. Without divine life within us, we fall utterly. In the confession of that truth is the beginning of wisdom.

Priding himself on the goodness of his manhood, Faber cruelly judges Juliet, all the while keeping hidden in his own heart an even worse sin. Good on the surface, Faber's hidden sin of the heart indeed typifies the wretchedness of all mankind. We are separated from God in sin, and only through salvation in Christ can this sin be washed away.

Like Faber, Juliet comes in contact with truth and, like him, rejects it. But as the story progresses, the roots of that salvation message probe ever deeper into her heart. As Faber eventually must face the bankruptcy of his own human goodness, Juliet must face the emptiness of her love for Faber outside the one true Love which creates all other loves. Elevating her husband to the level of a god, and seeking forgiveness for her own sins in his acceptance, she must painfully realize that in no man or relationship but only in Jesus Christ can come forgiveness from sins. Not until she makes confession—both in the sense of acknowledging sin and professing faith in Christ—is she released into the freedom to love as she was created to love.

In the Introduction to *The Curate's Awakening*, I commented that the book was more "spiritual" than some of the others with respect to themes and subject matter. In a similar vein, *The Lady's Confession* is a parable illuminating the state of man's sinful heart before God. It is the ideal companion to *The Curate's Awakening*, a parable on the nature of salvation. And like all MacDonald's books, truth comes in many layers. For on another level one can observe perhaps a parallel between the four soils of the Sower parable (Mark 4) and the five central characters of the story—Juliet, Faber, Dorothy, Drake, and Bevis. Though MacDonald does not make their responses so clear-cut as does our Lord in his parable, we nevertheless see contrasting elements of receptivity and growth which the gospel seed strikes when it comes into contact with the multifaceted human heart as represented by these five.

The book's ending is perhaps surprising, not typically MacDonald where all the threads and themes are resolved. Yet maybe it is the most appropriate ending MacDonald could have given to his parable on sin and man's need for God. For in the end every person must make his own choice. Each man and woman stand before God in the silence and emptiness of their own heart and must choose whether they will say yes or no to him. By leaving the ending as he did, MacDonald emphasized that point. In the same way that each reader must decide for himself what he thinks Faber's choice will be, MacDonald reveals the fact that each must make that choice for himself as well. And even MacDonald, as Faber's creator, cannot make the decision for the doctor. It remains Faber's alone.

As always, I welcome your responses, as I know the publisher does. I have received so many letters, in fact, that I have prepared a small pamphlet on George MacDonald which I would be happy to send on request.

Michael Phillips